PRAI[...]
O[...]

Th[...]

"This tenth bloom to b[...]
satisfying as any of the o[...]
Fans can rejoice in finding the outstanding features they've come to count on: intriguing historical details, double-crossing deceptions, complex characters, and plenty of romance." —*Library Journal* (starred review)

"With delectable wit and a deft hand at imaginative plotting, Willig expertly matches up the redoubtable, parasol-wielding Gwen with the perfect hero. The result is a completely captivating tale that fans of this long-running series will cherish." —*Booklist* (starred review)

"Another well-crafted, engaging thriller." —*Romantic Times*

"[A] witty series. . . . The writing is acerbic, arch, and funny . . . a welcome installment." —*Kirkus Reviews*

The Garden Intrigue

"Eloise, of course, is amazing, but it's truly the plot of *The Garden Intrigue* that shines . . . wonderful!" —Romance Junkies

"Enlightening and entertaining as always, and full of plenty of romance and intrigue." —*Library Journal*

"As fresh and charming as its floral theme." —*Kirkus Reviews*

"Humor, love, espionage—yet again there is absolutely *nothing* that this incredible author leaves out. . . . [These stories] just keep getting better and better every time!" —Once Upon a Romance

The Orchid Affair

"Supremely nerve-racking . . . successfully upholds the author's tradition of providing charming three-dimensional characters, lively action, [and] witty dialogue." —*Library Journal*

"Willig's sparkling series continues to elevate the Regency romance genre." —*Kirkus Reviews*

continued . . .

"Willig combines the atmosphere of the tempestuous era with the perfect touches of historical detail to round out the love story." —*Romantic Times*

The Betrayal of the Blood Lily

"Newcomers and loyal fans alike will love . . . Willig's signature mix of historical richness and whimsical humor." —*The Newark Star-Ledger*

"Willig hasn't lost her touch." —*Publishers Weekly*

"Willig injects a new energy in her already thriving, thrilling series, and presents the best entry to date." —*Booklist*

The Temptation of the Night Jasmine

"Jane Austen for the modern girl . . . sheer fun!" —*New York Times* bestselling author Christina Dodd

"An engaging historical romance, delightfully funny and sweet. . . . Romance's rosy glow tints even the spy adventure that unfolds . . . fine historical fiction." —*The Newark Star-Ledger*

"Another sultry spy tale. . . . The author's conflation of historical fact, quirky observations, and nicely rendered romances results in an elegant and grandly entertaining book." —*Publishers Weekly*

"[A] high-spirited and thoroughly enjoyable series." —*Kirkus Reviews*

The Seduction of the Crimson Rose

"Willig's series gets better with each addition, and her latest is filled with swashbuckling fun, romance, and intrigue." —*Booklist*

"Handily fulfills its promise of intrigue and romance." —*Publishers Weekly*

"There are few authors capable of matching Lauren Willig's ability to merge historical accuracy, heart-pounding romance, and biting wit." —*BookPage*

The Deception of the Emerald Ring

"History textbook meets *Bridget Jones*." —*Marie Claire*

"A fun and zany time warp full of history, digestible violence, and plenty of romance." —*New York Daily News*

"Heaving bodices, embellished history, and witty dialogue: What more could you ask for?" —*Kirkus Reviews*

"Smart . . . [a] fast-paced narrative with mistaken identities, double agents, and high-stakes espionage. . . . The historic action is taut and twisting."
—*Publishers Weekly*

The Masque of the Black Tulip

"Clever [and] playful. . . . What's most delicious about Willig's novels is that the damsels of 1803 bravely put it all on the line for love and country."
—*Detroit Free Press*

"Studded with clever literary and historical nuggets, this charming historical-contemporary romance moves back and forth in time."   —*USA Today*

"Willig has great fun with the conventions of the genre, throwing obstacles between her lovers at every opportunity . . . a great escape."
—*The Boston Globe*

The Secret History of the Pink Carnation

"A deftly hilarious, sexy novel."
—*New York Times* bestselling author Eloisa James

"A merry romp with never a dull moment! A fun read."
—*New York Times* bestselling author Mary Balogh

"This genre-bending read—a dash of chick lit with a historical twist—has it all: romance, mystery, and adventure. Pure fun!"
—*New York Times* bestselling author Meg Cabot

"Willig has an ear for quick wit and an eye for detail. Her fiction debut is chock-full of romance, sexual tension, espionage, adventure, and humor."
—*Library Journal*

"Willig's imaginative debut . . . is a decidedly delightful romp."   —*Booklist*

"Relentlessly effervescent prose . . . a sexy, smirking, determined-to-charm historical romance debut."   —*Kirkus Reviews*

"A delightful debut."   —Roundtable Reviews

The Mark of the Midnight Manzanilla

A PINK CARNATION NOVEL

LAUREN WILLIG

NEW AMERICAN LIBRARY

New American Library
Published by the Penguin Group
Penguin Group (USA) LLC, 375 Hudson Street,
New York, New York 10014

USA | Canada | UK | Ireland | Australia | New Zealand | India | South Africa | China
penguin.com
A Penguin Random House Company

First published by New American Library,
a division of Penguin Group (USA) LLC

First Printing, August 2014

 REGISTERED TRADEMARK—MARCA REGISTRADA

LIBRARY OF CONGRESS CATALOGING-IN-PUBLICATION DATA:
Willig, Lauren.
The mark of the midnight manzanilla: a Pink carnation novel/Lauren Willig.
p. cm.—(Pink carnation 11)
ISBN 978-0-451-41473-1 (paperback)
1. Vampires—Fiction. I. Title.
PS3623.I575M35 2014
813'.6—dc23   2014010559

Printed in the United States of America
10 9 8 7 6 5 4 3 2 1

Set in Granjon
Designed by Alissa Theodor

To my mother,
Rosette F. Willig,
for everything and more.

The
Mark of the
Midnight
Manzanilla

Prologue

Cambridge, 2004

"Vampire: Fact or Fiction?" announced Megan grandly.

An undergrad reading Kant in German raised a brow and went back to her critique of pure reason. The tourists at the table next to us edged their plastic chairs ever so slightly towards the other side, bumping into a potted plant in the process.

"So you've picked a title, then?" I said.

Megan shrugged. "It's a little over-the-top, but I thought, why not? It's almost Halloween, after all."

So it was. I'd been back in the U.S. for nearly three months now. We'd gone from the sticky heat of late August in Cambridge, the campus deserted except for the sleepy flies on the windowsills and a handful of stressed-out grad students in their carrels at Widener Library, to the Indian summer of September, when bewildered freshmen roamed the streets in defensive herds, turning up at the wrong buildings and crowding the tables at Au Bon Pain. It was October now. The freshmen had settled into their dorms; the upperclassmen were out and about, belatedly buying their course books at the Coop and arguing loudly about existentialism in the upstairs room of Café Algiers.

Summer seemed like a very long time ago. Sometimes, as I scurried from Widener to Robinson Hall, books clutched in one arm, a Vietnamese coffee from Toscanini's dripping on the other, it seemed hard to believe that I had ever left, had ever spent a year in England, had ever lived—albeit temporarily—in a Georgian manor in Sussex with an Englishman named Colin.

It sounds like something out of a chick flick, doesn't it? Take one American graduate student on her research year in England, wearing reasonably cute boots, add a set of family archives and the handsome but mysterious owner thereof. Cue dramatic music.

Of course, in real life, it was all a great deal more prosaic than that.

Admittedly, when I'd first met Colin, he'd done his best to impersonate Mr. Rochester, if Rochester had been blond and given to wearing an ancient Barbour jacket. Despite those impediments, Colin had managed to brood quite forbiddingly when I'd requested access to his family archives. He was rather protective of the family heritage, which contained a truly dramatic number of undercover agents.

There was a time when I'd wondered if Colin might be one himself.

But I was over that now. Mostly. In any case, the only agents of whom I was officially on the trail were all two centuries gone. My mission was to winkle out their escapades—and turn them into footnotes in my dissertation: *Aristocratic Espionage During the Wars with France, 1789–1815.*

With enough academese, even swashbuckling spies can be rendered dry as dust.

But that was just a front. The truth of the matter was that my interest had long since become less about the dissertation and more a personal involvement with the people whose escapades I was reconstructing, piecemeal, from a sometimes conflicting array of documents. I was meant to be studying all three of the major British spy leagues—the Scarlet Pimpernel, the Purple Gentian, and the Pink Carnation—but my interest had come to focus more and more narrowly on the Pink Carnation.

I could find all sorts of ways to justify it: the Carnation was in operation much longer, and therefore made a better case study; the League had experimented with different techniques and methods, which told us something about the evolution of aristocratic spying from an ad hoc endeavor to a quasi-professional enterprise. And, of course, the Carnation was a woman, one Miss Jane Wooliston, who, with the help of her erstwhile chaperone, Miss Gwendolyn Meadows, had hoodwinked Napoleon for close on a decade. It was so simple that it was genius. Who would suspect a demure lady of society to be fronting the most audacious undercover enterprise since Odysseus came up with the bright idea of knocking a few wooden slats together and calling them a horse?

At least, that was how the League of the Pink Carnation had operated during the first three years of its existence. I'd blithely assumed that the Pink Carnation had gone on that way, refining her technique without changing it. But documents I'd found just before I left England had held out the tantalizing prospect that, in fact, the Pink Carnation had precipitated a major shake-up at some point in 1805, switching from the existing League structure to something more like a solo agent.

I was itching to uncover more. Why had the Pink Carnation broken with her longtime partner and chaperone, Miss Gwendolyn Meadows, in 1805? Was it because of Miss Gwen's marriage and subsequent success as a novelist? Or was that just a guise? Were the Pink Carnation and Miss Gwen really still in partnership, albeit operating on different fronts, Miss Gwen in London, the Pink Carnation abroad?

It seemed as though every thread I followed led not just to another thread but to a whole skein of them, all waiting to be unraveled. But instead of unraveling them, here I was, back in the wrong Cambridge, laying waste my hour trying to drum Western Civ, 1650 to the Present, into the heads of two sections of uninterested undergrads, while also wrangling a bunch of disaffected teaching fellows. I'd promised to take the Head TF job for Western Civ, so dutifully back to the States I had come, leaving my mysteries unsolved.

And Colin back in England.

Megan said something. I gave a little shake of my head and forced myself to try to pay attention. "Sorry. What was that?"

Megan and I had gotten into the habit of a weekly Thursday lunch at Campo de Fiore, the tiny pizza place in the middle of the Holyoke Center, before sallying off to teach our respective Hist and Lit tutorials. Megan was the Lit, I was the Hist, but undergrads who hadn't done the reading were undergrads who hadn't done the reading however you looked at it. It was easier to deal with them after a fortifying lunch heavy on the carbohydrates and caffeine.

Sometimes we met for a restorative drink after as well, but this wasn't going to be one of those days.

Megan looked at me sympathetically. "No problem," she said, and took a bite of her potato pizza. Through a mouthful of spud and crust, she said indistinctly, "When does Colin get here?"

I checked my watch, which hadn't moved very far from the last time I had checked it. "His plane gets in around four."

By which time my apartment would be clean and sparkling, there would be groceries in the fridge, and all stray bits of spinach would have been removed from my teeth. Or at least the spinach bit. My tutorial ran from one to three. With any luck, it would take Colin a while to get a cab, thus giving me more time to repair the wear and tear of teaching and scrub the miscellaneous coffee stains off my person.

Megan leaned forward, the wooden beads of her necklace

narrowly missing the straw sticking out of her Diet Coke. "Are you nervous?"

Me? Nervous? I jabbed at an ice cube with my own straw. "We talk every day."

Some days longer than others. With Colin five hours ahead, we tended to speak at odd times; it was either insanely early my time or late at night his. Not to mention transcontinental rates being what they were, even with a good deal on a long-distance calling card. I was managing on a teaching fellow's income and Colin had a money-guzzling old house to support. Which meant, in sum, that four nights out of five, our phone calls were little more than a pro forma "just to hear your voice."

It's amazing how quickly someone familiar can start to feel alien and how pro forma that pro forma becomes.

I had left a toothbrush in the holder at Selwick Hall and two sweaters and a nightgown in "my" drawer. At Colin's insistence, I might add. It was as if we were both afraid that absence might break the fragile thing we had built between us, as if we might tether ourselves together across the Atlantic through the magical invocation of the bristles of an Oral-B and a J.Crew cashmere-merino blend.

Sometimes, I took comfort from the fact that my toothbrush was still there. Other times, in the twilight, when I was tired from teaching and alone in my little studio apartment, in those dreary moments when the sun has gone down but you haven't quite turned on the lights, a purple plastic toothbrush seemed a very fragile object on which to build my future happiness.

Nine out of ten dentists notwithstanding.

Megan checked her watch and grimaced. "Twelve forty-five," she said.

It was our fifteen-minute warning. Tutorial started at one. Office space being scarce, especially for the junior of the junior, we both taught our tutorials in the café at the Barker Center, the vast redbrick building that housed the English department.

I was a little jealous. The history department didn't have a café. We just had a black plastic coffeemaker that no one ever remembered to clean.

"At least we're in your territory today," I said, heaving my black leather satchel up on my shoulder.

In honor of Halloween, we had joined forces. We were teaching Le Fanu's *Carmilla*, and, of course, Bram Stoker's *Dracula*. With particular reference to gender politics and class considerations. This was Hist and Lit, after all. If you couldn't work the term "liminal" into your tutorial, you were doing it wrong.

Megan made the sort of face I make when people assume I'm a Victorianist. "Not really . . . People have already worked *Carmilla* and *Dracula* to death. I'm looking at the antecedent narratives. Earlier references to vampires in popular fiction," she translated.

Lit people tend to assume that Hist people are a little slow. From their point of view, we're practically social scientists, and everyone knows what those social scientists are like.

"Yep, understood," I said. "So, like, what?"

Most of the works she mentioned were completely unknown

to me. I let the catalogue of names wash over me as I crumpled my napkin onto my paper plate. I was trying to determine whether there was enough Coke left in my cup to justify taking it with me when I heard Megan say, "Then there's *The Convent of Orsino. . . .*"

The name acted on me like an electric shock. I nearly dropped my waxed-paper cup. "You're writing about *The Convent of Orsino?*"

Megan stopped with her own straw halfway to her lips. "You've heard about *The Convent of Orsino?*"

Had I heard of *The Convent of Orsino?*

It was a long and rather improbable story, involving family feuds and lost jewels, so I decided to boil it down to essentials. "The author was one of Colin's ancestors. Ancestresses. Whatever." I couldn't resist bragging a bit. "There's a great big ornate first edition at Selwick Hall."

Megan choked on the dregs of her Diet Coke. "I can't believe you actually got to hold a first edition of *The Convent of Orsino.*"

"Phrases that don't come up often . . . ," I murmured.

"This is great! You can help me out. I mean, Colin can help me out." Common sense tempered academic fervor. Megan shot me a sheepish glance. "If that's okay with you. I don't want to monopolize your Colin time."

"It depends on what you want him for," I said cheerfully.

Colin was supposed to be in town for four days—a very short time by some reckonings, a very long time by others. I hadn't known what to plan or not plan. In England, our days had simply meandered peacefully along: Colin had worked on the spy novel he was convinced would make him the next Ian Fleming, I had worked on my dissertation, and in the evenings we had watched silly movies or headed out to the Heavy Hart, ye olde local pub (trivia night on Tuesdays, chicken tikka on Thursdays).

Now that he was coming to my turf, I wasn't quite sure how we were meant to fill twenty-four hours a day.

Today was Thursday. Sunday was Halloween, and, incidentally, my birthday eve. I was an All Souls' Day baby, which was technically the reason for Colin's visit. We were also just a few weeks shy of our one-year anniversary. Colin had been hinting for several phone calls now at a "special surprise." I veered between expecting a proposal and a pair of thermal socks.

All right, maybe not the thermal socks (although they would be useful if I returned to Selwick Hall for the winter holiday), but I was trying not to get my hopes up, and thermal socks were the least romantic thing I could think of. Naturally, the more I told myself "thermal socks," the more I secretly convinced myself that Colin was going to show up with the Ancestral Ring of the Selwicks, prostrate himself on my none-too-clean floor, and beg for the honor of my hand.

Or something along those general lines.

There were a number of flaws to this fantasy. Among other things, if there ever had been an Ancestral Ring, I was reasonably sure Colin's mother would long since have traded it in for something sleek and trendy.

In an attempt at sanity, I said, "I'm sure we can make time for a coffee. What do you want to pick his brains about?"

"Anything he can tell me about this ancestor of his," said Megan, dodging a group of tourists who appeared to have meant to go to Au Bon Pain next door and were looking in vain for a connecting door.

"That's more my province than Colin's. What about her?"

Mrs. William Reid, née Miss Gwendolyn Meadows, had been the second-in-command of the Pink Carnation from 1803 through 1805. And I wasn't entirely convinced that their connection had ended with her marriage. That was part of what I intended to find out. If I could figure out how. The paper trail had dead-ended on me and I hadn't quite determined which tack to take next.

"Well . . ." Megan fingered her beads, the same way she did when trying to figure out how to explain a text to a group of undergrads. "Basically, what I'm looking at are the intersections between fact and fiction in early vampire narratives. Of course," she added hastily, "we all know that the vampire myth is merely a metaphor for sexual repression and inchoate class conflicts."

"Yup," I said, nodding encouragingly. "But . . ."

Reassured, Megan went on. "But there's a chicken-and-egg factor. You get vampire scares that lead to myths that lead to scares that lead to myths. Many of them predating *Dracula* by a fair amount."

Without having to consult, we detoured into Toscanini's for preclass coffees. The coffee in the Barker Center was of the college cafeteria variety, for emergency use only. "Where does *The Convent of Orsino* come into this? I'll have a large Vietnamese coffee, please."

"And I'll have a skim latte." Megan rooted in her wallet for cash, dropping an extra dollar in the tip jar. "I'd thought *The Convent of Orsino* was a perfect example of an antecedent event transmuted into a fictionalized narrative in a way that reified class and gender concerns."

My head was spinning a bit, so I seized on the easiest piece. "What antecedent event are you talking about?"

I'd spent a fair amount of time with *The Convent of Orsino*, and as far as I could tell, it was all fiction.

Well, mostly.

The book followed the exploits of Plumeria, the dashing chaperone, who teamed up with the aging-but-still-got-it Sir Magnifico to rescue Magnifico's insipid daughter, Amarantha, from the clutches of the sinister but attractive Knight of the Silver Tower, aka the vampire. I was pretty sure that Plumeria was a thinly veiled alter ego for Miss Gwen, and I strongly suspected that the Knight of the Silver Tower was the French spymaster the Chevalier de la Tour d'Argent—who, by the way, was not, as far as I could tell, any kind of undead. He had, however, committed the cardinal sin of pissing off Miss Gwen, and was therefore condemned to roam the ranks of vampire fiction for eternity as a spoony, moony, self-loathing creature of the night. In sparkly armor.

"That's just the problem," said Megan mournfully. "It turns

out it's the other way around. The book came first. And it was so perfect."

I took a long, bracing swig of my coffee, so strong that it made Starbucks taste like a distant second cousin to caffeine. "What was?"

Outside, the air was crisp and bracing, perfect jacket weather. We picked up our pace in an attempt to get to the Barker Center before our students did. There's always a little loss of moral high ground when the TF is five minutes late. And, trust me, we needed all the moral high ground we could get.

Breathlessly, Megan said, "There was a vampire scare in London—including a woman turning up dead with fang marks on her neck—and the author of *The Convent of Orsino* was all over it—but it looks like it happened *after* her book, not before."

"Whoa." Miss Gwen and vampires? I stumbled as my heel caught on a bit of uneven brickwork and just managed not to upend my coffee over my cream-colored sweater. "All over it how?"

I was amused by the idea of Miss Gwen as a sort of parasol-toting Van Helsing, but I couldn't help but wonder if there might be something more to it. Whenever people turned up dead around Miss Gwen, they tended to be connected in some way or another to French spy rings. *The Convent of Orsino* came out in 1806. If my hunch was right, then maybe the dissolution of her partnership with the Pink Carnation was exactly what I had expected it was, a front.

It would make a brilliant chapter. If it were true.

"There was this duke—," Megan began, and broke off as one of our students chugged up to us.

"Eloise? Megan?" She had the expression of contrition down pat. "I'm, like, SO sorry. . . ."

And it began.

"Don't worry," Megan was saying patiently. She gave me a shoot-me-now look over the girl's head. "I'm sure you can find some way to make up the work."

Grrr. The hands of the clock in the hall of the Barker Center clicked to one. Vampires were going to have to wait. And in three hours, my boyfriend was getting off a plane from England.

I thought of all the things I had intended to do before Colin arrived: shower, laundry, shove miscellaneous overdue library books into a coherent pile, go through the fridge to remove evidence of microwave dinners for one, buy fresh flowers to put into a vase (which led to the next item: buy a vase into which to put fresh flowers). Oh, yes, and bake cookies. Because, as we all know from *Clueless*, it's important to have something baking.

Then I thought about Miss Gwen and vampires.

If I left directly after tutorial and hightailed it home, I would have time for at least the shower and quite possibly the library books. After all, any information Megan might have about Miss Gwen's escapades in 1806 was already two hundred years old. It would keep for the weekend. It had been three long months since I had seen Colin. Surely, he deserved a little more consideration—

and possibly, some fresh flowers—than a batch of long-dead spies?

I caught up to Megan as we joined the students jostling their way into the café of the Barker Center.

I couldn't believe I was doing this, but . . .

"Do you have time for a very quick drink after tutorial?" I murmured. "I want to hear more about your vampire . . ."

Chapter One

London, 1806

"They say he's a vampire."

Sally Fitzhugh's friend Agnes trotted after her as Sally made a beeline for the French doors to the garden, driven by a restlessness she couldn't entirely explain. Behind her, she could hear the scraping of the musicians, the swish of fashionable fans. She just wanted out. Away from the heat, away from the smells, away from the petty gossip and murmurings.

It was October, and cold, but the ballroom was humid with the press of too many bodies in too small a place. The very mirrors seemed fogged with it, blurred and distorted. Even with her arms and neck bare, Sally felt uncomfortably warm in her silk and gauze gown.

The crisp October air hit Sally like a tonic, and, with it, Agnes's words. Had Agnes really said—

"A what?"

Agnes ducked the rapidly swinging door. "A bloodsucking creature of the night," she said helpfully as she followed Sally out towards the balustrade, away from the crush in Lord Vaughn's ballroom.

"I know what a vampire is. Everyone knows what they are." Ever since *The Convent of Orsino* (by a Lady) had taken the town by storm the previous spring, the ladies of the *ton* had become intimate experts on the topic. The men, just as sickeningly, had taken to powdering their faces pale and affecting red lip rouge. Sally found it distinctly ridiculous.

But, then, she was finding it all a little ridiculous just now: the too strong perfumes, the smug smiles, the whispering voices behind fans, the incredible arrogance of those powdered fops and perspiring ladies. It would serve them right if there were vampires in their midst. Not that such things existed, of course. Any bloodsucking that went on in the *ton* was purely of the metaphorical variety, although none the less draining for that.

Sally gripped the cool stone of the balustrade with both hands, breathing in deeply through her nose. She wasn't sure what ailed her. Back in the cloistered confines of Miss Climpson's Select Seminary, she had been itching to try her wings on the world, to flirt and laugh and bend beaux to her will. She knew exactly what it would be like: a cross between a Samuel Richardson novel and those notices one read in the paper, the ones that began with "Lady A— wore a gown of watered green silk." She would be the toast of London, taking the town by storm.

And why shouldn't she? She was, she knew, without false modesty, more than passably attractive. Quite a bit more, really. It didn't do to be disingenuous about such things. So what if Martin Frobisher called her a gilded beanpole? He was just sore because she made him look like the sniveling little thing he was—and jealous because his family hadn't two guineas to rub together. Proud, he called her. Well, yes, she was proud. She knew her own worth, both in character and in coin. What did it matter that her family had never thrown down a cloak for Elizabeth I or provided a mistress for Charles II? Just because they had never toadied for a title didn't mean that they weren't as good as anyone. They were certainly a sure sight better-looking, and her dowry was as big as anyone's.

Both of those, Sally knew, guaranteed her entrée into society—or her brother's name wasn't Turnip.

She had sallied off to London in the firm anticipation of champagne-filled evenings of compliments, in which she would hold court among her devoted and witty admirers.

Well, she had been right about the champagne, at least. She just hadn't expected it to taste quite so sour.

Even so, it was better than ratafia, the drink of young ladies, of which she had imbibed enough over the past year and a half to float a medium-sized royal barge. To be honest, she hadn't minded the ratafia at the first. And if her admirers were less witty and more waspish—well, she was too busy flirting her fan and enjoying her own wit to mind. It was only bit by bit, along the course of her first Season, that she began to realize that it all felt a little flat. The bright silks and satins looked best by candlelight, where the stains didn't show. The glittering jewels were too often paste. The fashionable gossip, which had seemed so terribly clever and scandalous in that first month, became nothing more than the endless repetition of a series of painfully similar *on dits*.

Did it really matter that Lucy Ponsonby had been seen *without her gloves* at Lady Beaufeatheringstone's latest ball? It was hardly a matter of international policy.

She was just in a mood, she told herself. Tired, cranky, weary. Too many nights of too many entertainments that weren't all that entertaining. It would get better. It had to get better. She didn't like feeling like this, so purposeless. So restless.

She had hoped that having her friends Lizzy and Agnes join her this year would help, that introducing them to society would provide some of the vim that she had felt last year, when it was all fresh and new. But Agnes didn't care much for such things, and Lizzy had rapidly, without much help from Sally, acquired her own circle.

Lizzy had, in fact, become something of a minor sensation in her own right. Part of it was due to her stepmother, Mrs. Reid. Mrs. Reid's novel, *The Convent of Orsino*, was the topic of conversation at all select soirees, her presence a coup for any hostess. People fought to send cards to her stepdaughter, in the hope that Mrs. Reid might attend, and—even better!—lose her temper and pink someone with her infamous sword parasol. A wound from Mrs. Reid was a sure sign of social success. But while Mrs. Reid's notoriety might have garnered Lizzy the invitations, the rest she had achieved on her own. At any party, one could find Lizzy surrounded by a fascinated group of men and women, telling hair-raising tales of her youth in India. Given that Lizzy had left India at the age of six, and spent the rest of her formative years first with a retired vicar's wife and then in the decidedly unexotic confines of Miss Climpson's Select Seminary, Sally strongly suspected that the larger part of those stories were apocryphal, taken right out of the novels they had smuggled under the covers at Miss Climpson's. Not that that made any difference to her audience.

It didn't hurt that the rumor had made its way around the *ton* that Lizzy's mother had been an Indian princess, complete with elephant and priceless jewels.

It was Sally who had started the rumor about Lizzy's mother being an Indian princess. Not the elephants. The elephants had come later, along with other embellishments that made the originator of the tale raise her brows and wrinkle her nose. People did come up with the most ridiculous things. . . .

But, still, it was all better than the truth, which was that Lizzy's mother had been a bazaar girl. A touch of royal blood rendered Lizzy interesting and exotic; without it, she would be stigmatized as nothing but the bastard brat of an insignificant

East India Company Colonel of little fortune and no birth. That was what Sally had reckoned when she started the rumor.

Of course, she hadn't reckoned on it running away from her like that.

She hadn't reckoned on being left behind.

That was silly. It wasn't as though Lizzy had left her. They still spent a great deal of time together. It was just ... When Sally had left Miss Climpson's for London, it had never occurred to her that Agnes and Lizzy would carry on without her, turning their trio into a duo. They had even had an adventure of their own—not that it was terribly much of an adventure, given that Lizzy and Agnes had run off the moment there was a hint of a French spy on the scene, disappearing for weeks and causing everyone a lot of bother finding them again. If Sally had been there, they would have routed the spy on their own, and saved everyone a great deal of trouble.

But she hadn't been there. As they had reminded her countless times. Not always intentionally, but in little ways—in jokes she didn't understand and in memories she didn't share. Sally was used to being the leader of their little trio. It felt very odd to be rendered de trop.

"—inconvenient diet," Agnes was saying. "Blood does stain so."

Belatedly, Sally pulled her attention back to Agnes. Unlike Sally, Agnes did not seem to be enjoying the cool night air. Her teeth were chattering slightly and her skin was turning a faint shade of blue that matched the color of her gown.

"Here," Sally said, and took the light shawl from her own shoulders and wrapped it around Agnes, who hadn't had the sense to bring her own. "What *are* you talking about?"

"The rumors," said Agnes, blinking innocently at Sally as she absently tucked the corners of the wrap beneath her arms. "Haven't you heard? They say he's a vampire."

"A vampire? Hardly." Sally paused to glower in the general direction of the ballroom. There was no love lost between her and their host. Lord Vaughn was not an admirer of Sally's brother, Turnip, which meant that Sally was not an admirer of Lord Vaughn. No one but Sally was allowed to insult Turnip. Still, even so . . . "Whatever else I may think of the man, Lord Vaughn looks perfectly corporeal to me. Those waistcoats are just an affectation."

It would be just like Lord Vaughn to set himself up as an undead creature of the night. He prided himself on being slightly sinister, going about in those black waistcoats with silver serpents, murmuring cryptic comments. It was, reflected Sally critically, all just a little too obvious.

"Not Lord Vaughn," said Agnes patiently. "The Duke of Belliston."

"The Duke of Who?" Lizzy joined them on the balcony, her bronze curls escaping from a wreath of flowers that had gone askew, like the halo of a naughty angel. There was a healthy glow in her cheeks and her brown eyes were bright.

"Belliston," said Agnes, palpably unaware of any social frissons or fissures. "In the house across the garden."

She gestured in the other direction, away from the crowded ballroom, past long rows of perfectly trimmed parterres.

Even in the waning season of the year, Lord Vaughn's shrubbery didn't have a leaf out of place. The garden was arranged in the French style, all gravel paths and geometric designs, scorning the more natural wilderness gardens coming into vogue. Above the close-clipped hedges and the marble statues glimmering white in the moonlight, Sally could just make out the outline of the great house across the way.

Unlike Lord Vaughn's, that garden had been allowed to run to seed, by either accident or design. Weeping willows trailed ghostly fingers over the dim outline of a pond on which no swans swam, while ivy climbed the walls of the house, dangling from the balconies, obscuring the windows. In the heart of London, the edifice had an eerie air of isolation.

It was the largest house in the square, larger by far than Lord Vaughn's. Sally felt a certain satisfaction at that thought. Lord Vaughn could put on all the airs he liked, but he still wasn't the biggest fish in the square. And by fish, she meant duke. The Duke of Belliston out-housed and outranked Vaughn.

He was also remarkably elusive. In her two Seasons in society, Sally had never met the man. There was some sort of story about him . . . something to do with a curse and his parents.

But vampires? Nonsense.

"Is that Belliston House?" Lizzy shook back her curls as she stared avidly at the house across the way. "I hadn't realized we were so close to the Lair of the Vampire."

Sally rolled her eyes at the idiocy of mankind. "Vampires are a myth. And not a particularly interesting one," she added repressively.

"People said the same thing about the Duke of Belliston," Agnes pointed out. "About his being a myth, I mean. But you can't deny there are lights in the windows."

That much was true. Through the ivy and the dust, a faint but distinct light shone.

"She has you there," said Lizzy. There was no denying that someone was in residence at Belliston House. Whoever—or whatever—that someone might be.

"Yes, but . . ." Sally made an impatient gesture with her hands. "Next you'll be telling me you saw a bat flying around his belfry."

Lizzy cocked her head, considering the urns that lined the roof of the house. "I think it's a crow."

"Did you know what a group of crows is called?" Agnes's voice dropped to a hushed whisper. "The collective term for a group of crows is—"

"Oh, no," said Sally.

"—*a murder,*" Agnes finished earnestly.

As an academic appellation it was just a little too atmospheric, especially with the moon silhouetted against the chimney pots, casting strange shadows through the abandoned garden. Sally felt a chill shiver its way down her spine, beneath the thin fabric of her gown and chemise.

Catching Lizzy's too-knowing eye, she hastily looked away, wishing she hadn't parted with her shawl.

There was no call for Lizzy to look at her that way. Chills were simply what one got when one stood on a balcony in a scoop-necked ball gown in the middle of October. It had nothing at all to do with the black bird flapping about the chimney pots.

Somewhere in the depths of the garden, an owl voiced its mournful cry.

"That"—Sally cast about for a suitably dampening adjective—"is absurd."

"No, truly," said Agnes. "It's a murder of crows and an unkindness of ravens."

That last, at least, was appropriate. Sally cast a glance back over her shoulder at the ballroom. "I'd say it's more an affectation of imbeciles."

Lizzy grinned at her. "You sound like my stepmother." Before Sally could decide whether that was an insult or not, Lizzy turned her attention back to the dark shell of Belliston House. Leaning her elbows on the balustrade, she said with relish, "They say he sucks the blood of unwary maidens."

Agnes considered this. "I imagine they're less trouble than wary ones."

"Utter rubbish," said Sally crisply. Before Agnes could argue with her, she added quickly, "Just because the man scorns society doesn't mean that he's an unholy creature of the night."

In fact, at the moment she would say it was rather a sign of his good sense.

"No one has seen him for seven years," Lizzy pointed out.

"Or was it ten? That's rather a long time for societal scorning unless he had some other motive in mind."

"Such as draining the blood of wary or unwary maidens?" Sally gave a delicate sniff. "I think not."

Agnes's face took on the distant look it acquired when she was parsing a difficult academic question. "Seven is a mystical number. . . ."

"So is three," said Sally. "Or five hundred and thirty-two." She had no idea about five hundred and thirty-two, but someone had to show a bit of sense. Sally pushed away from the balcony, her gauze overskirt catching on the carved edge of an acanthus leaf. "Whatever the Duke of Belliston is, he's just a man."

Lizzy's eyes glinted with mischief. "Prove it," she said.

Agnes looked in alarm from Lizzy to Sally and back again. "You don't mean—"

Lizzy nodded decisively. "Someone ought to go over there. In the interest of truth, of course." Her face was a picture of guileless innocence as she added delicately, "Unless, of course, you don't care to go."

They had played this game so many times before, in the safety of Miss Climpson's Select Seminary. Sally had never yet turned down a challenge, and Lizzy knew it.

"Why shouldn't I?" Sally made a show of indifference, even though she could feel the thrum of the blood through her veins, sending her pulse racing, making colors crisper and sounds clearer. "What could be more invigorating on a cool evening than a walk across a garden?"

Agnes looked at her in alarm. "Sally, you wouldn't. . . ."

Oh, wouldn't she? Sally caught Lizzy's grin and knew she understood, even if Agnes didn't.

"Don't worry," Sally said to Agnes. "I shan't do anything foolish. Anything else foolish," she amended. "I'll just peer through the window and report back. That's all."

Before Agnes could protest, Sally pushed her cameo bracelets up on her wrists and ran lightly down the path.

"Be—" and behind her, Sally heard Agnes's voice, soft and worried, on the night breeze. "Careful?"

Careful was just what she didn't want to be. She had missed this, the sense of being alive that came only from taking risks, from pushing the edges of the rules—all for good reason, of course. Always for good reason. They were nothing if not civic-minded, Sally told herself virtuously. But, oh, it felt good to be free of the leash of polite society, if only for a few stolen moments.

Gravel crunched beneath Sally's slippers. The cool October breeze lifted the flounces of her dress and set her golden curls dancing. Dimly, Sally was aware of Lizzy, on the bottom step, fidgeting with impatience, all eagerness to run across the garden herself; Agnes behind her, a pale presence leaning over the balustrade, prepared, despite her own doubts, to leap into the fray and fight bloodsucking creatures of the night on Sally's behalf should the occasion call for it.

Sally's heart swelled with affection for them. Sometimes, she wished they could go back to Miss Climpson's, back to the safety and security of the rambling school in Bath, where they all wore identical white muslin gowns and their greatest worry was who was to play whom in Miss Climpson's annual Christmas fiasco and whether it might be possible that someone was attempting to elope with the music master. Not that she would ever admit it to anyone. At Miss Climpson's, she had itched and fretted to be out in the world, but now that she was out, she had to admit that she was finding the world strangely flat.

But not tonight. Not now, with an adventure before her on the other side of Lord Vaughn's garden.

The formal parterres had been cleverly arranged to provide the sense of an endless vista, but, as was always the case with the Vaughns, the sense of spaciousness was an illusion; it was a London garden, and Sally was at the end of it in moments.

There was no wall separating Lord Vaughn's property from that of the Duke of Belliston, only a series of cypress trees. Their spindly shapes lent a funereal aspect to the scene, but they had one major benefit: there was plenty of space between them for one slender woman.

At the cypress border, Sally checked slightly. For all her bravado, there was something more than a little dodgy about willfully trespassing on someone else's property. It had been quite another thing to slip down to Miss Climpson's sitting room in the dead of night; the students did that so often it was practically an official extracurricular exercise.

But she couldn't turn back now, not with Lizzy watching. And it really couldn't do any harm just to creep up to the house and back. Admittedly, a white gown wasn't the best attire for creeping, but, if spotted, she could always raise her hands above her head and pretend to be a statue.

Which was, Sally realized, a plan worthy of her brother, Turnip.

With a shrug, she plunged through the cypress border. And came up short as a candle flame flared in front of her face.

For a moment, she had only a confused image of a dark form, silhouetted against the fronds of a weeping willow. Childhood memories of ghost stories surged through her mind, the horrible tales Nanny used to tell her, of faceless ghouls and headless horsemen and phantom monks in their transparent habits.

"Who is it?" she demanded, her voice high. But not with fear. It was just shortness of breath—that was all. "Show yourself."

A man swept aside the fronds of a weeping willow tree. "Show myself?" The man's voice was well-bred, and distinctly incredulous. "I should ask the same of you."

For a moment Sally froze, wildly recalling all the tales Agnes had recounted. The man's face was marble pale against the dark leaves, his features chiseled as if from stone, beautiful and stern.

The only sign of color was the single splotch of blood that marred the snowy whiteness of his cravat.

Chapter Two

Not blood. In the space of a heartbeat, Sally saw her own folly. Carmine. Merely red stone, carved with a device or sigil too faint to make out in the uncertain light.

Sally could feel her breathing return to normal. Just a man. Just a man in a garden. What she had taken to be a gibbering imp behind him revealed itself as nothing more than the marble statue of a satyr, overgrown with moss and cracked with time. The satyr presided over the empty basin of an ornamental pool, flanked by a weather-blasted marble bench, its base tangled with dark weeds.

Sally felt monumentally foolish. She didn't like being made to feel foolish.

"It isn't polite to creep up on people," Sally said sharply.

"Creep?" The man looked at her incredulously. Under the circumstances, Sally wasn't sure she could blame him. He stepped closer, holding his candle aloft. "*I* was simply enjoying my own garden."

The sudden shock of light made Sally wince. Also, he was holding it on her bad side.

"Which begs the question . . . ," the man said, in a tone that made the hairs on Sally's arms prickle with something other than cold. "What are you doing in my garden?"

Sally pressed her lips tightly together, refusing to be intimidated. "What are *you* doing—"

Sally stopped short. She couldn't very well ask him what he was doing in his own garden.

She drew herself up to her full height, letting the moonlight play off the rich gold of the cameo parure that adorned her neck, ears, and brow, and made a quick recovery. "What are you doing addressing me when we haven't been introduced?"

The Duke of Belliston—or, at least, Sally assumed it must be the Duke of Belliston—lowered his candle. "I would say," he said silkily, "that trespass was a good substitute for a formal introduction."

His hair had been allowed to grow down over his collar, curling slightly at the edges, the darkness of it contrasting with the pallor of his skin. He was even fairer than she was, which Sally took as a personal affront. She was accustomed to being the fairest of them all.

He stepped forward, the moonlight silvering his hair, making him look strangely ageless. As though he might have dwelt in this ruined garden for centuries, his eyes as dark and haunted as the night.

Behind him, the moss-grown satyr on its plinth seemed to leer at Sally.

"I am not trespassing," Sally said haughtily. "I was simply admiring your foliage."

The Duke of Belliston arched one brow. "Has anyone warned you that strange plants might have thorns?"

If she had wanted a lesson in horticulture, she would have consulted a gardener. "Has anyone ever told you that it is exceedingly annoying to speak in aphorisms?"

For a moment, a flicker of something that might have been amusement showed in his dark eyes. Amusement, or merely the reflected light of the candle. "Yes," he said. "It tends to truncate conversation quite effectively."

Sally wasn't accustomed to allowing herself to be truncated.

She took her time studying the scraggly shrubbery and empty flower beds. "Your gardener has been neglecting his duties."

The duke took a step forward. He was taller than she had realized, and he moved with a controlled grace that managed to be both elegant and slightly menacing. "There are gardens . . . and there are gardens."

His voice whirled around her like the slow swirl of a dark potion, conjuring up images of strange rites in midnight gardens, of night-blooming flowers and witches dancing under the full moon. There was a foreign flavor to it, a strange tang that blurred the edges of his accent, as exotic as a flower from distant shores.

What manner of man cloistered himself away from the world in a garden such as this?

A showy one, Sally told herself firmly, and made a pretense of contemplating the bleak remains of what must once have been a rather pretty little pleasure garden. "Your overgrowth is particularly overgrown," she said brightly. "Have you considered a scythe?"

The duke's heavy-lidded black eyes swept from the bottom of her gold-embroidered hem all the way up to the glimmering concoction of gold and coral around her neck.

At least, she assumed it was the necklace at which he was looking, and not the fine blue veins in her throat.

The duke stepped forward, fallen leaves rustling beneath his feet. The air in the garden felt suddenly very close, heavy with the scent of dead flowers. "Are you volunteering to wield it?"

Sally stumbled as she took a half step back, trying to pass it off with an airy gesture. "I toil not, neither do I scythe. But I am assured that they are quite effective at eradicating extraneous foliage."

"Perhaps," said the duke, and Sally found herself unable to look away from the eyes that were so very dark in his pale face, "I like my foliage just as it is."

Sally's voice was somewhat more breathless than she would have liked. "Even when it obstructs your view?"

"That," said the duke, "depends on what you wish to see."

"Or on what you wish to hide?" said Sally boldly.

She couldn't recall stepping forward, but she and the duke

were nose to nose. Or nose to chin, as the case might be. His cravat smelled faintly of French perfume, a haunting bouquet of exotic flowers.

For all the rumors, up close, there was nothing the least bit incorporeal about the duke. There was a faint scar on one side of his brow and a callus on his ungloved hand; she could feel the warmth of his skin through the dark stuff of his jacket. She felt an insane urge to reach out and lay her hand upon his chest, to feel if his heart was beating beneath the antique silver buttons of his waistcoat or whether that was merely the echo of her own elevated pulse.

"In that case," said the duke gently, and she could feel the brush of his breath against her cheek, "surely I wouldn't tell you."

Their gazes locked; the world around them receded to nothing.

Somewhere, not far away, a church bell tolled. The lonely knell broke over the garden, once, twice, and then again, breaking the spell that held her. Sally counted twelve.

Midnight.

She hadn't realized she had said it aloud until the duke said, "That is the accepted term."

He took a step back, and Sally became painfully aware of just how close they had been standing, her head tilted back like some silly ninny waiting to be kissed.

Sally hastily rearranged the angle of her chin, aiming for maximum hauteur. She was generally quite good at hauteur. It went with her height and the size of her dowry. But tonight she found herself at something of a loss.

"Forgive me if my hospitality"—the duke gave Sally a pointed look that brought the color into her cheeks—"seems lacking, but I have . . . an appointment. Shall I escort you back to the line of shrubbery, or may I trust you to make your own way?"

"I made it here without escort," said Sally tartly, before realizing that that didn't exactly help her case.

"I make the offer for your own protection." Sally caught a glimmer of something that might have been a smile. "Against ghosties and ghoulies and things that go bump in the night."

Oh, ha-ha. Very funny.

"Hmph," said Sally, in her best imitation of Mrs. Reid's infamous sniff. "The question you should be asking is, who will protect them from me?"

It was an excellent parting line, and Sally meant to use it to its full advantage. She turned on her heel with an exaggerated sweep of her demi-train. But one thing nagged at her. She knew she should leave it be, but . . .

Turning, Sally demanded, "Who makes appointments at midnight?"

The Duke of Belliston was standing just as she had left him, silhouetted against the dark shadows of the empty pool.

He essayed an ironical bow. "What better time for a creature of the night to travel?"

Lucien, Duke of Belliston, watched his trespasser as she stalked with great dignity as far as the cypress border, and then ruined it by glancing back over her shoulder.

To make sure, presumably, that he hadn't turned into a giant bat.

Lucien essayed an elegant bow.

The girl gave a loud and disapproving sniff and disappeared between two twisted trees, and Lucien allowed the grin that he had been repressing to spread across his face. Beasties and ghoulies and things that went bump in the night, indeed. It had been worth it, just to see her eyes widen and then narrow again. He hadn't been so amused since—

Since boarding the ship to return to England.

That thought was enough to wipe the smile off his face. Only a few weeks more, he reminded himself. Just a few weeks to sort through the yellowing papers in his father's study and the long-abandoned journals in his mother's workroom, to sift through moldering correspondence and mouse-eaten cards of invitation.

And then what? Back to New Orleans, to the home of his mother's sister? Lucien had been happy there, or something close to it, but it wasn't his home. The broad acres of his uncle's plantation were well managed by others, and he had no place in the insular society of the French Quarter. An English duke was as out of place there as a Creole in London.

In New Orleans, he was too English; at home, he was tainted by his mother's blood, by the tang of something foreign, and exotic, and more than a little bit French. His mother had come from Martinique, with the liquid accent of the islands, hair as dark as his, and pale skin warmed by the sun on distant shores. She had been considerably younger than his father.

Witchwoman's brat, the boys at school had taunted him.

Lucien's face hardened. Others might flirt with girls in gardens, but he had another task, a task too long delayed. He meant to see justice done, or, at least, some measure of it.

To his right, he could see the remains of his mother's greenhouse, the glass panes cracked and blackened with soot and grime, the frame warped by English winter weather. The broken panels gaped like a silent scream, leering like a demon's smile.

She had been a botanist, his mother, specializing in the plants of the tropics. Her greenhouse had bloomed with exotic specimens, warmed by braziers through the cold of the English winters. Among Lucien's earliest memories was his mother in the greenhouses at Hullingden, taking him from bloom to bloom, introducing each by name, warning him away from some, letting him crinkle and sniff others. Lucien had made mud pies in the rich garden loam while his mother had scribbled her notes in a flowing hand in the faintly scented brown ink she favored.

Lucien's grandfather had been a botanist too. He had taken Lucien's mother with him from Martinique to London to give a paper at the Royal Society—and it was there that Lucien's parents had met. His father had little interest in plants, but he, who had defied all the best matchmaking efforts of London's matrons, had displayed a great deal of interest in the bluestocking from Martinique. The duke was well past forty, at an age when London had despaired of seeing him married; Lucien's mother was barely twenty. But something in them had called each to each. They were married a mere three weeks later, with half of London in attendance to speculate and gawp.

An old man's fancy, they called her, but Lucien knew otherwise. His mother hadn't been like that; his parents hadn't been like that. He could remember them together, teasing and mocking, his mother inquiring after his father's activities in the government, his father displaying a valiant interest in his mother's cuttings and sectionings and who had insulted whom in which learned paper. Lucien could remember them sitting together on a bench in the garden at Hullingden, his mother's unpowdered head on his father's shoulder, the black curls falling long and free across his silver-brocade waistcoat as little Marie-Clarice batted her hands in a basket by their feet.

Lucien looked across the garden, at the dark bulk of Belliston House. For a moment, he could see it as it had been, the statues solid on their plinths, lithe goldfish swimming in the clear water of the fountain, hedges neatly trimmed, windows blazing with light. All gone now. Gone these past twelve years.

Lucien had been only twelve. He had been shunted off to school, left to stew and brood and avenge his honor with his fists as best he could on and off the playing fields of Eton. Those hadn't been pleasant years. He had been numb with shock and grief, and the concerted malice of his peers had caught him on the raw. He had escaped as soon as he could, first for the family seat, and then, when Uncle Henry had sent him back, where all the Uncle Henrys in the world couldn't reach him, all the way to his mother's family in America.

"Your grace." A rough voice pulled him back to the present, the guttural accents turning the title from an honorific into a grunt.

It was Jamison, who had served as caretaker of the house these past twelve years, and now, for want of a better option, butler and general factotum. His wife, once an under-housemaid, made a pretense of keeping the house, and served Lucien meals so consistently inedible that he was forced to conclude that either her taste buds had long since atrophied or she was engaged in a plot to slowly poison him with rancid pie.

Despite their inadequacies, there had been no call to go to the bother of hiring staff, the sort of staff the house had once boasted, the legions of maids and footmen, the well-starched butler and chattering scullions. He didn't intend to stay long.

Besides, it wasn't as though Lucien would be receiving callers. The only guests he was entertaining were long since dead.

With the exception of that girl in the garden.

"Your grace." As always, Jamison's weather-beaten face revealed nothing of his feelings. His loose-lipped visage and stooped shoulders suggested ancestry of the simian variety, but he had been head gardener in Lucien's parents' day. More importantly, he was the only one of the staff to stay on, after—

After.

Lucien's life was divided into two halves: before and after. There was no need to specify the event.

Never one to waste time on niceties, Jamison got right to the point. "You have callers."

He spat on the last word, which might have been an opinion as to their guests or merely his habitual form of communication.

"At midnight?" Lucien heard himself echoing the girl in the garden. But she was right. Midnight was a deuced odd time for anyone to come calling.

Jamison merely directed another wad of spittle towards a spot just to the left of Lucien's right shoe.

"All right, then," said Lucien. "I suppose it's too much to ask whether you showed them in?"

But Jamison had already departed. Buttling was not among his core competencies.

Curious despite himself, Lucien retraced his steps along the crumbling flagstone path and let himself in by a little door in the side of the house, a door once meant for the comings and goings of servants, but which, in their absence, had proved a convenient means of ingress for the master of the house. Especially when he wished to enter without being seen.

For a moment, he wondered if the girl with the golden hair had chosen to essay another approach, having been banned from the garden. Was it was a weakness in himself that he rather hoped she had? His self-appointed task might be a noble one, but that didn't make it any less lonely.

Jamison had left the callers standing in the hall, which, Lucien supposed, was rather what one got when one visited, unheralded, at midnight. There were four of them: a young man in high shirt points, an older man with his hair clubbed back in the old style, a matron in the finest stare of style, egret feathers bristling from a turban of Nile green satin.

And a young woman, a fillet of filigree shining in her gently curling hair.

"—disgraceful!" the older woman was saying. But Lucien had eyes only for the young woman.

He felt that dislocation again, that curious overlay of past and present. In place of the slender woman in the hall, he saw a little girl in a white dress with a sash embroidered with posies, her chubby hands grasping a bouquet of dandelions.

Lucien stepped out from behind the suit of armor. "Marie-Clarice," he said.

All four turned to stare at him as though the suit of armor had suddenly taken to its legs and staggered forward to greet them.

Marie-Clarice stared at him, with eyes that were too dark for her pale face. She had inherited their father's fair coloring, but their mother's eyes, deep-set and black, the same eyes that Lucien saw in the mirror every morning.

"So it is true," she said distantly. Her eyes narrowed and her voice hardened. "It is you."

There seemed very little to say to that except, "Yes."

How else did one fill nine missing years?

"Well!" said Aunt Winifred, her stays creaking ominously beneath her satin gown as she drew in an indignant breath. "One would think you might have allowed your own family to hear of your return from your own hand, rather than leaving it to the mouths of common gossips—"

"We're delighted," Uncle Henry intervened, shooting his wife a hard look. A little too heartily, he said, "Welcome home, my boy. Welcome home."

Lucien's cousin, Hal, his hair the same silver-gilt that Uncle Henry's had once been, did nothing but stare, his jaw dropping until it connected with the top fold of his elaborately tied cravat.

They were all fair. The Caldicotts had been breeding fair-haired, light-eyed, and pink-cheeked since time immemorial, a testament to their Saxon forebears. Next to them, Lucien felt, as he always had, a cuckoo in the nest. It was an unfortunate mischance that he was the cuckoo who bore the title.

"Hello," Lucien said inadequately.

His sister took a step forward. Their mother had been petite, but Marie-Clarice had inherited the Caldicott height, as well as the family's famed silver-gilt hair. Only her eyes belonged to their mother.

"Did you mean to call?" she inquired dangerously. "Or were we not to be privileged with the pleasure of your company?"

Every word stung like the lash of a whip, all the more so for being—Lucien had to admit—deserved.

"I had thought you would have been at Hullingden," he ventured.

Hullingden was the primary family seat. Lucien had grown up there, had roamed those woods and explored those secret passageways. It had been, for the bulk of his childhood, his entire world; Belliston House, in London, was a faraway place he knew of only from his parents' conversation.

The estate had been passed into the stewardship of Uncle Henry until such time as Lucien came of age.

By the time Lucien came of age, he was already halfway across the world.

He ought, he knew, to have presented himself at Hullingden first. It wasn't much good for the prodigal to return without making his presence known. But the idea of passing through those portals again had filled him with a fine sweat of fear. Belliston House was different. It was bland. It was safe.

"It's your sister's first Season." Aunt Winifred sailed into the fray, her feathers bobbing ominously. "Naturally, we are in London. As you would have known had you shown any of the consideration due as the Head of the House."

Lucien could hear the capital letters as she pronounced it and the bite of venom behind it.

"But what," Aunt Winifred added, addressing herself to the suit of armor, "can one expect?"

From the witchwoman's brat.

The boys at Eton weren't the only ones to have cast slurs on Lucien's parentage; Aunt Winifred had been more subtle, but no less vicious. It was one of the reasons that Lucien had bolted when he had. Without his parents in it, Hullingden hadn't been home; with Aunt Winifred in it, it had become a form of prison. Aunt Winifred had made it quite clear that she thought it a sad mistake on the part of Fate to allow the dukedom to fall to so unworthy a creature as Lucien, the debased product of a sad mésalliance.

One would think she might be a bit more pleased that Lucien had obliged her by removing himself.

"We would have consulted you," said Uncle Henry mildly, "but we supposed you abroad."

The gentle reproach in Uncle Henry's voice was worse than the vitriol in Aunt Winifred's.

Lucien looked from one hostile face to the next, at a loss as to what to say. Yes, it had been a childish trick to bolt, as he had, all those years ago. He could see that now. But he had never imagined his presence being missed. In fact, quite the contrary. Uncle Henry had the care of Hullingden and of Marie-Clarice; if Lucien had thought of it, he had imagined it all meandering on just as it had. He had never thought of himself as having any part of it, or as shirking by being away. He had never thought of Marie-Clarice as growing older; in his head, she was eternally a child of six, in the nursery with her governess.

Lucien took a tentative step towards her. "Marie-Clarice——"

"Clarissa," she corrected him sharply, her accent very proper, very correct. Very English.

"Clarissa," he amended. "You are . . . well?"

He didn't know her, this woman with the proud face and the narrow, angry eyes. But, then, he'd never known her. Not well. She had been a child when he left, too much younger to be of much interest to a boy of fifteen, and particularly a boy so occupied with his own wrongs as he had been. She had seemed happy enough at Hullingden.

Hullingden, a paradise in Lucien's memory, turned so suddenly and unexpectedly into a nightmare.

Had he been wrong? Lucien had told himself he was obliging them all by staying away, by failing to inflict upon them his unwanted presence. He had assumed that Marie-Clarice would be happy enough without him.

She didn't look particularly happy right now.

"Very well," she said, in clipped tones.

"Her ball is in two days' time," said Aunt Winifred. Her hard round eyes swept the dusty hall. "It *ought* to have been at Belliston House."

From far away, Lucien could hear the echo of his mother's voice, a half-remembered snippet of conversation.

Winifred will never forgive Henry for not being the duke.

And his father, responding in his own, dry way. *No, my love. Winifred will never forgive you for being my duchess.*

They had spoken in French. They always spoke in French at home, his father's the elegant accents of Versailles, his mother's the rolling cadences of her island home.

"I have no desire for a ball at Belliston House," said Marie-Clarice—Clarissa—flatly.

Lucien felt himself the center of a circle of censorious eyes. "The house isn't really in any condition to hold an entertainment," he said mildly. "From what I've seen of such things."

It seemed like a sacrilege to invite a herd of strangers to trample through the ashes of his past. He was too busy doing that himself.

"Nonsense," said Aunt Winifred, her bosom swelling to new and impossible proportions. She was a tall, thin woman, but, like a toad, she could inflate to several times her own size when the occasion called for it. "What do men know of such things? It's no large matter to have the servants soap the chandeliers and shake out the rugs. It's a scandal for the daughter of the duke not to have her ball in her own family home."

She made Lucien feel as though he were personally responsible for trampling on a litter of particularly adorable puppies.

"I have no desire for a ball at Belliston House," repeated Clarissa, in a tight, hard voice.

"Your family heritage—," began Aunt Winifred stridently.

"The ball is in two days," said Uncle Henry wearily. "The cards have gone out already."

Lucien looked at him with gratitude.

"All the same," Uncle Henry added, looking to Lucien, "we do trust we will see you there."

It was more a command than a request.

In a gentler tone, Uncle Henry added, "It would mean a great deal to us to have you join us."

The last thing Lucien wanted was to go out into society. But, with the weight of four pairs of Caldicott eyes upon him, there was little he could do but say, "I will not fail you."

"Haven't you?" said Aunt Winifred. And then, "Come, Clarissa."

Clarissa went, pausing only to give Lucien a long, hard look on her way out. "Welcome home," she said.

Her welcome did not sound particularly welcoming.

Uncle Henry squeezed his shoulder in passing. "It's good to have you back, my boy."

"Thank you," said Lucien, his throat tight with a tangle of emotions. Uncle Henry, of all of them, sounded as though he meant it.

The only one left was Hal.

Hal had been eleven when Lucien left. Now he was a young man, with his fine, fair hair cut fashionably short, and his waistcoat generously adorned with jangling fobs. Once upon a time, he had been Lucien's shadow, tagging along after him to the stable and the Home Woods, filching tarts from the kitchen as a signal of his devotion, always ready to take the junior part in any drama.

Now he looked at Lucien with hurt, accusing eyes. "I didn't believe it when they told me," he said, in a low voice.

"Believe—"

"That you had come back." Hal's voice broke on the last word. He gave a bitter laugh. It made him sound, thought Lucien, very young. "But, then, I didn't believe it when you left, either. Just like that. Without a word."

If he had left word, they would have found him and made him come back. But Lucien couldn't say that.

"I'm sorry?" he ventured.

"Sorry," his cousin echoed, with all the scorn of twenty. "And now, I suppose, you expect to waltz right in and have everything just as it was." His voice went up. "Well, it isn't. And it can't be."

"No," agreed Lucien, thinking of Marie-Clarice's cold, hard eyes, of his mother's grave, his father's portrait on the wall, "it can't be."

Hal gave Lucien one last, suspicious look. "Mock all you like," he said furiously, "but you'll see. We don't want you here."

And he slammed the heavy door behind him.

"I don't want to be here either," said Lucien. But Hal was already gone.

No use to explain that he couldn't leave. Not yet. Not until he brought his parents' murderer to justice.

But in the meantime, it seemed that he had a ball to attend.

Chapter Three

*L*ady Clarissa Caldicott's ball was held in Richmond, at the home of Lord Henry Caldicott and his wife.

The trip from London had taken even longer than usual, due to the glut of carriages on the road. The circular drive before the house was jammed, and the pale marble stairs were all but invisible due to the procession of ladies and gentlemen making their way up to the great doorway that loomed between two tall flambeaux.

Sally, Lizzy, and Agnes zigzagged their way up the stairs, trailing behind Sally's sister-in-law, Arabella, who had been tasked with chaperoning them for the evening, and Sally's brother, Turnip, who bounded enthusiastically ahead to clear a path for them, like a particularly energetic golden retriever.

Technically, both Lizzy and Agnes were meant to be under the eye of Lizzy's stepmother, Mrs. Reid, the former Miss Gwen. But ever since it had come out that Miss Gwen was the author of *The Covent of Orsino*, she couldn't go anywhere without being mobbed by admirers.

Miss Gwen did not admire her admirers.

And when Miss Gwen did not admire, she tended to apply the pointier portion of her parasol to whichever bit of anatomy was nearest. Matrimony and the arrival of an infant daughter had done nothing to blunt the sharp end of Miss Gwen's tongue or her parasol. Colonel Reid was suspected of having taken it upon himself to supply his wife with an even larger collection of sharp-edged accessories, although, when taxed about this by those with sore extremities, he generally disclaimed responsibility with an innocence entirely at odds with the glint in his eye.

It was thought safer for everyone concerned if Miss Gwen accompany the girls as infrequently as possible.

It was particularly fortunate that she hadn't accompanied them this evening, as it seemed that all of London's fops and fribbles were out in force. By the time Sally had fought her way up the stairs, she was hot, rumpled, and generally annoyed.

"Retiring room?" Sally bellowed to Lizzy. It wasn't meant to be a bellow, but the din was such that even private conversations required stentorian tones.

If Sally had wondered why London's elite hadn't quibbled at rattling all the way out to Richmond, the answer soon became clear: the ladies' retiring room was buzzing with the rumor that the Ghoul of Belliston Hall was due to put in an appearance.

"It's not a hall—it's a house," commented Sally in annoyance to Lizzy, as they made the necessary repairs to their appearances.

"Just be glad they're not calling it an abbey." Lizzy leaned forward, admiring the effect of her emerald-and-filigree earrings. They weren't at all the thing for a girl in her first Season, but the stepdaughter of the author of *The Convent of Orsino* was allowed to be just a little bit outrageous. Sally's own blue-enamel-and-seed-pearl set, a gift from her brother, Turnip, seemed decidedly bland in comparison.

"In order to be an abbey," said Agnes, looking at them owlishly in the mirror, "the house would have had to have belonged to a religious institution of that order. *Were* there monks on the site of Belliston House?"

Sally rolled her eyes. "Why not just say there's an ancient druid burial ground and have done?"

"An ancient druid burial ground?" The girl next to them, repairing a microscopic tear in her flounce, dropped her pins. "Oh, my! That explains so much. Did you hear—"

And she turned to the woman on her other side to gush out the latest intelligence.

Sally regarded them both with a jaundiced eye. "Piffle," she said.

Lizzy's lips twitched. "Would you care to share your real feelings?"

The Mark of the Midnight Manzanilla ❦ 51

Behind them, two other women were exchanging the latest *on dits* about the Duke of Belliston. "—a jagged scar across his face!" Delia Cathcart was saying. "They say you'll know him because his eyes glow red . . . when he's about to *feed*."

"It's not at all surprising," returned Georgiana Thynne, looking superior, "when you think what they say about his mother. . . ."

What did they say about his mother?

"They say"—Delia leaned forward, the words coming out in a rush—"that the reason no one has seen him all these years is that the family has kept him confined. In a *crypt*." She shivered deliciously.

"I wager you all of next quarter's allowance that you don't have the courage to dance with him," said Lucy Ponsonby, with a titter.

"I couldn't," Delia said, clasping her plump hands to her bosom. "I just couldn't."

"I don't know," said Georgiana Thynne. "For a whole quarter's allowance? There's a hat I've been wanting that Mama refuses to buy. . . ."

"Yes," said Delia, bumping into Sally in her enthusiasm. Sally frowned at her, but she didn't pay the least bit of attention. "But what if he were to *set his mark upon you*?"

"It's the curse," said Lucy Ponsonby, pronouncing the word with relish. She preened in the mirror. "The curse of the Caldicotts. I don't care how large his lands are. I wouldn't have him if he were the last duke in London, and I told that to my mama just this morning. Mama, I said—"

"What makes her think he'd have her?" Sally whispered to Lizzy. She hadn't seen buckteeth like that since her beloved pony, Bucky the Bucktooth, had gone off to that good pasture in the sky.

"Well," said Lizzy innocently, "with that hideous scar across his face and the hunchback and clubfoot—not to mention the curse—I imagine he can't be picky."

"He's not hunchbacked," snapped Sally. "In fact he's quite—"

Handsome? He wasn't handsome in the way society assessed such things: his hair was too long, his eyes too deep, his lips too full, his features too marked. All of him was just too . . . too. He was like the embers on the hearth, burning from within.

Infuriating? Intriguing?

"Quite?" Lizzy's ears perked up.

"Presentable," said Sally quellingly. "Quite presentable."

Lizzy looked at her knowingly. "As good-looking as all that?"

"Hmph." No other sound was adequate to express her feelings. Sally drove a pearl comb into her hair with more force than necessary. "All of this is worse than nonsense—it's *unkind*."

Normally, Sally enjoyed a spot of gossip as much as the next girl, but this wasn't innocent chitter chatter of the who-danced-with-whom variety. This was the sort of hysterical speculation that drove villagers out in the dead of night armed with garden implements to essay a spot of castle burning.

She turned to glower at the oblivious women behind them. "Besides, he isn't like that."

Lizzy linked an arm through hers. "What is he like, then?" she asked.

Mysterious. Terribly mysterious.

The word rose unbidden to Sally's mind, along with the memory of a wilderness of a garden, willows weeping above a frost-blasted fountain, and a black-garbed figure in its midst. He had been other things—enigmatic, infuriating, more than a little bit sardonic—but the primary word that came to mind was "mysterious." He looked as though he had grown out of the fallen leaves and moss-covered stones, like a creature of shadow and moonlight, condemned to lonely durance in his haunted castle.

All nonsense, of course. Next thing one knew, she'd be mooning over *The Convent of Orsino* and begging Miss Gwen for her autograph.

"Human," said Sally tartly. "And very much alive."

Alive and quipping. It still rankled that she had allowed him to seize the last word. No one, but no one, was allowed to best Miss Sally Fitzhugh. Not even reclusive dukes rumored to be vampires.

Particularly not reclusive dukes rumored to be vampires.

Sally had spent the rest of the evening meticulously constructing pithy parting lines, none of which were the least bit of use after the fact.

"I can't imagine the duke would be here," said Sally loftily.

"It isn't at all the sort of affair one would expect creatures of the night to frequent."

Best time for creatures of the night to travel, indeed!

"It is after dark," said Lizzy impishly.

Returning from behind one of the screens, Agnes looked from one to the other in surprise. "But, of course, the duke would be here. Didn't you know? Lady Clarissa Caldicott is his sister."

"I knew that," said Sally quickly. And maybe she had, at one point. *Debrett's Peerage* had been required reading at Miss Climpson's, right there next to the Bible. Miss Climpson believed in books that began with "begat." "I just didn't think he looked much like a Caldicott."

"What does a Caldicott look like?" asked Agnes.

Sally wafted a hand. "Fair. Bland. Unobjectionable."

Hal Caldicott was just her age and a member of her brother's club; Sally had danced with him from time to time. He was everything that was conventional and predictable: he drove his phaeton too fast, he wore too many capes on his coat, he played for high stakes, he tortured his cravat into elaborate styles, all in the most inoffensive way possible. In short, all the usual rites of passage of a young man of good fortune and limited imagination. Sally found him quite pleasant and entirely uninteresting.

Belliston, on the other hand . . . There was something dark and brooding about the very name "Belliston." Something with a hint of passion to it.

Rather like the duke.

"Do vampires *have* sisters?" asked Lizzy with feigned innocence.

"This one does," said Agnes earnestly. Pursing her lips, she recited, "Lucien, sixth Duke of Belliston, and Lady Clarissa Caldicott are the sole surviving offspring of the fifth Duke of Belliston, and his wife, the former Hortense de la Pagerie."

Sally looked narrowly at Agnes. "Sole surviving—does that mean there were others?"

Agnes looked a little sheepish. "I don't think so. It just sounded better that way."

"Unless you think he ate them?" suggested Lizzy.

Agnes's pale brows drew together. "I don't think vampires are meant to eat people. They just . . ."

"Nibble?" provided Lizzy.

Another two women pushed past them, arm in arm. "—druid curse!" Sally could hear one saying, in strictest confidence, at the top of her lungs.

"I thought we had ascertained that there are no vampires," said Sally, in her best imitation of Miss Gwendolyn Meadows. There were times when she really did wish that she owned a sword parasol.

Lizzy narrowed her brown eyes. "Even so, there must be something wrong with the man. Why stay so secluded all these years? Why hide from society?"

"Perhaps he simply doesn't like them," said Sally. She wasn't sure why she felt so defensive on the duke's behalf. It wasn't as though he had been particularly warm or welcoming to her—unless one considered sarcasm a sign of regard.

Maybe it was that he was a challenge, her own private challenge, not to be shared with anyone else.

Which was, of course, equally ridiculous, given that she was unlikely to see the man ever again, current rumor notwithstanding.

"We should be getting back," Sally said. She could see Arabella looking for them, with her perturbed-chaperone face on. Arabella enjoyed chaperoning just about as much as Sally enjoyed being chaperoned; Sally knew she would much rather be home, watching her daughter, Parsnip, attempt new aerial feats with a spoonful of mushy peas. "They're sure to begin the dancing soon."

"Hmm." Lizzy raised a hand in greeting to Lady Vaughn just to watch Lady Vaughn do her best imitation of a block of ice. That task accomplished, she turned back to Sally. "You can't avoid me forever, you know. You've been remarkably chary with the details of your tête-à-tête."

Sally shot a warning glare at Lizzy, but it was too late. Arabella might look as meek as milk, but she had ears like a hawk. If hawks had ears. Sally wasn't sure, ornithology not having been prominently featured in the curriculum of Miss Climpson's Select Seminary.

"Tête-á-tête?" said Arabella, in a deceptively mild voice.

Lizzy looked from Sally to Arabella and scented danger.

"Oh, goodness," she said, her eyes wide and innocent. "Has my flounce torn? I must go and see to it."

Sally wondered if Miss Gwen would consider the loan of her infamous sword parasol. Just for use on Lizzy. She would make sure to clean it thoroughly before she returned it.

"Did you see Lady Vaughn snub Lizzy?" Sally said quickly. There was nothing like a good diversion.

Arabella was not to be diverted. "Lady Vaughn snubs everybody. What was that about a tête-à-tête?"

"Tete a whatsis?" Sally's brother, Turnip, appeared, balancing five glasses of ratafia, two in each hand and one under his chin, adding an extra dent to his cravat and a trail of sticky liquid down his waistcoat. He apportioned the beverages among the three ladies, and looked in some confusion to the place where Lizzy had been standing. "Where's your friend?"

"Departed," said Sally bitterly. "Decamped. Deserted."

"With a hey and a ho and a hey nonny no," agreed Turnip. He looked at the extraneous glass of ratafia, gave a philosophical shrug, and drained the glass himself. He glanced up to see all three women looking at him. He grinned sheepishly at his wife. "Sounded like a verse, don'tcha know."

"Yes," said Sally sourly. "Ratafia brings poetry into everyone's lives."

"Leave a kiss but in the cup and I'll not ask for thingummy," said Turnip, looking soulfully at Arabella.

Arabella blew her husband a kiss over her fan.

Sally rolled her eyes, but she took advantage of her chaperone's momentary distraction to ask, "What do you know about the curse of the Caldicotts?"

Arabella raised her eyebrows slightly, signaling that she knew exactly what Sally was doing. The tête-à-tête discussion would be resumed at a later time—but not in front of Turnip, and not in the middle of a crowded ballroom. Arabella would never think of taking Sally to task in public, a fact of which Sally took shameless advantage.

"I shouldn't have thought you would pay any attention to that sort of flummery," Arabella said mildly.

"I'm not," said Sally indignantly. "I mean, I haven't. I was just curious." She squirmed a little under her chaperone's too acute gaze. "And, yes, I know what they say about curiosity and cats."

"Speak of the devil," said Turnip heartily. He raised a hand and flapped it in the direction of someone behind Sally's back. "Caldicott. I say! Caldicott!"

A tingle like lightning ran down Sally's spine. She turned slowly, frantically trying to get her expression under control. Should she look aloof? Amused? Sweetly angelic? Or—

Oh. It wasn't the duke at all, just plain old Hal Caldicott, who was, to be fair, neither plain nor old. But he wasn't the duke.

Hal had been making a beeline across the ballroom. At Turnip's enthusiastic hail, he feinted sideways, as if trying to decide whether there was still time to make a run for it. As Turnip

bellowed his name again—this time with a loud "halloo!"—
Caldicott bowed to the inevitable and made his way to their side
with a marked lack of enthusiasm.

"Fitzhugh," he said.

"Off your feed, what, old bean?" said Turnip sympathetically. "You don't look at all the thing."

For once Turnip was right. The normally good-humored
Hal looked as though he hadn't slept in a week. His blond hair,
usually brushed into a Corinthian crop, was straight and stringy;
his cravat was clean and crisply starched, but crookedly tied; and
his watch chain boasted only half the usual number of fobs.
There were purple circles under his eyes and his fingers beat a
nervous tattoo against his thighs.

If Sally had to guess, she would wager that he had been playing too deeply at the gaming tables. She looked him up and
down with an experienced eye. He had the look of a man who
had been badly dipped and was trying to figure out which was
worse: braving his father or going to the moneylenders.

Hal Caldicott forced a smile. "I'm quite all right. Mrs. Fitzhugh. Miss Fitzhugh."

He bowed over Arabella's hand, then Sally's. His gloved
hand was cold against Sally's lace mitt.

Turnip dealt him a resounding whack on the back in the accepted male gesture of affection. "Come to ask my sister to dance?"

There were times. . . . After that, the poor man could hardly
do otherwise, when it was quite obvious it had never been his
object.

Pointedly ignoring Turnip, Sally turned to Hal Caldicott, intending to afford him an honorable retreat. "Aren't you opening the dancing with your cousin?"

The rumor in the ladies' retiring room was that a betrothal was on the verge of being declared between the Honorable Harold and his cousin, Lady Clarissa.

Certainly, Hal squired his cousin frequently enough, although Sally had never been able to determine any signs of partiality between the two. Affection, yes. Partiality, no. The two sentiments were quite different. After a Season and a half, Sally considered herself a connoisseur.

Deep lines formed on either side of Hal's mouth. He fidgeted with a cameo fob. "I was to have opened the ball with my cousin, but—"

"—my brother shamelessly waylaid you on your way to her side?" Sally provided, with a pointed glance at Turnip.

"—but I was cut out." The words came out a little too loudly against the first scrapings of the musicians' instruments. In the awkward silence that followed, Hal's color rose slightly, and he said, a bit indistinctly, "Would you do me the honor of this dance, Miss Fitzhugh? I should be delighted."

Turnip opened his mouth to say something. Arabella threaded her arm through his and gently but firmly led him away.

Thank you, Sally mouthed. Turnip always meant well. It was just the execution that was the problem. Scenting gossip, Sally said soothingly, "There must have been some mistake. If the order was already set . . ."

"I'm surprised you haven't heard," said Hal Caldicott bitterly. "You must be the only one in London who hasn't."

Men were so prone to exaggeration. "Heard what?"

"There," Hal said, uttering the word as though it left a bad taste in his mouth. He gestured towards the dance floor, where the first set was starting to form, the lady of the hour at the fore.

Lady Clarissa Caldicott looked like an ice princess, with her silver blond hair and her black, black eyes, the effect intensified by a white gauze slip frosted with silver embroidery. Something about her reminded Sally of a winter wood, the bare branches dark against the glittering snow.

There was nothing the least bit frosty about the man standing beside her. Beneath his black jacket, his waistcoat was a deep crimson, like a full-blown rose; the same carnelian stickpin smoldered in the snowy folds of his cravat.

As he straightened from the ritual bow, Sally caught his eye. For a moment, their eyes locked, his as dark and deep-set as she remembered, the sort of eyes that burned right through you.

For a moment, Sally thought it was just the ringing in her ears that made the room seem suddenly still. But then the duke rose, and their gazes broke, and Sally realized it wasn't her ears at all. The room *had* gone still.

All the little conversations, all the gossip and greetings going on in clumps around the room, were extinguished as, one by one, everyone turned to stare at the man in the middle of the floor.

For once, rumor had it right. The Ghoul of Belliston Hall had emerged from his lair.

"You see?" In the silence, Hal's voice sounded unnaturally harsh. "Break out the fatted calf. My cousin, the duke, has come home."

The prodigal wasn't having a very pleasant time of it.

If there was any fatted calf, it had long since grown cold. The gossipmongers might have exulted in his appearance, but Lucien's own family was treating him with a mixture of resentment (Hal), forbearance (Aunt Winifred), and chilly civility (his sister). The only one who appeared genuinely pleased to have him back was Uncle Henry, but even his bonhomie was rendered thin by his all too obvious attempts to allay the behavior of the others.

Lucien couldn't tell whether his relations were more furious with him for leaving or for coming back.

One woman made the sign against the evil eye; another swooned as he crossed her path. Yes, his valet, Patrice, had told him that there were silly rumors circulating about his being some sort of bloodsucking creature of the night, but Lucien had assumed it was—largely—a joke.

Apparently not.

The only person who looked him in the eye was the blond girl who had invaded his garden two nights ago. Lucien saw her giving him a frank examination as he came up from his bow.

"Who is the woman in pink?" he asked abruptly.

Clarissa placed a hand correctly on his arm as he led her to the front of the line for the dance. "Which one?"

Lucien decided not to attempt describing the shade. As he watched, the girl and her partner took their place farther down the line. Drily, he said, "The one dancing with Hal."

Clarissa looked and shrugged. "I don't know. I only came down from Hullingden two weeks ago."

Clarissa dropped into a deep curtsy, and the rest of the women followed her lead, one by one, all down the line. It was a distinctly dizzying effect.

The blond girl said something across the line to Hal. Lucien found himself wondering what it was.

The musicians struck up the first chords of the dance. It was, mercifully, one that Lucien knew. "Were you happy there? At Hullingden?"

The familiar name sat uneasily on his tongue. For so very long, he had avoided speaking or thinking of his home. Except in dreams. One couldn't help one's dreams.

Clarissa looked straight ahead as they stepped forward and then back. "Why wouldn't I have been?"

Because their world had been torn out from around them in the space of a day.

Perhaps Clarissa had felt it less. Her life at Hullingden hadn't changed as much as his; she had seen less of their parents, still wrapped in the protective cocoon of the nursery. Lucien's father had been heard to opine that a child didn't become interesting until he had attained the age of reason. It wasn't until Lucien was seven or eight that their father had begun to take an interest, to coach Lucien in the ways of the world with witty stories and dry asides.

Even so. Even away in the nursery, Clarissa must have felt the difference, the howling void left by their parents' deaths, and, even more so, by the manner of their dying.

Lucien felt a wave of remorse. "I should have taken you with me when I left."

Even as he said it, he knew it for the flummery it was. Marie-Clarice had been all of nine when he had run off. At the time, he'd had no clear idea where he was going, other than away. Away from the cold dorms of Eton, away from Uncle Henry's well-meaning but fumbling attempts to take his father's place, away from memories that had turned to nightmares.

Bolting in the dead of night, with one portmanteau and ten guineas to his name, Lucien had harbored vague notions of finding his mother's family in Martinique. It had been nearly two years before he had made his way by circuitous routes to his mother's sister in New Orleans.

If he were being honest, Lucien would have to admit that he had enjoyed those two years. He'd wandered from port to port, seeing curious and strange sights, learning a smattering of languages—the foul bits—and generally going to all the sorts of places a young gentleman wasn't supposed to see on his Grand Tour.

He had arrived in New Orleans intending to stay a month; instead, he had stayed close to seven years. Tante Berthe wasn't at all like his mother. He remembered his mother as a combination of intense pragmatism and quicksilver wit, someone out of the ordinary, wry and wise. Tante Berthe had the pragmatism, but not that quicksilver quality. She made up for it with a streak of strong sentimentalism that covered a genuine warmth. She had gathered Lucien to her bosom, both literally and figuratively, making him free of her home, showering him with sugared cakes and strong coffee, pressing him to consider himself a sibling to his cousins.

For nearly seven years, Lucien had lived in the Francophone society of Louisiana, relishing the strangeness of it, the burned taste of the coffee, the strange spices in the food, the flamboyant wardrobes and even more flamboyant manners. He had danced at their balls and fenced in their salons.

Would Clarissa have come if he had sent for her? In retrospect, Lucien knew it had been impossible. Uncle Henry was her guardian. Which meant, in practice, that Aunt Winifred was her guardian. She would never have allowed it.

But he might at least have tried.

Clarissa afforded him a wintry smile. "How very kind of you. It's a bit late for that, don't you think?"

It was a bit late for many things. Month by month, year by year, Lucien had promised himself that he would return to England to seek justice for their parents—but it was easy enough to drag it out and put it off, letting himself be seduced by the easy life of the bayou.

Lucien fumbled for the words. "When I left—I was a fifteen-year-old boy." Burning with a sense of injustice and anger at the world. No one listened to a fifteen-year-old boy, not even if that boy was a duke. They nodded, and smiled, and patted him on the head, and packed him away to school, while his parents' blood still cried out for justice. "I never meant to stay away for as long as I have."

Clarissa turned her face away. "There's no need to explain."

In profile, her face was eerily like their father's, the lean, fine-boned lines, the aquiline nose. A feminine version, but with the same blade-keen elegance, refined over the centuries.

"But there is." He had never thought of what it meant to her, left behind. A little girl in a nursery was nothing to a boy of fifteen. "I was remiss in my duty to you. And, most of all, I failed *them*. Our parents."

"I try not to think of them." The pattern of the dance parted them and brought them together again. Clarissa's eyes were fixed on the far reaches of the ballroom, searching—for what?

A portrait of Aunt Winifred, pug-faced in puce, smirked down at them from above the mantel.

If their parents were alive, this dance would be at Belliston House, with the paired portraits of their parents looking down from the wall, his father in his powdered wig and silver-embroidered ice blue waistcoat, his mother laughing down at them, her dark hair, unpowdered, in long curls hanging over her shoulders, one elbow leaning on a marble pedestal, a scroll unrolling from her hand, the frame of her greenhouse behind her.

Those portraits were dull with dust, hanging behind tattered curtains in the empty ballroom of Belliston House, his father's sharp-edged smile and his mother's laughter filmed by the haze of memory.

"Do you remember any of it?" Lucien asked. His hand touched hers, palm to palm, and then parted again. They had danced together when she was a chubby-legged toddler, clap in and clap out and ring around the rosy, under Nurse's approving eye. "Do you remember *Maman* teaching you your letters? She drew a book for you, with a garland of flowers around each letter. A is for apple-blossom—"

Clarissa swept her skirts away, twisting around the next person down the line.

"And the smell of papa's powder," Lucien persisted. "What was it?"

"Violet." Clarissa shut her lips tightly on the word, but it was too late. Lucien could see the cracks in the ice, the memories that she had claimed to have shut away.

"And there was the song that *Maman* always sang to us. About a shepherd, searching for his sheep in the rain." He could remember it, painfully and vividly, their mother, when he was very young, or ill, laying a cool hand against his cheek, singing softly. *"Il pleut, il pleut, bergere. . . ."*

"*Stop.*" There was a faint flush on Clarissa's pale cheeks. She modulated her tone, forcing a smile for the benefit of their audience. "It's all past. Over."

"Not for me." The dance had drawn to a close. Lucien halted in front of his sister. "Not until we find out who killed them."

Clarissa looked at him as though he were an idiot. "Our mother killed our father and then herself," she said flatly. "What more do you wish to know?"

Chapter Four

It had been a very long time since anyone had said that to Lucien's face.

The fixed social smile on his sister's face only made the impact worse.

"Do you wish to refine upon that?" Clarissa was still smiling, smiling. It was a smile of teeth, not eyes. "I don't."

Lucien felt as though someone had just reached into his chest and squeezed.

"Can you really believe it?" he asked softly. It seemed macabre that all around them the musicians were still playing and people were still dancing and laughing, while old corpses were being exhumed, brutally and painfully. "Yes, I know that was what people said, but . . ."

They claimed she had killed him, that his mother had taken a tincture made from the fruit of the manzanilla plant and fed it to his father in his tea. Fatal for him and for her as well, when she drank from the same pot.

It had been politely papered over, of course. One didn't openly accuse a duchess of murder. Not even a dead duchess of questionable extraction. "Accident" was the official verdict. But society knew and society judged and society found the duchess guilty.

Marie-Clarice had been younger than he when their parents had died, her memories fewer, but surely there must be some lingering trace of affection, some loyalty.

There was no trace of warmth in his sister's eyes. "What reason have I to believe otherwise?" Flippantly, she added, "We are a cursed race. We have the seeds of evil within us. Haven't you heard?"

"That's nonsense. Who told you that?" Lucien didn't need to wait for the answer. "Aunt Winifred? I suppose she told you some faradiddle about dark arts and foreign charms."

Clarissa turned her head away. "I don't want to talk about it." The figures of the dance separated them and brought them together again. "Aunt Winifred never said a word."

No, she didn't need to. Not directly. She might not have said a hard word, but she had never said a kind one either.

"I won't leave it at this," Lucien said conversationally. If his sister could play at that game, so could he. He smiled, lazily, baring his teeth for the delectation of the watching crowd. Let them see how pointy they could be. "I intend to prove her innocence."

"Oh?" Clarissa made no effort to hide her disbelief. "How?"

Hands joined, they stepped towards each other, then away again.

"That's my affair," Lucien prevaricated.

The truth of the matter was that after a fortnight of searching, he hadn't stumbled upon anything worth reporting. Just the artifacts of a life ended too soon. Poignant, but not probative.

"I am already on the trail of the real killer," Lucien said glibly. It was just a little lie, after all. He was on the trail. He just didn't quite know where that trail led.

"You would do better to leave." The musicians played the final chord, and his sister sank neatly into a curtsy. She looked up at him with shadowed eyes. "While you still can."

Whatever else Aunt Winifred had done, she clearly hadn't censored his sister's reading material. Clarissa had been reading far too many horrid novels.

"While I still can?" echoed Lucien, with a faint edge of exasperation in his voice. "What is that supposed to mean?"

This wasn't that blasted book everyone was talking about; this was their parents. And it was all very real. There was no need for dramatic flourishes and enigmatic utterances.

His sister ignored him. She held out a hand to the man to Lucien's right. "Ah, Mr. Tholmondelay," she said. "I believe I owe you this dance."

She smiled sweetly at the newcomer, as if she hadn't just

been croaking warnings like a wizened crone two minutes past. The next set was a lively country dance. Lucien left his sister skipping and hopping with the enthusiastic Mr. Tholmondelay. Short of dragging her out of the line and demanding answers, there was nothing else he could do.

He suspected she didn't have any. Answers, that was. Just more nonsense straight out of the pages of *The Convent of Whatever It Was*. Vampires, enigmatic warnings . . . Had everyone in London gone mad in the years he'd been away?

He had been amused when Patrice told him of the rumors generated by his reclusiveness, amused and slightly scornful. People would believe anything. Now, in the light of Clarissa's chilling words, Lucien found his scorn tinged with a genuine edge of concern. Cursed race? Seeds of evil? What manner of nonsense had they been feeding her?

From his long-ago school days, he could hear the echo. *Witchwoman's brat. Murderess's brat.*

He had borne their taunting at the time, but he'd had no idea that the whispers had persisted, or that they had morphed and twisted into something quite so intricate. And insane. So he was meant to be an undead creature of the night because his mother came from a cursed race?

He'd like to see someone tell Tante Berthe she was cursed. She would dose them with wormwood and turn them out to dry.

Now, that was a satisfying image.

No, thought Lucien, sobering. There was nothing the least bit occult about the events of twelve years past. It was all quite brutally, sordidly human. Just because the murderer had slipped poison into their tea rather than driving a knife through their flesh didn't make it any less corporeal. There had been no incantations chanted, no chickens slaughtered. It was murder, plain and simple.

If there was ever anything simple about murder.

Even now, after all these years, Lucien still couldn't fathom who might have wanted to kill his parents—and who might have hated his mother enough to do so in such a way as to make sure that all suspicion fell to her. Had it been malice? Or merely expedience? Foreign and scornful of society, Lucien's mother made a tidy scapegoat.

Lucien had been over it again and again, a million times in his nightmares. The means was clear, but motive eluded him. Had the target been his mother? His father? Both? He had been only twelve at the time, his world confined to the schoolroom and the nursery. He knew enough to know that his father had been a senior member of His Majesty's government, wielding a quite disproportionate influence on foreign affairs. There was no doubt that he had his political rivals. One might even call them enemies. But would any of them have killed?

In a duel, perhaps. His father's compatriots were men of their generation, quick to see a slight, quick to draw their swords. But a dawn affair of honor was a far cry from poison in one's tea.

There was no honor to poison.

As for his mother . . . Yes, she had her rivals and detractors.

Even in the schoolroom, Lucien had been well aware that his mother wasn't exactly in the common mode. And it hadn't taken Aunt Winifred long to make clear that his mother had been nothing that had been desirable in a duchess. But it seemed equally absurd to try to imagine a disappointed candidate for his father's hand taking the desperate expedient of eliminating her rival, and in such a way that Lucien's father might, too, sip of the poisoned brew. As he had.

It was no good. He was drifting in circles, around and around, theorizing with insufficient evidence.

It was time to seek help.

Lucien made his way from the dance floor, trying to ignore the exaggerated reactions of his uncle's guests as he navigated the crowded room. Was that girl really peering at his teeth? Yes. Yes, she was.

The idiocy of mankind never ceased to impress him, and that was after six months spent at sea, sharing a berth with a deckhand fondly known as Foolish Pete.

A quick scan of the ballroom assured Lucien that his quarry had already beaten a retreat from the dancing. That didn't matter; Lucien was reasonably sure he knew where to find him.

He had spent a month at his uncle's house the winter he was fourteen, when he was sent down from Eton for fighting. It might have been a decade ago, but the contours of the house were impressed upon his memory. Lucien made his way without faltering out of the ballroom, through an anteroom, around a corridor, and up a short flight of three steps that led to a narrow back hallway. Uncle Henry's study was at the back of the house, away from the noise and hubbub of the grand rooms that Aunt Winifred used to overawe her acquaintances.

Aunt Winifred was the daughter of a successful soap seller from Ipswich. A very successful soap seller. Her money had purchased the Richmond house and supported a level of opulence that Lucien's father had always found more than a little bit ridiculous.

Lucien stopped at the door of Uncle Henry's study, overcome with memory. Coming to Richmond with his parents, his father tapping his cane impatiently against the floor of the carriage, his mother in a hat with cherry-colored ribbons. They had forced Lucien into a blue velvet suit with a wide lace collar.

"We mustn't disappoint Winifred," his father had mocked, and his mother told him he was too bad, in a voice full of laughter.

The memory brought with it a familiar surge of anger and loss. Lucien's father hadn't been a young man; he might have been gone by now in the normal course of things. Why had someone felt the need to hasten the process? And in such a way?

This was why he had stayed away so long. In New Orleans, the ghosts were bearable. Here . . .

Lucien took a deep breath and turned the knob of the study door.

Uncle Henry was there, his back to Lucien, tucking something away in a hidey-hole next to the fireplace. The house was too modern to have a priest's hole or secret panels; Aunt Winifred must have ordered one put in, along with the linenfold paneling and portraits of other people's ancestors.

"Uncle Henry?"

"Lucien!" The panel beside the fireplace snapped shut. Turning, Uncle Henry scrubbed his hand on the side of his breeches. "What are you doing here? Shouldn't you be in the ballroom, enjoying yourself?"

"If such affairs are one's idea of enjoyment," said Lucien, closing the study door behind him.

Uncle Henry smiled wryly. "I confess, my boy, they aren't mine, either. But the ladies set great store by such things." His tone suggested a charming conspiracy, man to man. He patted the back of a heavily carved pseudo-Tudor chair, piled with lumpy red velvet cushions. "I know I ought to urge you to sally forth and do your pretty with the ladies—but there's claret enough for two if you feel like sharing my solitude."

"Thank you." Lucien moved cautiously into the room. Just being there made him feel like a delinquent schoolboy again, about to be called to account for being sent down from Eton. "I had hoped I might trouble you for a moment."

Poking at the small fire in the grate, Uncle Henry looked a little wary. "There could never be trouble where you are concerned."

"That's more kind than true," Lucien said, taking the seat Uncle Henry indicated. He had been nothing but trouble as far as Uncle Henry was concerned.

Poor Uncle Henry. In retrospect, Lucien could see that he

had done his best by him. He had tried, so diligently, to give Lucien an education fitting his station. It wasn't his fault that Lucien hadn't given a fig for his station. He hadn't given a fig for anything back then. He had been angry and raw and spoiling for a fight with the world. It didn't help that his voice kept going back and forth between registers.

It hadn't been pleasant being thirteen. Or fourteen or fifteen.

Uncle Henry handed Lucien a glass. "To better times," he said diplomatically. "We put it about that you had retired to your estates in Scotland. We thought it better that people believe you were of a retiring disposition than . . ."

"Than so entirely blind to my responsibilities?"

Uncle Henry looked slightly embarrassed. "You were very young." The corners of his mouth crinkled. "What am I saying? You still are very young. Looking at you and Hal . . . I've never felt quite so old! I'll be taking to my chair before you know it, being wheeled out to take the waters."

"You never age, sir," said Lucien politely. It wasn't entirely a lie. The silver blended neatly with the blond in Uncle Henry's hair, and an active life kept him fit and vigorous, more fit than Lucien's father, who had been given to what Uncle Henry had discreetly termed "the dissipations of London life."

"All the same," said Uncle Henry, settling back in the worn cushions of his chair with evident relief, "I shall be glad to hand the reins to a younger man."

Lucien winced. "About that. As you may have guessed, I've returned to—"

"To take your rightful place, I should hope. You should, you know," Uncle Henry added, before Lucien could protest. "It's past time."

"It never felt like mine," said Lucien honestly. The duke? That was someone else. That was his father. As for Lucien . . . He wasn't quite sure who or what he was. Part of him had been stuck in place, like a cracked clock, ever since that dreadful night twelve years ago.

"But it is yours." Uncle Henry set his glass down on the table with a decided air. "As soon as this nonsense about your sister's Season is over, I'll take you up to Hullingden and show you the accounts. I can assure you, you'll find everything just as it should be."

"I never doubted it." Whatever else one might say of Uncle Henry, he was deeply devoted to the ducal patrimony. Hullingden and its tenants had undoubtedly fared better under his stewardship than they would have under Lucien's inexpert care.

In the normal course of things, Lucien ought to have learned the management of his lands at his father's side. But his father had always been more interested in politics than land management. He had been content to leave the care of his estates to Uncle Henry, whom his father had once likened, in one of his more caustic moods, to a faithful old dog, trotting loyally back with someone else's kill.

Quietly, Uncle Henry said, "When you fled—I felt that I had betrayed your father's last trust. It has eaten at me all these years. There was only one thing he had asked of me, and I failed him in it."

Lucien had never thought before of his uncle's sentiments. He had only viewed him as an obstacle in his path. "In this instance, failure was forced upon you."

"Shall I consider that an apology?" A hint of a smile lightened Uncle Henry's lips. "Your father never liked to apologize either."

For a moment, the two men were silent, occupied with shared memories.

Then Uncle Henry, flexing his shoulders, pushed himself upright in his chair, and said, "Either way, it will be a relief to return the estates to your hands. Hullingden has been too long without a master."

For the first time, Lucien felt a twinge of guilt for what he was about to do. But there was no point in raising false hopes.

"I didn't come back for that—or to take my seat in the Lords," Lucien said, forestalling Uncle Henry's next comment. "I've come to see justice done."

Uncle Henry looked pained.

"You know it as well as I." Lucien leaned forward, his voice clipped and hard as he said, "Someone has evaded justice for twelve years. I intend to see he doesn't do so any longer."

Uncle Henry rubbed his forehead with the heel of his hand. "I don't want to set a damper on your finer feelings, but isn't it a bit late in the day to enact a Greek tragedy? Blood doesn't call to blood except on the stage. And that didn't go very well for Hamlet, as I recall."

Or for anyone else. If Lucien remembered correctly, pretty much everyone ended up dead by the final act.

"I hardly intend to litter London with bodies," said Lucien. "All I want is to know why. Why would someone do that to them? And don't try to tell me it was my mother," he added fiercely. "She didn't have it in her to hurt a spider."

Uncle Henry looked away, at the fire crackling merrily in the grate. "That isn't entirely true. She had it in her to do any amount of violence. Oh, yes, she did"—he raised a hand as Lucien opened his mouth to protest—"to anyone who tried to harm you or your father."

Lucien was left with his mouth open, caught off guard.

"Yes," said Uncle Henry quietly. "I have always wondered too."

Lucien recovered his voice. "But, then, why— All those years ago, you were in a position to do something. They would have listened to you." Lucien's hands had balled themselves into fists. He forced himself to relax them, to sound less like the schoolboy he had been. "Why didn't you demand an investigation?"

Uncle Henry made a helpless gesture. "What was the use? Even if I might suspect—" He caught himself up short. "Society had already judged your mother and found her guilty. And you know how people are when they get an idea in their heads."

Lucien leaned forward, peering narrowly at his uncle. "You know something, don't you? What aren't you telling me?"

Uncle Henry frowned at an invisible speck of dust on his sleeve. "Nothing of any substance. I never had any proof. . . ." He lifted his head abruptly. "Are you sure you want to hear it? It's all over and gone, years ago. Better to let sleeping dogs lie."

"Those sleeping dogs have a sharp bite," said Lucien caustically.

What was it that Clarissa had called them? The tainted seed of a cursed race? The legacy of their parents' murders followed them still.

"Sharper awake, I would think." Uncle Henry shook his head. "Speaking of dogs, the old setter bitch at Hullingden just had a new litter. If you would like your pick—"

The attempt to change the subject was too obvious to be effective. "What do you know about my parents' deaths?"

"I wouldn't say *know*. Suspect. Not know." Uncle Henry took a deep swig from his glass of claret and made a face over it. "Not as good as I'd thought. No, no, don't look like that. I'm just getting to it. Even after all this time, I do not find any of this easy to relate."

Lucien shook his head as his uncle tipped the decanter in the direction of his glass. "I do not find it easy to hear," he said stiffly.

"But you would have it, nonetheless?" Uncle Henry looked at him with something like resignation. "You are so very much like your father. Not in looks—there's no denying that you favor your mother's people—but in temperament. He could never abandon a point either."

Lucien smiled crookedly. "Perhaps it was because he was never wrong."

"That," said Uncle Henry, "is just what your father would have said." His own smile faded. "But he was wrong. Fatally wrong. If I had seen it sooner, I would have warned him—but what good would it have done? He would never have listened." He set the decanter aside and leaned forward, his glass cradled between his hands. "How much do you know of the situation in Martinique the year—the year your parents died?"

The question was such a non sequitur that Lucien choked on his own claret.

"Nothing," Lucien said guardedly. "My mother had maintained no ties to that part of the world."

Except for the manzanilla tree in the greenhouse. The death apple, they called it, and with good cause. It had been the fruit of the tree that had killed her.

"Or so she would have had us believe."

"What are you implying?" Lucien asked sharply.

He wasn't in the mood for any far-fetched theories about Creole conjuring and voodoo magic gone wrong. His mother had been a child of the Enlightenment, a devotee of science, a disciple of reason. She would have laughed such ideas to scorn.

Uncle Henry's nails beat a soft tattoo against the side of his glass. "You were just a boy, but even you must have been aware of the tumult of the times. There was bloody revolution across the channel, governments rising and falling. . . . Do you remember your grandfather—your mother's father?"

"A little." Granpere had been quite old already by the time Lucien had been born, or at least he had seemed so to Lucien. But though he was white-haired and wizened, he had the energy of a much younger man. "And?"

"Your grandfather had radical notions. He meant well, bless him," said Uncle Henry quickly. "There wasn't an ounce of harm in him. But he dealt in natural philosophy, not in the daily affairs of men. I'm sure his plants never beheaded their fellows," he added, in a misguided attempt at humor. He looked up at Lucien. "You know, he divided his plantation among his slaves. It didn't make him a popular fellow among the planters of Martinique, I imagine."

"No, I imagine not," said Lucien. "How does all of this touch on my parents?"

Uncle Henry sighed. "Your mother . . . inherited her father's views. She was a very outspoken advocate of the early phases of the revolution in France."

"So were many," said Lucien guardedly. "Including Mr. Charles James Fox."

"I'm not saying it was out of the ordinary." Uncle Henry looked into the flames of the fire. "After all, who could say then how matters would play out? No one could have imagined it. Although by the time of which we speak . . . well, that is as it was."

"Forgive me, sir," said Lucien, doing his best to be polite, "but I find your reasoning oblique."

Uncle Henry lifted his glass, letting the firelight play off the deep red liquid. "Let me be plain, then. In the spring of 1794, the revolutionaries abolished slavery. The monarchists in Martinique appealed to us for help. They were afraid of invasion, insurrection. . . . Naturally, we came to their aid." He looked up at Lucien. "Your mother's sympathies were, in this instance, with the other side."

This wasn't much of a surprise. "My mother was a great believer in the *Rights of Man*."

The firelight cast long shadows across Uncle Henry's face. Long lines formed on either side of his mouth.

"It was your father who had oversight for the planning of the expedition. It was all meant to be quite secret: the number of ships, our tactics, the timing of our attack—all of it information for which the French were quite eager."

The implication was clear. Lucien stared incredulously at Uncle Henry. "My father was a Tory, sir."

"Your father could deny your mother nothing," snapped Uncle Henry. He slumped back in his chair, saying heavily, "I am not saying that your father was involved in this matter. Good God, Lucien, do you think I would care to believe ill of my own brother? But your father tended to turn a blind eye where your mother was concerned. He loved her past reason."

"What are you trying to say?" Lucien asked tightly.

"If you must have it . . . Your mother was passing information to the French," Uncle Henry said baldly. "Information she received from your father."

His mother, a spy? "My mother was a botanist." Plants seldom took sides in the affairs of nations.

"With strong political views. I am sure she meant well by it," Uncle Henry added clumsily. "She had no idea—how could she?—that it would end as it did."

Setting his glass down, Uncle Henry looked intently at Lucien. "I have always believed that it was her contact who killed her. Who killed them both."

Chapter Five

"Her contact?" Lucien echoed.

Spies . . . contacts . . . The whole story was fantastical. Lucien dug back into his memories, his mother in her greenhouse, his father in his bookroom, both engaged in their respective pursuits, light streaming through the long windows. Whenever he remembered the house of his youth, he remembered light, glinting off the glass panes, sparkling off the mirrors, catching the curves of the gilded picture frames.

Everything had been airy and open, no place for clandestine meetings or murmured secrets.

As for his parents, the very idea of his mother betraying his father's trust in that way—it just didn't bear considering. They had been the very picture of marital harmony.

Unless it was just that, a picture, a construction of artifice and illusion. Pictures, by their very nature, lied.

"That's absurd," Lucien said flatly. He had the evidence of his own eyes, didn't he?

For the few hours a day in which his parents had visited his schoolroom. What about all those other hours? What about all those aspects of their lives of which he knew nothing?

"Is it?" Uncle Henry looked grave. "You were very young at the time, too young, perhaps, to realize how high feelings ran. And your mother . . . She was never one to mask her beliefs."

"True." That much, Lucien couldn't argue with; both parents had been outspoken in their beliefs. Their debates seemed to delight them both, his father's cynical pragmatism pitted against his mother's more abstract ideals. "But belief and action are very different things."

"For some, perhaps," said Uncle Henry quietly. He rose, using the poker to stir the coals on the grate. Ash sifted down, the smell acrid in the small room. "For some."

Lucien opened his mouth to argue. And closed it again.

He couldn't believe that his mother would ever have betrayed his father's trust in the normal course of things—but what if the freedom of an island of men weighed on the other side of the balance? It didn't take much imagination to see where a few paltry snippets of information would seem a minor price to pay.

Even if it meant placing his father's honor in jeopardy?

Everything Lucien had thought black-and-white was suddenly murky; his head ached as it had the first summer he had spent in Louisiana, when he had contracted marsh fever and woken to find that his tongue was too big for his mouth and the sun made his eyes ache.

"What made you suspect my mother of . . . relaying information?" Lucien asked gruffly.

Uncle Henry paused with the poker in his hand. After a moment he said, "Small things. Your father complained of papers gone missing, his desk disarranged. He was always very nice in his arrangements."

"The servants—," Lucien began.

"Knew better than to touch your father's papers." Uncle Henry replaced the poker in its stand. "Your mother seemed . . . distracted those last few months. Distraught. Her behavior was erratic. She pleaded a headache and retired early from the theater but returned home late. On another day, I came across her in a part of town she didn't usually frequent—inquiring after a rare plant, she told me, but then why not take the carriage?"

"I don't remember any of this," said Lucien frankly.

"Why would you? You were in the schoolroom. Although," Uncle Henry added thoughtfully, "there was that tutor of yours. What was his name?"

"Sherry," Lucien said. "Thomas Sheridan."

He hadn't thought about Sherry in years, although he had missed him sorely when he found himself shipped off to Eton after his parents' deaths. Sherry had neither browbeaten the pupil nor toadied to the future duke; from the first, he had treated Lucien as an equal, engaging him in debate, taking him on expeditions, forcing him to articulate his ideas and challenge his own preconceptions.

Sherry's regime had done much to exercise his mind, but it had left him entirely unprepared for all the pettifoggery of public school.

That had been one of the nastier rumors set about after his parents had died: that his mother had been in the throes of an affair with Sherry, that the two of them had plotted to do away with the duke.

Lucien looked narrowly at his uncle, but Uncle Henry was lost in his own memories. He stood before the fire, staring into the flames.

"Sheridan," said Uncle Henry. "That was it. She picked that tutor for you herself, you know, out of nowhere. A young man. An Irishman."

Yes, Sherry had been young, probably not much older than Lucien was now. Lucien remembered him with his wavy hair always escaping from its queue, his cravat askew, and ink stains on his cuffs. Sherry's face had been too long to be handsome, but he made up for what he lacked in looks with the liveliness of his expression.

Lucien had a fleeting image of his mother in consultation with Sherry, the two of them standing by the window embrasure in the schoolroom. His mother was a small woman and Sherry had been tall; she had had to tilt her head up to speak to him, her profile limned in the light streaming through the casement.

They had shared many ideals, his mother and Sherry. Had they shared more than ideals?

Lucien felt cold beneath his heavy brocade waistcoat. "Being Irish is hardly an indictment."

"It is when the Irishman is involved in incendiary circles," said Uncle Henry frankly. He looked at Lucien's face and enlightenment dawned. "You didn't think I was going to bring up that nonsense about— Good God, my boy! Do you think I would accuse your mother of *that*?"

Despite himself, Lucien felt himself relax a little before the full impact of Uncle Henry's words kicked in.

No. Not of infidelity. "Just of another kind of betrayal," he said.

Uncle Henry clasped his hands behind his back. "She might not have seen it as such. Your father was always so . . . urbane. She might not have realized the depth of his convictions."

"Putting a peer of the realm at risk of being convicted of treason is hardly a small thing," said Lucien sharply. His father had been, as his uncle said, urbane, but he hadn't held his honor cheap. "You think Sherry was—was in league with foreign forces?"

Uncle Henry heaved a sigh that seemed to come straight from his boots. "It might explain why your mother hired him so precipitously." His expression turned wry. "Ignoring, I might add, all the fine candidates I proffered for her perusal."

Lucien was not amused. "And you think he killed her."

There were deep lines on either side of Uncle Henry's mouth. "It was a possibility, yes, but—"

"But you had no proof." Lucien's fingers were digging into his knees, making wrinkles in the smooth fabric of his breeches. Why was Uncle Henry telling him this only now? Why not twelve years ago, when something might have been done? Of course, twelve years ago, he had been only a boy, but Uncle Henry might have told someone, someone with the authority to investigate. "Why didn't you confide your suspicions to the magistrate?"

Uncle Henry's expression was gently reproachful; he made Lucien feel like a boy caught speaking out of turn. "Do you remember the magistrate in charge of the case?"

"Sir Matthew Egerton." The name came out of the depths of Lucien's memory. A middle-aged man in a brown coat and an old-fashioned bagwig, with a round, rather florid face. "We didn't get on."

"No," said Uncle Henry drily, "I don't imagine you did. Sir Matthew had made up his mind that it was a crime of passion." Uncle Henry added reflectively, "He did not have much use for women. He considered them hysterical creatures, prone to murdering their husbands."

"All the same. Why not present him with your evidence?"

"And drag your father's name into the mire?" There was the ring of steel beneath Uncle Henry's words. At Lucien's glance, Uncle Henry gentled his tone. "Under the circumstances, I was not inclined to press Sir Matthew to greater efforts. The less known about the whole distasteful affair, the better." The corners of his lips twisted. "I had a hard enough time getting him to bring in a verdict of accident."

"Was that better?" Lucien's throat felt tight. "Letting the world believe that my mother killed my father?"

Uncle Henry's shoulders slumped. "You were twelve years old. These decisions weren't yours to make. What were my choices? I could see your father mocked as a cuckold—or scorned as a traitor." A coal broke and hissed against the grate. In the silence, Uncle Henry said quietly, "I chose the lesser of two evils."

"And their killer went free," said Lucien bitterly.

He made to rise, but Uncle Henry clapped a hand on his shoulder. "If you imagine that hasn't haunted me all these years, then you aren't the man I thought you were. Oh, yes. I see them in my nightmares, still, crying for justice." His hand fell away. "But it's too late now."

"Is it?" Lucien demanded. He rose unsteadily. His legs felt uncertain beneath him, and the room was wreathed in a haze. He caught at the back of the chair to steady himself. "If this is true—if the man is still alive, I'll find him. I'll find him and I'll settle the score."

Uncle Henry looked at Lucien for a long, considering moment.

Lucien met his eyes unflinchingly.

Uncle Henry's gaze dropped first. "Be careful. One Duke of Belliston has already died at the hands of these weasels." His expression turned wry. "It would seem like carelessness to lose another."

Sally had lost her duke.

"Do tell me more about your stoat breeding program," she said, smiling up at her dance partner as she tried to angle just a little bit to the left.

The Duke of Belliston had disappeared through those doors a good half hour ago and hadn't come back.

The idea that he might have departed for good made the evening feel strangely flat. She wasn't done with him yet. She had at least seventeen opening lines prepared, each wittier than the last.

So far, her quest to discover the duke's dark secrets had not met with unparalleled success. There were certainly plenty of rumors circulating, but what with all the slaughtered chickens and Gypsy curses, Sally was having a hard time separating fact from fiction. Miss Gwen's fiction, to be precise. Some of the theories being shared were lifted straight from the pages of *The Convent of Orsino*, which, as far as Sally knew, was a work of fiction, not a tell-all biography of the life and times of the Duke of Belliston.

She wanted to know about the man, not the myth. Where had he been all these years? Why did he lurk in overgrown gardens? And what was it that his sister had said that had made him look like thunder?

Their meeting the other night had piqued her curiosity. And if there was one thing Sally couldn't endure, it was being piqued.

"You mustn't believe everything you hear," Mr. Fitzwarren announced.

Sally looked at him sharply. "About—?"

"About stoats." Mr. Fitzwarren shook his flaming red head. "People have the oddest ideas about them."

Sally didn't have any ideas about them at all. "I'm afraid I've never met a stoat," she said apologetically.

"They don't seem to get about much." Mr. Fitzwarren seemed genuinely bewildered by this state of affairs.

"Have you attempted popularizing them as pets?" Sally asked politely, her attention on the back of the ballroom. She wasn't the only one. Half the people in the room seemed to be glancing over their shoulders for the duke; the other half contented themselves with gossiping about him.

"Would you like one?" Mr. Fitzwarren asked eagerly. "I can give you Lady Florence."

Mr. Fitzwarren appeared to be looking at her expectantly. Sally shook herself back to the present. "Lady Florence who?"

"Lady Florence Oblong." When Sally looked at him in puzzlement, Mr. Fitzwarren explained, "That's the name of the stoat."

"I see." What Sally didn't see was any sign of the duke. Blast.

On the other hand, the people dancing behind them were having a rather fascinating whispered conversation about the wrong the duke's mother had done. It appeared to have something to do with . . . sacrificing chickens? Really, the acoustics in this room were dreadful.

"She's a very genteel stoat." What on earth was Mr. Fitzwarren on about? Oh, yes, Lady Florence Oblong. The stoat. "She's very dainty about her kills."

Two words Sally hadn't expected to hear in the same sentence. "I'm sure she's a paragon among stoats."

"Oh, yes, she is! You see, stoats—"

Sally stepped down hard on her own hem. "Oh, dear! Will you excuse me, Mr. Fitzwarren? I seem to have torn the hem of my gown. Clumsy, clumsy me. I simply must make the necessary repairs."

Sally waggled her fingers and staged her retreat before Mr. Fitzwarren could inform her that stoats, not having gowns, would never have this sort of problem. A very sweet man, Mr. Fitzwarren, but a bit single-minded. She couldn't imagine anyone being that passionate about weasels, but, then, thought Sally tolerantly, there was no accounting for taste. It could be worse. It could be minks. Sally wrinkled her nose. Or poultry. She detested poultry. Nasty clucking things.

Rather like the gossips of the *ton*.

As Sally made her way towards the retiring room—after all, she wouldn't want to hurt Mr. Fitzwarren's feelings by not making repairs, even if there was nothing to repair—a rustling noise like the crackle of fallen leaves started at one end of the room and began to spread.

Sally felt a tingle of anticipation, like the bubbles in a glass of champagne, prickling against her fingers, making her stand straighter, hold her head a little higher. As casually as she could, she turned her head ever so slightly, and there he was, just a little bit different from every other man in the ballroom, his hair a little longer, his coat a little tighter, his cravat tied in a way that was somehow both more casual and slightly foreign, that single blot of crimson in the center, giving rise to a thousand whispers.

The duke had returned to the ballroom.

Sally released her pent-up breath in a long sigh, and then felt rather silly as she realized that a dozen others were doing the exact same thing. Not that it was at all the same. Unlike the others, she had met him.

And she still had a score to settle.

Instinctively, Sally looked for Agnes. But Agnes was with Lizzy, at the fringe of a circle of young Corinthians, all of whom seemed to be laughing uproariously at something Lizzy had just said. Sally started in their direction, and then just as abruptly stopped. They wouldn't thank her for interrupting. And for what?

Sally looked for her sister-in-law, but Arabella was dancing with Turnip, laughing up at him as he twirled her in extravagant loops.

Sally felt something twist in her chest. She smiled at them, but it was a bittersweet smile, with something wistful around the edges.

Which was silly. Sally turned away, giving the skirts of her dress a little shake. She couldn't have asked for a better sister-in-law. Really, she should be congratulating herself on seeing her brother so well settled. If it hadn't been for her intervention, the two of them would never have made a match of it, as she might, in fact, have made a point of reminding the concerned parties a time or two. Or twenty. She was delighted that they had found such happiness in each other.

So why did she suddenly feel so low?

Maybe it was that something about the way that her brother was beaming at his wife made her feel more than a little bit *de trop*. If she went up to them, she knew, Turnip would tease her and Arabella would fuss over her. Their affection for each other was such that it left room for other people. But—Sally struggled with a nameless sensation of discontent—it was a secondhand affection. They came first with each other now. Which was as it should be.

But it still left Sally feeling strangely lonely and more than a little bit disgruntled. She missed feeling needed.

Sally rolled her eyes at herself. Any more of this and she'd turn herself into a watering pot. She straightened her shawl and readjusted her bracelets. What she needed was a project.

Such as a duke.

The duke was standing all by himself at the back of the room, doing his best to look brooding and mysterious, or as brooding and mysterious as one could in a well-lit ballroom with footmen pestering people by pushing champagne at them.

The man was in dire need of a little friendly advice—and who better than Sally to deliver it? Really, it would be a kindness, not to mention a shot in the eye to Delia Cathcart and Lucy Ponsonby and all the others whispering and gossiping and spreading their ridiculous rumors.

Sally cast a glance over her shoulder at her chaperone. Arabella was still occupied with Turnip.

Besides, Sally reassured herself, it didn't really count as a breach of etiquette to address the duke, since, after all, they had met before. In a manner of speaking.

Having thus comfortably settled the matter for herself, Sally set forth with a swish of her skirts and her head held high.

If the duke wouldn't come to her, she would just have to go to the duke.

Chapter Six

"Hello," someone said, rather insistently.

It took a moment for Lucien to realize he was being addressed. There was a blond girl standing in front of him, tapping her slippered foot impatiently against the parquet floor. She looked, he realized, rather familiar.

"Oh," he said. His tongue felt fuzzy, even though he had imbibed only a few sips of Uncle Henry's claret. "It's you."

Under the dizzying light of a hundred candles, her hair was even brighter than it had appeared in the garden, the true gold of new-minted guineas.

The girl was undaunted by his grudging greeting.

"Sally Fitzhugh. Of the Norfolk Fitzhughs. *Not* the Hertfordshire Fitzhughs." She seemed quite insistent about that. Before Lucien could respond, she peered closely at him. "Are you quite all right?"

"All right?" The very idea was so alien that Lucien didn't know what to say. He was inclined to laugh, but he was afraid that, once started, he wouldn't be able to stop.

What in the devil was in that claret of Uncle Henry's?

He shouldn't blame the claret. It wasn't the drink that had set him reeling.

There was no proof; Uncle Henry had been quite clear about that. It was all speculation and inference. But while Lucien didn't precisely believe his uncle's accusations, he didn't precisely disbelieve them either. And that was the problem. He was neither here nor there; he had been stripped of the comfort of his convictions and left entirely at sea.

Miss Fitzhugh cocked her head. "Let me be more specific. Are you about to swoon? Because, if so, I should like to step out of the way."

"Am I about to— Good Lord, no!"

"You were looking more than a little bit wobbly," said Miss Fitzhugh importantly. "Should you have need for it, I have a vinaigrette in my reticule."

"I assure you, I have no need for a vinaigrette," said Lucien, with some asperity. "If I were to be . . . *wobbly* . . . any wobbliness is purely a wobbliness of the spirit."

"Would your spirit like my vinaigrette, then? Because you do seem to need something."

"A swift blow to the head," Lucien muttered. Maybe then he'd wake up and find he'd imagined all of this.

"Pardon?"

"Nothing." His uncle Philippe had warned him that when one went poking around in the past, one might stir up smelly fish. Or something like that. The idiom had been both pungent and in French. Lucien had brushed the words aside, convinced that they didn't apply to him. He had been so sure of the justice of his cause. He was going to sally off to England, prove his mother's innocence, and— Well, he hadn't quite thought what was going to happen after that, but whatever it was involved a certain amount of smug self-satisfaction.

So much for that.

Lucien bowed to Miss Fitzhugh, taking refuge in pomposity. "Your concern does you credit, but I can assure you that your tender ministrations are entirely unnecessary."

"I never minister unnecessarily," said Miss Fitzhugh indignantly. "That would be a waste of both your time and mine. You look like death."

That was the last thing he needed, more rumors about his supposed career as a creature of the night. "Not that again."

Miss Fitzhugh pursed her lips. "What I meant is that you look a bit like you just staggered up from a prolonged illness while still in the weak-tea-and-porridge phase."

It was a rather vivid image. Lucien's lips reluctantly turned up at the corners. "I'm not sure that's an improvement."

"No," agreed Miss Fitzhugh. "If you tasted my nurse's porridge, you would agree that death was by far the better option. At least death wouldn't taste like *glue*."

Her words surprised a laugh out of him. It was a little rusty, but a laugh all the same. "I won't ask how you know what glue tastes like," Lucien said.

Cocking her head, Miss Fitzhugh said with satisfaction, "That's better. You look quite different when you smile, you know. Much less otherworldly."

Lucien regarded her narrowly. "Are you attempting to jolly me?"

Miss Fitzhugh didn't seem the least bit offended by the accusation. "Someone needs to. Otherwise those vultures will just go on speculating about your nocturnal habits." She subjected Lucien to a frank appraisal. "You really aren't doing yourself any favors by standing alone and scowling."

"Perhaps I wanted to stand alone and scowl."

"Don't be silly," said Miss Fitzhugh serenely. "No one wants to stand alone and scowl. It's simply the last resort of the socially inadept."

Lucien found himself without words.

"You see?" said Miss Fitzhugh blithely. "Someone needs to show you how to get on."

And she was volunteering herself for the task? Lucien recovered his voice. "I do not need—"

He staggered as someone bumped against him, hard enough to make him stumble.

Miss Fitzhugh grabbed his arm. "If you're going to swoon—"

"I am not going to swoon." Three people turned their heads to stare. Lucien lowered his voice. "Someone bumped into me."

He turned his head to look, but no one was there. There was, however, a folded piece of paper on the floor at his feet. Written on the side, in bold black lettering, was, simply, BELLISTON.

"I think that's for you," said Miss Fitzhugh helpfully.

Lucien scooped it up before she could reach for it and shook it open. The cream-colored paper was heavy, of good quality, the ink a rich black, but the handwriting was as shaky as if the author had penned it in the throes of ague, on a ship, in a strong wind.

I know something you will wish to know. Meet me on the south balcony at midnight.

There was no signature.

Lucien glanced behind him. Too late. Three women who had been staring looked away hastily, and one of them pretended to swoon, but short of checking the fingers of all the partygoers for ink, he had no way of telling who had dropped the note.

Something you will wish to know . . . He hadn't made any secret of his intentions; he'd spent the years before he left England loudly voicing his plan to exonerate his parents. Someone might have got wind of the inquiries he'd had Patrice making, or overheard him speaking with Clarissa on the dance floor.

"The balcony? At midnight?" Miss Fitzhugh peered shamelessly over his arm. "How trite. Really, people have no imagination."

Lucien crumpled the note in his hand. He felt irritable and edgy, half-anticipation, half-fear. "First my garden and now my correspondence? Haven't you heard of the term 'privacy'?"

"If you leave them lying about . . ."

"My garden," said Lucien, "happens to be attached to my house. And my note was in my hand."

"Which was right under my nose," Miss Fitzhugh pointed out.

Lucien raised a brow. That nose had moved a few judicious inches in the right direction.

Miss Fitzhugh was undaunted. She trotted along beside him as he made for the balcony. "I could hardly help seeing. And, really, it's quite a good thing for you that I did."

"Oh, really?" It was, if the ornate clock on the mantel was correct, ten minutes to midnight. Miss Fitzhugh was right about one thing: midnight was a rather hackneyed time for an assignation.

Not that Lucien would give her the satisfaction of telling her so.

"It's probably a thrill-seeker who wishes to be able to brag that she spent a few moments alone with the vampire," Miss Fitzhugh said sagely, keeping pace with him stride for stride. "Either that, or a coronet seeker who wishes to be able to claim that she spent a few moments alone with a duke. You have no idea—*no idea*—of the lengths to which some women will go. Or the heights," she added. "Lucy Ponsonby once scaled a wall in an attempt to ensnare a marquess."

"A wall," said Lucien flatly.

"Admittedly, it wasn't a very *high* wall. It was more of a

fence, really. But I'm sure you'll agree that the principle remains the same. And a duke," she added portentously, "is higher than a marquess."

Wouldn't that depend on the height of the wall on which he was standing? "Meaning—"

"That you really must take care not to be compromised," advised Miss Fitzhugh importantly. "I shouldn't think that would be the sort of wife you would want."

Lucien stopped short in front of the French doors. "I don't want a wife at all."

"Well, then," said Miss Fitzhugh. She opened her eyes wide, and Lucien could see the glint of satisfaction in them. "You'd best not go out there alone."

There was a flaw in her logic the size of a very high wall, but Lucien was sufficiently discombobulated that he couldn't find it.

"Isn't there a rule about young ladies on balconies?" Lucien asked desperately, as Miss Fitzhugh slipped past him.

Miss Fitzhugh looked back over her shoulder, one long curl bouncing expressively. "It's all right as long as we're in sight of the ballroom," she said airily, so airily that Lucien was reasonably sure she was lying. "Besides, my chaperone is right over there."

If her chaperone was the fair-haired woman with a harried expression who was currently scanning the ballroom with two little furrows between her eyes, then Lucien rather suspected that it was not, in fact, all right.

"Is that your chaperone?"

"Shhh!" said Miss Fitzhugh, rapidly grasping the gilded door handle. "She's probably just looking for—for some more ratafia. Mmm, ratafia." She held open the door to the balcony. "Don't you have an assignation to keep?"

"Assignations are generally better kept alone," said Lucien repressively, although at this point he had to admit that he would be rather disappointed if Miss Fitzhugh were to decamp. As a means of distraction, she was remarkably effective.

"Pooh," said Miss Fitzhugh, and preceded him through the French doors.

Lucien caught up with her just past a large Vanbrugh urn. "Why are you so eager to leave the ballroom?" Turn and turn about was fair play. "Don't tell me it's all altruistic interest in my humble affairs."

"Of course not," said Miss Fitzhugh, entirely unruffled. "Your affairs would never be humble. Now, then, if you had instigated an assignation, where would you wait?"

Miss Fitzhugh paused halfway down the balcony, surveying the scene with a busy air. On either side of her, red roses bloomed improbably in marble urns, hothouse flowers transplanted for the evening to enliven the unrelieved gray of the long stretch of stone. In the chill of the night, the flowers were already beginning to droop and fall, scattering red petals like drops of blood.

The urns stretched out at regular intervals along the balcony, into infinity, punctuated only by marble benches, the sides curled and scrolled. They looked, thought Lucien, distinctly uncomfortable.

There was no sign of life on the balcony.

"It's just as likely that there's no one here at all," Lucien said, as much for himself as for Miss Fitzhugh.

His back was tense with a combination of anticipation and trepidation, his ears tuned for the slightest noise.

I know something you will wish to know.

Lucien squinted down the length of the balcony. If someone was there, it was just as likely to be Miss Fitzhugh's hypothetical thrill-seeker, looking for an assignation with the vampire, or that wall-climbing woman, trying her luck with a duke. There was no reason to assume that it had anything to do with . . . anything else.

Except for the hairs on the back of his neck, which prickled with expectation and cold.

"There," said Miss Fitzhugh suddenly, tugging at his arm.

"Where?"

Out in the deserted gardens, an owl hooted. Just on the other side of the French doors were light and noise, the thrum of voices and footfalls, but from where he stood, all that was strangely muted, like a voice heard in a dream. Moonlight reflected eerily off the pitted surface of the balustrade, lending an unearthly gleam to the landscape.

"Don't you see?" Miss Fitzhugh whispered. "She's sitting on that bench. Waiting. For you."

She pointed all the way down to the right, far away from the reflected light of the ballroom windows. Among the shadows, Lucien caught a hint of white.

"I'll just wait here," she added, pulling her light wrap around her shoulders. "In case you need me."

"How generous," said Lucien drily. He had managed his own affairs before the intervention of Miss Fitzhugh.

Admittedly, he didn't seem to be managing them very well.

There was certainly something at the end of the balcony, although whether or not it was, as Miss Fitzhugh claimed, a seated woman, Lucien couldn't tell. At first, he thought it might merely be someone's discarded wrap, a shimmer of spangled fabric against the stark gray stone of the balcony. But no. Miss Fitzhugh was right. As he approached, he saw a foot dangling beneath the fabric, a small foot in an impractical satin slipper, stained with some dark stuff.

Lucien's footfalls were heavy against the flagstones, but the woman made no move to rise.

"Hello?" said Lucien tentatively.

The woman appeared to have fallen asleep. She lay on the hard marble bench as though it were upholstered in the softest of velvet, her diaphanous white skirts falling gracefully around her legs. Her head had fallen back a little against the scrolled arm of the bench, her long black curls partly obscuring her face.

In her lightly clasped hands rested a straggling bouquet of pale flowers.

Like a funeral wreath.

The full moon lent an uncanny clarity to the scene. Or maybe that was some long-buried, atavistic reaction, sharpening his senses. Lucien took a step forward, his own footfall echoing in his ears.

The fabric of the woman's dress was pathetically thin for the weather, the neckline cut low, but she betrayed no signs of cold. She lay entirely still, as still as the empty fountains and deserted paths of the garden. Her eyes were closed, her lips ever so slightly parted.

Lucien didn't need to hold a mirror to those lips to know that there was no breath between them, but he held out a hand all the same. Just because.

"What is it?" There was a series of light footfalls on the flagstones. Miss Fitzhugh came to a stop behind him, her shadow touching the other woman's tousled skirts. "Why are you—"

She broke off, her eyes widening, her mouth rounding into a silent "Oh."

In the silence, Lucien could hear the rustle of fabric as Miss Fitzhugh's chest rose and fell, and the small, damp noise as she swallowed. Hard. "Is that . . . Are those . . ."

"Yes," said Lucien.

In the hollow between the lace ruffle of her dress and the dark fall of her hair, the woman's skin was a clear, pale white.

Aside from the two red marks at the side of her throat.

Chapter Seven

"Is she . . ." Sally's throat felt tight.

She stared at the woman on the marble bench, her flowing draperies arranged so carefully around her. So peaceful. So still.

The duke drew his hand back. Sally watched as he rubbed the palm against his waistcoat. "Yes."

"Oh." For once in her life, Sally didn't know what to say. All she could do was stare and stare.

Dead. She had never seen a dead person before. Well, unless one counted her great-aunt Adelaide, and one hardly did, because she had been properly in a coffin and not just lying there on a slab of marble like a princess out of a storybook waiting to be awakened by true love's kiss. But nothing was going to wake this woman. That chest would never rise and fall; those eyes would never open. She would never wiggle herself upright on that marble bench and shake out those long skirts.

Sally found her eye caught by the flowing folds of fabric, by the long, dark stripes and blotches that made an eccentric pattern down the sides and along the hem. She caught herself staring at it, trying to make sense of it. Anything but look at that cold, still face. And those two red marks on her neck. It was an odd sort of pattern, with no symmetry or order to it.

Only it wasn't a pattern at all. That was blood. Lots of blood. Long ribbons of blood, staining the woman's dress and marking her shoes, twisting down her sides and caking her hem.

There was bile at the back of Sally's throat and a ringing in her ears; her hands felt cold and damp, but she couldn't look away. All she could see was those long ribbons of blood, twisting and twining towards her. . . .

The duke caught Sally around the shoulders. "Where's that vinaigrette?" he said roughly.

Sally wiggled in his grasp. "I'm not swooning." She wasn't really. The world had just gone a bit hazy for a moment. "I just—tripped on my own hem."

The duke looked skeptical, but he removed his arm all the same. Sally rather wished he hadn't. Without the warmth of his body, the night air crawled along her bare arms like a cold, dead hand.

Like the hand of the woman, dangling by her side, the fingers small, smaller than Sally's, fine-boned and white.

"I had never—," Sally said wonderingly, and then caught herself. "She looks asleep." Asleep and peaceful.

But for the blood staining her skirt.

Sally swallowed, hard.

"I should get you inside," said the duke.

Sally drew herself up. "No. No. I'm quite all right. Really."

She wasn't going to swoon, not in front of the duke. She could feel her nails making sharp half circles in her palms and forced herself to relax her hands, finger by finger.

Didn't she pride herself on her cool head in a crisis? Of course, in the past, her crises had been limited to propping up falling scenery in amateur theatricals and talking her way out of French exercises. For all that she thought herself a woman of the world, she had really lived a rather sheltered existence.

Someone had placed flowers in the woman's hands. It wasn't an elegant bouquet. The stems were uneven, bound untidily in a trailing yellow ribbon. The flowers themselves were simple white flowers with a yellow dot in the center.

"Daisies," said Sally. "She's holding daisies."

There was something poignant and sad about those simple flowers in the woman's still, white hand. They were meant to be plucked in sun-washed summer meadows and twisted into chains. They didn't belong here in the chill autumn night any more than the woman, with her inappropriately light dress, belonged here, cold and dead on a marble bench.

The duke's voice seemed to come from a long way away. "Those aren't daisies."

*There's rosemary—that's for remembrance. . . . There's a daisy.
I would give you some violets, but they withered all when my father
died.*

The duke looked at her oddly. Sally hadn't realized she'd
spoken out loud.

"I saw *Hamlet* last week," she said inconsequentially. "At the
Pudding Lane Theatre."

The duke made a little grunting sound deep in his throat,
and turned his frown back to the woman in front of him, who
did, even disregarding the flowers, look rather like Ophelia, but
for the fact that Ophelia had been fair-haired where this woman's long curls were a stark and startling black. Ophelia had
worn just such a gown as this, white and flowing, dusted with
something that gave it just a bit of a shimmer, so that when
Ophelia whirled across the stage, the folds of her gown swirled
and sparkled with her.

But that had been theater and this was real.

Sally rubbed her gloved hands against her bare arms, fighting to keep her voice steady. "Who is she?"

The fabric of her gown, elegant from a distance, was flimsy
and cheap, far too thin for the late October chill. There was
kohl darkening her lashes and red, red rouge on her lips.

"I have no idea." The duke, who had been kneeling by the
bench, pushed himself up, standing so abruptly that he almost
stumbled.

What was that in his hand? "Oh?" said Sally.

Whatever it was, the duke was holding it down by his side,

cupped in one palm. "I've never seen her before," he said rapidly. "She's a stranger to me."

There was a saying: what I say three times is true. Did that mean twice was a lie?

Sally positioned herself between the duke and the woman on the bench. "Either she summoned you here herself or someone meant you to find her. If she was the author of the note . . ."

If she was the author of the note, then she had met someone she hadn't expected on the balcony.

"Are you accusing me?" The duke looked down at Sally with the advantage of height afforded him by her flat slippers. "Go on. Be direct about it. Don't mince words."

"I'm not accusing you." Not yet. Sally stepped up to the duke, the stones underfoot cold through her thin slippers. The air was sickly sweet with the scent of overblown roses. The wind rose, whipping Sally's hair around her face. "If you know *anything*—"

"Are you hoping I'll break down and confess?" Beneath the duke's mockery, Sally could hear the thrum of frustration. "Are you planning to return me to the ballroom in irons? Or will you merely run a stake through my heart?"

Sally glared at him. "A woman is dead," she said. *Dead*, the echo came back to them from the withered gardens. *Dead*. "This isn't a joke."

"No. It's not." The duke's expression was bleak in the moonlight. For a moment, just for a moment, Sally thought she detected some genuine emotion, until he added provocatively, "If you had any sense, you would run away—before I make you my next meal."

The breeze snapped at Sally's ankles, blowing her dress close to her legs. Her necklace seemed to burn against her throat. She wrapped her arms tightly around herself.

"Don't be ridiculous," she said belligerently. "Do you really think I believe such nonsense?"

"I don't know." The duke's fingers curled around her chin, forcing her face up towards his. He looked at her with hooded eyes. "I don't know anything about you. Other than that you have a strange habit of appearing at inopportune moments."

Was he implying . . . ? No. That was unthinkable.

"Well, I know this about you," Sally said tartly. She poked him in the chest with one finger, hard enough that the duke released his grasp. "Your teeth are no pointier than mine."

"Didn't you hear?" said the duke silkily. "I come from a cursed race."

A little frisson of fear crawled along Sally's spine. She was alone in the dark with a dead woman and a man who might have killed once, might be ready to kill again.

With his pointy, pointy teeth? Sally got hold of herself. The duke was trying to scare her away; she was sure of it. And it wasn't going to work. She refused to give him the satisfaction of turning and bolting.

"I don't believe in curses," said Sally flatly.

"What do you believe in?" The words were a challenge.

The duke's eyes were on hers, dark beneath their heavy lids.

They exerted a magnetic effect. Sally could imagine an innocent falling prey to those eyes, losing herself in those depths, dark as midnight, and just as dangerous.

Of course, Sally wasn't that sort of ninny. Fortunately.

"Malignant human agency," Sally said succinctly, and had the satisfaction of seeing the duke blink. "That's what I believe in. It wasn't a curse that did this to this poor woman. It was a person." Seizing her advantage, she pounced. "What's in your hand?"

The duke drew his hand back, but Sally was too fast for him. After a moment of confused fumbling, Sally emerged triumphant. Dancing away from the duke, she held an object up in one gloved hand, the moonlight winking off a smooth enamel surface.

"It's a . . . snuffbox." She couldn't quite keep the disappointment out of her voice.

"Brilliantly spotted," drawled the duke.

He made a grab for it, but Sally drew it back. She squinted at the intricately detailed surface. "With a coat of arms on it. Your coat of arms?"

Agnes would undoubtedly have known. Sally only guessed, but the guess hit home. Extending his hand, the duke said stiffly, "If you would return that to me—"

Return? She was fairly certain she had seen him scoop it up from beside the woman's body. "Is it yours?"

She watched the duke's face. Unfortunately, he was standing with his back to the light, but she could still see him press his lips together hard, weighing his responses, before saying curtly, "I don't take snuff. May I have that, please?"

"Why, if it's not yours?" Sally flipped the lid open, and saw the duke make a quick, convulsive movement with one hand.

"Is there—," he asked, and then stopped himself. His lips pressed tightly together. "I had thought there might be a message. Inside."

Sally felt around, just to make sure. "There's nothing." Not even a few grains of desiccated snuff. Only the portrait of a woman, painted on the underside of the lid. A woman with long black curls, wearing a light white gown. "Who is she?"

She half expected the duke to deny any knowledge. He looked at the portrait with lidded eyes. "My mother."

Sally's eyes flew to the duke in surprise. "But—" The woman on the bench couldn't be any older than Sally. "Then, she isn't . . . ?"

"No. May I have that now?" In the tone of one speaking much against his will, the duke added, tersely, "The box belonged to my father. I haven't seen it since— For a very long time."

"Then what was it doing here? Next to—?" She glanced sideways, and broke off, her tongue tangling on the words. For a moment she had nearly forgotten. Recovering herself, Sally said tartly, "Unless your father has returned from the grave."

"To suck the blood of his victims?" The duke's voice vibrated with frustration. "Damn it all. Damn it all to hell."

The words struck an unfortunate note. Sally looked from the woman to the duke and back again. In the moonlight, the fang marks on her neck seemed obscenely red, the same red as the rouge on her lips, far more red than the blood streaking her dress, which had dried to a dark brown, almost black.

"They're fake." Sally's eyes went to the duke's face as a horrible surmise began to form. She fought a rising wave of nausea. "The fang marks."

"They may be fake," said the duke, "but whoever she is, she's most genuinely dead." He shook his head slightly. "The proper authorities will have to be told. Whoever they might be."

"Wait." Sally grabbed his arm before he could head towards the door. "Don't you see?"

The duke paused, frowning down at her. "See what?"

Sally's fingers dug into the fabric of his sleeve. "That note—the snuffbox—the fang marks," she said breathlessly. "Someone wanted you here. Someone means to make it look as though you did this."

The duke's arm stiffened beneath her fingers. His face was shadowed. "Me."

"You." Sally's blood thrummed in her veins, every sense on alert. "Who else? You're the only vampire in London." She looked the duke in the eye, her face serious. "Your father's snuffbox was insurance."

Their eyes locked; they stood frozen together. Sally could see the duke's throat work beneath the folds of his cravat.

"That's—," he began, then stopped. His head lifted. He stood like that for a moment, his expression abstracted. "The blood," he said.

"What about the blood?" If he was trying to convince her that he was a vampire . . .

"Years ago. I was on a merchantman that was boarded by a French frigate," the duke said conversationally. "There was blood, blood everywhere. You could smell it. But here—"

Sally sniffed experimentally. "All I smell are those roses."

Before she could stop him, the duke pulled away, dropping to his knees by the bench. "If she were just killed," he said rapidly, "there should be blood everywhere. Puddles of it."

"There's blood on her dress." The sight of it made Sally feel more than a little bit wobbly, not that she would let the duke know that.

The duke was not so squeamish. He touched a finger to the woman's hem. "Dried." He rubbed his fingers together. "Or mostly dried."

Sally looked down at the duke's dark head, keeping her own pale skirts well out of the way of the woman's. "What are you saying?"

The duke rose slowly to his feet, brushing off his hands on his breeches. "She wasn't killed here. Someone brought her here. Someone brought her here and laid her out."

In the darkness of the garden, twigs crackled as something scrambled up a tree. Leaves rustled in the wind. Sally glanced over her shoulder, her eyes flicking back and forth, wondering who might be out there, hidden under cover of those trees. Waiting.

"He—" Sally's voice sounded strange to her own ears. "He arranged her."

It was grotesque. Macabre. Sally cupped her elbows in her gloved hands, hugging herself.

Whoever it was had laid the woman out on this bench, fanning her skirts out around her, arranging her hair, pressing that pitiful bouquet of flowers into her lifeless hands.

Sally looked down at her, at that strangely peaceful face, the eyes staring up into nothingness. There was something odd about her hairline; it skewed to one side, and there was an auburn wisp that had escaped beneath the black.

A wig. The woman was wearing a wig.

Had she put it on herself or had it been placed on her—after?

"It's disgusting," Sally said huskily. "It's inhuman."

The duke's expression was remote as he gazed down at the woman. "Yes."

Indignation kindled in Sally's breast; she could feel the warmth of it in her cheeks, in her hands, making her see red, as red as that poor dead girl's rouged neck.

Sally turned to the duke. "You can't be seen here," she said fiercely, shooing him towards the door. "You can't be here when she's found. I'll raise the alarm. No one needs to know you were here."

"What are you doing?"

"Preventing a miscarriage of justice." Even as she said it, Sally knew she was doing the right thing. Light danced off her bracelets as she waved her hands. "There's a girl with curly brown hair and green earrings. Lizzy Reid. Find her. Tell her I said to dance with you. People will think you were in the ball-room the whole time."

The duke pulled back. "Someone will have seen me leave with you."

"Then I'll say I sent you back inside to fetch my shawl. Or my fan. That's it," she said decidedly. "I dropped my fan in the ballroom and dispatched you to bring it to me."

"Because it's so warm on the balcony?" The duke frowned down at her. "There's no need for all this subterfuge. If we just go to the proper authorities—"

"They'll clap you in irons. And whoever did this will *win*." The thought made Sally want to spit. "We can't let that happen. I'll raise the alarm. You have to go. Now. Before anyone sees you here."

The duke stubbornly refused to move. "And leave you here alone?"

Sally gave him an exasperated look. "No one is going to sus-pect me of killing her."

The duke's fingers closed lightly over her forearms. He gave her a little shake. "Did it occur to you that someone who killed once might kill again?"

It hadn't, actually.

Sally drew a deep breath, marshaling all her courage. "No one has any cause to kill *me*," she said haughtily.

The fleeting hint of a smile lightened the grim set of the duke's lips. "Are you so sure of that?"

Before Sally could retort, the sound of voices arrested her

attention. Down the balcony, the doors to the ballroom were opening. She could see only a woman's skirt, the outline of a man's form behind her.

"Quickly!" Sally gave the duke a little push, and then realized that she was pushing the wrong way, straight towards the couple by the door. At any moment, they would step out . . . and see the duke looming over the body of a murdered woman. She hastily reversed course, shooing him in the opposite direction. "Not that way. You'll have to go over the balcony. Well? What are you waiting for?"

"A moment to draw breath?"

"Draw breath later," Sally said tartly. She thought for a moment and added, "And call on me. Tomorrow. Number Twenty-two Upper Brook Street."

The couple were stepping through the door, their light conversation in stark contrast to the dark tableau on the balcony.

Sally flapped her hands at the duke, but he hung back, his head tilted slightly to one side, his eyes searching her face. "Why are you championing me?"

She scarcely knew herself. Sally gave a little shrug. "Call it a sense of fair play. Now *go*."

To her surprise, the duke grasped her hand and raised it to his lips.

"Thank you," he said.

Before Sally could gather her wits to reply, he gave her fingers one last squeeze, then let go. Bracing a hand on the balustrade, he swung himself over the balcony. His dark clothes blended with the shadows. The only sign of his passage was a slight crunch as he landed on the gravel path below. And then . . . nothing.

Sally peered anxiously over the balustrade, but she couldn't make out any sign of the duke. He had disappeared into the shadows, leaving her alone with the murdered woman.

The rush of energy that had fueled her faded along with the duke, leaving her feeling very cold and more than a little bit uncertain. The events of the evening rolled through her mind: the crowded warmth of the dance floor, Lizzy and Agnes in the center of a group of laughing beaux, the duke standing alone by the edge of the ballroom. This might, Sally thought uneasily, be rather more of an adventure than she had bargained for.

How long had it been since she had left the ballroom? It felt like hours, but she knew that in reality it couldn't have been more than ten minutes, fifteen at most.

She could still feel the press of the duke's lips against her hand.

She had been so sure, a moment ago, that she was doing the right thing, but now, with the woman's pale eyes staring sightlessly up at her, she couldn't repress a slight shiver of unease.

Had she just let a killer go free?

No. Sally frowned into the darkness. She was quite sure of her own instincts, and all of them told her that the duke was innocent.

Which meant that they had a killer to catch.

On the other end of the balcony, Hal Caldicott held the door open for Georgiana Thynne. At any moment, they would step across the threshold and spot Sally's pale dress. Sally stiffened her spine. Tomorrow, the duke would have some explaining to do. But now, Sally had a body to discover.

Dropping to her knees beside the bench, Sally filled her lungs and let out a bloodcurdling shriek.

Chapter Eight

Cambridge, 2004

"*E*eek!"

I let out a squeak, dropping my bag on my foot as a hideously misshapen figure loomed up from behind the mailboxes.

The bulb had burned out again, turning the dirty beige walls to a sinister orange. Mine was the last door on the hall, tucked into a little cul-de-sac behind the mailboxes, out of reach of the feeble light from the window on the stairwell.

The hunchback lurched towards me.

"That's not quite the greeting I was expecting," said the Oxford-inflected tones of my boyfriend.

I blinked, my eyes adjusting to the gloom. Yes, that was my boyfriend, propped against the doorframe. The strange blob behind him resolved itself into a Barbour jacket draped over the handle of a wheelie suitcase.

Not a hump.

"You're early," I said weakly. "I mean, yay! You're here."

I flung my arms around his neck, burying my nose in the shoulder of his sweater, breathing in the familiar scents of Colin, falling leaves and shaving soap and crinkly old paper lining the bottoms of dresser drawers. The sweater was scratchy against my cheek, but I didn't mind. It smelled like Selwick Hall.

Colin's arms tightened around me, his nose nuzzling my hair.

"Here I am," he confirmed, and let go. "After a very easy flight. And you've been . . . ?"

"I caught a drink with Megan after class." I dug in my bag for my keys, feeling thoroughly discombobulated. This wasn't quite how I'd meant the reunion to go. "And by 'drink,' I mean coffee."

I hadn't wanted to be blotto for Colin-greeting, so we'd abandoned Grafton Street in favor of the Starbucks on Church Street. Pumpkin spice lattes had seemed like an appropriate beverage for the discussion of vampires.

Colin bent his head towards mine. "I can smell it in your hair," he said, and I could hear the smile in his voice. Colin was well aware of my latte habit. He'd been dragged to every Costa Coffee within a fifty-mile radius of Selwick Hall.

"Eau de caffeine," I said, and pushed open the door to my tiny studio apartment. "Welcome!"

It felt a bit weird to be treating Colin as a visitor when we'd been living together for months in England.

But we'd been living together on his turf, not mine.

He bumped his wheelie over the threshold. The doorway was smack in the middle of the room, on the dividing line between my living area and my sleeping area. I'd stuck bookshelves down the center of the studio to mark out the difference between the two, but it was purely a nominal barrier; Colin's head was higher than the highest shelf. The whole was smaller than Colin's bedroom at Selwick Hall.

"It's nice," said Colin, stifling a yawn with the back of his hand.

"It's cozy," I replied, a little stiffly. I caught myself wanting to explain that this was actually reasonably large for Harvard Square, that property values were different in the wilds of West Sussex and across the street from Harvard Yard. "Anyway! Just leave your bag wherever."

There wasn't much wherever to leave it. Colin seemed to take up an inordinate amount of floor space. I could see him looking dubiously at my bed. My single bed. It doubled as spare couch and work space, but that didn't change its overall square footage.

All the more reason to snuggle?

Maybe having Colin stay with me hadn't been the best idea. New England was full of adorable little inns. We could have gone to a bed-and-breakfast up in the Berkshires, with blue-berry muffins for breakfast and a big four-poster with brass knobs and a patchwork quilt, with leaf-peeping and apple pick-ing and the sounds of sleigh bells in the snow. Well, not the snow, but the rest of it.

But I'd wanted to show Colin what my life was like. Partly just because, but also as a diagnostic. If we were going to stay together, we were going to have to work out some way to bridge the continental divide. We'd lived his life together; could he live mine?

One thing was clear: if he was going to live mine, I was go-ing to have to get a bigger bed. And possibly a larger apartment.

I shoved the wheelie into the corner, next to the blanket chest that lived at the foot of my bed, and dumped the folder Megan had given me down on top of it. "Are you hungry? Thirsty? Sleepy?"

"All three." Colin wrapped his arms around my waist and rested his cheek against my hair. "But mostly glad to see you."

"Me too." I felt some of the frenetic energy dissipate as I leaned my head against his chest. In a slightly muffled voice I said, "I hate that we only have four days."

"On the bright side," said Colin, "we have four days."

"Fair point." I removed my nose from his collarbone, tipping my head back so I could see his face. "What would you like to do? Do you need a nap?"

Reluctantly releasing me, Colin raised a brow. "I think I can stagger on for an hour or two more."

It was at moments like this that I loved him so much it hurt.

It's always the silly little things, isn't it? A quirk of expression, a tone of voice. In Colin's case, just the indefinable Colin-ness of him. I knew that he was longing to conk out. Colin was, left to himself, an early riser; he'd been on the road all day; he'd probably already been fed a number of meals on little plastic trays with reckless disregard to (a) the actual time of day and (b) the recipient's state of wakefulness. But he would come out with me anyway, because he knew I was itching to take him out and about in my world.

"There's a pub a few blocks away . . . ," I said, trying to sound as though it was just a suggestion.

I had it all planned out. For tonight, since Colin was tired, I had chosen a comfortable dive bar for drinks and sandwiches. Tomorrow, we could do fancy cocktails at Casablanca, the restaurant in the basement of Café Algiers, Indian food at my favorite Indian place across the street from the K school, followed by dessert and chocolate martinis at Finale, the dessert place down the block from the Holyoke Center.

Saturday night was the Dudley House Halloween Costume Ball, and, incidentally, my sort-of birthday eve. Since my actual birthday was Monday, the day Colin flew back, we were celebrating Birthday Eve Observed on Saturday night. And then a quiet night in on Sunday. Colin had looked into staying for my birthday proper, but the vagaries of airline pricing had been against us. For some absurd reason, the ticket was far cheaper on the Monday than the Tuesday. And what was a day here or there?

In between prebirthday festivities, there would be visits to the history department and the Harvard Coop, a walk by the river, brunch with my friends Liz and Jenny, and various other representative activities designed to place my existence in Cambridge in the best possible light.

Of course, if I were really trying to give Colin an accurate view of my life, these activities would include sprinting from the library to the Barker Center and back again, retail therapy via the sale rack at Ann Taylor, eating take-out burritos with one hand while grading papers with the other, and getting blotto on red wine at Grafton Street.

Maybe that would have been better. Maybe that would make Colin feel a part of my life here, the way I had been part of his in England.

But we had only four days. . . .

"The pub would be brilliant," said Colin promptly, and I gave his arm an extra squeeze, just because.

"After you," I said with a flourish.

"No, after you," said Colin gravely, trying to move aside to let me pass, and hip-bumping his wheelie in the process.

Megan's folder made a slow slide towards the floor, spewing papers.

We both lunged for it at the same time, cracking heads in the process.

"Ow," I said, lurching back to my feet.

Crouched on the floor, Colin grimaced. "Sorry."

"No. No, it's fine." I surreptitiously touched a hand to my forehead. I was sure I would stop seeing stars in a moment.

"I'll get these for you, shall I?" offered Colin.

"That seems wise," I murmured, and perched gingerly on the arm of the love seat. The love seat was secondhand, and not the sturdiest construction in creation.

Which reminded me that I ought to warn Colin about that. And about the desk chair, which was held together by one of its original four screws. And the coffeemaker that liked to spew coffee in odd directions.

Basically, my apartment was a health hazard.

"Um, can I get you anything?" I offered the top of Colin's head. "Water? Booze?" Other than that, the options were limited.

"Didn't you want to go to the pub?" Colin asked absently, holding up one of Megan's printouts. He glanced up over his shoulder. "A little light reading for Halloween?"

"A little— Oh, right. I haven't really looked at those yet."

Megan, in an excess of generosity, had entrusted me with the folder containing her notes on the Ghoul of Belliston Hall, that being, apparently, the name that the press had given to Britain's first vampire.

Edging carefully between Colin's knee and the bookcase, I plunked myself down on the floor on the other side of the puddle of papers and craned my neck to catch a glimpse of the one in Colin's hands. "The year *The Convent of Orsino* came out, there was a vampire scare in London. A woman was found dead with fang marks on her neck."

"That explains this, then." Colin obligingly held the paper out towards me.

I scooted in closer, or as close as I could with the bookshelf getting in the way. The page was a photocopy of what looked like a Gillray cartoon. I could recognize the classic Gillray figures, tall and wasp-waisted—and the telltale smudges of the Widener copy machines, each of which had its own unique pattern of grime.

Gillray knew his stuff. Even in blurry black and white, there was something deeply chilling about the scene. A woman lay upon a marble bench with scrolled ends, one arm flung gracefully behind her head, the other dangling down to the stone flags of the floor. The thin fabric of her dress showcased the lines of her legs; the long, dark curls of her hair twined sinuously along her bosom. Roses bloomed from large marble urns on either side of her, like something out of the imagination of Edward Gorey.

One might have thought she was asleep, but for the man crouched behind her. His long black cloak was furled high around his neck, and his back was turned away so that we saw him only in profile and in shadow—a nice way of avoiding an action for libel.

Gillray being Gillray, he hadn't resisted the urge to lampoon the thrill-seekers. You could see them, crowded into the door from the balcony, craning to see over one another, their expressions more rapacious by far than that of the supposed vampire.

I gave a little shiver. "The word of the day is 'macabre.' Or, as I used to pronounce it when I was little, mack-a-bray."

"Mack-a-bray, indeed," Colin agreed. He set the paper aside. "Is this for the dissertation, or purely for your amusement?"

"Possibly the former, probably the latter."

Megan hadn't been able to tell me much. The Duke of Bel-liston had been suspected of the murder of an unknown woman who had turned up dead on the balcony of his uncle's house. The press had drawn the obvious parallels to *The Convent of Orsino*: beneath the cartoon Colin had been holding was an-other, in which the Duke of Belliston—at least, I assumed that was the Duke of Belliston—was portrayed as the Knight of the Silver Tower, sparkling armor and all.

"I'm trying to figure out whether there's anything dissertation-worthy in it." I drew my legs up and wrapped my arms around my knees. The heels of my boots added new scrapes to the hardwood floor. "Miss Gwen's book sparked a vampire craze—so the question is, was the duke a crazed ad-mirer of Miss Gwen's writing—"

"Had he *read* it?" murmured Colin.

"Hey, that's your ancestress you're talking about. And it was the bestselling book of 1806."

Colin shook his head. "Heaven help us all."

"Pretty much." Personally, I didn't think *The Convent of Or-sino* was that bad, once one got past the purpler-than-purple prose, but I wasn't going to say so. Colin was currently writing his own potboiler, of the guns, drugs, and car crashes variety, and it seemed to have unleashed a deep vein of criticism in my boyfriend. "Anyway, the question is, was the duke a nutcase—"

Colin leafed through the rest of Megan's photocopies. "In-breeding has been known to produce such things."

"—*or*"—I was determined to finish my sentence this time—"was this a deliberate attempt to taunt Miss Gwen? The whole vampire thing, I mean."

Colin looked up from a lurid headline from *The Speculator*, the nineteenth century's answer to the *National Enquirer*.

"Come again?"

Okay, admittedly, I hadn't put that well. I hugged my knees closer to my chest. "What if someone was deliberately trying to pique Miss Gwen's interest? The Pink Carnation had gone into deep cover. What if someone used a faux vampire kill to get Miss Gwen to draw her out?"

Colin massaged his temples with his fingers. "I think I left my brain in the lost luggage at Heathrow," he said apologetically.

"Sorry." I scrambled to my feet, using the edge of the blanket chest to haul myself up. "You must be exhausted. And hungry. And here I am talking at you."

"With," Colin corrected me, rising with considerably more grace. At least, until he bumped a knee on the blanket chest. I winced in sympathy. " 'With,' not 'at.' "

"Let's get you a drink," I suggested. And out of my apartment, which, with Colin in it, seemed more and more like a maze designed for a midget.

"Yes," Colin agreed, slinging his Barbour on, and narrowly missing karate-chopping my bookshelf. "I'm sure this will all make more sense after a pint or two."

"Or not." I gave his arm a quick hug before letting go to open the door. This time, Colin wisely didn't try to help. "It's just a theory. I haven't done the research yet. And, anyway, I'm not really supposed to be adding new material at this point. It's all about writing up."

In the gloom of the hallway, Colin's expression was inscrutable. He slung his hands into the deep pockets of his Barbour. "So you're almost done, then?"

"'Done' is a relative term." We made our way down the narrow staircase, into the narrow hall, decorated in an unattractive combo of yellow and a red that had taken on the rusty shade of dried blood. I ducked my head so that my hair fell in front of my face. "I gave my advisor the first ten chapters. The ones I wrote at Selwick Hall."

Me on my bulky green laptop in the library, Colin on his desktop in his study, late-summer sun slanting through the long windows, the scent of the roses from the garden heavy in the air.

The October air bit at my neck. I pulled my collar closer.

"Good on you," said Colin, and if he didn't sound quite as enthusiastic as he could have, well, that was probably a function of jet lag, and the wind that had whipped up, choking off his words, making him hunch down into his jacket.

I looked at him anxiously, swiping at the hair that the wind blew into my eyes. "I hope you don't mind. I have a meeting with my advisor tomorrow afternoon." It was the only time that had worked for Professor Tompkins. Advisors were never there until you didn't want them to be, at which time they suddenly became strangely insistent. "It shouldn't take long. Especially on a Friday."

"That's fine."

"I can give you the keys to the apartment, so you're not housebound while I'm away. Or you can go to the Peabody. They have a new exhibit up. Or—"

"It's fine," Colin repeated, as we dodged someone wanting us to sign a petition, and passed the inevitable Goth teenagers hanging out next to Out of Town News. "I'm sure I'll find something to entertain myself."

"Mm-hmm." I swallowed what I had been about to say. "I just hate that this is cutting into our time together."

Colin reached out and twined his fingers through mine. Even in the cold, his hands were warm. "This is your work," he said matter-of-factly. "Of course you have to see him."

We passed Tealuxe and the obligatory Urban Outfitters, with its display of glow-in-the-dark bobblehead Jesus dolls and fatigue chic at civilian prices. The late-afternoon sun had faded into twilight, taking the warmth of the day with it. There was something terribly melancholy about Cambridge on an autumn evening. Or maybe it was any autumn evening, anywhere, with that sense of things slipping away.

I held tight to Colin's hand. "I'll keep it brief," I promised. "It should be just a yes/no on those chapters. He just needs to tell me if I'm on the right track so I can keep going."

"And then?" That was another of Colin's strengths. He listened. He'd spent a lot of time listening to me babble on about my work in the months we were together. This dissertation was as much his as mine; he'd been part of it every step of the way.

Well, almost every step of the way.

I took a deep breath. "If he likes it—there's a shot I could submit for June."

Even as I said it, I wished I hadn't. The words felt like a jinx. But there it was: vampires aside, I was scarily close to finishing. The chapters I'd given my advisor represented a good two-thirds of my outline. Discovering what had happened to the Pink Carnation would be nice, but it wasn't necessary for the dissertation, which dealt less with personalities and more with mechanisms. Or, at least, that was the idea. My advisor was big on mechanisms, not so much on personalities. I'd tried to tamp down the fascination I felt for the individuals and make it look like I was merely mining them for their methodologies.

"Will I have to call you Doctor?" Colin's voice was warm against the chill air, like hot cider with a kick of brandy in it.

"Please!" I said. "Only the pretentious do that. Besides, it's only the first step. I may not be ready to submit in June. Who knows."

The shadows seemed to press around us as we crossed the green in front of Peet's Coffee, the same Peet's Coffee where I had my weekly writing dates with my friend Liz. As counterintuitive as it might seem, I didn't want to think about finishing. I'd gotten used to life as a grad student. As a grad student, I could pick up and spend three months in England. Once I was on the job market—what then? It was one thing to try to imagine Colin sharing my life in Cambridge, here and there, for a week at a time. But what would happen after that? The future was a large, frightening blank.

Jobs for historians of modern Britain weren't exactly thick on the ground. I would have to go where I had to go.

But I didn't want to think about that now, not with Colin here, with our own future so uncertain and unsettled.

"There's a good shot that even if I finish this year, I'll stay on in Cambridge another year," I said, dodging a group of drunk B-school students who were staggering out of the depths of Grendal's Den, having evidently started their weekend early. "It'll be too late to go on the job market, so what usually happens is that they dredge up a job here as a Hist and Lit lecturer. I'm already teaching in Hist and Lit, so that's an easy option for me."

"So you'll stay where you are?" Colin's collar was up against the wind, giving me an obstructed view of his face.

"Possibly in a larger apartment," I said, and grimaced at the needy note in my voice. "Anyway. Here we are. One pub. As promised."

Shays was really a business school hangout, rather than a grad school one, but I'd thought Colin would prefer the sticky floor and round beer mats to the beige trendiness of Grafton Street. It was also one of the few places with an outdoor seating section, a tiny little sunken patio right off JFK Street. In a week or two, the unsteady metal chairs and tables would be dragged inside as the world battened down for winter, but right now it was just warm enough to sit outside with a glass of tannic-tasting red wine and enjoy the nip in the air and an arm around the shoulders.

Most of the tables were already occupied by students celebrating an extended weekend with Thursday-night drinks, including a group that had pulled three tables together. We managed to snag one to ourselves, off to the side, still bearing the dirty glasses and crumpled check of the previous party.

Colin neatly moved the detritus out of the way. "Gin and tonic?" he said, with the air of a man who knows.

"Er—red wine, actually," I said apologetically. "Whatever they have for their house plonk. No, sit. They'll come to us."

Colin sank back down in his chair, and I found myself missing the Heavy Hart, where we had our regular routine, G&T for me, a pint for Colin, order at the bar, and ladies' room to the back. Maybe it was that Colin was jet-lagged, maybe it was that I was tired, but our reunion felt oddly uneven, one minute comfortable and familiar, the next stiff and awkward, as if we were strangers on a train, forced into the false intimacy of sharing a limited space.

"How are things at Selwick Hall?" I asked quickly, eager to bring us back onto familiar ground.

Colin readjusted his cardboard beer mat. "Fine."

What is it about the word "fine" that always makes it sound quite the contrary? As if "fine" were a synonym for "altogether crappy and thank you for not inquiring further."

I shifted forward, making the iron table rock against the uneven flagstones of the patio. "Is everything okay?"

"Brilliant." Colin glanced up. "Where's that waitress?"

Serving a rowdy group of business school students, already dressed for Halloween. I counted one witch, one pirate, and at least two slutty vampires, one of whom was already several sheets to the wind.

"She'll be here in a minute." Fighting a sense of impending doom, I asked, "Is Joan Plowden-Plugge still seeing Nigel Dempster?"

Joan was the girl next door, although anyone less girl-next-door-ish would be hard to imagine. Fortunately, her designs on Colin appeared to have been quenched when she started dating Colin's sister's evil ex.

Our lives were very complicated sometimes. Don't even get me started on the rest of Colin's family.

Colin raised a hand to flag down the waitress. "I assume so. I made it a point not to find out."

I nodded vigorously. "As long as they're keeping each other occupied."

My breath made little puffs of air in the evening chill. It was about ten degrees too cold to be sitting outside. But that wasn't the sole source of the chill. What was going on with Colin? He might just be tired. He might. But all my antennae were quivering, like Miss Clavel in the Madeline books, who woke up in the middle of the night, sure that something was not quite right.

Something wasn't quite right here. I just wasn't sure what it was. It wasn't that Colin hadn't seemed glad to see me. He had. He wouldn't have hauled all the way out here just to break up with me, would he? No.

At least, I didn't think so.

No. Definitely no. Or if he had, he would have done it right away, and then removed himself to a hotel. He wouldn't have smooched me like we were still a thing and left his suitcase by my bed. That wasn't Colin. He was honorable to a fault, and, for a male, remarkably straightforward about his feelings. When he bothered to express them.

Which meant that it was something else.

I waited while Colin placed our orders, frantically going through our conversation in my mind, trying to isolate the moment when he had pulled his classic hedgehog impression. My dissertation? He'd told me he didn't mind my putting his family stories out there—not that there was terribly much risk, given that (a) it tended to take a good five years to get from dissertation to book, and another few years on top of that for the academic presses to grind their way to publication, via a slow boat to China, and (b) the circulation would probably be roughly ten academic libraries, four cranky reviewers, and my mother.

"Is Jeremy behaving himself?" I asked. Colin's stepfather had been a source of some drama in the not too distant past. He had designs on Colin's home. Which he'd claimed he'd abandoned in the spirit of familial entente, but . . .

"As far as I can tell." Colin's stony expression relaxed somewhat. "There haven't been any more break-ins, if that's what you mean."

"That's a relief," I lied. Jeremy would have been an easy one. We'd dealt with Jeremy before.

Maybe Colin was just tired. Maybe that was all it was.

The waitress plunked our drinks down in front of us, making the table rock dangerously. I plucked up my glass of wine before the suspiciously viscous liquid could slosh over the sides.

"To your visit," I said, a little too heartily, lifting my glass to Colin.

"To your meeting tomorrow." Colin tipped his pint in my direction. There was a crash from the neighboring table as one of the Slutty Vampires caught her feet in the paving and went catapulting over her own chair. "And to vampires."

Chapter Nine

London, 1806

*H*onor commanded that Lucien present himself, as promised, at Miss Fitzhugh's residence the next day.

Pride, however, dictated that he not do so too promptly.

It was midafternoon by the time Lucien set off for Brook
Street, easily evading the pursuit of a large man whose clumsy
attempts at surveillance marked him unmistakably as a Bow
Street Runner. The encounter did little to improve Lucien's
mood. Did the authorities really believe that he was a creature
of the night who assuaged his bloodlust by supping from the
veins of females wearing too much lip rouge? He hadn't con-
ducted an examination of the body, but he would have been

willing to wager that the cause of death was more likely a knife in the back than a tooth in the throat.

The whole affair stank to high heaven.

Between the rumors, the note, and the disposition of the body, Lucien had the uneasy sensation that he was the prime actor in a drama whose script was known to everyone but him. He wouldn't have been surprised to have touched the body to find that the flesh was wax, an elaborate prop in a play being enacted around him for purposes unknown to him.

And what was Miss Fitzhugh's role in all this? Last night, there had been no time to do anything but take her at her word; he had been over the balcony before he could question her advice or her motives.

But the hours had passed and his head had cooled and Lucien found himself reexamining, with increasing disquiet, his brief acquaintance with Miss Sally Fitzhugh.

If that was even her name. He had only her word for it, after all.

It was the presumed Miss Fitzhugh who had, by her own admission, appeared in his garden the other night, and it was Miss Fitzhugh who had boldly presented herself to Lucien the night before. Was it mere officiousness or something more, something sinister? Her presence by his side at the exact moment the note was dropped began to seem something more than coincidence.

Lucien conjured up the image of Miss Fitzhugh's elegant figure and guinea-gold hair. In her pale gown, with her hair arranged in ringlets, she was the perfect image of a debutante—but for the disconcerting directness of her conversation.

She couldn't be his mother's mysterious contact; she was too young. An actress, hired for the occasion? A confederate? The daughter of the original spy?

No matter how Lucien turned the matter over in his mind, the pieces wouldn't fit. If Miss Fitzhugh were part of a dastardly scheme designed to implicate him in murder, one would think she would have raised the alarm and drawn half the ballroom to their side, not urged him over the balcony.

Unless, of course, that was merely a piece of the plot. In the wee hours of the morning, in his gloomy bedchamber in his parents' abandoned mansion, Lucien's paranoid imaginings ran rampant. What if the object weren't his arrest, but this very meeting? The corpse might have been wax, the entire scenario designed to draw him out, to catch him off his guard.

As he made his way across town, through a mist that drifted across the cobbles and hugged the trees, Lucien wondered just what he was likely to find at Number Twenty-two Brook Street. Miss Fitzhugh? Or a trap of some kind?

If it was the latter, Lucien thought grimly, let them do their worst. He would welcome the opportunity to meet his adversary face-to-face. He had some questions that wanted answering—and a sword in his cane.

The town house on Brook Street hardly presented a sinister aspect. Light shone in bright patches through the windows, fighting bravely against the gloom of a rainy afternoon. Lucien could see a drawing room through the drapes, with a pianoforte in one corner and some rather appallingly pink upholstery embroidered with carnations. It all looked entirely respectable and reasonably benign, but he kept a tight grip on his cane as he rapped on the door, half expecting a skeleton to tumble out at him, or someone in chains to gibber from the attic.

"Yeth?" A man in black opened the door, regarding him with what might have been either a squint of suspicion or merely the result of extreme myopia.

Lucien peered over the man's shoulder, waiting for an ambush, but saw only a gold-framed mirror and what looked like a child's fallen toy. The house smelled pleasantly of dried flowers, beeswax candles, and lemon oil. Lucien wasn't entirely sure what duplicity was meant to smell like, but he doubted it was lemon oil.

Unless, of course, this was a false address and he would find himself encountering an entirely unknown family rather than the mysterious Miss Fitzhugh.

In his grandest voice, he said, "Tell Miss Fitzhugh that the Duke of Belliston is here to see her."

"Your grathe." The butler bent low with an audible creaking of bones. "Ith your grathe would be tho kind . . ."

Lucien stalked into the hallway. "Is Miss Fitzhugh at home?" he asked suspiciously.

There was the smell of something baking, something involving apples and cinnamon. The scent made his stomach rumble. Lucien sternly silenced it.

"Mith Thally ith otherwithe occupied," the butler informed him. He appeared to have a bit of a limp as well as a lisp. "Ith your grathe would be tho good?"

The butler gestured Lucien into a parlor notably lacking in thugs, armaments, or instruments of torture—unless one counted the tall harp in one corner—assured him that Mith would be with him prethently, and limped off to fetch Lucien refreshment.

It was all suspiciously unsuspicious.

A pair of double doors to Lucien's right opened onto another parlor. "Well, *really*," Lucien heard Miss Fitzhugh exclaim, in tones of distinct annoyance.

Looking through a keyhole would have been undignified. A gap between the doors, however, was quite a different matter.

Lucien positioned himself comfortably at the gap, through which he could see Miss Fitzhugh gesticulating with considerable vigor, her slender fingers fluttering. There was a man in the room with her. Lucien could make out only a frock coat of a dull brown and close-cropped gray hair, thinning in the back.

"Really, Sir Matthew," chirped Miss Fitzhugh. She sounded entirely unlike the decisive woman who had ordered Lucien off the balcony. "I can't think what I can tell you that I didn't tell everyone last night."

The man drew a notebook out of his pocket and flipped it open. Licking a finger, he thumbed through the papers.

Lucien froze, transported to another place, another time. Standing in his mother's greenhouse, as the magistrate in the case licked his finger and flipped through his notes, the susurration of the pages grating against Lucien's raw nerves.

The man turned, and Lucien knew there was no doubt as to his identity. The magistrate in charge of his parents' case had worn a bagwig, while this man was close shorn. That man had been corpulent and red-faced; this man's jowls had begun to sag. But they were undoubtedly one and the same.

Lucien should know. He had dogged Sir Matthew's footsteps, haunted his doorstep. The magistrate had shook him off as he might a flea. Upon hearing that Lucien had discovered his parents' bodies, Sir Matthew had fired off a series of curt questions at Lucien, and then dismissed him to the schoolroom, refusing to answer his questions, turning a deaf ear to pleas that he be told what was going on. *Ask your tutor*, he had said curtly.

But Sherry was already gone, gone the morning after Lucien's parents died, and there was no one for Lucien to ask. Only Uncle Henry, who had squeezed his shoulder and looked sad and told him to go on, there was a good boy.

Confused and alone, Lucien had been forced to piece together what had happened, bit by bit, from a patchwork of gossip and half-heard conversations. It would have meant so very much if Sir Matthew had taken half an hour, ten minutes even, to sit down with him and tell him frankly what had happened, what he believed to have happened. Instead, he had left Lucien in an agony of doubt and uncertainty.

Lucien had been to hell and back; Sir Matthew didn't look as if he had missed a hot dinner.

A wave of blinding anger assaulted Lucien, enough to make his knees shake.

Consulting his notes, Sir Matthew recited, " 'Dreadful, just dreadful. Oh, heavens, it was dreadful.' " He looked up at Miss Fitzhugh over his spectacles. "Do you have anything to add to that statement, Miss Fitzhugh?"

Miss Fitzhugh lifted her chin imperiously. "It was a frightful experience. And I cannot believe you are being so unkind as to ask me to revisit it." She clasped her hands to her chest in a manner reminiscent of Mrs. Siddons. "Have you no finer feelings, sir?"

The magistrate looked pained. "What I have, Miss Fitzhugh, is a woman murdered."

And, from the looks of it, a massive headache.

Lucien's own head wasn't feeling too clever. Sir Matthew was the magistrate they'd summoned to deal with the matter of the murdered girl? He supposed it made a certain amount of sense; Uncle Henry would have been familiar with him from Lucien's parents' case all those years ago. All the same, it filled Lucien with a deep sense of foreboding.

Sir Matthew, as he recalled, had preferred to judge first, investigate later.

If he knew that Lucien had been there on that balcony . . .

"Well, it isn't *my* fault I happened to discover her," declared Miss Fitzhugh, managing to sound quite as empty-headed as any debutante could wish. "It might just as well have been anyone!"

"But it wasn't anyone, Miss Fitzhugh," said Sir Matthew, with exaggerated patience. "It was you. And—"

"I do call it *most* unfair."

Sir Matthew made himself heard over her by dint of main force. "—And yours is the only testimony we have as to the killer."

"Well, really." Miss Fitzhugh gave a theatrical shiver. "Whoever it was, I am quite sure he had a hunch. And a limp. And possibly a harelip."

What the devil? Taking care not to jar the doors, Lucien pressed his eye to the gap.

The harelip proved too much for Sir Matthew. "Are these attributes the evidence of your own eyes or the products of speculation?"

Miss Fitzhugh opened her eyes wide. "Shouldn't a villain look like a villain, Sir Matthew?"

"Sadly," said Sir Matthew drily, "most of them do not." He looked at Miss Fitzhugh sternly over the pages of his notebook. "Do you know the Duke of Belliston?"

Lucien tensed, waiting.

"Oh, but of course!" Miss Fitzhugh gave a little hop of excitement. "Who doesn't know about the Duke of Belliston?"

Sir Matthew's pen, which had begun to move, paused again. "That wasn't precisely what I—"

"Everyone was talking about him last night. *Everyone.* You do know that he was kept chained in an attic until he broke free? It's all on account of the Gypsy curse, you know."

"The—" Sir Matthew appeared to be having difficulty speaking.

"The Gypsy curse," repeated Miss Fitzhugh, checking to see if he was writing it down. "That's G-Y, not G-I. I do respect a good Gypsy curse, don't you? There's no sense in having a curse by halves. It was all over the ballroom last night, how the duke had been cursed in his cradle. Or maybe it was the duke's mother who had been cursed in her cradle? And, then"—Miss Fitzhugh lowered her voice confidingly—"there are all those dead chickens."

Sir Matthew appeared to be in the early stage of apoplexy. His jowls quivered alarmingly. "Dead *chickens?*"

"I don't like to talk about the chickens," said Miss Fitzhugh darkly.

It was almost enough to make Lucien feel sorry for Sir Matthew. Almost. Through the gap in the door, Lucien eyed Miss Fitzhugh speculatively, trying to figure out just what she was playing at.

Sir Matthew appeared to be having similar thoughts.

"Miss Fitzhugh," the magistrate said severely, "you do realize that obstructing the prosecution of a crime is a serious charge?"

Miss Fitzhugh drew herself up to her full height and looked down her nose at the magistrate. "I have already told you precisely what occurred. I ventured onto the balcony for air and happened upon that poor, poor woman. It was, I can assure you, *most* unsettling." She added spiritedly, "I am not accustomed to frequenting establishments with corpses on the balcony. It is *most* untidy."

Sir Matthew closed his notebook with a distinct snap. "Yes. Yes, I suppose one might call it that." He drew a handkerchief across his brow. Returning the crumpled cloth to his waistcoat pocket, the magistrate harrumphed with all the majesty of the law. "Forgive me if I tell you that I find your account of the evening's events unenlightening, Miss Fitzhugh. Distinctly unenlightening."

"Do you know," said Miss Fitzhugh, opening her eyes wide, "I had wondered why they didn't bother to light the torches on the balcony."

"Sally," said someone quellingly.

A woman whom Lucien hadn't noticed before rose from a rose and gold settee in the corner of the room. She was dressed modestly in a pale blue wool dress with a high neck and white trim on the collar and sleeves, her blond hair in soft waves beneath a white lace cap.

The second woman held out a hand to the magistrate. "Sir Matthew, we shouldn't wish to take up any more of your time. I am quite sure that if Sally recalls anything—anything at all"—this with a stern look at Miss Fitzhugh—"she will notify you at once."

Sir Matthew was still trying to regain his lost dignity. "I do not think you appreciate the seriousness of this matter."

"Oh, we do," said Miss Fitzhugh, a little too enthusiastically. "We do."

"Hmph." With one last, suspicious glance at Miss Fitzhugh, Sir Matthew took his leave.

Lucien deemed it prudent to draw out of sight as the butler escorted the magistrate to the front door.

Why hadn't Miss Fitzhugh told him that Lucien had been on the balcony? It seemed impossible that her motives could be purely altruistic. But Lucien was increasingly hard-pressed to arrive at another alternative.

Unless she was merely off her bean. That would explain a great deal.

"The Duke of Bellithton," the butler intoned, and flung the connecting doors wide, revealing a pleasant parlor with a fire crackling merrily on the grate. The wall above the mantel was occupied by a charming family portrait featuring a blond man with an execrable waistcoat and a marked resemblance to Miss Fitzhugh beaming down at a woman holding an infant in a lacy white dress. A novel lay open on the settee and a plate of biscuits sat on a small, round table.

Anything less like a den of intrigue, Lucien couldn't imagine.

The two ladies turned in Lucien's direction. Miss Fitzhugh looked him up and down. "You're late."

"Didn't you know that creatures of the night cannot travel by day?"

"It is still day," pointed out Miss Fitzhugh. "It is merely somewhat later in the day."

"Sally," said the woman in the white lace cap, whom Lucien recognized as the harried-looking chaperone of the night before. She was also, quite clearly, the woman featured in the portrait above the mantel.

Miss Fitzhugh threaded an arm through that of the woman in the white lace cap. "This," said Miss Fitzhugh fondly, "is my sister, Mrs. Fitzhugh. Arabella, may I present to you the Duke of Belliston?"

"Fangs and all," said Lucien pleasantly.

Miss Fitzhugh sniffed.

Arabella Fitzhugh smiled at him. She had a pleasant-featured face, somewhat tired about the eyes. "Duke," she said. Her voice was soft and well-bred. "You are very kind to call."

There was something rather disarming to being called kind. "I understood the summons was somewhat in the nature of a command," said Lucien.

"Don't be silly," said Miss Fitzhugh impatiently. "We have much to discuss."

Lucien eyed her warily. "Yes, we do." Such as why she had lied to the magistrate about the events of the night before.

Mrs. Fitzhugh intervened. "Would you care for some tea? Perhaps some apple cake?"

Lucien's mouth began to water. It had been rather a while since breakfast. He caught himself before he could be diverted by the smell of cinnamon. "No, thank you. I—"

He was balked by a ululating cry that filled the hall, followed by the sound of pounding feet. The door banged against the wall. Lucien whirled, looking for danger.

Instead, he saw a very chubby infant moving at an alarming

speed on short and unsteady legs, its face and hands smeared with a viscous red substance.

The child was rapidly followed by a nursemaid, her cap askew, her white apron streaked with gore. The nursemaid came to a stop, breathless, resting her hands against her knees as she panted, "Mistress! Mistress, I tried to stop her, but—"

"I know." Mrs. Fitzhugh swept the gory infant into her arms, transferring a great deal of the red and sticky substance to the front of her dress.

Miss Fitzhugh prudently moved her muslin skirts out of the way.

It looked like the slaughter of the innocents but for the fact that the innocent was awake, and clapping her chubby hands with every appearance of delight.

In which case, that probably wasn't blood. Lucien felt his breathing slowly return to normal.

Holding the infant out at arm's length, Mrs. Fitzhugh surveyed the carnage with an experienced eye. "Has Parsnip got into the jam tarts again?"

Lucien inferred from the context that Parsnip was not, in fact, a root vegetable, but the angelic-looking infant chuckling and clucking in her mother's arms.

"It was the raspberry," said the nursemaid, in tones of doom.

"I don't know how she does it," murmured Mrs. Fitzhugh. She looked down at the baby, who appeared to have rubbed jam into her own ears, her hair, and, now, all along the front of her mother's dress.

The child bared her tiny teeth in a delighted grin. There were raspberry seeds stuck between the two front teeth. Lucien detected a very strong resemblance to Miss Sally Fitzhugh. Particularly around the eyes, which were dancing with mischief.

Mrs. Fitzhugh hefted the begrimed child onto her shoulder. "Duke, if you will pardon me—?"

Sally Fitzhugh wafted a hand at her sister-in-law. "Do take all the time you need. I am sure I shall have no difficulty entertaining the duke in your absence."

Lucien wasn't sure that "entertain" was the correct verb.

Mrs. Fitzhugh appeared to harbor similar doubts. Clasping her child expertly around the knees, she fixed Sally with a meaningful look. "I will return momentarily."

"Naturally," said Miss Fitzhugh, with an air of wounded innocence.

Parsnip waved a plump hand at them over her mother's shoulder. The child's gurglings and the nurse's continued complaints receded down the corridor. Miss Fitzhugh looked fondly after them.

"Isn't she delightful?" Miss Fitzhugh said proudly.

"Delightful," echoed Lucien, feeling himself at a disadvantage. "Miss Fitzhugh, I—"

"I know," said Miss Fitzhugh, seating herself on a settee, with a sweep of her skirts. "You wish to thank me. There's no need."

Thanking really hadn't been at the forefront of Lucien's

mind. Abandoning any attempt to proceed logically, he said shortly, "Why did you lie to Sir Matthew?"

Miss Fitzhugh looked at him quizzically. "I didn't lie, precisely. I merely edited the facts a bit."

Edit? The term Lucien would have used was "obscure." Or perhaps "obfuscate."

Lucien decided not to quibble about words. "Why conceal my presence?"

"I should think that would be obvious."

It was all about as obvious as mud. Lucien braced a hand against the mantel. "Not to me."

With great patience, Miss Fitzhugh said, "If Sir Matthew were to apprehend you, how should we go about finding the real killer?"

Lucien blinked at Miss Fitzhugh, who was sitting quite peacefully on the settee, her sprigged muslin skirts fanned out around her, her hands folded demurely in her lap, looking the very picture of innocent maidenhood. "We?"

"Well, who else is going to do it? Left to himself, Sir Matthew would simply arrest you and have done with it. It's pure laziness, of course. I'm sure that's what the killer was counting on. Most people can't be trusted to look outside the obvious." Miss Fitzhugh gave her skirts a little twitch with a flick of her wrist. "Obviously."

Lucien's head was swimming. "Not to discount the obvious . . . how do you know I didn't do it?"

Miss Fitzhugh regarded him pityingly. "If you had, you would hardly have implicated yourself, now, would you?"

For some reason, her calm assumption of his innocence grated on Lucien's nerves. "Unless I assumed that others would arrive at that same conclusion."

Miss Fitzhugh raised a blond brow. "Implicating yourself to exonerate yourself? It seems needlessly twisty. Besides," she added serenely, "you haven't a hunch *or* a harelip."

"I left them in my other waistcoat." Lucien paused, taking a moment to get his thoughts back in order. Miss Fitzhugh had a remarkable ability to lead him off along verbal byways. Doing his best to keep it all as simple as possible, he said, "Explain to me. Why this excessive interest in my affairs?"

"I would hardly call it *excessive*." Miss Fitzhugh looked reproachfully at him. "Really, I consider it quite civic-minded."

"I'm hardly a public charity." Lucien forced himself back to the point. "You've sought me out twice now. Three times if one counts today. Since meeting you, I have been accused of vampirism and implicated in a murder. Would you care to comment?"

"That's really not quite fair," protested Miss Fitzhugh. "Everyone was saying you were a vampire long before I— Wait. Are you saying—? Do you really think that I had something to do with—"

For once, Miss Sally Fitzhugh appeared to be bereft of speech.

"It does look rather suspicious, you have to agree," Lucien said gruffly.

"No, I don't!" Miss Fitzhugh popped up off the settee. There were two bright patches of color in her cheeks. "I do call that ungrateful. Here I am, trying to save you from the noose, and— You can't really think I had anything to do with that poor woman's death? Do I look like a cold-blooded murderess?"

Her bosom swelled with indignation, attaining impressive proportions.

"Not cold-blooded, no," said Lucien. He felt himself losing the thread of conversation and forced himself to divert his attention back to her face. "You must admit the timing was suspicious."

"The timing," Miss Fitzhugh shot back at him, "was exceedingly unfortunate. For me. Do you think I *liked* stumbling upon that poor woman? It was excessively unpleasant."

The two of them stared at each other for a long moment, the words ringing in the air between them, incongruous in the cinnamon-scented parlor.

The fire faded from Miss Fitzhugh's face. "The more so for her. Whoever she is. Was." She looked down at her hands, worrying at her lower lip with white, even teeth. "I keep forgetting that. That it's not just a sort of puzzle. That she was a person. And now she isn't."

The words stopped Lucien cold.

"Yes," he said, feeling a bit as though she'd just punched him in the gut.

He hadn't stopped to think about the murdered woman at all, except for her role in relation to himself. And he certainly hadn't considered the feelings of Miss Fitzhugh. He remembered her face last night on the balcony, pale and wide-eyed. She'd been more than a little bit unsteady on her feet, babbling nonsense about rosemary for remembrance. No one would have blamed her for going off in a fit of the vapors.

But she hadn't.

And Lucien felt like the worst sort of heel.

"Well, then." Miss Fitzhugh gathered herself together. With a sniff, she gave a little toss of her head. "I suppose I should be flattered. No one has ever suspected me of skulduggery before."

"That," said Lucien slowly, "I find hard to believe."

He found himself looking at her, really looking at her, for the first time, not just as a girl in his garden or as that woman on the balcony, but as a person in her own right. In the peaceful parlor, in her demure gown, she looked like any debutante at home. But Miss Fitzhugh, Lucien was beginning to learn, was a debutante with a difference.

It was like picking up a bunch of daisies to discover that they were, in fact, a rather rare sort of orchid.

Miss Fitzhugh turned away from his scrutiny, sweeping one long curl back over her shoulder. "Do you know what *I* believe?" she said tartly.

"I suspect I'm going to hear it," murmured Lucien.

Miss Fitzhugh pointedly disregarded that comment. "I believe that someone put about that ridiculous vampire rumor on purpose." She turned back towards him, her blue eyes intent. "It's terribly easy to start a rumor as long as one whispers a word in the right ears. *Especially* if one specifies that it's all in strictest confidence."

She spoke as one who knew.

"All right," said Lucien, seating himself in a pink-patterned chair. "Then what?"

Miss Fitzhugh looked at him with approval. "Then we have to answer one question." She paused for dramatic effect. "Who wants to see you hanged?"

Chapter Ten

"Beheaded," said Lucien. He remembered that much from his long-ago history lessons. "They behead peers. They don't hang them."

"Because that is infinitely preferable," said Miss Fitzhugh caustically. She waved a hand. "All right, then, who has reason to want your head severed from your shoulders?"

Lucien looked bemusedly at Miss Fitzhugh. "Are you always this direct?"

"I find it saves time—which you are currently wasting." Miss Fitzhugh rubbed her slender hands together. "It's a rather clever way to commit murder, don't you think?" she said admiringly. "Death by jury. By implicating you for another murder, the murderer manages to see you dead without taking the blame himself. You'd be both dead *and* discredited. It's really a quite well thought-out plan."

"Forgive me if I fail to share your enthusiasm." Lucien was finding this talk of his own demise more than a little disconcerting.

"Do sit down." Miss Fitzhugh flapped a hand at a chair next to the settee. "It's impossible to think with you looming like that."

Lucien seated himself gingerly on the chair, a spindly gilt affair with the seat resting on the heads of two rather bored-looking sphinxes.

"That's better." Miss Fitzhugh settled herself more comfortably against the cushions of the settee, saying, in a tone of worldly wisdom, "Now. In the ordinary course of things, one would suspect your heir of having designs on your fortune. Who *is* your heir?"

"My uncle Henry," Lucien responded mechanically.

Even as he said it, he knew that the very idea was absurd. Uncle Henry was a well-established man of middle years who had never, as far as Lucien could discern, harbored any designs on the ducal title. He certainly wasn't in need of the money. Aunt Winifred had been a considerable heiress.

Lucien shook his head. "I can't imagine Uncle Henry going about trying to drop large stones on my head. It's a plot out of a bad novel."

"Fiction borrows from life," said Miss Fitzhugh wisely. "If heirs didn't resort to plotting skulduggery, it would never have become such a popular theme. Who next?"

"My cousin. Hal." And that was even more laughable.

Apparently Miss Fitzhugh felt the same way.

"Hal Caldicott?" Miss Fitzhugh wrinkled her nose. "He belongs to the same club as my brother. I've known him for ages. It is rather difficult to imagine him engineering something quite so Byzantine. I wouldn't have thought he would have the initiative."

Lucien found it equally unlikely. He remembered the little boy he had known, running along behind him, Will Scarlet to his Robin Hood. He thought of Hal's angry face, in the hall of Belliston House three days before.

Hurt, yes. Betrayed, yes.

Hal, murdering young ladies, slinging them over his shoulder, and dropping them on balconies? No, no, and no again.

"Not Hal," Lucien said. "Besides, he's due to inherit a small fortune from his mother's people. Unless Uncle Henry has squandered it all on wine, women, and farming equipment."

Miss Fitzhugh looked at him speculatively. "In that case—"

"No," said Lucien.

"All right, then," said Miss Fitzhugh. "If your heir doesn't want to shuffle you off this mortal coil, who does? And don't tell me you have no idea, because I won't believe you. I saw your face when you received that note." She leaned forward, doing her best impression of a bloodhound. "What did you expect to find on that balcony?"

"Not that," said Lucien.

Miss Fitzhugh rolled her eyes. "That much was clear." She looked at him shrewdly. "But you were expecting something; otherwise you would never have been so swift to respond to that note."

"Yes," said Lucien slowly. He couldn't have put into words quite what those expectations had been. After Uncle Henry's revelations, nothing seemed impossible. "I was expecting . . . a message."

And he had received it. Just not the message he had expected.

"Yes?" Miss Fitzhugh prompted.

Lucien looked at her, at her bright blue eyes and expectant face. The sitting room was warm from the fire on the grate, the bright light of the candles keeping the mist and fog at bay. The scent of cinnamon was strong in the air, mingled with lemon oil and lavender.

There had been no one to speak to last night. In truth, there had been no one to speak to since he had departed from New Orleans, with the exception of his valet, Patrice—and with Patrice, there was always the inevitable barrier caused by the fact that he was master and Patrice was servant, and if Lucien didn't remember his place, Patrice certainly remembered his. How long had it been since he had had a real friend, a confidant? Someone to whom to pour out all the tangled thoughts in his head?

The urge to unburden himself warred with the habit of discretion.

Lucien contented himself with saying, "I have been making inquiries into matters about which people might rather I not inquire."

Miss Fitzhugh was having none of it. With excessive politeness, she inquired, "What matter of matters might these matters be?"

Lucien felt a reluctant grin lift the corners of his lips. "You're going to think it sounds mad. I think it sounds mad."

"Don't worry," said Miss Fitzhugh reassuringly. "I have a very high tolerance for insanity. It runs in my family."

Was that meant to be reassuring? Not that he had anything to crow about. He, after all, was the one with a family curse. And, apparently, dead chickens. "Do you know anything about my parents?"

Miss Fitzhugh perked up. "They died?"

"They were murdered."

"Oh." The blunt words made Miss Fitzhugh's eyes widen. Surprise was followed by speculation, and, then, something else entirely. She leaned forward and rested her hand on the arm of his chair. "Poor old thing. You haven't had an easy time of it, have you?"

Lucien didn't know what to say. He'd expected shock, yes. Repulsion. Or ghoulish curiosity. Those were the usual reactions. But not sympathy.

Clearing a throat that felt suddenly tight, Lucien shrugged.

"I wouldn't recommend it as an experience." He looked up at Miss Fitzhugh. "Where are your parents?"

"Not dead," she said promptly, and then grimaced, as if she realized how that sounded. "They're quite innocently occupied in Norfolk. My mother doesn't like town."

"Then this house—"

"Belongs to my brother, Turnip," she said easily. She wrinkled her nose at the drapes. "He had it all redecorated a few years ago in an Egypto–Pink Carnation theme. I was rather hoping Arabella would take it all in hand, but then there was Parsnip, and—here we are."

She sighed, with a put-upon air, but there was no mistaking the depth of affection behind it, or the pride in her voice when she mentioned Parsnip.

Lucien's chest tightened. He could remember, dimly, a time when his own family had been like that.

Recovering himself, he said, "Turnip . . . Parsnip . . . Is everyone in your family named for a vegetable?"

"Turnip is really Reginald. And Parsnip is Jane. But Reggie's friends got in the habit of calling him Turnip. And then when little Jane was born . . ."

Miss Fitzhugh glanced up at the portrait over the mantelpiece, a little smile curving her lips.

As Lucien watched, the smile turned wistful around the edges. Straightening her shoulders, she turned back to Lucien and said brightly, "Well, it all seemed rather inevitable, really."

Lucien found himself watching her closely, trying to get a

hint of what lay beneath that confident exterior. "No one has taken to calling you Carrot? Or Rutabaga?"

"No," said Miss Fitzhugh quellingly. "But we weren't meant to be speaking of me. We were meant to be determining who is trying to secure your demise."

"I wish you would stop saying that," murmured Lucien.

"Ignoring unpleasantness seldom makes it go away." Miss Fitzhugh considered for a moment. "Except in the case of history compositions, which really isn't at all applicable in this instance. So, you see, you would do better to tell me."

There was something lacking in that logic, but the urge to confide was too strong to split hairs.

"I was told yesterday that my mother—" Lucien had trouble getting his lips around the words. He forced himself to spit it out. "That my mother was engaged in funneling secrets to the French. That she was a spy."

"They do get in everywhere, don't they?" said Miss Fitzhugh soothingly. As Lucien gaped at her, she added, in measured tones, "Spies, I mean. Really, they're worse than moths. We had a terrible problem with them at my school."

"Moths?"

"Spies. They were smuggling messages in— Never mind all that." Miss Fitzhugh sat back on the settee and folded her hands in her lap. "As you see, I am not without experience in these matters."

Lucien shook his head. He supposed it shouldn't have surprised him. Nothing about Miss Fitzhugh was as he had thought it would be. "You make it all sound so . . . commonplace."

"Every situation is unique, of course," Miss Fitzhugh said airily. She leaned forward, looking at him searchingly. "Do you believe your mother was a spy?"

In his gut? No. But he was learning that his gut wasn't a very reliable organ when it came to making large life decisions. Uncle Henry was right about one thing: there was far more to his parents' lives than his twelve-year-old self had known. While he had been blissfully roaming the woods at Hullingden, they might have pursued intrigues of which he knew nothing.

"It is not an impossibility," Lucien said stiffly. And then, "My uncle believes her contact killed her, and my father, too, all those years ago."

Miss Fitzhugh's head came up. "There's a rather large flaw in that theory. Why would her contact kill her? It does seem rather imprudent to dispatch the goose that lays the golden eggs."

Lucien brushed that aside. "He might have learned all he needed to know." His face darkened. "Or he might have feared that my mother might unmask him."

"I see." Miss Fitzhugh gnawed on her lower lip, nodding thoughtfully. "And if you were to begin to poke around in the circumstances surrounding her death . . . Yes, I can see why someone might want to put a stop to that."

"Yes." Now that the barrier had been breached, the words

poured out. "That woman last night. Those weren't daisies in her hand. Those were manzanilla flowers."

Miss Fitzhugh looked at him blankly.

Sometimes he forgot that not everyone knew. He had been over it so many times that he had every detail memorized.

Lucien said bleakly, "That was what killed them. Manzanilla bark in their tea."

He didn't need to explain further. "That was the message." Miss Fitzhugh gave a little shiver. "*She* was the message."

Lucien nodded, his lips tight. "A warning to me not to inquire further."

Miss Fitzhugh pressed her fingers to her temples. "Rather hard on that poor woman, I should think. Why her? Why kill her in particular?"

Lucien looked at her helplessly. "I wasn't lying. I haven't any idea who she was." Other than the superficial resemblance to his mother, an illusion created by the long black curls. "I can't stop wondering. Did she have something to tell me? Was that why she was killed? Whoever she was."

"It's not impossible, I suppose." Miss Fitzhugh was silent, her brow furrowed. "When I saw her, with those flowers, for a moment, I thought I recognized— But, no. It's gone." She looked up at Lucien. "This is all a little . . . unreal, isn't it?"

Lucien made a feeble attempt at humor. "I thought you were accustomed to spies."

Miss Fitzhugh tossed her hair. "Spies, yes. Dead bodies, no. Unless . . . there is another possibility. What if this had nothing to do with you at all? What if someone wanted that woman dead?"

Lucien looked at her askance. "Then why summon me?"

Miss Fitzhugh pursed her lips, considering. "You do make a convenient scapegoat. It would be rather clever, really. Everyone would be so busy attending to you that they would never bother to ask about *her*."

Which was precisely what they had been doing.

Lucien felt a sudden lightness. It would make him feel considerably less guilty to know that this woman's death, though still tragic, wasn't on his conscience.

Then Lucien felt the weight of reality descend on him, depressing his spirits. "It won't work," he said. "Why deck her with manzanilla flowers? And my father's snuffbox . . ."

"Which might well have been your snuffbox," Miss Fitzhugh pointed out. "It had the Belliston coat of arms on it. That was all anyone would have noticed."

It was a tempting theory. "Her hair," said Lucien. Long black curls. "Her hair had been arranged to look like my mother's."

Miss Fitzhugh sat up straighter in her chair. "That wasn't her hair. That was a wig. Didn't you notice? Under it, her hair was lighter. Reddish. I suppose," she added doubtfully, "that she might have worn the wig herself, to disguise her identity."

"Or the killer brought it for her. Along with the other things." Lucien remembered the girl on the balcony, so carefully arranged on that marble bench, with the improbably red roses on either side, his father's snuffbox by her foot. The thought of it filled him with disgust. He pushed himself off his chair and paced rapidly towards the fireplace. "It's sick—that's what it is. Not just to kill her, but then to arrange her. Arrange her and stage her . . ."

Miss Fitzhugh looked at him sharply. "What did you say?"

Lucien looked down at her, startled. "I said it's sick."

"No, after that." Miss Fitzhugh rose from the settee, her skirt rustling. In the sudden silence, a piece of coal broke on the grate. "What did you say after that?"

Lucien hardly remembered. "Something about arranging her?"

"Staging her." Miss Fitzhugh was staring at him like a medieval peasant confronted with a conjurer. She turned in an agitated circle, murmuring, *"Rosemary, that's for remembrance. Pray you, love, remember. And there is pansies, that's for thoughts. . . ."*

"Are you quite all right?" Perhaps that comment about insanity in the family hadn't been in jest after all. Lucien looked over his shoulder at the doorway. Should he call Mrs. Fitzhugh? The nurse?

Miss Fitzhugh looked at him, her eyes blazing, two spots of color high on her cheeks. She looked remarkably handsome, if slightly demented.

"Ha!" she crowed. She gave a little dance of triumph, her skirts swishing around her legs. "I knew I had remembered that for a reason!"

"Hamlet?" inquired Lucien cautiously.

"No, Ophelia." Miss Fitzhugh lifted her head and looked

him directly in the eye, her expression more than a little bit smug. "I know who she was."

The Pudding Lane Theatre was located in a cul-de-sac not far from Covent Garden. As the crow flew, it wasn't terribly far from Brook Street. Via narrow streets clogged with the usual traffic of carts and carriages, the journey was considerably longer.

Sally leaned over the edge of the phaeton. "Are you sure you shouldn't have taken the lane to the left? If you'd like, I could—"

"I'm not letting you drive," said the duke, moving the reins to his other hand.

Well, then. "I'm really quite an excellent whip," Sally informed him. "I can drive to an inch."

Or, if not to an inch, at least to two or three inches. There had been only one little incident with that farm cart back in Norfolk, and, really, if people insisted on driving smack in the center of the road, what could they expect?

"Besides," Sally added, moving to firmer ground, "who discovered that woman's identity?"

"Presumed identity," the duke corrected her. He looked at her sideways. "I shouldn't have let you come with me, should I?"

Let? Hmph. "There is nothing the least bit improper about taking a drive with a gentleman in an open carriage," said Sally loftily.

The duke maneuvered competently around a hansom cab.

"Then why did you tell your butler that you were going shopping for laces with—?"

"Lizzy," provided Sally.

The duke raised a brow.

Sally looked at the duke with wide, innocent eyes. "I might be buying laces with Lizzy."

It had seemed like a good excuse at the time. She had needed something to tell Quimby as she dashed out the door behind the duke and she doubted that "chasing murderers with the Duke of Belliston" would have quite the same soothing effect on her sister-in-law.

"But you're not," said the duke, betraying a dampening tendency towards literality.

"A mere technicality. All I said was that I *would* be buying laces with Lizzy." The duke failed to register comprehension. Sally sighed. "I have no doubt that at some point in the future, I will buy laces, most likely in the company of Lizzy. Even if she does tend, regrettably, to have rather unfortunate tastes when it comes to trim." Sally made a show of readjusting her kid leather driving gloves. "I never made any representations that the buying of lace would occur today."

"I believe the word for that," said the duke, "is lying."

"Nonsense. It's merely misdirection."

Sally could have sworn she saw a little smile lurking around the corner of the duke's mouth. "Which is another word for . . ."

Some people had no gratitude.

Some people had also missed the proper turn. "There," said

Sally, pointing. "There's Pudding Lane. You'll have to circle around and go back."

"Hmm," said the duke. He looked at her from under the curly brim of his hat. "Misdirection, you said?"

Yes, that was definitely a smile. Despite herself, Sally found herself smiling back, struck by how the duke's whole face changed when he smiled.

The duke reined the horses in. The smile faded from his eyes. "It's not too late, you know. I can still bring you back home."

"Don't be silly," said Sally. "I didn't come all this way simply for the pleasure of a drive in the rain."

The duke regarded her seriously. "If I had any decency, I wouldn't embroil you in this."

"I'm already embroiled," said Sally simply. She had been embroiled from the moment she had stepped out onto that balcony. No, before that. She had been embroiled from the moment she had heard Agnes call the duke a vampire. What blue-blooded English girl could resist a challenge like that? "Everyone knows I found the body."

"Which I deeply regret," said the duke. He turned to look at her more fully, resting his hand on the backboard behind her shoulder. "If I had had the wit last night to send you back inside . . ."

"Yes, yes," said Sally impatiently. "That's all very chivalrous. But I'm certainly not going to let you tackle a killer alone. In a manner of speaking," she added quickly. "I am happy to leave all physical exertion to you."

Fisticuffs were both undignified and hard on one's wardrobe. Several years ago, thinking it seemed rather romantic, Sally had badgered Turnip to instruct her in the use of an épée, but had discarded the exercise after discovering that it was, indeed, exercise.

The duke seemed to be having trouble controlling his emotion. "How very generous of you."

Sally suspected she was being mocked. "Do I seem like the sort of person who would let a killer run free?"

The duke regained control of his face. "If I were a murderer," he said gravely, "I would make sure to confine my murderous activities to regions far from your vicinity."

"Hmph," said Sally. Since she wasn't sure whether to be flattered or insulted, she decided to ignore the comment entirely. "That's the theater, there," she said unnecessarily.

In the gray afternoon light, it looked much smaller and shabbier than it had at night, with the flambeaux blazing on either side and the cul-de-sac crowded with the carriages and sedan chairs of the fashionable. The neoclassical facade had a rather down-in-the-mouth air, the marble weathered and chipped. The theater had opened only three years before, as a rival to the Theatre Royal in Drury Lane, but, despite a brief fad the previous year, it had enjoyed only modest success.

The duke came around to hand her down. His hand closed firmly around hers. "No second thoughts?"

"What can possibly be the harm in inquiring into an actress?" Sally replied airily. "If I'm wrong, there's no harm done."

And if she was right . . .

Sensing that the duke was about to muster that objection, Sally added hastily, "Besides, I've always rather wanted to see what a theater looks like during the day."

The answer to that appeared to be "unimpressive." The lobby seemed smaller, somehow, without the usual crowd of people. Only a handful of candles blazed in the great chandeliers, just enough to alleviate the worst of the gloom. It was chilly, too, with a cold that seeped through the stones.

"Oh, my prophetic soul!" rumbled a voice that seemed to echo off the grimed giltwork on the ceiling.

"Yes, yes," said another voice, in more prosaic tones. "That's all very well, but it's the wrong play. Bother it, Kenyan, can't you wait until after rehearsal to hit the bottle?"

The duke's eyes narrowed. "That sounds like . . ."

"A rehearsal in progress," said Sally with satisfaction, following after the duke as he pushed through the velvet curtains separating the lobby from the pit.

Sure enough, on the abandoned stage stood two actors. Sally recognized the leading man as Hamlet in *Hamlet* and Mr. Sleazle in *The Tutelage of Scandal*. The actress was unknown to her, gaily dressed in a frock that lurched at fashion but missed by about three flounces too many.

Seen up close, without the usual distractions of the other theatergoers, the theater was, Sally concluded critically, not all that much more sophisticated a setup than Miss Climpson's annual amateur theatricals.

To be fair, the sets leaning against the back of the stage, awaiting proper deployment, did seem to be somewhat sturdier. At Miss Climpson's, the actors had labored under constant danger of toppling scenery. Abigail Dimsdale had spent a week in the infirmary after being lobbed in the head by Juliet's tower, which, it turned out, was not designed to be taken topically.

Ah, memories.

Sally turned to share her recollections with the duke, but he was already halfway down the aisle.

"It was only—hic!—one." The leading man's tones were just as mellifluous as Sally remembered, if slightly impaired by a bad case of the hiccups.

"Can't you stay off the sauce, Ned?" The woman onstage with him set a hand on her hip. " 'Ow—I mean, how a woman's supposed to work with—"

"All right." There was a third man, standing facing the stage, his back towards Sally, a sheaf of papers in his hand. His voice had a reluctant edge of amusement. "The play we are meant to be rehearsing, Mr. Kenyan, is *The Rogue's Progress*. Do you think you can remember that?"

The player essayed a sweeping bow, marred only by a bit of a stumble. "Sir," he swore, "I shall *be* that rogue and progress as no rogue has progressed before."

"That's just what I was telling Mr. Quentin," said the woman ungratefully. "If you'd leave off pinching me—I mean, pinching my—bum and learn your bloody lines— Oh! Hello, there!" She caught sight of the duke, in his caped coat and curly-brimmed hat, and mustered a truly impressive simper, as well as a marked change in her accent. "Were you lookin'—looking—for someone particular, sir?"

Well, really, thought Sally, feeling more than a little put out. *She needn't sound as though she assumed the duke was there for her.*

The third man turned in the direction of his visitors. Unlike the actors, who were turned out in a facsimile of the fashionable mode, he wore a simple brown coat that was nearly the same color as his short-cropped hair, his cravat loosely tied. He had a long face with a wide, humorous mouth.

"Forgive me. I'm afraid you find us in some disarray." He stepped forward, one hand extended, a question in his voice. "I am Mr. Quentin."

He spoke the name as though they were meant to know who he was. A playbill was lying discarded on one of the benches. *Hamlet, with additional dialogue by Mr. T. S. Quentin.* That was it. Mr. T. S. Quentin, playwright and proprietor.

Sally turned to the duke, but the duke was staring at Mr. Quentin, staring like Hamlet confronted with his father's ghost.

"Sherry?" he said.

Chapter Eleven

"Lucien?" said Mr. Quentin incredulously. "If I didn't think my eyes deceived me . . . It is! By all that's holy— Lucien!"

He looked as though he would have stepped forward to embrace him, but the duke stepped back.

Mr. Quentin recovered himself quickly. "I forgot. It's Belliston now, isn't it?"

The duke's face was hard as marble. "Yes."

"I take it you're acquainted?" said Sally, who didn't like to be left out of things.

"Acquainted?" Mr. Quentin's face broke into a broad smile. "I taught this lad his numbers."

Sally looked to the duke. "You never told me your old . . . tutor?"—In the half-light of the empty theater, Mr. Quentin hardly looked old enough to have been the duke's tutor, with his long, lean frame and carelessly cropped hair. That was, until one noticed the fine lines at the sides of his eyes and lips—"tutor was the proprietor at Pudding Lane! One would think you might have mentioned that."

The duke's gaze never wavered from Mr. Quentin's face. "You've changed your name."

Mr. Quentin opened his hands. "There was already one man in the world of theater named Sheridan. There didn't seem room enough for two." His voice changed; the creases at the corners of his eyes deepened. "But you, Lucien. I left you a boy and now you're a man grown! How have you been?"

The duke didn't return his smile. "As well as could be expected." His voice was clipped and very ducal. "How long have you been . . . here?"

"It's five years now since I struck out on my own. Before that I was with my cousin, Richard, at Drury Lane." When the duke didn't respond, Mr. Quentin tried again: "You'll remember I always did have a taste for the theater. I haven't the talent to tread the boards, but I'm not a bad hand at turning a phrase."

The duke was not inclined to share tender reminiscences. "All this time, you were all of a mile away."

Mr. Quentin's keen brown eyes softened. He set his script down on a stand. "I wanted to visit, you know. I tried, more than once, after . . . They told me you'd gone away to school."

"Of course you did," said the duke satirically. "That's why you left without a word."

"Do you think I didn't want to say good-bye?" Mr. Quentin's long face looked even longer. "I'd have stayed with you if I could—"

"I'm sure," said the duke unpleasantly. Before Mr. Quentin could protest, the duke said, "But we haven't come about that."

"So this isn't a social call, then?" Making a valiant attempt to redeem the situation, Mr. Quentin turned to Sally. "Our accommodations aren't the most opulent, but I can offer you a dish of tea to chase the chill away, Miss—"

"Miss Fitzhugh." It belatedly occurred to Sally that since she wasn't supposed to be here, perhaps it would have been wiser to give a false name. Oh, well. She'd remember for next time.

Besides, there was something she rather liked about Mr. Quentin. And someone needed to maintain the social amenities.

She held out a hand. "I very much enjoyed your *Hamlet*, Mr. Quentin. I much preferred your ending to the original."

Mr. Quentin's strained expression relaxed a trifle. "Did you, now? If only the critics agreed. They seemed to take umbrage at it."

"Critics." Sally dismissed those worthies with a wave of her hand. "I thought a wedding was much tidier than having the stage littered with dead bodies. It was very affecting when Ophelia came back to life. In fact—"

The duke cleared his throat. Twice.

Oh, right. The memory of their purpose sobered Sally. Unfortunately, it was only onstage that dead bodies rose to take a bow.

"In fact," she amended what she had been about to say, "we're looking for your Ophelia."

"That would be me," announced the actress on the stage, who had been following their colloquy with interest, her colleague having lapsed into sodden slumber beneath the tower of Elsinore Castle. "*I'm* his Ophelia, so I am."

She was not, on any account, the woman Sally had seen in the role last week. Her hair might have been red, but that brassy shade had never come from nature.

"Your other Ophelia," Sally said firmly.

"You mean Miss Logan." Mr. Quentin's eyes snaked over to the duke, who was still doing his best impression of a Doric column. Recalling himself, he dragged his attention back to Sally, mustering a rueful smile. "I hate to disoblige, but I'm afraid she's left us. As you can see"—his gesture encompassed the other Ophelia—"it has left us in some disarray."

"There ain't nothing wrong with my array," protested Ophelia stridently.

"Lovely as always!" called Mr. Quentin soothingly. In an undertone, he added, "Molly usually plays our saucy serving wenches. But with Fanny gone so suddenly and her understudy taken to her bed with a broken leg . . . well, you see the bind we're in. You aren't by any chance an actress, are you, Miss Fitzhugh?"

"Well . . ." Did playing the Angel of the Lord in Miss Climpson's Christmas festivities count?

"No," said the duke flatly. "She's not."

Sally sent him a reproachful look.

Mr. Quentin's eyes crinkled. "You'll not take offense, will you, if I tell you that's a pity?" He ruined the compliment by adding, "We're sorely in need of a new leading lady." He cast a covert glance at Molly. "*Another* new leading lady."

"Mr. Quentin—" Sally jumped in quickly, before Molly could remonstrate. "Just when did Fanny leave you?"

The playwright looked puzzled, but answered readily enough. "It was two days ago—which is why you see us here, rehearsing now. She'd an offer from a better prospect and away she went, without so much as a thank-you or a by-your-leave."

"Is that so?" said the duke grimly.

Mr. Quentin glanced swiftly at the duke. "Why all this interest in our Fanny?" The playwright's brows drew together. "You don't mean to tell me, Lucien, that you were our Fanny's mysterious protector?"

"Her— No!"

Mr. Quentin fingered the pages of his script. "I'll not deny that she could be a taking little baggage when she chose. And she was certainly easy on the eyes. But . . . I'd never thought you were one to be so taken in."

"Neither would I," said the duke, and Sally had the impression he was referring to something else entirely. He said shortly, "I never met your Fanny. Not to speak to."

Mr. Quentin looked frankly confused, and Sally couldn't blame him. "Then why—?"

"We believe she was murdered," said Sally. "That is, we

know a woman was murdered. We believe she was your Miss Logan."

Somehow, that hadn't come out quite as succinctly as she'd intended.

"I found her," Sally added. "I'd seen her in *Hamlet* last week and— Well. Here we are."

Just one big happy family.

"I see." Mr. Quentin looked deeply shaken. "Are you sure— No, of course you are. How very unpleasant for you, Miss Fitzhugh."

"More unpleasant for Miss Logan." The duke was watching his old tutor closely. "What do you have to say for yourself?"

Mr. Quentin drew himself slowly up. He was roughly of a height with the duke, but his lanky frame made him seem taller. "What are you implying?"

The duke's voice was hard. "You do seem to leave a trail of bodies in your wake. First my parents. Now Miss Logan."

Sally frowned at her duke. Really, if he was going to make these sorts of accusations, he ought to consult with her first, so they could coordinate their strategy. In Brook Street, he'd told her that spies had done away with his parents. Admittedly, it did seem rather dodgy that their murdered woman had led them straight to the duke's old tutor—and even dodgier if he had, in fact, fled the scene—but Sally had a hard time imagining the playwright as a cold-blooded killer.

On the other hand, a man who would rewrite Shakespeare would shrink from nothing.

"A trail . . ." Mr. Quentin shook his head in disbelief. He pressed his fingers to his temple. "Would I kill my own leading lady?"

"I don't know. You tell me."

"I may not have particularly liked Fanny, but she knew her lines and she pleased the punters." Mr. Quentin gestured emphatically towards the stage. "You've seen the alternative."

"Oy!" said Molly.

Mr. Quentin turned to Sally. "Are you sure—are you quite sure—that it was Fanny?"

"It did seem to be she," Sally hedged.

The light had been dim and she hadn't looked all that hard. She had seen Miss Logan only from a distance, on the stage.

She would feel excessively foolish if Miss Logan were, right now, sitting in comfort, drinking a dish of tea, in some warm lodging.

Sally grasped at a convenient straw. "You say Miss Logan disappeared?"

"Left," Mr. Quentin amended. "Left. She gave me her notice herself."

The duke was standing quietly, a little off to the side. "And who do you have to corroborate that?"

"No one. Only my own word of honor."

"From a man with no name," retorted the duke.

"He's a man with three names," Sally pointed out helpfully. "He's merely rearranged the order of them."

Neither man paid any attention to her.

Mr. Quentin's eyes moved over his former charge, subjecting him to a long, thorough scrutiny. "You've changed."

The duke didn't blink. "You haven't."

"I wish I could think you meant that as a compliment." Mr. Quentin tugged at his ink-stained sleeves. "If I could change the past, Lucien, I would do so. Believe me. But I was young then, as young as you are now—and when they said to go, I went. Don't you think I've regretted it?"

The duke's Adam's apple bobbed beneath his cravat, but all he said was, "Tell me about Fanny Logan."

"The devil with Fanny Logan," said Mr. Quentin impatiently. "Her kind are a shilling the dozen: a girl on the make with a pretty face and grasping fingers. I don't mean to speak ill of the dead—if she is dead—but Fanny was the sort who'd have trampled her own mother for the sake of something shiny."

The duke's expression didn't change. "And what of my mother? What did she do to deserve to die?"

"Oy!" called Molly from the stage. "My shoes are beginning to pinch something fierce."

"Take the rest of the day for yourself," said Mr. Quentin, without taking his eyes from the duke. "We're done here." And then, "I would never have hurt your mother."

The duke raised a brow. "Oh?"

On the stage, Hamlet snored.

Mr. Quentin shook his head in a helpless gesture. "All right, then. Let's be blunt. Man to man. You're old enough for me to say it. I was more than a little bit in love with her."

The duke's lips were white around the edges. "They said as much at the time. I didn't believe it."

"It wasn't like that. She was my Gloriana—my Faerie Queene. Everything that was great and good. And unobtainable." Lost in memories, Mr. Quentin looked ten years younger, a boy with a boy's enthusiasms. He looked up, his expression disarmingly frank. "She'd never have returned the sentiment. It was a boy's love, nothing more. I was hardly older than you are yourself at the time. If that."

"You had some knowledge of botany," the duke said stubbornly. "You could have prepared that fatal draught."

"And for what?" The pages of the script crumpled beneath Mr. Quentin's fingers. His knuckles were white against the dark wood of the stand. "I was *happy* at Hullingden. Your father gave me free use of his library; I even liked teaching you, precocious brat that you were."

There was no mistaking the affection beneath the insult. Sally saw something like pain cross the duke's face.

So did Mr. Quentin. He pressed his point home. "Why would I ruin it all? Why would I make it all go away?"

The duke's voice was tight. "Two women, Sherry. Both with connections to you." After a pause, he said, "That woman—Fanny—was dressed up in a black wig. Someone had left my father's snuffbox by her body."

Mr. Quentin recoiled as though he had been struck. "I swear to you, Lucien, I knew nothing about it." And then, in a quieter voice, "Did you think I kept your father's box—as a trophy?"

"I don't know what to think." The duke stepped back, drawing the folds of his dark cloak around him.

Sally opened her mouth to say something, and closed it again. Something in the duke's face precluded easy raillery.

"I'll tell you what I know," said Mr. Quentin. He smoothed the crumpled pages of his script with one hand, in an absent-minded gesture. His hands were large and long-fingered, with calluses on the right hand from holding a pen. Large enough hands to subdue a small woman, especially if she wasn't expecting foul play. "After Tuesday's performance, Fanny announced to me that she wouldn't be appearing again. She said she was moving on to better things—a new protector, I assumed." He bowed towards Sally. "My apologies, Miss Fitzhugh. Such arrangements are common in the world of the theater."

"Naturally," said Sally grandly, trying to look as though she discussed such affairs all the time. "A new protector? Does that mean there was an old one?"

Mr. Quentin's lips twisted wryly. "With such a one, Miss Fitzhugh, there is always a protector. As to his identity . . . Fanny was always close-lipped about her affairs." A shadow crossed his face. "She was convinced she was destined for greater things. She thought her face would be her fortune."

Sally thought of the woman's face as she had last seen it, garishly adorned with lip rouge, glassy-eyed in death, and she shivered. True, she might be wrong; it might have been another woman entirely, but . . . She shivered again.

"Here." The duke unfurled his driving cape from around his shoulders. "Take this."

Before she could protest, a heavy weight of wool enveloped her, smelling a great deal of wet, and a little bit of the duke's cologne. The duke's arms slid around her shoulders to fasten the clasp at her neck. As Sally turned to look up at him, the side of his gloved hand brushed her cheek in an unintentional caress.

Their eyes met over her shoulder. The duke looked, thought Sally, as though he'd lost something incredibly dear.

Sherry, he'd said, and there had been such a wealth of confusion and affection in that one word.

How would she have felt, two years ago, if Arabella had slipped Turnip a poisoned Christmas pudding and then fled? Like someone had torn the heart right out of her chest, that was how. Hurt. Confused. Angry. And too proud to say it.

Without thinking, Sally reached up and covered the duke's gloved hand with hers.

"It is a bit nippy in here." Mr. Quentin's voice was carefully neutral.

Sally dropped her hand. The duke stepped quickly away.

"Thank you," said Sally primly. "It is, indeed, rather chilly." Gathering together the folds of the cloak and her dignity, she turned a beady-eyed stare on Mr. Quentin. "You were telling us of Miss Logan?"

"Yes." Mr. Quentin rubbed his forehead, looking deeply weary. "There isn't terribly more to say. She told me she would be here today to clear out her dressing room—but she never came." There was a pregnant silence. "Now I know why."

"Her dressing room." Sally nearly tripped over the folds of the duke's cloak. "Is it still as it was?"

"You can look at it if you like," offered Mr. Quentin doubtfully.

"We like," said Sally promptly, and took the duke by the arm, dragging him forward before Mr. Quentin could change his mind. "Show us the way."

Perversely, Sally found herself hoping that their woman wasn't Miss Logan after all, that there would be something in her dressing room to corroborate Mr. Quentin's claim that she had simply left, of her own volition. She wasn't quite sure what that something would be: it was too much to hope that the woman would have left a signed affidavit stating that she had left, thank you very much, and wasn't at all lying dead in the morgue with fang marks on her neck.

Would that take the wounded look from the duke's eyes? Probably not. But it might go some way towards helping.

Mr. Quentin led them through a door in the side of the stage, down a short corridor, and through an unmarked door. Unlike the front of the stage, which was gaudily decorated, the back regions were dusty and unadorned. Inside the dressing room was another matter entirely. The windowless room was crammed with fashionable furniture, all just a little shabby, the upholstery just a little worn, the giltwork just a little chipped.

The dressing table was cluttered with paint pots. Paste jewelry glittered in the light of Mr. Quentin's lantern, hanging off the side of the mirror, fallen on the floor, decorating the hems of gowns and the heels of shoes. Great bouquets filled the vases at various places throughout the room, enveloping the small space with the sickly sweet smell of half-dead flowers.

Pinned roughly to the wall was a series of engravings, the sort one saw in stationers' shops with the faces of the current beauties on them. These all featured the same woman in different poses.

"She was so proud of those pictures," Mr. Quentin said roughly. He cleared his throat. "Don't mind me. Just a touch of the grippe."

"That's she," said the duke. Sally wasn't quite so sure, but his voice brooked no disagreement. "That's the woman we found."

Mr. Quentin set the lantern ceremoniously on a small table. "I'll leave you to it, then," he said tactfully. He turned to the duke. "Lucien . . ."

"We can see ourselves out." The duke busied himself with drawing off his driving gloves. As an afterthought, he added, "If you recall anything that might be of use to the investigation, I suggest you contact Sir Matthew Egerton."

There was regret on Mr. Quentin's face, but he accepted the dismissal without demur. "I shall." Pausing in the doorway, he subjected his former charge to one last, long look. "If you need me, my door is always open to you."

The door closed behind him.

Sally looked at the duke, her lips pursed.

"These doors are always open to anyone," said the duke defensively. "Here." He thrust a pile of tumbled costumes into Sally's arms. "I'm not sure what we're looking for, but since we're here, we might as well look."

"You were very rude." Sally dumped the pile on a stool and went to the dressing table instead. "I like him."

"Oh, yes, he's very likable," said the duke disagreeably. "Actors generally are."

"He's not an actor; he told us so himself." Sally looked at the duke over her shoulder. "You wouldn't be so disagreeable if your feelings weren't wounded."

The duke disappeared behind a large embroidered screen. His voice, slightly muffled, emerged from behind the frame. "There are three people dead. That's hardly a little case of wounded feelings."

Sally sat gingerly down at the dead woman's dressing table. There was a fascinating array of paints laid out on a silver tray and, next to them, a box of cherrywood, inlaid with mother-of-pearl, far nicer than anything else in the room. "I thought you said spies murdered your mother."

The duke's head popped over the top of the screen. "What *Mr. Quentin* isn't telling you is that he was a member of a series of revolutionary societies."

Sally poked at the box, looking for secret compartments. She had one rather like this. If one pressed in just the right way . . . "That's hardly illegal."

"Actually," said the duke, "it is. But that's beside the point. My mother had a contact. How do we know it wasn't Sherry? How do we know he didn't leave because his work there was done?"

"Or," suggested Sally, carefully keeping her voice matter-of-fact, "he might have left because he was dismissed."

The duke shook his disembodied head. With the dark waves of his hair disordered around his face, he looked more than ever like a poet's romantic ideal of a tortured hero. "And now we have a dead woman who worked for him. We have only his word for it that this Fanny even had a protector."

Sally's fingernail hit a crack in the wood and a little drawer popped out of the cherrywood box.

"His word and these letters," she said smugly.

Chapter Twelve

"I have a box just like this," said Miss Fitzhugh cheerfully, as she neatly dispatched the blue ribbon holding together the packet of papers. "So, naturally, as soon as I saw this one . . . Goodness, did people really *do* such things? I can see why she tucked these out of sight. Her protector appeared to have a pet name for her—"

"I'll take those." Lucien plucked the papers out of her hands.

Miss Fitzhugh was certainly right about the nature of the documents. The first one, dated six months before, began with the words "I burn." The subsequent elaboration made clear that the writer wasn't referring to a freak cooking accident.

Lucien flipped the paper over. With some disappointment, he said, "There's no signature."

Miss Fitzhugh sat back on the stool. "No, and I'm not surprised! Would you put your name on that?"

Looking down at her, Lucien raised a brow, his voice rich with amusement. "I would prefer to voice such sentiments in person rather than committing them to print."

"Do you— Well, never mind." Miss Fitzhugh hid her blushes in a brisk reorganization of Miss Logan's paint pots. "At any event, there's your protector. I mean, Fanny's protector. Goodness, it is close in here, isn't it? You would think they would have arranged for a window."

"Mmm," said Lucien, busily scanning Miss Logan's correspondence. The letters certainly bore out Sherry's story—and his reading of Fanny Logan's character.

Not that that proved anything, Lucien told himself hastily. It was still just too much of a coincidence, Sherry appearing out of nowhere, after all this time. Sherry, who had belonged to subversive societies. Sherry, who had been in love with his mother. Sherry, who had left without a word.

In this, at least, though, Sherry had been telling the truth.

Miss Fitzhugh was craning her neck, trying to see over his arm. "You're holding them too high," she protested.

"I'm trying to spare your blushes," said Lucien drily.

Miss Fitzhugh sniffed. "I'm hardly so naïve as *that*."

Lucien lifted his eyes from the letters. "No?" he said lazily, and had the satisfaction of watching Miss Fitzhugh bristle.

Miss Fitzhugh lifted her chin. "I am in my second Season,"

she said importantly. And then, when Lucien merely raised a brow, she said, "People talk."

"Talk," said Lucien, "was not what Miss Logan's protector had in mind."

This time, Miss Fitzhugh didn't go pink. Instead she said, with admirable self-possession, "No. I don't imagine it was her conversation that attracted him."

She tilted her head up at Lucien, as if to say, *So there.*

She looked delightfully smug, her blue eyes bright with satisfaction, her very pose an unspoken challenge.

In fact, she looked like a woman waiting to be kissed. And if she weren't the innocent she claimed not to be—which she was, Lucien reminded himself, however many Seasons she might have had—he wouldn't have the least bit of compunction about taking her up on that offer.

All it would take was one step, one step forward, and then he could slide his hand beneath that artfully arranged hair, beneath that single curl that bobbed and bounced and drew the eye to the sleek line of her neck, rising above the demure braid collar of her walking dress. He would drop to one knee in front of that silly little stool and kiss the smile from the corners of her eyes. He would kiss the tender spot at the side of her neck, and the pulse in the hollow of her wrist, where her glove parted from her sleeve.

And then, when desire replaced surprise, when her breath quickened and her eyelids flickered, he would draw her down towards him and kiss those ripe red lips, kiss them until the papers fluttered unheeded to the floor around them, kiss them until neither of them remembered why they were there, or anything but that they were.

"Duke?" Miss Fitzhugh was watching him with bright eyes. She waved a hand. "Belliston? Are you quite all right?"

Lucien tugged at his collar. She was right. It was rather close in here. "Perfectly," he said. "I'm just—thinking." That was it. Thinking.

"Is there any clue in there to his identity?" Miss Fitzhugh leaned forward, her bosom molding the supple material of her dress.

His? Oh, yes. Miss Logan's protector. Lucien gave himself a little shake. He hadn't felt this randy since his Louisiana cousins had taken him, a raw seventeen, to their favorite little house of pleasure. He'd walked around in a happy haze for a week.

And he should absolutely not be picturing Miss Fitzhugh wearing a boned corset and draping herself across a red velvet settee.

Lucien hastily directed his attention back to the letters. "Whoever he was, she seems to have kept him on a short leash." Some imp prompted him to add, "Metaphorically speaking."

Miss Fitzhugh narrowed her eyes at him, but didn't ask what she was clearly burning to ask. Instead, she pursed her lips speculatively. "What if she pushed him past bearing?"

It was a tempting theory. "It sounds as though she was bleeding the poor devil dry." Lucien glanced down at the smudged pages. The writing grew more irregular as the correspondence progressed and the author grew correspondingly desperate. "She set a high price on her favors."

Miss Fitzhugh looked down at her hands, her expression troubled. "That isn't much of an epitaph, is it?"

"If Sherry was telling the truth, it's a just one." The old nickname slipped out without his meaning it to, bringing with it a stab of raw pain.

He'd scarcely thought of Sherry all these years, but now that he was here, all the old emotions came coursing back. Sherry had been the closest thing he'd had to a brother. The man had been telling the truth when he said he'd been scarcely older than Lucien was now; he'd been fresh out of university, just old enough to be worldly, but young enough to be a friend as well as a tutor. Lucien had looked up to him, had striven to emulate him in all things.

Against the greater tragedy of his parents' deaths, Sherry's defection had been a small wound. But it had ached all the same. Lucien had lost his parents, his confidant, and his home, all in the same week.

It was hard to speak to this new Sherry—to Mr. Quentin—without remembering the man he had known, without instinctively trusting him.

His own memories betrayed him. He'd remembered his childhood at Hullingden as a halcyon time, his parents devoted, his tutor a trusted companion. But his mother had been selling information, and Sherry—Sherry might have been plotting goodness only knew what.

Lucien shoved the letters into his waistcoat pocket. "It's past four. We should be getting back." Before Miss Fitzhugh could protest, he said provocatively, "You must be done buying laces by now."

"Buying— Oh. Right." Miss Fitzhugh took his hand and let him help her to her feet. "With any luck, Parsnip will have got into another pot of jam. They won't have any notion that I'm gone." Changing the subject, she said, "Tell me about Mr. Quentin."

"He was Mr. Sheridan when I knew him. Sherry." It was easier to think of the man they had met in the theater as Mr. Quentin, a different creature entirely from his own Sherry. Lucien shrugged. "There's nothing to tell. You know as much as I do."

"No," said Miss Fitzhugh, "I don't. Not if you won't confide in me."

What was there to confide? "My mother was a spy and my old tutor is most likely a cold-blooded killer." Lucien retrieved his cloak from the chair on which Miss Fitzhugh had deposited it and swirled it around his shoulders. "I should have stayed on the other side of the ocean."

He had been happy in New Orleans. As happy as one could be in perpetual exile, with unfinished business left behind.

"Was that where you were?" Miss Fitzhugh lifted the lantern that Sherry had left with them. Strange shadows played along the walls of the narrow corridor. "Gossip has it that you were chained in an attic. Or in the family crypt."

"Gossip was wrong." His parents had been laid to rest in the crypt, beneath marble slabs with their names engraved in the stone, the lettering fresh and raw beside the graves of his ancestors.

"Obviously," said Miss Fitzhugh. Skirting a pile of sandbags, she pressed her advantage. "And you might be wrong about Mr. Quentin. Whoever arranged that body has a twisty sort of mind."

"Theatrical." The word was bitter in Lucien's mouth.

"Yes. I mean—no!" Miss Fitzhugh paused, the lantern suspended in her hand. "If I were a theatrical impresario, the last thing I would do would be to draw attention to myself by killing one of my own actresses. Or if I were to kill one of my own actresses, I would be sure to do so in a way that didn't draw any attention to me."

"That's just what was done," said Lucien wearily. "She was left in Richmond. Her appearance was altered. If you hadn't recognized her, we'd never have traced her back to Pudding Lane." He could hear rustling and scratching behind them, undoubtedly mice in the wainscoting. "Didn't someone once say that the simplest solution is usually the best?"

"Yes, a person with no imagination." Miss Fitzhugh discarded Occam's razor without a qualm. "The simplest solution is merely the path of least resistance. It doesn't mean it's *right*."

Lucien walked faster. They ought to be in the wings by now, but the corridor went on and on, piles of scenery propped against the walls, dressing room doors on either side. "Why are you so determined to defend him?"

Miss Fitzhugh hurried to keep up, one hand holding her skirts, the other the lantern. "Because you cared for him once. Would your own instincts lie?"

His instincts were the last thing he'd trust right now. The corridor dead-ended on a door with a heavy latch. They had taken the wrong turning. He couldn't even do a simple little thing like get them out of the theater right.

Lucien's frustration expanded to encompass the door, the corridor, the whole situation. Backed into a corner, he said shortly, "My instincts are about as honest as a harlot's kiss."

"Well, then." Miss Fitzhugh's skirts brushed his legs as she wormed her way around him. "This isn't the stage."

"No," agreed Lucien. Behind them, bits of discarded scenery littered the corridor like the debris of a shattered world: fallen columns jostled with stone towers; stairs leading to nowhere loomed above chaise longues upholstered in tattered velvet. "We should be able to get out this way."

Lucien gave the latch an experimental rattle. The door held fast, the metal latch clanking against the wood.

Behind them, there was a loud crack. The lantern swayed wildly as Miss Fitzhugh swung around, setting the shadows leaping, strange shapes looming and dancing all along the corridor. Dust rose in the air, the motes turning a demonic orange in the lantern light, making Lucien's eyes water and his throat sting.

Inhaling deeply, Miss Fitzhugh lowered the lantern. "It's a bit of scenery. I must have brushed it with my skirt as I passed."

"Yes, that must be it," Lucien agreed.

Was it his imagination, or could he smell the cloying scent of dead flowers, stronger now than it had been before?

He peered down the corridor, but all was still now. Even the rustling and scrabbling in the wainscoting had stopped. It was all as silent as the grave.

"It's rather odd without the actors, isn't it?" said Miss Fitzhugh. She craned her neck to look over her shoulder. "A little . . . eerie."

As if in answer, something creaked behind them.

"Old buildings settle, don't they?" said Miss Fitzhugh gamely.

Lucien slid his hand into the secret pocket of his cloak, reaching for his pistol. He was sure it was all their imaginations, the result of the strange lighting, the fragments of a hundred illusions, but, just to be safe . . . "This building isn't that old."

He gave the latch another tug, and this time the door gave, opening with a tremendous screech that made Miss Fitzhugh draw in her breath.

Cold air came rushing in, along with fingers of mist that swirled along the tops of Lucien's boots and plucked at his hair.

"We've come out at the side," said Miss Fitzhugh. There was a cobbled courtyard, the stones all but obscured by a low-hanging fog. She reached to hang the lantern on a hook on the wall, and then thought better of it. Dark hadn't yet fallen, but the gray sky lent only a thin, pale light that barely penetrated the rising mist. "I'm sure Mr. Quentin won't mind if we borrow this."

"Let's get you home," said Lucien, possessing himself of her arm. "It's later than I like."

The sound of his bootheels echoed eerily behind them as they hurried across the courtyard. The swish of Miss Fitzhugh's long skirts against her half boots sounded like the whispers of a hundred malicious tongues.

Someone had lit the two tall flambeaux in front of the theater. The light lent a demonic orange tint to the purple mist swirling around them as they stumbled their way to the place where the carriage had been.

Miss Fitzhugh set the lantern down with a thump on a hitching post. "I thought you'd left the phaeton here."

So had he.

"It must have been farther down the street," said Lucien, with more confidence than he felt. Safe enough at night, when the alley was thronged with theatergoers, the area felt less salubrious by day, especially wrapped in the all-enveloping mist. The buildings across the street were all dark and shuttered; the black windows like a dozen winking eyes.

"What was that?" Miss Fitzhugh's hand slid from his arm. Lucien could hear the whisper of her skirt, the patter of her boots as she took a couple of swift steps, her violet pelisse blending into the fog. "Who's there?"

Lucien's instincts screamed danger. He snagged her by the arm before she could disappear into the mist. She swung around, coming up hard against his chest. "Ouch!"

"Sorry." Lucien didn't let go. He hadn't realized he had been holding his breath until he let it out. "What were you doing, wandering off like that?"

"I didn't wander off. Didn't you see . . . ? There was a man. A masked man. Following us." Miss Fitzhugh squirmed in his grip, straining her head to look back over her shoulder. "If you let me go, I might still catch him."

"I don't see anyone." Lucien's hands closed around her elbows, drawing her closer as he looked over her shoulders, scanning for danger.

"He was there." Miss Fitzhugh squinted into the fog. "I'm sure of it—well, mostly sure of it."

"Mist plays strange tricks." So did their killer. For a moment, he'd almost forgotten why they were here. Lucien swung around, keeping Miss Fitzhugh in the shelter of his arm. "There doesn't seem to be anyone there now."

"Nooo . . ." Miss Fitzhugh sounded distinctly disappointed. She murmured something that seemed to include the words "if only" and "sword parasol."

Lucien placed a hand protectively on the small of her back, glancing back over his shoulder with a frown. "Let's find that phaeton. We must have got turned around in the mist."

"Yes," said Miss Fitzhugh, sounding distinctly unconvinced. "That's it."

Lucien scooped up the lantern. "If not," he said, with more confidence than he felt, "we'll find a hansom cab."

"On a rainy Friday? It's impossible to hail a hansom at this hour." Miss Fitzhugh's breath was short as she hurried to match his pace. "Or so I've been told," she added quickly, from which Lucien gathered that young ladies weren't meant to be hailing hansoms. "Oh, look! There's the phaeton."

Lucien could hear the relief in her voice. It was echoed in his own. "If we'd come out the front, we'd have seen it right away."

The horses stamped their feet against the cobbles, whinnying faintly as they approached. The small boy he'd paid to watch them appeared to have decamped, leaving the reins lying looped on the seat.

"Belliston . . ." Miss Fitzhugh's hand closed on his sleeve. "What's that?"

The seat of the carriage was scattered with small white blossoms, slightly crushed, and a smattering of glossy dark green leaves.

"Don't touch those!" Lucien grabbed her hand before she could reach into the carriage. "Those leaves. They'll give you a nasty rash." And that was the best possible outcome. Lucien's voice sounded strange to his own ears as he said, "They're manzanilla leaves. They're highly toxic."

Ingested, the sap caused a nasty, prolonged death.

He should know. He had seen it.

"Oh," said Miss Fitzhugh, her eyes meeting his with sudden comprehension. And then, "There's a note."

"I'll get that." Lucien reached gingerly with his gloved hand, plucking up the folded piece of paper by a corner. It had been sealed with a single blob of red wax. In the center of the wax was something that might have been a flower, or merely a squiggle.

The wax was still warm.

Handing it carefully, he broke the seal, Miss Fitzhugh's breath warm against his cheek as she leaned close, straining to see over his arm.

"What is it? What does it—" She rocked back on her heels. "Oh."

Stay away, it said, in shaky block letters. And then, in letters from which the ink blurred and dripped like drops of blood: *Or she'll be next.*

Chapter Thirteen

Cambridge, 2004

The next afternoon, I stumbled up the stairs to the second floor of Robinson Hall, my third cup of coffee clutched in my hand, feeling distinctly bleary and out of sorts.

It wasn't just jet lag. Colin was, even for Colin, behaving oddly. He was abrupt, he was abstracted, he was affectionate one minute, he was out to lunch the next.

In this case, literally. Around one o'clock, he had announced that he had errands to run, gave me a quick kiss on the lips, and, for lack of a better word, fled.

Not that I could blame him. The day so far had been a painful exercise in overcompensation. As Colin had pointed out when I'd leapt over him to get to the coffeemaker, he was perfectly capable of making his own cup of coffee. He was even perfectly capable of making my cup of coffee. At Selwick Hall, he almost invariably did. He was the early riser; I was the snooze-button queen. There was usually coffee perked and waiting for me by the time I staggered downstairs.

At Selwick Hall.

I rubbed my aching shoulder with one hand. I hadn't shared a twin bed since college. Clearly, in college, I had been a good deal less geriatric. I felt like a wizened crone, all kinks and crooked back. As for Colin, he'd wound up hanging so far off the edge of the bed, he was practically on the floor.

So much for close and snuggly.

In this case, close and snuggly had turned a bit claustrophobic. I was beginning to realize that part of what made our relationship work so well in the past was that we'd both had our own space, both literally and figuratively. When we'd been together, it had been a joyous thing, not a game of sardines.

Okay, it was only for three more nights. We'd figure it out. The point was that we were together!

No matter how many exclamation marks I added, I couldn't quite work up the requisite enthusiasm. It wasn't that I didn't want Colin to be there. I did. It was just that I wanted everything to be as it had been before. That comfortable. That easy.

I couldn't quite shake the conviction that Colin was hiding something. Or, if not hiding, at least not sharing.

It wasn't just the midafternoon errands, species unknown.

Colin had woken before me that morning. That wasn't unusual. Colin always woke before me. What was unusual was that I'd woken to find flowers on the kitchen table, a bunch of anemic daisies in cellophane, with a note that was already slightly damp from floral leakage. The note—all three words, signed just with his initial in classic Colin mode—made me smile. The flowers, not so much, and not just because they looked like they were in the last gasp of consumption. Colin generally wasn't the flower-buying kind.

His buying me flowers was as unnatural as . . . well, as my making him coffee.

Stopping to poke my head into the little cubbyhole of my mailbox, I sighed. We were both behaving like weirdos. It was, I supposed, to be expected, given that we hadn't seen each other for three months. It might not even have been that bad if I hadn't imagined his visit as something out of a Calvin Klein ad, all joyful cavorting on a black-and-white beach.

Obsession, by Eloise.

I had various theories. Jeremy had done something dastardly and Colin was feeling too sheepish to tell me. (Likely.) Colin's mother had swooped back into his life in her disastrous way and made him feel crappy. (Highly likely.) Colin was secretly a spy, and his visit was a cover for a secret mission. (Unlikely.) My birthday surprise was an engagement ring and Colin was having preproposal jitters. (Highly unlikely.)

Or, pointed out a sensible voice in the back of my head, it might just be that I was nervous about seeing my advisor, and it was easier to create dramas about Colin than face the fact that I was (a) terrified that Professor Tompkins would hate my chapters, and (b) terrified that he wouldn't.

Transference, that was what my best friend in college called it. Stressed out about an exam? Break up with your boyfriend. Procrastinating over a paper? Obsess over a crush.

I'd thought I'd grown out of that sort of thing.

Apparently not.

There was nothing in my cubby but a flyer inviting me to a conference titled "Representations of Gender in the Transatlantic World." Having procrastinated all I could, I hitched my bag a little higher on my shoulder and tromped off through the grad student lounge, waving to the department administrator—she who wielded the all-powerful professor signature stamps. (What? You thought professors actually bother to sign their own grade reports?) If this meeting went well, someday I might have my own rubber signature stamp.

Senior grad students and junior faculty had their offices down in the basement, windowless cubicles separated by cardboard, down by the vending machine that never worked. In a literal representation of the food chain, senior faculty were graced with offices in the corners and crannies of the second floor, tucked away behind the student lounge, past the grad student mailboxes.

And very senior faculty? They had the skyboxes, offices at the top of a flight of stairs that led incongruously up out of the middle of the grad student lounge, with windows looking down onto the lounge below. It made gossiping about our advisors a bit rough, knowing they were up there, looking down.

Which was, presumably, the idea.

My advisor had one of the skyboxes. Harvard had swiped him from Columbia ten years ago in a much-publicized act of academic piracy. Dr. Tompkins was, not to put too fine a point on it, rather a big deal in the field. And he knew it, too.

I trudged up the narrow flight of stairs to an even narrower hallway, my bag weighing heavily on my shoulder. I don't know why I'd felt the need to bring all two hundred pages of my fledgling dissertation with me. It just made me feel more prepared. It also weighed a ton. But that was good, right? Weighty was what we academics went for. Page forty-three had more footnotes than text.

Megan's file on vampires was in there, too, but I wasn't sure I was going to show that. Not yet. Not until I had something more solid to tell him. My advisor was a political historian, which meant he went in for hard facts and tended to sneer at anything that smacked of cultural history, or, even worse, theory. He wasn't a big fan of the Hist and Lit program except inasmuch as it tended to provide employment to his students.

I could hear my advisor's voice within, but no one seemed to be crying, so I had to assume it wasn't a student-teacher meeting.

I checked my watch. Three thirty. On the dot. I rapped gently on the door.

"Just a minute." Yep, he was definitely on the phone. If I scooted closer, I could catch some of the conversation.

I heard the name "Steve" and leaned closer.

Steve was one of my advisor's older students. He'd long since graduated, but once a Tompkins student, always a Tompkins student. We were all of the lineage of Tompkins, and he plotted his legacy accordingly, maneuvering his academic offspring with the ruthlessness of a sixteenth-century monarch who harbored dynastic ambitions.

Professor Tompkins had a reputation for moving his students around like pawns on a chessboard, positioning them not necessarily according to their own interests or desires, but as part of a master plan of his own devising. Admittedly, the master plan accrued to the greater good of the individuals involved. Eventually.

"Stanford," I heard through the door.

So it was true about that tenure-track position opening up at Stanford. There had been rumors that Professor Dubinsky, one of the monuments in the field (girth as well as reputation), was planning to retire, opening a spot. Don't get me wrong. I didn't have a shot at it. There would be fifty scholars on it faster than goldfish on fish food. But if I knew my advisor, Professor Tompkins was going to make a bid to get that job for Steve, who had graduated five years ago and currently had a junior faculty position at Catholic University in D.C., which would open up the Catholic job for Jessica, who was currently at the University of Oklahoma.

Which made it increasingly likely that Professor Tompkins would try to push me towards Oklahoma. That was the way his mind worked.

The Tompkins Dynastic Plan would be great for me five or six years down the road, when I was Steve, and there was a job opening at NYU or Princeton. Not necessarily so great right now.

It was already more than six hours to England from Cambridge. It would be much longer from Oklahoma.

On the other side of the door, Professor Tompkins moved on from Steve's job prospects to a prolonged gossip fest about various colleagues. After five minutes, I took my ear away from the door. After fifteen minutes, I was slumped on the floor, leafing through Megan's file, when my advisor finally called, "Come in!"

I scrambled to my feet and blundered through the door, bag banging against my knee. This was a familiar routine. Professor Tompkins didn't believe in rising from his desk to greet visitors; he simply swiveled in his chair to realign himself. He also didn't believe in showing people out; departing guests were advised to shut the door behind them, and, sometimes, to show in the next person.

Inside, Dr. Tompkins's office was standard-issue circa 1980: beige carpet, shelves stapled unevenly to the wall, a rickety, round Formica table (which looked suspiciously like my parents' old kitchen table) that served as conference table for grad student tutorials, or, as they were called in the department, Reading Groups. The desk was little more than a countertop, set against the far wall, under the window that looked out onto the grad student lounge.

Such were the heights to which all grad students aspired.

I dropped my bag on the floor and lowered myself into one of the sagging black swivel chairs.

"Happy Halloween!" I chirped.

My advisor grunted at me. This time, he hadn't even bothered to swivel. He was squinting at his computer screen, giving me a good view of the back of his head. "Damn thing is frozen again," he grumbled.

That, I could sympathize with. "I hate when that happens."

Professor Tompkins glanced back over his shoulder at me. His hair stood up in two tufts on either side of his head, like one of the grumpy Muppets. "I don't suppose you know how to fix it?"

That would be the day. "No. Sorry." I help up my hands. "Luddite."

Professor Tompkins's eyes narrowed. Uh-oh. Poor choice of phrase. My advisor's thing was the Chartists. He had published groundbreaking work on the Chartists. It irked him beyond reason that the Luddites got more press just because they had a catchy name.

Also, they bashed machines, which does rather resonate with anyone whose computer has frozen in the middle of sending an e-mail.

My advisor swiveled around so that he was facing the conference table rather than the desk. "I read your pages."

Pages. It made it sound like I'd handed him four pages of loose-leaf paper, rather than three hundred double-spaced pages larded with footnotes.

"Thank you!" I said effusively. "I really appreciate your making the time."

"Mmmph," said my advisor, and squinted at a pile of dog-eared pages that I recognized, vaguely, as the pristine manuscript I had dropped off last month. It appeared to have had ice cream spilled over it in the interim.

He turned a page, then another.

"So," I said, clasping and unclasping my hands in my lap. "Is Steve going for the Stanford job?"

"Stanford will work nicely for Steve," Professor Tompkins said briefly, as though it were a done thing. Perhaps it was. One of Professor Tompkins's old drinking buddies was on the search committee.

Other academics fell into two categories: drinking buddies or sworn enemies. Professor Tompkins hadn't placed a student at Yale in years, due to a two-decades-old rivalry based on his Yale counterpart's borrowing his tie without asking, back in grad school. On such small things do academic careers rise and fall.

Professor Tompkins turned another page. I shifted uncomfortably in my chair, and not just because the springs were gone.

"So . . . ," I said, "what do you think?"

I wasn't hoping for kudos, just for an okay. I knew that my topic wasn't Professor Tompkins's cup of tea—or, in his case, can of diet root beer.

He was really a Victorianist. I'd come out of undergrad intending to work on the eighteenth century, specifically Jacobitism. But, academia being as it is, the eighteenth century tended to fall between the cracks, with the Tudor/Stuart folks on one end and the Modern Britain guys on the other. The Napoleonic Wars had been a compromise option, close enough to my advisor's field to make him less cranky, but still part of "the Long Eighteenth Century" for me.

Despite a lingering interest in Jacobites, I'd come to love my adopted topic.

Professor Tompkins, not so much. He would have been much happier supervising a dissertation on midcentury popular political movements, not enterprising aristocrats with quizzing glasses and a knack for disguise.

But it was what it was, and, having okayed the topic three years ago, he was honor-bound to see it through.

Professor Tompkins looked up from his perusal. "Your source base is too heavily weighted to one collection."

I hadn't seen that one coming.

"You mean the Selwick papers?" I could feel a guilty flush covering my cheeks, which was silly. It wasn't like I'd used the archives as an excuse to stay near Colin, mining a dead source. It was the other way around. Those archives were a treasure trove. Even if Colin had been knock-kneed and squinty-eyed with fish breath, I would have stuck around.

Not, however, in his bedroom.

"Yes," said my advisor. "That." And then, ominously, "You don't want to rely too heavily on one set of papers."

What about the Paston letters? What about all those other

scholars who had made their careers out of one good cache of documents?

"I do have other sources," I said quickly, pulling my chair up closer to the table. "Corroborative sources. If you'll look, you'll see that most of the material relating to the Pink Carnation's activities in Ireland comes from the collections of the British Library. I found the background on the Black Tulip in the Vaughn Collection. As for the Indian angle—"

Professor Tompkins held up a hand to stop my babble. "I'm not saying you didn't do your work—"

Wasn't he?

"—but even allowing for the diversity of sources, the argument itself is . . . one-sided."

There was a chip in the Formica tabletop. I traced the familiar contours with one finger. "Do you mean that there isn't enough about the French secret service? If you'll look, Chapter Eight is all about the conflicting structures of the French intelligence agencies and their attempt to combat English infiltrators in Paris."

I'd found those documents at the archives of the Prefecture of Police, and nearly got my poor boyfriend arrested when he came looking for me and wandered into the wrong corridor by accident.

"Yes, yes," said Professor Tompkins. "I read the chapter. You've done an admirable job of assembling your material. I hadn't thought you would be able to find this much."

It would have been nicer if he hadn't sounded quite so depressed about it.

I scooted my chair closer, trying to read his notes upside down. "Is it too long? I can cut it down."

"That's not it." Professor Tompkins kicked back in his chair, frowning at me over his glasses. "You've certainly done a thorough job. You've mustered your sources. Your writing is clear and concise."

This sounded like the beginning of the sort of comment I wrote on B papers, getting in a bit of praise before going for the whammy. "But?"

Professor Tompkins shook his head, his eyes on the scattered pages of my dissertation. "It's like Bud Bailyn says——"

Professor Bailyn wasn't just a monument in the department; he was one of the rocks on which it was built. He taught the requisite Practice of History class, in which his catchphrase was . . .

"So what?" I filled in for him, feeling like I'd just swallowed a massive ball of lead. "What's the point? But there *is* a point. The point is . . ."

"Yes?" Professor Tompkins waited, giving me a chance to hang myself.

The lead ball in my throat grew to bowling ball proportions. I really hadn't been prepared for this.

"The point is that it happened," I said desperately. Wasn't that enough? Wasn't that what we were meant to do, to reconstruct the past, make it accessible to future generations? "It happened and no one has assembled the pieces to prove it before. I'm—I'm filling a gap in the historiography."

Professor Tompkins looked deeply sympathetic, a fact that filled me with more foreboding than anything else. If he saw any merit in the project, he'd be snarky, prodding me on to the conclusions he'd already concluded.

"That's all very well," he said patiently, "if you're content with a career teaching at a fourth-tier academic institution."

Ouch.

My advisor shuffled the papers together, depositing them in a heap on the table. "But if you want one of the better jobs—I'm afraid you'll need something more."

"I see."

I didn't see. I wasn't entirely sure what he was telling me. Or, rather, I was, but I just didn't know how to process it. I felt like I'd been blindsided. He'd okayed this dissertation. He'd known what I was doing. If it wasn't enough—why hadn't he told me three years ago, before I'd invested a chunk of my life in researching a topic that was, apparently, a direct route to academic self-immolation?

"I can work on it." My throat felt dry. "I can come up with a new angle." My eyes fell on Megan's folder, sticking out of my bag. At random, I said, "I just came across some new material, about vampires. The Black Tulip used the vampire myth—"

"No," said my advisor. "No."

He was a slight man, but his voice could fill a lecture hall without a microphone. In a small office, the effect was even more impressive.

"Don't you see?" said Professor Tompkins kindly, and my heart hit the beige carpet, because if he was being kind, then it was really all over. "That's just the problem."

"Vampires?" I said, in a feeble, doomed attempt at humor.

"In a manner of speaking. Vampires, dukes, spies with cutesy names . . ." Taking off his glasses, Professor Tompkins set them on the table. "I'm afraid it all just reads too much like fiction."

Chapter Fourteen

London, 1806

"What a cheap trick," said Miss Fitzhugh indignantly.

"It's not a trick. It's a warning." Lucien handed her down from the phaeton at Brook Street, keeping a wary eye out for stray bits of manzanilla. He had brushed the seat of the phaeton with a fallen tree branch, making sure none of the leaves remained, but he still felt itchy around the wrists and neck.

"Warning, hmph." Miss Fitzhugh had a flinty look in her eye as she stomped towards the house. "It's an insult—that's what it is. A few bits of foliage and I'm meant to run screaming into the mist? Really."

She hadn't seen what that foliage could do. Lucien had.

What next? Extract of manzanilla in her tea? A death apple left temptingly on a plate?

Lucien had a sudden image of Miss Fitzhugh doubled over, a fallen apple by her side, her complexion mottled, her mouth opening and closing in silent gasps of pain so violent that it robbed the sufferer of the ability to scream.

Lucien cut around her, blocking her path. "Poisonous foliage. Poisonous foliage from a man who has killed before." Gruffly, he said, "I don't want to see you laid out on a marble slab."

"I don't want to see me laid out on a marble slab either. But I refuse"—her chest expanded with the force of the sentiment— "I *refuse* to allow this ruffian to run free."

She broke off as a door banged open and an authoritative voice snapped, "Young lady! Get yourself inside! At once!"

A tall, thin woman in the largest purple turban Lucien had ever seen stood in the door.

As an afterthought, she pointed a finger at Lucien. "You, too."

The candles were still lit and the smell of cinnamon was still rich in the air, but the hall, which had seemed fairly large when Lucien was last there, was crowded with a profusion of people.

"Thank goodness," said Mrs. Fitzhugh, hurrying forward. She had jam in her hair and a worried expression on her face. Beneath the jam, relief warred with annoyance. "Your brother has been roaming the streets of the city looking for you."

"It wasn't really a roam. It was more of a ramble. Almost an amble." The large blond man tried to gesticulate, and then remembered he was holding an infant. He gave Parsnip a little bounce. "We knew Aunt Sally would turn up all right and tight, didn't we, Parsnip, old thing?"

A slender brunette rushed forward. "They say it's not safe to be out right now because of the—" She caught sight of Lucien and broke off, flushing.

"The vampire," finished a young woman with curly brown hair, favoring Lucien with a frank stare. "But you seem to have brought him with you."

At the word "vampire," the nursery maid went into strong hysterics in the corner and had to be ministered to by the butler.

"Thank you, Agnes and Lizzy," said Miss Fitzhugh. Turning to Lucien, she said, "I don't believe you've met Miss Wooliston and Miss Reid. They, of course, know all about you."

Little Parsnip waved her chubby arms from the safety of Turnip's arm, adding her vocal—if incoherent—voice to the din.

"I take full responsibility—" Lucien attempted to get a word in edgewise, but his voice was drowned out in the general cacophony, with everyone rattling on about rambling, roaming, and the feeding habits of vampires and other large woodland creatures.

"Enough!" snapped the woman in the purple turban, her voice cracking off the neatly papered walls like a boomerang. She glowered at Miss Fitzhugh. "Well, missy? What do you have to say for yourself?"

Lucien stepped forward to take the blame. "I—"

Miss Fitzhugh cut him off. "The Duke of Belliston was kind

enough to take me for a drive." She handed her gloves and bon-net off to the butler. "Thank you, Quimby. That will be all."

Lucien was impressed. Her chaperone wasn't.

"I thought," said Arabella Fitzhugh pointedly, "that you were buying laces with Lizzy. At least, that is what you gave Quimby to believe."

Miss Fitzhugh looked reproachfully at the girl with curls. Lizzy gave a little shrug. "If you had told me . . ."

"All a misunderstanding," Miss Fitzhugh said airily. "Oh, goodness, Parsnip, have you grown since this morning? Come give Auntie a kiss. It must be all that raspberry jam, don't you think?"

Her beatific smile fooled no one.

The large blond man, who Lucien presumed had to be Miss Fitzhugh's brother, Turnip, hoisted Parsnip higher on his shoul-der and attempted to muster a grave expression. "Not at all the thing, you know, going off with strange dukes."

Miss Fitzhugh assumed her most innocent expression. "You mustn't believe all those rumors. He's really not all that strange once you get to know him."

Arabella Fitzhugh pressed her eyes briefly closed. "Sally . . ."

"All right. All right!" A good campaigner knew when she was outmaneuvered. Miss Fitzhugh readjusted the cuffs of her pelisse. "If you must know, there were certain exigencies that necessitated our . . . bending the rules of propriety. We have SPIES."

Parsnip gave a little bounce in her father's arms.

"Again?" Arabella Fitzhugh looked as though she had the headache.

"And you didn't tell me?" demanded Lizzy indignantly.

"You had your own spies," said Miss Fitzhugh to Lizzy. Turning to Lucien, she said patiently, "You see, I told you we had experience with this sort of thing. Really, it's quite fortunate that I wandered into your garden. I can't imagine what you would have done without me."

Lucien felt a reluctant smile tweak the corners of his lips. "I can't imagine either."

Ever since Miss Fitzhugh had traipsed into his life, he felt as though he'd been standing at the center of a whirlwind. What would he have done without her? He'd probably be squatting in a cell in Newgate, Lucien realized grimly. But for Miss Fitzhugh's prompt intervention the night before, he would, as their mysterious malefactor had planned, have been found hovering over the body of a murdered woman with fang marks on her neck.

He did not imagine that would have gone well for him.

All the same, Miss Fitzhugh's family was right. He had no business dragging her down into his own murky past and even murkier present. His troubles had branched out like the hydra, growing new heads as he attempted to lop off the old.

Lucien looked around the assemblage. "I feel as though I ought to crave your pardon. These are my—" He couldn't quite bring himself to say "spies." "My troubles. I never meant to enmesh Miss Fitzhugh."

Turnip Fitzhugh gave his daughter a hearty bounce. "Oh, Sally enmeshes herself. Never known her to stay away from troubles. Or spies. Or iced cakes," he added darkly.

"If you wanted those cakes—," Miss Fitzhugh said hotly.

"We'll have Cook make more cakes," Arabella Fitzhugh intervened. "How do you know there are spies?"

Turnip Fitzhugh looked at Lucien keenly. "Haven't been going about leaving messages in puddings again, have they?"

"Puddings?" Lucien wondered if he had misheard.

"I'll explain later," said Miss Fitzhugh to Lucien. Her expression became serious as she turned back to her family. "It wasn't anything so benign as pudding, I'm afraid. Do you remember that woman on the balcony last night?"

Arabella Fitzhugh reached out to touch her daughter's soft cheek. "It isn't the sort of thing one easily forgets."

"They say she had fang marks on her neck." That was from the taller girl, Miss Wooliston.

"She had." Miss Fitzhugh took a deep breath. "We think that the woman last night was killed in an attempt to prevent the duke from unmasking his mother's killer, who may or may not be the spy to whom his mother was sending information back in the 1790s. The murdered woman was dressed up in a black wig to look like the duchess. And," she added triumphantly, "she was adorned with *flowers*."

Lucien wasn't quite sure how the others in the room had followed that. He was having trouble making sense of it, and he had been there.

The woman in the purple turban looked sharply at Miss Fitzhugh. "A black wig, you say?"

"I realize it all sounds a little strange," Lucien began, feeling a bit as though he were sinking slowly but inexorably into marshy ground.

The woman in purple wafted that aside. "You did right to summon me," she said grandly.

Lucien looked at her in confusion. "But we didn't summon you."

"Well, then, you ought to have," retorted the woman in purple. "Fortunately, Fate remedied your oversight for you."

Miss Fitzhugh stepped in before Lucien's head could start spinning. "This is Mrs. Reid," she explained. "The author of *The Convent of Orsino*."

Lucien regarded the purple-garbed woman with a distinct lack of enthusiasm. "You—you wrote that book?"

Mrs. Reid looked down her nose at him. "This is no time for autographs, young man."

An autograph? Lucien wanted an apology.

"If—" Lucien was having trouble finding his voice. "If—"

Mrs. Reid's skirts whipped like a lash as she stalked in an arcane pattern around the room. "Hush. I'm thinking." She rounded on Miss Fitzhugh. "What else?"

Miss Fitzhugh looked to Lucien for corroboration. "Well, there was a masked man who followed us in the mist and decided to deck the duke's carriage with a tasteful arrangement of flowers and leaves. Poisonous leaves," she added, for Lucien's benefit.

"I really don't like the sound of this," said Arabella Fitzhugh.

Lucien regarded her with gratitude. It was good to know that there was at least one person in the room who didn't view stalking spies as an invigorating alternative to hunting foxes.

"I'll go to Sir Matthew Egerton in the morning and tell him the whole," Lucien said rapidly. "In the meantime, if Miss Fitzhugh were to retire to the country for a week . . . ?"

"Sir Matthew? The man is worse than useless." The purple feathers adorning the neck of Mrs. Reid's gown quivered ominously. "Besides, even if he weren't, he wouldn't be able to help you against the Black Tulip."

The name seemed to echo through the far reaches of the room.

Turnip Fitzhugh looked hastily over his shoulder; Lizzy Reid's eyes opened wide with surprise; Agnes Wooliston gasped.

Parsnip yawned.

"The who?" inquired Lucien.

Mrs. Reid's nostrils flared at this display of ignorance. "The Black Tulip is only the most deadly spy ever unleashed by the French."

Turnip Fitzhugh turned to his wife. "I had a spot of bother with one of his agents once." His brow furrowed in reminiscence. "Seemed like an awfully decent sort of woman until she started taking knives out of her hair."

"Lovely," said Lucien. That was all this situation needed. Medusa with cutlery. "Are you sure we're dealing with this . . ."

"Black Tulip," provided Miss Fitzhugh helpfully. She stepped closer to Lucien, a one-woman private guard. She regarded him with a mixture of amusement and admiration. "When you embroil yourself with spies, you don't do it by halves, do you?"

Lucien looked at Mrs. Reid. "What makes you think it's this Tulip character?"

He couldn't quite bring himself to say the whole name. It sounded too much like something out of the pages of Mrs. Reid's novel.

"The Black Tulip was in operation in the nineties. He had a habit of leaving calling cards behind."

"Flowers?" inquired Lucien.

Mrs. Reid gave him a quelling look. She wasn't accustomed to being interrupted right in the middle of a dramatic pause. "There were flowers. . . . And there were the flowers the Tulip carved into the flesh of his victims."

"Charming," said Miss Fitzhugh.

"No," said Mrs. Reid. "It wasn't."

"Our flowers," said Lucien hastily, "were quite real." Quite real and quite deadly. "And our note was written on paper." Not carved into flesh.

Although, was that really so different from the fang marks painted on the actress's neck?

"He didn't always carve his sign," said Mrs. Reid, looking rather put out. "And he always chose black-haired confederates.

Female black-haired confederates. They were his Petals of the Tulip."

Mrs. Reid uttered the name in thrilling tones.

Lucien decided not to share his opinion that "petals of the tulip" sounded more like a sultan's collection of concubines than a dangerous gang of assassins.

Turnip Fitzhugh raised a hand. "Er . . . ah . . . don't like to put the fly in the ointment and all that, don't you know . . . but isn't the Tulip dead?"

That struck Lucien as a highly legitimate objection.

"Unless his ghost has returned from an unquiet grave, seeking revenge on those mortals who have disturbed his rest," offered Miss Fitzhugh blandly. When the others turned to look at her, she held up her hands, palms out. "We have vampires. Why not ghosts?"

Despite himself, Lucien found himself swallowing a smile. "It is all rather . . . fantastical."

Until one remembered that a woman had been killed the night before.

Mrs. Reid glared impartially at Miss Fitzhugh and Lucien. "The Black Tulip is no laughing matter, young man." She began pacing rapidly across the marble floor. "I have always believed reports of the Tulip's death to be highly overstated. You say the man you saw in the mist was masked?"

"The masked man in the mist," murmured Turnip Fitzhugh. "Has a bit of a ring to it, what?"

"The Tulip," said Mrs. Reid, thumping the floor with the

point of her parasol, "was caught in an explosion of his own devising."

"Hoist by his own petard, and all that," said Turnip cheerfully. "Deuced dangerous things, petards."

Mrs. Reid raised her voice to be heard over the extraneous commentary. "The Tulip would, if he survived, have been scarred. Hideously scarred." She allowed that to sink in before adding, "I do not imagine that can have done much to improve his temperament. Yes?"

That last was to the butler, who had appeared through the green baize door and was hovering on the edge of the group, holding a package in front of him in a rather gingerly fashion. "Thith wath delivered for Mith Thally."

The parcel was wrapped in brown paper with a series of holes making an abstract pattern along the top. It appeared to be vibrating.

"I say," said Mr. Fitzhugh. "What's making it go all thingummy?"

"Don't touch that!" Lucien said, and threw himself between Miss Fitzhugh and the box, at the same time that Mrs. Reid struck at the box with her parasol, sending it tumbling to the ground. The string holding it shut burst.

Lucien thrust Miss Fitzhugh behind him and waited for the worst.

A small, brown object leapt out and streaked across the floor, releasing a strange, musky odor as it went. Mr. Fitzhugh lunged for the animal. Lizzy Reid coughed and held her nose. Agnes Wooliston clutched at her skirts. Parsnip clapped her hands in delight, laughing a joyful, gummy laugh.

Slowly, Lucien lowered his arms.

"What," said Mrs. Reid, in tones of doom, "was that?"

Miss Fitzhugh's face was buried in her hands, her shoulders shaking.

Lucien bent over her. She was doubled over, her entire body quivering. Lucien regarded her with concern.

"Miss Fitzhugh?" he said gently.

It had, after all, been a very trying two days.

Miss Fitzhugh lifted her head, and Lucien saw that she was shaking with laughter. She lifted one hand unsteadily to her damp eyes, blotting tears of mirth.

"I believe," Miss Fitzhugh said unevenly, "that that is a st-st—"

"A what?" demanded Mrs. Reid.

"A stoat!" Miss Fitzhugh finally gasped out, and collapsed into another spasm of uncontrollable mirth.

"Small, weasel-like creature, don't you know," said Mr. Fitzhugh sagely. He dealt his sister a resounding whack on the back. "Like to eat rodents and lop the heads off bunnies and all that."

The stoat, meanwhile, had taken refuge behind a bust of Charles I, and was regarding them all suspiciously from just above the martyred king's lace collar.

Lucien couldn't help himself. His lips began to twitch. He could feel a laugh fighting to work its way out of the back of his throat.

Miss Fitzhugh's voice trembled with laughter. Her eyes met Lucien's. "I have been told that she's a very well-behaved stoat."

"I know I shouldn't ask," said Arabella Fitzhugh, "but why have you been sent a stoat?"

"Because she doesn't like poultry?" Agnes Wooliston ventured.

Miss Fitzhugh sent a reproachful look at her friend. "Do *not* mention the chickens."

"I believe stoats eat chickens," said Lucien thoughtfully.

"Really?" Miss Fitzhugh looked at him with interest. "What excellent news. Come here, you charming creature."

She held out her arms to the stoat, which went chirping and chittering its way across the polished floor. Miss Fitzhugh scooped it neatly up, holding it this way and that to admire its little face and sleek fur. The two regarded each other with mutual fascination.

"I had a monkey once," announced Lizzy Reid.

"A monkey isn't a stoat," said Miss Fitzhugh, stroking her new pet's sleek fur. "I rather think we'll start a fashion, won't we, Lady Florence? You shall go beautifully with my winter wardrobe."

Like Mrs. Fitzhugh, Lucien knew he shouldn't ask, but he couldn't help himself. "Lady who?"

Miss Fitzhugh stopped admiring her stoat long enough to

hand him a note that had been tied with a ribbon to the stoat's neck.

Dear Miss Fitzhugh, ran the text. *This is your stoat, Lady Florence Oblong. I do hope you get along. Yours truly, Archibald Fitzwarren. P.S. . . .*

" 'She prefers bunnies but mice will do,' " Lucien read aloud.

Miss Fitzhugh looked at the butler with wide eyes. "You will see to it, won't you, Quimby?"

Quimby looked deeply pained.

"*No*, Parsnip," said Mrs. Fitzhugh firmly, and pulled her daughter's hand away from the stoat's dangling tail.

Lucien looked quizzically at Miss Fitzhugh. "Do your admirers often send you stoats?"

Miss Fitzhugh chucked Lady Florence under the chin. "Most of them confine themselves to flowers."

The reference to flowers had a sobering effect on both of them.

"Poisonous ones," said Lucien quietly.

Mrs. Reid poked Miss Fitzhugh with her parasol. "Stop mooning over that creature and use the wits God gave you. We have a spy to catch. And I," she added smugly, "have a plan."

Why did Lucien feel a deep sense of foreboding?

"Does this plan involve going to the proper authorities?" he inquired.

"Young man," said Mrs. Reid, looking at him repressively, "*I* am the proper authorities."

"I thought she was a novelist," murmured Lucien, moving closer to Miss Fitzhugh.

"Mrs. Reid," explained Miss Fitzhugh, looking up from her stoat, "used to be second-in-command to the Pink Carnation. The Pink Carnation is—"

"Yes, I've heard of the Carnation." He hadn't paid much attention, but he had heard of the Pink Carnation. Lucien looked at Mrs. Reid with new interest. He had always assumed that spies would be less . . . purple.

"The Carnation will need to be notified," Mrs. Reid said briskly. She turned sharply to Lucien. "You say your mother worked with the Black Tulip in the nineties?"

"It is a possibility." He felt honor-bound to add, "There might have been an intermediary."

Her mysterious "contact." Who might or might not have been Sherry.

Miss Fitzhugh looked at him sympathetically.

"Either way"—Mrs. Reid brooded beneath her turban—"if the Tulip feels the need to distinguish you with his attentions, there must be something he fears that you might find. Where are your mother's effects?"

Lucien was beginning to be accustomed to Mrs. Reid's abrupt form of communication. "Some are here in London. Most are up north. At Hullingden."

The name fell off his tongue like something out of myth. Camelot. Lyonesse. Hullingden.

It felt nearly as far away and out of reach as the other two.

"Then," said Mrs. Reid, as if it were the simplest thing in the world, "we shall have to go to Hullingden."

"My uncle is in residence there now," Lucien hedged. "I've been away for some time."

Mrs. Reid smiled a smile that made Lucien think of crocodiles. "Then what could possibly be more natural than that you would bring your betrothed?"

She turned and looked straight at Miss Fitzhugh.

"I—" Miss Fitzhugh blinked as the stoat whisked its tail against her chin. "Betrothed?"

"What Miss Fitzhugh said," said Lucien. "Are you implying—?"

Mrs. Reid looked down her nose at them both. "I never imply. It takes far too much time. Yes, yes, this shall work quite nicely. You bring your betrothed; your betrothed brings her chaperone—I will be her chaperone," she added, for the sake of those who needed everything spelled out, "and you will give me full access to your mother's papers. Nothing could be simpler."

"Aside from the small matter of matrimony," Lucien felt obliged to point out.

"I say," said Turnip Fitzhugh. "You can't just go marrying a chap off like that. Not without his consent."

"But marrying me off is perfectly all right?" demanded Miss Fitzhugh with some aspersion.

"No one is marrying anyone," said Arabella Fitzhugh soothingly, and then spoiled it by adding, "Yet."

"Is a betrothal entirely necessary?" demanded Miss Fitzhugh shrilly.

Her sister-in-law regarded her with some sympathy. "It is if you want to dash off without a chaperone."

Miss Fitzhugh's eyes narrowed. "A simple *I told you so* would have sufficed." She looked around the room and, finding no support, turned to Lucien. "This—this is absurd! We've known each other all of a week! We can't possibly—"

Mrs. Reid looked at her reprovingly. "You act as though no one has ever entered into a betrothal of convenience before."

For once, Miss Fitzhugh appeared to be beyond words. From her shoulder, her stoat let out a low growl of either sympathy or hunger.

In the resulting silence, Lucien finally found his voice. "It's not a bad plan."

Miss Fitzhugh stared at him. "Not a bad plan?"

It wasn't a bad plan. It was an absolutely insane plan. But it had a certain reckless appeal. And there were unintended benefits.

"The village outside Hullingden is small." It wasn't even a village; it was more of a hamlet. "Any strangers will be easily identifiable. If anyone attempts to follow us, we have a better chance of spotting them than we would in London."

"You seem to be forgetting the small matter of our nuptials," Miss Fitzhugh said testily.

"Not nuptials, betrothal." Her relations were right; she couldn't dash around chasing spies without a chaperone. And

Lucien found he very much wanted her company. He had been dreading the idea of returning to Hullingden, of seeing it, and himself, changed. With Miss Fitzhugh, however, whatever his homecoming was, it wouldn't be dull. "And you can always cry off later. She can cry off, can't she?"

"On grounds of vampirism?" suggested the irrepressible Lizzy.

"That isn't funny," snapped Miss Fitzhugh.

Lucien moved to stand in front of her, creating a small circle of privacy. If one didn't count the stoat, that was. It was watching from Miss Fitzhugh's shoulder with every indication of interest.

Lucien turned his back on the others, looking intently at Miss Fitzhugh. "Do you mind terribly? Being betrothed?"

Lucien found that her response mattered, very much. His palms felt sweaty beneath the leather of his driving gloves.

Miss Fitzhugh's eyes darted to one side, then the other. She pressed her lips tightly together. "I haven't much choice, have I? It seems to have been decided for me."

"You have every choice," said Lucien firmly. He wouldn't let her be bullied into anything, no matter how much he might want it. "What's the standard phrase? You are fully cognizant of the honor I do you, but cannot now find it in your heart, and so forth?"

"And leave you to face the Black Tulip alone? No." Miss Fitzhugh threw back her shoulders, seriously discommoding her stoat in the process. "You're right. It isn't such a dreadful plan."

Lucien let out a breath he hadn't realized he had been holding. "I should go to my aunt and uncle and apprise them of our impending visit."

"And of your betrothal," snapped Mrs. Reid, from behind him.

Lucien's eyes met Miss Fitzhugh's. He cocked a brow. "And of our betrothal."

Miss Fitzhugh's face relaxed into a reluctant smile.

"In that case," said Miss Fitzhugh, "I imagine you had better call me Sally."

Chapter Fifteen

Lucien Charles Edward Henry Caldicott, Duke of Belliston, Marquess of Stanyon, Baron Riversham, and Heredity Lord High Marshall of the West Marsh
and
Miss Sarah Fitzhugh.
A marriage has been arranged between Lucien, 6th Duke of Belliston, and Miss Sarah Fitzhugh, only daughter of Mr. and Mrs. Peregrine Fitzhugh of Parva Magna, Norfolk.

—The Morning Post

20 October 1806
Ghoul of B—H— to wed! A betrothal has been announced between

London's most mysterious peer and eccentric heiress, Miss S—F— (Sister of a certain sporting gentleman whose antics have appeared between these pages before. See December 30, 1803: *Has Our Turnip Made a Pudding of Himself? Full details on Page 8.*)

Recommended wedding gifts for the happy pair include garlic, wooden staves, and a large supply of scarves.

Will the new duchess survive the betrothal with her neck intact?

—*The Speculator*

20 October 1806

Correspondence following the Beaufeatheringstone Ball on 26 October 1806:

Miss Lucy Ponsonby to
Miss Delia Cathcart

Sally Fitzhugh, a duchess? It just makes me sick to think of it. As if it weren't bad enough when Mary Alsworthy brought Lord Vaughn up to scratch (although Mama says there was something quite dodgy about that, not that we'll ever know now).

Well, that's some good at least. It was quite insufferable watching Mary put on airs about being a countess—as if we should all scrape and bow!—and now that Miss Fitzhugh has carried off the prize.

*Not that I would have the duke at any price.
How any woman of sensibility could even
think—but, then, you know what they say about
the Fitzhughs. They're not quite right, are they?
It is appalling the way Sally waltzes about with
that furry thing draped over her shoulder. And
there was no excuse for the way she was
giggling—giggling!—behind her fan with the
duke at Lady Beaufeatheringstone's ball last
night.*

*Really, there's nothing the least bit amusing
about soul-sucking creatures of the night. And
one certainly shouldn't look quite so much as
though one were actually enjoying their
company. . . .*

The Dowager Duchess of
Dovedale to Lady Beaufeatheringstone

*Good stuff in that Fitzhugh gel. She reminds me
of me.*

*As for Belliston, if I were fifty years
younger . . .*

I'd still be too old for him.

Ha!

Lady Henry Caldicott to Mrs. Ponsonby

*... I know I need not tell you my sentiments on
hearing of Lucien's ill-advised betrothal. Such a
common creature—all of that brassy blond hair
and that unfortunate brother. And that weasel ... !
Words fail me.*

[Omitted for reasons of space: four pages in which Lady
Henry proves that words do not, indeed, fail her when it comes
to enumerating the flaws of Miss Sally Fitzhugh.]

*Really, it is most unfortunate, although not in the
least unexpected, given Lucien's father's disastrous
choice of a bride.*

*Even so, I suppose I shall have to lend my
countenance to the match. Lucien has expressed
his desire to bring his bride to Hullingden. He
shows not the slightest consideration for the
inconvenience caused by having to remove from
London at the height of the Season. But there you
are, it is his father all over again. Nothing would
do but he would have what he wanted when he
wanted it, and never mind the bother to those
around him. If he had had any consideration, he
would never have married at all, and I would not
be forced to the imperative of arranging*

entertainments for appalling young women with garden pests as pets.

If that Lucien had never been born . . .

But no one will be able to say I haven't done my best by my nephew. I have plans in train for a masquerade ball to be held at Hullingden on All Hallows' Eve.

And beyond that, I do not see what I can be expected to do. . . .

Miss Sally Fitzhugh to Lucien, Duke of Belliston (via footman)

All is in readiness for Hullingden! At least, Miss Gwen says it is, and it's generally safer not to question her. Although I really have no idea why we need an entire trunk filled with billiard balls.

When do you depart?

Lucien, Duke of Belliston to Miss Sally Fitzhugh

I leave tomorrow morning.

Will you be bringing your weasel?

Miss Sally Fitzhugh to Lucien, Duke of Belliston

She's not a weasel. She's a stoat.

Lucien, Duke of Belliston to Miss Sally Fitzhugh

A weasel by any other name . . .

Mrs. Reid (née Miss Gwendolyn Meadows) to Miss Sally Fitzhugh and Lucien, Duke of Belliston

Kindly stop tiring the footmen. You may flirt all you like once we arrive at Hullingden. In the meantime, I have messages to send. . . .

Mrs. Reid to An Undisclosed Location

[This message has been redacted by the request of the Pink Carnation.]

Chapter Sixteen

Miss Sally Fitzhugh arrived at the hamlet of Hullingden with her chaperone, her maid, and her pet stoat.

Of the three, the stoat was the least excited by their arrival. Ensconced in her own mahogany traveling case with ormolu accents, Lady Florence Oblong blinked lazily and then went back to chewing her own tail.

As they left London behind, the gloom of the metropolis gave way to the sort of brilliant autumn weather that made summer seem distinctly overrated. The air was crisp and cool, rich with the tang of mulch and fallen apples; the leaves flaunted their showiest orange, crimson, and gold; and the faint, sweet sound of a small brook singing as it tumbled over stones could be heard in the distance.

Hullingden, they were helpfully informed by the innkeeper at the local hostelry, the Cockeyed Crow, was the name of both the village and the castle. He had offered them directions, down a long and rambling way edged with tall trees that looked as though they had been old when William the Conqueror was young.

"A castle." Sally raised her brows, but her chaperone only emitted a distracted sniff, her maid was asleep in the corner of the carriage, and Lady Florence appeared to be engaged in an extensive toilette.

Sally hadn't expected a castle.

The word conjured up images of ruined towers on deserted hillsides, with White Ladies stalking the battlements and maidens sighing from the parapets, the filmy white fabric of their skirts billowing in the moonlight.

Which, Sally decided critically, was most likely to cause the maiden in question to come down with a bad cold. There was nothing romantic about a case of the sniffles.

Nor was there anything eerie about the landscape. The gatekeeper ought to have been tall and gaunt with cavernous cheeks and sunken eyes. Instead, he was a distinctly jolly individual who didn't seem to have missed a meal in some time. The gatehouse was just as stony as one could desire, but there was nothing ruinous about it. There were lace curtains at the windows and the smell of something baking coming from the chimney.

The smell made Sally's mouth water. They hadn't had nuncheon when they stopped for directions at the Cockeyed Crow, and it had been some time since breakfast.

She was itching to quiz the duke about their destination, but he had ridden ahead, to see to the preparations for their reception, he had said, although Sally suspected it was really to escape Miss Gwen, who all too clearly viewed the prospect of a long journey in a closed carriage as an opportunity to grill the duke on everything he remembered about his mother's activities twelve years ago.

Not the duke. Lucien. Sally kept forgetting that, just as she kept forgetting that in the eyes of the world, they were about to be joined in holy matrimony until death did they part.

Her death, that was.

There were, apparently, already wagers at White's on whether she would survive the honeymoon. The news had made Sally's blood boil, and caused her brother, Turnip, to duck, fling up his hands, and say hastily, "Hold your fire, Sal! Ain't the thing to shoot the messenger, don't you know!"

In the ballrooms of London, the announcement of Sally's betrothal had been greeted with equal parts envy and pity.

"Well, I certainly wouldn't trade places with you," Lucy Ponsonby had announced.

"I should hope not," Sally had retorted. "The Belliston sapphires wouldn't go with your coloring at all."

Sally had no idea whether the Bellistons had rubies, sapphires, or a collection of small bits of gravel, but she did have the satisfaction of seeing Lucy Ponsonby's eyes turn a gratifying shade of green.

Harder to deal with had been the tongue-tied sympathy of

the good-hearted and small-brained, all of whom seemed to assume she was selling herself to a monster for a title.

"Have you taken a good look at the duke?" Sally had said acidly to the fifth of these inquiries, and stalked off to the ladies' retiring room for a good fume at Agnes, which would have been markedly more satisfying if Agnes hadn't responded with a tentative "You can still cry off, you know. Before you go to Hullingden."

Sally had regarded her friend with some aspersion. "I'm hardly about to be flung into an oubliette in my nightdress!"

"Well, noooo...," Agnes admitted. "Not in your nightdress."

It was nice to know that her friends thought her betrothed would wait until she was properly attired to subject her to strange and arcane tortures.

The memory still made Sally fume. Had any of them, including her so-called friends, taken the time to examine the duke? Had any of them spoken to him? If it weren't for those ridiculous rumors, they would all be panting to be the object of his attentions. For heaven's sake, the man was the image of the romantic ideal, with all that tousled dark hair, and that sensitive mouth that could turn so easily from a grimace to a crooked smile. Sally couldn't deny that she took a certain satisfaction in the attractive picture they made entering a ballroom together, even if most of their grand entrances were marred by Lucien murmuring something droll, making her snort ratafia up her nose.

There was nothing quite so unpleasant as ratafia up one's nose.

As for Lucien, he was very pleasant, indeed. Sometimes a little too pleasant. He was the perfect companion—attentive, courteous, with a dry, sardonic wit. But Sally couldn't help feeling that there was something else hidden away behind that civilized facade. Not—and here she spared a dark thought for Lucy Ponsonby—an insatiable lust for blood, but something held in reserve, some mystery deep at the heart of him that she itched to unravel. Sometimes he would look at her with those dark, deep-set eyes, and she would sense a flicker of . . . well, something. Something that fizzed through her like forbidden champagne.

Perhaps here, in his family home, she would find that window into his soul, the key that would unlock his reserve.

Not, of course, that she was meant to be unlocking anything, Sally hastily reminded herself. This betrothal was a contrivance of convenience. It didn't matter if the duke's lips turned up at the corners, or if she could still remember the brush of his gloved hand against her cheek as he had fastened his cloak around her neck. He was, Sally reminded herself bracingly, a good soul in a tight spot, and she was here to help. That was all.

And to prevent a homicidal spy from marauding across the countryside. It wouldn't do to forget the homicidal spy.

"Look," Sally said quickly, more to distract herself than anything else. "That must be the castle. Do you see? There. Through the trees."

Miss Gwen looked at her over her spectacles. "What else did you expect to see? The leaning tower of Pisa?"

"It doesn't look terribly castle-like," said Sally. There weren't any battlements, at least none that she could see. There was a vast dome in the center, and two symmetrical wings stretching out to either side.

"Castles are as castles are," said Miss Gwen austerely.

Sally looked at her sideways. "That doesn't mean anything at all."

She thought she heard a chuckle from beneath the maid's white cap, but when she looked, the woman was just as she had been before, slack-jawed in sleep, her large buckteeth protruding over her bottom lip.

Lucien was waiting for them at the foot of the stairs below a distinctly Palladian portico. Standing by himself at the center of the vast circular drive, his dark coat contrasting with the pale stone of the castle, he looked, thought Sally, particularly alone.

Not anymore. Leaning through the window, Sally gave an enthusiastic wave, and saw Lucien's lips lift in response.

He held out a hand to help her down. "Welcome to Hullingden." He looked at her sideways. "I would have assembled the servants to greet you, but I thought, under the circumstances—"

"No," said Sally quickly, feeling suddenly shy. "That's quite all right. After all—well—"

After all, she wasn't here to stay. Grimacing, she lifted her eyes to the duke's. "Forgive me. I've never been mock-betrothed before. I'm not quite sure how one goes about it."

"Neither have I," agreed her mock-betrothed, lifting her fingers to his lips in greeting. Sally could feel the brush of his lips through the fine leather of her glove. "We'll just have to muddle along, won't we?"

"Yes. Muddle. Of course."

Sally appeared to be doing brilliantly at it. She was muddled already.

"It was a very long drive," she said defensively.

"You're here now," said Lucien, looking at her with those fine, dark eyes.

"Yes, and we have *much* to discuss."

"Would you like to freshen up first?" Lucien relieved her of Lady Florence's traveling case.

Sally glanced back over her shoulder at her chaperone.

"Go on," said Miss Gwen imperiously. "I shall see to the disposition of our baggage." To the duke, she added, "You may inform your aunt that I shall not be joining you for dinner. I will require a cold collation to be delivered to my room along with a pot of tea, steeped for precisely five minutes. Not six minutes shall you steep, nor four, but five."

"I shall be sure to relay that," replied Lucien, with remarkable forbearance. "I should hate to think that your tea might be steeped for only three—or," he added, in a tone of great seriousness, "as much as seven."

"China tea, *not* India." That having been settled, Miss Gwen pointed her parasol at one of the footmen who had hurried forward. "You! Not so fast. Careful with that!"

There were a number of oddly shaped parcels that Sally suspected contained something other than Miss Gwen's wardrobe. Sally also wasn't sure exactly why they had needed to travel with a large trunk full of nothing but billiard balls—which seemed rather pointless without a billiard table—but since questioning Miss Gwen was an exercise in futility at best and parasol-poking at worst, Sally decided it was wiser not to ask.

Leaving Miss Gwen to it, Sally took Lucien's arm and let him lead her up the enormous stone staircase, into a hall that seemed to stretch all the way up to the heavens. Or, at least, to the center of the vast dome several stories above.

Sally tilted her head back to stare at the nymphs dancing in baroque splendor miles above. Above the nymphs, panels of stained glass created a complex interplay of light and color. The effect ought to have been daunting, but instead it felt welcoming, almost playful.

"Goodness," Sally said. The word was entirely inadequate to express her sentiments. "I expected wooden beams and moldering banners."

"We have those too." There was no mistaking the pride in Lucien's voice. "In the old part of the castle. This is the new wing. My great-grandfather had it put up around the Tudor core of the house."

"Is there nothing older than that?" said Sally, doing her best to sound blasé, although it was hard when the light danced with colored flecks from the stained glass far above and the floor was an intricate mosaic of colored marble and semiprecious stones that seemed to dance and shimmer beneath her feet.

"We do have a rather fine Norman chapel. Other than that, no. The stones of the old castle are shoring up pigsties between here and Leicester."

"Fortunate for the pigs," said Sally, trying not to stare.

Of course, she knew that to be a duke meant something more than a grand title, but she had never seen it so forcibly expressed as in the hall of Belliston Castle. There were none of the impressive battle murals or Roman statuary that she had seen elsewhere, all designed to remind the viewer of the owner's ancient lineage. The dukes of Belliston didn't go in for that sort of obvious display. They didn't need to.

It was incredibly impressive and more than a little bit daunting.

The Fitzhughs were quite an old family, but their accomplishments were limited to getting off a boat from France in the Conqueror's train, spotting a pleasant plot of land, and staying there. They were, as Turnip liked to point out, awfully good at staying.

Lucien looked entirely at home in the grand hall. He shouldn't have. The soaring marble seemed to demand the red heels and elaborately brocaded frock coats of the previous century, and Lucien was dressed in buckskins and top boots. But on him, the casual costume looked just right. The nymphs simpering on their pedestals certainly didn't seem to mind.

"I take it you don't have the same prejudice against pigs that you do against poultry?" said Lucien. Amusement glinted in his dark eyes like sunlight through stained glass.

Sally gathered her wits about her. "I am positively persecuted by poultry."

"Frequently frowned upon by fowl?" offered Lucien.

Sally swept into the hall, her skirt making a satisfying swish. "Horribly harassed by hens," she said triumphantly.

"How immeasurably fowl for you," murmured her betrothed.

Sally plucked Lady Florence's case from Lucien's grasp. "That was dreadful," she said sternly.

"I know," said Lucien. He smiled at her, with his eyes as well as his lips. "Welcome to Hullingden."

It seemed a little silly to say "thank you," so Sally made a show of regarding her surroundings and said, "It's not what I'm accustomed to, but I shall contrive to make do."

"My humble hall is honored," said Lucien solemnly, but she could see the amusement in his eyes.

He looked as though he was about to say something else, but a series of heavy footfalls broke through the sun-dappled silence of the hall, and a harsh voice shrilled, "Lucien! You didn't tell me Miss Fitzhugh had arrived."

The acoustics hadn't been designed for such brassy tones; the words hung discordantly in the air, like notes played by the wrong sort of instrument.

All the light faded from Lucien's eyes. It was as though a

cloud had come over the sun. Very politely, very correctly, he said, "Aunt Winifred, I believe you know my betrothed, Miss Fitzhugh?"

At Miss Climpson's deportment classes, the girls had been taught a range of curtsies, from the obeisance due to royalty to a bob so slight as to be a snub.

Sally dipped her knees in the very slightest of curtsies, her back very straight. "Lady Henry," she said.

Lady Florence poked her head out of her box and regarded her hostess critically. Sally didn't blame her. That shade of mauve was exceedingly unbecoming to a mature complexion.

Lady Henry ignored Sally. She fixed a basilisk stare on Lady Florence and declared in tones of extreme outrage, "You don't mean that creature to stay in the house!" Then she turned to the butler and ordered, "Dabney, take that weasel to the stables."

Sally deftly shifted the carrying case to her other hand. "Lady Florence won't be the least bit of trouble, I promise you." In illustration, she scratched Lady Florence's head with one gloved finger. She couldn't resist adding, "This will be her home, after all."

The butler, Dabney, cleared his throat. "If I may say, Miss, that is a very fine stoat."

The sentiment earned him a hard look from Lady Henry and Sally's wholehearted appreciation. Sally sensed an ally in the butler, and not just because he had the good taste to admire her stoat.

"Yes, she is, isn't she?" Sally relinquished Lady Florence's case to the butler, who accepted it with gratifying reverence. "Will you see her safely stowed in my room? I wouldn't think of entrusting her to anyone else." She turned to her betrothed. "Now. I am simply aching to see your castle."

Lady Henry stepped forward, her heels cracking against the marble floor. "You will find, Miss Fitzhugh," she said, with an entirely unconvincing smile, "that we have your room prepared for you. I am sure you will wish to rest—and wash—before seeing the castle."

Sally did rather want both of those things, or, at least, the washing bit, but if Lady Henry had told her the sky was blue, she would have strongly inveighed for its being rather a fine shade of pink. "Not at all," she said airily. "After being cooped in that carriage for two days, I couldn't endure the thought of a moment more spent within four walls, even such fine walls as these."

Lady Henry's eyes hardened, but her fixed smile never wavered. "I am afraid I cannot spare myself to show you the grounds at present. When one gets up a party at such short notice, there are a myriad of details to be seen to—but you wouldn't know about that." Having relegated Sally to the ranks of those without great estates to be seen to, she added, in the air of one making a great concession, "Perhaps tomorrow, if the weather is fine . . ."

"I wouldn't think of putting you out," said Sally. She batted her eyelashes at her betrothed. "I'm sure Lucien wouldn't mind showing me his grounds, would you, dearest? I wouldn't *think* of seeing Hullingden for the first time with anyone else."

Lady Henry gave her a look that promised reprisals. "Dinner is served at five," she said frostily. "We do not keep town hours at Hullingden."

And with that, she swept out, undoubtedly to strew Sally's bed with tacks.

"'We do not keep town hours at Hullingden,'" Sally mimicked. "Goodness, is she always so warm and friendly?"

Lucien appeared resigned to her frankness. "Just to me. And my . . ."

"Associates?" suggested Sally. It was a much less charged term than any others that came to mind. It felt appropriately impersonal. Not that she was feeling particularly impersonal at the moment. All of her fighting instincts had been aroused on Lucien's behalf. "Did your aunt ask your permission before she appointed herself chatelaine of Hullingden, or did she simply move in?"

"The latter." Offering her his arm, Lucien led her to the side of the hall, through one of the many arches below the great dome. "Do you really want to see the grounds?"

"Why not?" Her blood was boiling and a walk in the crisp autumn air would be refreshing. Not to mention that she could speak more frankly once out from under the duke's roof. "She treats your house as though it were her own."

The archway led into a long gallery studded with statuary, glittering with mirrors. "I was away for a very long time."

"You're making excuses for her," protested Sally.

Lucien looked down at her wryly. "One tends to be more just

to those one doesn't like. And, to be fair," he added, "Aunt Winifred has kept Hullingden very well."

Sally couldn't fault the woman's housekeeping. Each bezel on each chandelier was polished to a sheen, every mirror dazzling in its clarity. Sally could see herself and her duke reflected again and again, into infinity, walking arm in arm, like a pair in a painting.

Lucien, with his long hair and tightly tailored jacket, had a slightly foreign air that seemed to suit the baroque opulence of the gallery. He would, thought Sally, have made a rather good cavalier, all curly hair and plumed hat, ready to gallop off to defend his king.

"Where were you all that time?" Sally asked curiously.

The gallery gave way to a pair of glass doors, leading out onto a carefully sculpted terrace. Fountains stretched in front of them, dry now, the statues carefully covered in burlap sacking. In summer, Sally could see, the view would be brilliant, a visual echo of the room they had just left, with all the water glinting and glittering like glass.

Lucien helped Sally down a short flight of stairs. "At school, at first. Later, here and there."

Gravel crunched beneath their feet as they made their way between expertly trimmed shrubs. There were empty spaces where pots that had been meant to hold orange trees had already been taken inside for winter.

"Here and there." Sally widened her eyes. "Oh, my. How terribly descriptive. If we're going to be betrothed, I'm going to need to know something more than that."

It wasn't just curiosity, she told herself virtuously. As his betrothed, wouldn't she be expected to know more? When one adopted a role, one shouldn't do it by halves.

Besides, she wanted to know where he had really been all those years.

She half expected him to fob her off with a wry comment, but instead he said, "If you must know, I ran away."

"In the dead of night with a packet on your back?"

"It was midafternoon, actually. And the packet was by my side." Sally flapped a hand at the duke, and he relented, saying, "Other than that, yes. I stole away from school and stowed away on a ship to the West Indies."

"That sounds very daring," said Sally, thinking that in fact it sounded rather sad. She had slipped away from Miss Climpson's any number of times, but never farther than the Sydney Gardens. The truth was, she had liked her life too much to want to leave it.

Lucien's lips quirked. "More daring than romantic. I was seasick for the first month."

It was at moments like these that it was impossible not to like Lucien. So many of the masculine members of the *ton* tended to take their own dignity far too seriously. At the same time, Sally recognized the self-mocking humor for the dodge it was.

She refused to be diverted.

"And after that?"

The corners of her betrothed's eyes crinkled. "I made the mistake of partaking of the ship's provisions and was sick for another two." He shook his head in reminiscence. "I have the greatest respect for the men of the navy. Mine is not a seafaring nature."

Sally had condescended to be taken out in a rowboat once. The experience had not been a success. She could still smell the lake water in her hair.

"If God had meant us to take to the water, he would have given us fins." A stray twig had fallen by the side of one of the fountains. Sally scooped it up, breaking off the little twiglets on the side. "Why the West Indies?"

Lucien's measured pace didn't falter. "I was looking for my mother's family." He led Sally off to the left, away from the long vista of fountains, beneath an arbor that, in summer, would undoubtedly be rich with roses. "My mother was from Martinique. Her father had come to England with her, but she still had a brother and sister on the island. Or so I believed. My information was somewhat out of date."

The words were matter-of-fact, but Sally found herself worrying about the boy he had been, alone in a strange land. In all her life, she had never been without the support of family close by. There was always Turnip to come galumphing to her rescue, or her friends at Miss Climpson's, there for a bit of light plotting. She couldn't imagine what it was to be so entirely alone.

"What did you do then?"

"I nearly came back here with my tail between my legs. It was a close-run thing." Lucien's voice was light, but there was something in his eyes that suggested the situation hadn't been at all amusing at the time. "Instead, I followed my mother's sister to Louisiana. She had married a planter in New Orleans. I've been there ever since."

"What a lot of places you've been." Hearing about Lucien's adventures made Sally feel very small. Her world had, until recently, been limited to the confines of Miss Climpson's Select Seminary. She had been meant to go to Paris, but then the hostilities had started again, and she hadn't. "I imagine few of them could hold a candle to this."

They were off the gravel paths now, on a winding circuit that took them through a carefully contrived woodland. There was a pillared temple on a hill, and a pond that glinted with gold in the sunlight. Sally imagined that there must be swans on it in summer. The whole was a meticulously crafted idyll, designed for a Phyllida and whatever that shepherd's name was to flirt and frolic.

"No, they couldn't." Lucien breathed deeply of the crisp autumn air, scented lightly with woodsmoke. From their vantage point, Sally could see an orchard, the trees still heavy with red fruit, and a series of succession houses, their glass walls hinting at treasures within. Behind them, the elegant facade of the castle shimmered against the deep blue sky like something out of a fairy tale. "When I was away, I'd thought I was exaggerating it in my memory, making it something more than it was."

"You must have missed it terribly," said Sally, keeping her voice neutral.

Lucien's step slowed as they wandered up the hill, encountering old landmarks, old memories. "That's where we played at Robin Hood, my cousin and I. Poor Hal was always Alan-a-Dale, and sometimes the sheriff as well. We used to steal sweetmeats from the kitchen."

"And distribute them to the poor?"

"I'm afraid we weren't that public-spirited. We had a tree fort. We would retreat there and gloat over our spoils." Lucien turned, his eyes roaming greedily over the landscape, drinking it in like a man perishing of thirst. "That's where I shot my first rabbit, right there. And up there, past that third tree to the left, that's where we had our tree fort."

"Mmm." Sally wasn't looking at the remains of the tree fort; she was looking at the duke. "If you loved it so much, why did you stay away so long?"

The light faded from Lucien's eyes. He shrugged. "Why does any boy go roaming? Wanderlust, I suppose."

Sally didn't believe that for a moment.

"But you're back now," she said. And about time, too.

"For the moment." Lucien's smile was perfectly pleasant, but Sally could practically hear the locks clicking shut as the great iron door of his reserve closed once again between them. "I'm afraid I've strayed from our task. You're not here to admire the view."

"Ye-es," said Sally reluctantly. She'd nearly forgotten that they had a killer to catch. "It all feels rather unreal, doesn't it?"

Corpses and killers and spies belonged to the smog of London, not to this rural idyll.

Lucien seemed to catch her meaning. *"Et in Arcadia ego,"* he said soberly.

They hadn't taught Latin at Miss Climpson's. "Which means?"

"It means, 'Even in Arcadia, there am I.' Even here, among all this beauty, is death." Something about Lucien's expression suggested more than a symbolic significance.

The words made Sally feel cold beneath her elaborately frogged pelisse. For some reason, she had assumed his parents had died in London. Not here. "Was this where—"

"Yes," said Lucien shortly. He pointed at the white-pillared temple on the hill. "Right there." And then, just when Sally thought it couldn't get any worse: "I was the one who found them."

Chapter Seventeen

"Oh," said Sally. She pressed a hand to her lips. "Oh. Oh, dear. No wonder— I'm so sorry."

In the face of her sympathy, Lucien felt like a fraud.

For a full ten minutes—twenty even—he had forgotten their purpose. He had looked at the landscape and remembered, not those grim final hours but the happy ones. Eluding his nurse to play hide-and-seek with the squirrels in the Home Woods; reaching a chubby baby hand for the trumpet of one of the statues in the fountain, then tumbling with a splash into the water. Even the folly on the hill had been, for a moment, not the location of his parents' deaths, but the center of a hundred childhood games.

The folly had been fitted out for light entertainments, with table and chairs, and a reflecting pool stocked with goldfish. He had flopped and splashed in that pool as a child; it had been a stream to be forded, or the home of Jonah's whale, depending on the day and his fancy. When his parents weren't in London, they liked to take refreshment there, and Lucien could always be sure of finding sweetmeats or cakes.

There had been sweetmeats that day, scattered across the ground. Crumbs of cake and shards of porcelain, his father's silver-headed cane tumbled to the ground, his mother's skirts crumpled around her like a fallen handkerchief. Lucien's father had been dead already, his lips peeled back in a soundless grimace, his blue eyes open and staring.

His mother had been alive still, just. He had watched, helpless, as the life had faded from her eyes.

Somehow Lucien mustered a shrug. "I wouldn't recommend it as an experience."

It had been a summer day; the scents of the flowers and the chirping of the birds had seemed obscene in contrast with the desolation within.

Et in Arcadia ego.

Lucien breathed deep of the autumn air, of the scent of mulch and loam, of damp tree trunks and wet leaves. There were no flowers here now, and the birds sang a different tune. The ghosts of the past were just that, ghosts, relics of his memory, as insubstantial as the breeze that ruffled the bright ribbon on Sally's bonnet.

Beneath the brim, her blue eyes were bright with concern.

She was, Lucien knew, going to ask him about it. But what was there to say? *If I had come upon them sooner, my parents might still be alive?* The sense of his inadequacy, his failure, haunted him. That he should inherit Hullingden upon his father's death, along with all his father's dignities and titles—that seemed more wrong still.

He hadn't even been able to avenge their shades by bringing their murderer to justice. What right did he have to sit in his father's chair and dine at his father's table?

He didn't deserve Hullingden, and he certainly didn't deserve Miss Fitzhugh's sympathy.

But Lucien couldn't find the words to say that, so, instead, he offered Sally his arm. "Shall we dress for dinner? Aunt Winifred can't abide tardiness."

Sally scowled at him. "Don't," she said fiercely. "There's no need to pretend to be all stoic." She gestured over her shoulder. "There's no one else here. It's just the birds and the squirrels. You can say what you like. Punch the trees if you like. I'll be the only one to hear it."

"I have no desire to assault the foliage," said Lucien mildly.

Sally set her hands on her hips. "You know perfectly well what I mean. It was a vile, vile thing that happened to you, and here you are, all—ducal. Did you ever take the time to mourn?"

Alone, by himself, in his narrow bed in the dormitory at school, shivering with cold and suppressed tears, trying so hard to keep the sound muffled in his pillow, lest the others hear and taunt him. Uncle Henry, ruffling his hair and telling him to buck up, there's a good boy. Aunt Winifred, saying tartly that a parent's death was a commonplace thing and one didn't see her snuffling about her parents' demises.

Tante Berthe had slopped him over with sympathy, with embraces and exclamations, and then hurried off to supervise supper.

"All the time," said Lucien repressively. "Every day."

Only it wasn't entirely true, was it? Their faces had ossified in his memory, hardening into a set likeness, portraits rather than people. He had clung to the prospect of justice, but lost the fact of them.

And justice, even justice, would never bring them back.

A wave of bleakness swept over him, harsh as winter. It was like losing them all over again, that awareness that whatever he did, it was too late now. It had been too late twelve years ago.

He had been too late.

Lucien turned abruptly away from the summer house and set off back the way they had come, covering the ground in long strides. "There's no need to fuss. I'm quite all right."

Sally hurried after him, her skirt rustling against the grass. There were no fallen leaves to catch at her hem; one of the army of gardeners must have raked them up, raked them as soon as they had fallen. Nothing could be allowed to mar the perfection of the landscape.

"Don't be ridiculous. Of course you're not." Sally caught up with him by an artistically weathered arch. "There's no need to be stoic for me."

"I'm not." Lucien was being stoic for himself, because if he didn't, he didn't know what might come out.

Sally reached for his hand. He could feel the press of her fingers against his as she said earnestly, "Just because this isn't a real betrothal doesn't mean I don't care."

Sally's head was tilted up towards him, her gloved hand warm on his. The gloves were a primrose yellow, a bright splash of color against his dark coat.

For a moment, Lucien felt himself responding to the pressure of those slim fingers. But then the impact of her words hit him. *Not a real betrothal.* Of course, it wasn't. It was a sham, and at the end of it they would go their separate ways.

"Save your sympathy." Lucien realized just how harsh that sounded and forced his lips into an unconvincing smile. "We haven't time for it. Not with spies lurking in the shrubbery."

"I think that's a gardener." Sally looked expectantly at Lucien. When he didn't respond in kind, she bit her lip, looking at him with concern. The hand holding his tightened briefly. "If you change your mind—"

"I know where to find you," said Lucien lightly, and raised her hand to his lips in the Continental style. "But for now, I should leave you to your toilette. If anyone is late for dinner, Aunt Winifred unleashes the gargoyles."

Sally looked as though she wanted to argue, but she knew when to pick her battles. Instead, she looked archly over her shoulder, saying with mock seriousness, "It isn't kind to speak of my chaperone that way."

And with that, she whisked back through the door that led to the Hall of Mirrors, leaving Lucien behind her, choking on a laugh.

His betrothed, Lucien had noticed, did like to have the last word.

His mock betrothed, he reminded himself. Only his mock-betrothed. Repeating that to himself, Lucien retired to the ducal chamber to allow Patrice to dress him for dinner.

It felt strange to be in the suite of rooms he still thought of as his father's, and stranger still when Uncle Henry gestured him to the place at the head of the table, in the great state dining room decorated with murals of the daring deeds of Bellistons past.

Lucien took the chair at the head of the table with studied nonchalance, trying to pretend that he had meant to do so all along. He had never eaten in this room before; as a boy, his meals had been taken in the nursery or, when the mood struck his mother, alfresco in the gardens. He felt like an impostor in his father's place.

He wasn't the only one who seemed to think so. Aunt Winifred's air was even frostier than usual, and it wasn't hard to guess the reason why. In his absence, it was Uncle Henry who occupied the seat at the head of the table.

Aunt Winifred, Lucien reflected, wouldn't in the least have minded if he had been swallowed by a sea serpent en route to the West Indies all those years ago.

As it was, she was regarding Miss Fitzhugh with a distinctly territorial air. "I'm sure this isn't what you are used to, Miss Fitzhugh," she said regally.

"No, it isn't," said Sally frankly. She had changed into a dress of pale blue satin covered with silver net; pearls glimmered at her throat and ears. "The dining room at Parva Magna is much better lit. Have you thought of adding a few torchères?"

Aunt Winifred's mouth opened in outrage.

Uncle Henry jumped in. "I'm so sorry Hal couldn't be here to greet you," he said for at least the fifth time. Hal's place sat empty at Clarissa's right hand, a provincial Siege Perilous. "He was detained in town."

"He is in such demand," said Aunt Winifred pointedly.

She looked meaningfully at Clarissa.

Clarissa applied herself to her soup.

The soup, Lucien had noted, was both tasteless and tepid, despite the regal tureen appointed for its transportation from the kitchens, which were, as Lucien recalled, about a mile away through a maze of corridors that would have daunted the Minotaur.

Sally gingerly sampled her soup and set her spoon down again. To Lucien, she said, "Have you thought of renovating the kitchens to bring them closer to the dining room?"

"I—," began Lucien, but Aunt Winifred cut him off.

"The arrangements at Hullingden are just as they should be." Aunt Winifred smiled so fixedly at Sally that Lucien suspected she was having fantasies of running Sally through with her fish knife. "You, of course, would not understand what it is to manage a house such as this."

"No," Sally agreed demurely, directing herself to Lucien. "Parva Magna is much more modern. We haven't your disadvantages. Oh, dear. Are you quite all right?"

"Quite," said Lucien in strangled tones.

Uncle Henry cast a quick look at his wife. "If you would like to learn more of Hullingden's history, Miss Fitzhugh, I—"

Aunt Winifred's bosom swelled. "The cost of maintaining a house such as Hullingden, Miss Fitzhugh, is more than you might imagine, even without the addition of such costly renovations as you propose."

Uncle Henry cast Lucien an apologetic look. "The revenues of the estate have been down over the past few years," he said, in a conciliatory way. "There was the roof to be releaded and the old moat to be drained, not to mention the tenants' houses . . ."

"I'm sure everything is just as it should be," said Lucien quickly.

"You see?" said Aunt Winifred to Sally. "Renovations are quite out of the question. Even if they were wanted."

"Oh, that's no matter." Sally smiled sweetly and dipped her soupspoon into her bowl. "My dowry is quite appallingly large."

Aunt Winifred's spoon clanked against her bowl.

Sally looked reprovingly at Lucien. "Oh, dear. We really *must* do something about that cough of yours."

Lucien forced himself to swallow his laughter. "Don't worry. It's probably just plague," he said nonchalantly. Turning to his sister, he said, "I hope we haven't caused you to miss too many entertainments in London?"

Aunt Winifred answered for her. "If Clarissa cannot go to

London, London must come to Clarissa. I have," she said coyly, "sent out a few more cards for your betrothal ball."

Lucien's eyes met Sally's. The more fanfare surrounding their betrothal, the harder it would be to cry off. "I had thought it was meant to be a small party."

"Really," said Sally brightly. "How very kind of you. That sounds like a great deal of bother. I wouldn't want to put you to any trouble. Given the great effort of managing a house such as Hullingden."

"It won't be a large party," Aunt Winifred said, in the air of one making a great concession. "I have only sent out two hundred cards."

"Oh," said Sally weakly. "Only two hundred."

"I can't imagine many people will want to come all the way out to Leicestershire for an evening's entertainment," said Lucien reassuringly.

Sally's lips settled into a grim line. "For this," she said, "they will come."

Lucien was rather afraid she was right.

"Won't they be afraid to travel on All Hallows' Eve?" he asked hopefully. "Highwaymen are bad enough, but when one adds ghosts and ghouls . . ."

"We," said Aunt Winifred repressively, "do not celebrate such pagan festivities."

"As boys," interposed Uncle Henry, "we used to bob for apples. Some of the tenant farmers carve lanterns out of turnips. Rather gruesome ones, too."

"Tenants," said Aunt Winifred dismissively.

Sally leaned forward, the milky surface of her pearls catching the light. "Don't they say that's the night on which ghosts walk?"

"I think they're meant to float," offered Lucien.

His betrothed nodded decidedly. "Preferably on battlements. Do you have any battlements tucked away in the old wing? If so, I will be sure to avoid them on All Hallows' Eve."

"We do not need an occasion for the ghosts to walk at Hullingden." Clarissa spoke for the first time, her voice as sharp and clear as glass. "They are with us all the time."

After that cheerful statement, no one showed any inclination to linger over the repast.

The ladies left the gentlemen to their port, but since the gentlemen consisted only of Lucien and his uncle and the empty seat that Hal had been meant to fill, they engaged in no more than a ceremonial glass before rejoining the rest of the party in the Blue Salon, a large and rather chilly apartment in the new wing.

Lucien found his betrothed in a corner of the salon, below an ornamental arch supplemented with a drape of blue velvet that made her fair hair seem ever brighter. "Miss Fitzhugh—"

"Sally," she corrected him. "If we're to make this betrothal believable, we must play our parts properly."

Just how properly? Her hair was twisted up in a Grecian knot, the artfully arranged curls leaving her neck and shoulders bare. He could see the pulse beating at the base of her throat, the tender hollows of her neck, and, below, the slope of her breasts rising from the scooped neck of her dress.

If this were a real betrothal . . . He still shouldn't be thinking the sorts of things he was thinking.

Sally's lashes glittered gold at the tips. The shimmer drew the eye. Her words, however, were dishearteningly prosaic. "You should speak to your sister."

"My sister?" Lucien glanced over his shoulder at his sister, who seemed to be doing her best impression of Patience on a Monument, smiling at Grief. "Because she might know something?"

"Because she's unhappy. And you," Sally said, as though that explained it all, "are her brother."

Lucien opened his mouth to point out that he barely knew Clarissa.

And then closed it again. He remembered the easy affection between Sally and her brother. In her world, brothers looked out for their sisters. It was as simple as that.

Lucien found that he couldn't bring himself to disillusion her.

And maybe she was right. Maybe it was as simple as that.

Meekly, he said, "All right."

"Now?"

Next week would be better. Or the week after that. He might be able to schedule a tooth extraction in the interim.

"Now," Lucien said resignedly. Before he marched off to do his duty, though, he couldn't resist saying, "At dinner . . . were you determined to give Aunt Winifred an apoplexy?"

Sally bared her teeth in Aunt Winifred's general direction. "It wasn't my original ambition, but I am finding the prospect increasingly attractive. What an appalling woman!"

It didn't help that Lucien agreed wholeheartedly. "She has been a very good steward to Hullingden."

"If stewardship consists of re-covering chairs and choosing drapes. You can tell she hasn't the least feeling for the spirit of the place."

"Don't you mean spirits?" said Lucien, and went off to corner his sister before Sally could think up a crushing retort.

Clarissa's silver-gilt head was bent over her embroidery as Lucien crossed the salon. Unlike Sally, she didn't favor the curls currently in fashion. Her hair was braided into an elaborate knot that looked like a coronet.

For all Sally's warm sentiments, this woman was a stranger to him, as much a stranger as any woman one might meet in a ballroom. He knew nothing of her, or what her life had been these past twelve years.

And that, as his sister had pointed out to him last week, was entirely his own fault. He had believed he was punishing himself with his self-imposed exile; it had never occurred to him that he might be hurting his sister as well.

Feeling doubly guilty, Lucien claimed the seat next to his sister. "Might I beg a moment of your time?"

Clarissa set aside her embroidery. "I have no other pressing commitments at present."

She looked up at him, and, for a moment, Lucien saw the

little girl she had been, with her pale wisps of hair and those great, dark eyes.

The polished words he had meant to utter fled, and he found himself saying instead, "What's wrong, Clarrie? If I can make it right, I will."

It appeared that that had been absolutely the wrong thing to say.

"Make it right?" His sister looked at him incredulously. "It was all right until you came home and ruined everything. And now here you are, with your intended, making eyes at one another across the dinner table, and I'm meant to wish you happy and pretend that everything is just as it should be. It's not fair."

Making eyes at one another?

The words were rolling out, one after another. "It's not fair to flaunt your happiness in front of me when you've cost me my—" Clarissa pressed her fingers to her temples. "I'm sorry. I don't know what I'm saying." She mustered a stiff little smile. "Will you allow me to wish you happy and return to my needlework?"

"No," said Lucien bluntly. He reached over her needlework to try to take her hand, but she moved it out of reach. "How am I the cause of your unhappiness?"

In profile, Clarissa's nose was just a little too long for beauty. She had their father's features, but on their father, the long bones had been lightened by a well-developed sense of humor. There were no leavening laugh lines on Clarissa's face.

"Do you remember Adam Standish?" she said abruptly.

"Not well." He had been closer to Clarissa's age than Lucien's. "At Broome Hall?"

"Yes." She looked down at her needlework, her eyes fixed on the elaborate pattern of leaves and flowers. The leaves looked uncannily like those of the manzanilla. "We were betrothed."

"No one told me." Lucien still wasn't sure what he had to do with any of this.

"Of course they hadn't," said Clarissa impatiently. "We hadn't announced it. Aunt Winifred insisted I have a Season first." She made a face at their aunt, looking more like the little girl Lucien had remembered. "It was hardly out of the goodness of her heart. She's determined to marry me off to Hal. Not that Hal is having any of it, thank heavens."

"What went wrong?"

Clarissa cast a quick, furtive look over her shoulder to make sure the elders weren't listening. "You. All those rumors. People started talking about the family and curses. . . ." Her lip curled. "Adam didn't even have the basic decency to tell me himself. Just a horrible, stiff, formal letter saying that his parents wouldn't hear of his marrying into such a family."

" 'Such a family'? You're the daughter of a duke."

"Yes, but no one here ever really *liked* Papa," Clarissa said, picking distractedly at her embroidery. "He didn't hunt; he didn't shoot; he was always dressed in the height of fashion. . . . And then there was *Maman.*" Her voice was rich with condemnation.

True, the good matrons of the county had never taken to

their mother. She was too foreign, too different; her interests weren't theirs. Their mother had never minded. She had never seemed to know or care that there was a position she was meant to fill.

It had mattered only afterwards.

Lucien would have liked to argue with Clarissa, to take their mother's part. His memories of their mother sparkled like prisms in the sunlight: impromptu excursions into the woods, swimming lessons in the reflecting pool, picnics and outings, unexpected trips to London, where they would descend on the big house in St. James and take the servants unawares, with Holland covers over the furniture like ghosts.

His sister had been younger, so she remembered none of the good; she only suffered the legacy of the bad.

Witchwoman's brat.

"If he feels that way," Lucien said with false heartiness, "you're better out of it."

Clarissa plucked at the edges of her embroidery with unsteady hands. "Maybe I should marry Hal. At least we would know where we stand."

"And endure a lifetime of Aunt Winifred?" Lucien was only half joking. His sister had had enough of that regime already. He thought he knew whence many of her attitudes about their parents had come. "There must be something better."

"Is there?" Clarissa looked up at him sideways. "I suppose you must think so—with your Miss Fitzhugh."

Lucien was tempted to tell her the truth, if that might soothe some of Clarissa's hurt, but a modicum of common sense held him back. Wounded animals tended to strike out at friend and foe alike.

Clarissa stabbed the needle through the cloth. "I imagine by the time she's through with it, Hullingden will hardly be recognizable."

She sounded so much like Aunt Winifred that Lucien looked at her in surprise. "Moving the kitchens is hardly the same as tearing down the battlements."

Across the room, he could see Sally looking at them expectantly. Sally, who had told him that it was his duty to comfort his sister. She might be a little outspoken at times, perhaps even a little imperious—all right, very imperious—but there wasn't a mean-spirited bone in her body. Her meddling was all kindly meant.

She certainly didn't deserve to be stabbed in the back by the very woman she had sent him to help.

Sharply, Lucien said, "Perhaps a little change is just what Hullingden needs. As you say, we've allowed the spirits of the past too much sway."

"As you like." Setting her needlework aside, Clarissa rose from her seat. "Then I suppose I shouldn't tell your Miss Fitzhugh that Aunt Winifred put her in the Haunted Chamber?"

Chapter Eighteen

Sally's room looked like it hadn't been slept in since the last time Queen Elizabeth had paid a formal call.

The bed was of the baronial variety, with vast carved posts, and hangings that could be drawn shut to keep out drafts, mice, and the odd ghost. The casement windows, with their leaded glass, appeared to have been designed to keep out the light and let in the draft. They rattled ominously as the wind rose, straining against the catches that held them fast and causing the candles in their tall stands to gutter.

It was all very atmospheric and entirely inconvenient.

When Lady Henry had delivered Sally to her room, she had told her, in smug tones, that she hoped Sally wouldn't mind being in the Haunted Chamber. The implication being, of course, that she would run howling off into the night and never darken their casements again. Sally didn't believe in spooks, and even if she had, she doubted any spook would have the poor sense to haunt a chamber known as the Haunted Chamber. It showed a distinct lack of initiative. She was, Sally was quite sure, more in danger of being pickled from the smoke blowing back down the chimney than of being visited by midnight specters.

If she were staying, one of the first things she would do would be to order the chimneys rebuilt. There was no reason for them to smoke the way they did. Some larger flues, more modern chimney pots—really, this room could be quite cozy without a haze of smoke.

And then there was that dining room. It was foolish for the family to have to choke through cold soup for the sake of dining in baronial state when they were *en famille*. There were a dozen small chambers that didn't seem to be doing anything in particular, all of them closer to the kitchens. One might easily be turned into a family dining room while the kitchens were being reconsidered.

Even she couldn't redesign the kitchens without having seen them, but she'd wager that they were of the subterranean, late-medieval variety, with huge fireplaces designed for roasting whatever the lord of the manor happened to haul in over his saddle. A nice modern kitchen, that was what was needed, connected to the house by a covered gallery so that the food didn't turn to ice in winter. And think of all the work it would make for local masons!

If she were staying. Which she wasn't.

Sally retrieved her hairbrush and plied it so vigorously that her hair crackled. This faux betrothal was proving more complicated than she had expected. She knew she shouldn't be making these sorts of plans; it wasn't her place. But every word Lady Henry had said just made Sally itch to whip Hullingden Castle into shape, to turn it into the kind of home it could be—the kind of home Lucien needed.

There had been no mistaking the pride and affection in his voice as he had shown her around the gardens. Sally set down her brush with a *thunk*. The duke belonged here, even if Lady Henry didn't think so.

Even if his own family treated him like an unwanted guest.

It was no wonder Lucien had run away. His uncle treated him with an anxious affection of the sort designed to make a healthy male twitchy; his aunt accorded him the heavy-handed courtesy owed an uninvited visitor. As for his sister—Sally had been inclined to be sympathetic at first, but she was coming to believe that what Clarissa Caldicott needed was a good dose of salts.

She wasn't the one who had found her parents' bodies.

Really, had no one thought of Lucien in all this? Had no one taken the time to inquire after his feelings, to make him feel welcome in his own home? The very thought of it made Sally's blood boil. They all treated him like an inconvenience, and the worst of it was that he, poor man, just sat back and let them do it. Vampire, ha! The man was too good-natured for his own good. He let them all run roughshod over him, and apologized to them for doing it.

Someone, Sally decided grimly, needed to do something.

She coughed as another gust of smoke blew back down into the room.

Starting with the chimneys.

Shaking back her hair, she pulled her dressing gown around her shoulders, and went to peer ineffectually around the fire screen. The wind was whistling back down the chimney, producing more smoke than heat. There must have been a bird caught in the flue. Sally could hear a rustling and scrabbling that seemed to echo from behind the stones.

A bird? Or mice? Sally wrinkled her nose. She really wasn't the least bit fond of mice. Ghosts were one thing; rodents quite another. Ghosts didn't chew one's pillow and leave nasty droppings in one's shoes.

The scrabbling was louder now. It sounded almost like . . . footsteps. Sally lifted the poker, edging closer to the fireplace. If that was a mouse, it had awfully large feet. And was wearing boots.

Nursery rhymes to the contrary, mice, in Sally's experience, did not generally go shod.

The tapestry hanging to the right of the fireplace undulated in the draft, a draft that seemed to come from nowhere. The candles guttered and sputtered as the sound of the wind whistling down the chimney resolved itself into a low moan, a moan that sounded like someone, in a rasping voice, calling, "Sally . . . Sally . . ."

Oh, for heaven's sake! This was absurd. Thoroughly annoyed with herself, Sally marched forward and yanked the tapestry aside. It gave easily on its gold bar, revealing a wall of solid stone.

Or was it? On one side of the tapestry, the window embrasure was a good three feet deep, deep enough for a wide window seat. On the other, the fireplace stretched back. That left a considerable space unaccounted for.

Feeling rather foolish, Sally poked tentatively at the stone. The wall creaked. She poked again, harder. When that didn't work, she shoved.

With a low groan, the wall swung forward, revealing an alcove liberally festooned with cobwebs.

There was, mercifully, no skeleton in chains. That, Sally decided, feeling more than a little giddy, would have been a bit much. But there was the burned end of an old torch set into a bracket and a flight of stone stairs that spiraled down into regions unknown.

Tightening the sash of her dressing down, Sally wedged the door open with the handle of her hairbrush, caught up a candle, and stuck a spare in her sash, just in case she needed an extra. The stairs were of stone, hollowed at the center from long use. One of the staircases of the original castle? Sally wouldn't have been surprised. She picked her way carefully around the central shaft, debris crunching beneath her slippers.

Her lips tightened. The sound of it was rather like the scratching and scrabbling she had heard from the chimney.

Had she been put in that chamber because it was haunted, or because it could conveniently be made to appear so?

The stairs branched off in multiple directions, a warren of passageways. But there was light coming from one side and one side only. Sally rather regretted not having had the forethought to appropriate one of Miss Gwen's sword parasols. Oh, well; if she didn't have a weapon, at least she had her dignity. She regarded the ruffles on her sleeves. Her dressing gown was of rich blue velvet, edged with ruffles of Valenciennes lace. It was quite fetching. It was not very intimidating.

She would just have to make up for her attire with the force of her personality.

Whoever it was hadn't even bothered to close the secret door all the way behind her. (Sally had her suspicions as to the identity of the malefactor. Haunted Chamber, indeed!) Ahead, she could see the back of a heavy tapestry much like the one in her room.

Gathering her skirts and her dignity around her, Sally swept the fabric aside, announcing, "I know what you're doing!"

The duke was seated in a broad chair before the fire, a book in his hand. He had divested himself of his evening attire, and wore, instead, a dressing gown in an exotic pattern on crimson silk. The firelight danced off his dark hair and eyes and shimmered against the liquid in the glass by his side.

He blinked, frowned, and blinked again. He closed his book over his finger. "Going to bed?" he asked mildly.

Lucien's betrothed came to an abrupt stop in the center of the floor, leaving the tapestry flapping behind her. She was dressed for bed, in a dressing gown of rich blue velvet, with a cascade of lace at the sleeves, her fair hair falling around her shoulders and halfway down her back. Loose, it was perfectly straight, with no hint of the curls she affected for fashion's sake.

She appeared to be nearly as surprised as he was, which didn't seem quite fair, given the fact that she was the one who had come bursting out of the wall.

Unless . . . Lucien glanced at the decanter beside him. No. He realized he didn't have a very hard head, but he was hardly going to be hallucinating on half a glass of claret.

And if he were to hallucinate, he decided, his hallucination would not have included the dressing gown.

His betrothed opened her mouth and then closed it again. "What are you doing here?" she asked suspiciously.

Lucien looked around him. "The last time I checked, this was my room. Which begs the question, what are you doing here?" The fabric of the dressing gown molded rather nicely to her legs. Lucien wasn't gentleman enough to ignore that fact. "Not that I'm objecting, mind you."

"I—" Sally frowned at him, looking this way and that, as

though she suspected him of hiding malefactors in the corners. "You weren't just scrabbling in the tunnels behind my room and making moaning noises?"

Lucien put his book aside. "I can say with some assurance that I was not." He cocked a brow. "Moaning noises?"

Sally set her hands on her hips, scrutinizing his room. "It sounded like someone calling my name."

The ducal chambers were located on an inner courtyard, shielded from the elements, but even here the wind whistled along the window frames. Hullingden had a multitude of nighttime noises. Lucien had half forgotten that in his time away. "Are you sure it wasn't the wind?"

"Absolutely not. Or—mostly not." Sally chewed on her lower lip. "I can tell the difference between my name and a breeze. Did you know that there was a secret stair behind my room?"

"It's hardly that secret." Lucien hadn't thought about them for years, but the passages in the walls had been a boon to a small boy, perfect for evading bedtime, mushy peas, and other unpleasantness. He gave the paneling an affectionate pat. "The walls of Hullingden are riddled with passageways. Stairs, priests' holes, subterranean tunnels—we have them all."

"Well, it was secret to me." Sally folded her arms across her chest, making the fabric of her dressing gown gape in interesting ways. Lucien caught a glimpse of the nightdress below, a fine linen not best suited to chilly castles in October. "Have you thought of affixing labels to these passages, for the edification of the unwary? Or do you prefer to surprise your guests with nocturnal visitations?"

"I," Lucien pointed out, justifiably, "am not the one roaming the night." He managed to drag his eyes away from her more obvious assets, and frowned. "Why do you have a candle stuck in your sash?"

Sally put a hand defensively to the wax at her waist. "I didn't know how far the stair would go. I didn't want to be caught in subterranean caverns without a candle."

"That was very resourceful of you." Lucien did his best to contain his grin, but he wasn't entirely successful.

"I believe in being prepared for every eventuality," said Sally grandly. She looked pointedly at Lucien. "Every foreseeable eventuality. I did *not* foresee that the stair would end in your bedchamber."

"I'm crushed," said Lucien cheerfully. "You were expecting an oubliette, perhaps? Or a subterranean chamber lined with corpses?"

His betrothed's lashes flickered guiltily.

Lucien snorted with laughter. "I don't have to ask what you've been reading."

Sally tossed her hair back over one shoulder. "If you will line the walls with secret passageways . . . ," she said sternly.

"I'll make sure to add a skeleton or two, just for form," Lucien promised. "Would you like some cobwebs as well?"

Sally flicked with distaste at a smudge on one sleeve. "Those you have," she said, sounding distinctly disgruntled.

Lucien couldn't resist. "If you will disappear down secret passageways . . ."

Sally gave him a look. Changing the subject, she gestured to something behind him. "Is that the Belliston coat of arms?"

Lucien glanced back over his shoulder, but all he saw was the ducal bed, raised on its own dais. It took him a moment to realize that she was referring to the massive representation of the Belliston coat of arms, carved in bas-relief on the bed frame and painted in gaudy red, blue, and gold. It loomed out from between the gathered bed curtains: the two halves of a broken sword forming a triangle beneath which one could see three stylized drops of blood.

The craftsman who had carved it long ago had not stinted on the blood.

The motto running across the scroll on the bottom read, "Bludde wyll owt."

"Yes, it's one of them."

Sally walked over to the dais, trailed her blue velvet skirts behind her, and squinted into the gloom beneath the bed curtains. The mattress creaked as she rested one hand against the foot of the bed, craning her neck for a better view. "It's quite . . . sanguinary."

"Sanguinary," Lucien echoed, as the mattress creaked again. "I suppose so."

It belatedly occurred to Lucien that this was, perhaps, not the most orthodox of interviews. Admittedly, Sally's robe was of a heavy, opaque fabric, but all it would take would be one tug—not that he was thinking of doing the tugging—on that sash to reveal what looked like a very thin nightdress below.

And there *was* that very large bed, conveniently placed right behind them.

Sally looked back at Lucien over her shoulder, her golden hair a bright spot in the dark room. "Have you considered a nice heraldic beast? A lion perhaps? Or a gryphon?"

"Or a fluffy bunny?" Lucien said blandly. He stepped forward to offer her a hand. "It's not quite as gruesome as it seems."

"Not quite?" Sally looped up her trailing flounces in one hand, resting her other hand lightly in his. Ungloved, her fingers were long and slender, and very white against his sun-darkened skin. "Blood will out?"

It took Lucien a moment to remember what they were talking about. "One of my ancestors backed Henry Tudor on Bosworth Field. The story goes that he was run through three times. Each time he staggered to his feet and resumed fighting. When the new king thanked him, he is said to have replied, 'I regret that I have but three drops of my heart's blood to give for my sovereign.' Then he promptly collapsed."

"I see." Sally perched on the edge of a red velvet settee, her blue velvet skirts fanning out around her. "How very distressing for him."

"Not very." Reminiscent amusement creased Lucien's lips.

His father might not have been terribly invested in the day-to-day running of the estate, but he had been a limitless repository of family stories, particularly of the saltier variety. "He was nursed back to health by the daughter of the local baron, who bore a very blond child nine months later."

Sally raised her brows. "In*deed*."

Lucien caught himself up short. "I really shouldn't have told you that, should I? In fact"—he looked down at Sally, who had made herself quite comfortable on the settee and showed every intention of staying for some time—"you really shouldn't be here."

Sally dismissed that with a wave of her hand. "Such things do go on." She leaned back, tilting her head up at him. "Was this child your ancestor?"

Lucien coughed. "I'm afraid not. As a token of the king's gratitude, he was offered a royal ward who came with several nice castles and a number of serfs."

"That's appalling," said Sally indignantly.

Lucien held up his hands. "One doesn't acquire a dukedom by being nice."

His betrothed looked at him narrowly. "One doesn't hold on to one by being nice, either."

Lucien tensed. "What does that mean? You can hardly be advising me to go out and exercise my droit du seigneur. I mean—" Damn.

"Don't be silly," Sally said sternly.

Did she have no idea what a tempting picture she made,

halfway reclining on the settee, with her hair loose around her shoulders?

Lucien shoved his hands in the pockets of his dressing gown. "You should be going back to your room," he said gruffly.

Sally rose, her robe gaping distractingly. "Because you don't want to hear what I have to say?"

"Because I— Did you hear that?" Lucien spun on one heel.

Sally tagged along after him. "You can't avoid me that easily." From the recesses of the wall came a thud, followed by a low moan. "Oh. *That.*"

Lucien strode to the tapestry and lifted one corner. "It came from the passage."

"Maybe it's the wind," said Sally pointedly.

That didn't sound like the wind; it was a low muttering. Almost like . . . an incantation. Lucien looked at his betrothed over his shoulder. "That wasn't the wind."

Sally didn't waste time on "I told you so." "I'll get the candle," she said briskly. "Would you like to go first?"

"Like" wasn't exactly the operative term. Lucien opened his mouth to suggest that she stay behind, then thought better of it. Some lost causes were noble; others were just lost. "That case, on the table. There are two pistols. Hand one to me."

"And the other?" said Sally, proffering the case.

Lucien offered it to her, butt first. "Try not to shoot me in the back."

Together, they ducked behind the tapestry and through the

gap in the paneling. There was a mechanism that controlled it—Lucien remembered that much—but someone appeared to have forced the lock so it wouldn't catch. The door easily swung open.

He hadn't remembered the passageways being quite so grim. Or so cold.

The skirt of Sally's robe brushed against his ankles. He could feel her breath against his ear. "Do you see anything?"

There was another thud, followed by muttering.

Lucien paused, pistol cocked. "If that's a French spy," he murmured, "it's a remarkably clumsy one."

He could feel Sally's fingers on the belt of his dressing gown. "Miss Gwen did say that he was hideously maimed," she whispered.

A misshapen shadow lurched into view, moving with a shambling, uneven gait.

Lucien leveled his pistol. "Drop your arms and show yourself," he commanded.

"Drop my—" The voice was young, English, and more than a little bit slurred. The shadow resolved itself into a man in a caped greatcoat. Hal Caldicott tripped over the hem of his cloak. "Lucien?"

Sally let out a gusty breath. "So much for spies."

Lucien lowered his pistol. "Hal? I thought you were in town?"

"I am— I mean, I was. I mean . . ." Hal floundered in the folds of his cape.

Lucien leaned down and gave his cousin a hand up. As he did, Hal's eyes focused hazily on Sally.

"Miss Fitzhugh? What are you doing— Oh." A look of drunken comprehension spread across his face. It stopped somewhere just short of a leer. "Oh."

Sally reflexively tightened the belt of her dressing gown. Lucien resisted the urge to wipe the leer off his cousin's face.

"It's not what you think," Lucien said grimly.

Hal held up his hands. "Not thinking anything at all. None of my business what you do with your own—"

"Betrothed?" supplied Lucien repressively.

"Just so." Hal looked owlishly at Sally around Lucien's arm. "Nuptials coming up and all that . . . No one . . . blame you for anticipatin' . . ."

Sally leaned forward and glowered at Hal. "I am not here," she said succinctly. "Do you understand me, Mr. Caldicott? I am not here. I was not here. I have never been here."

A foolish grin spread across Hal's face. He made an attempt to stand, and would have stumbled, but for Lucien's supporting arm. "Oh, I understand."

"No, you don't," said Lucien wearily.

Sally took matters into her own hands. "I am a figment of your imagination. Do you hear me? A figment."

Hal winced as the candle flame danced across his dilated pupils. "Awfully loud for a figment," he complained.

"He's foxed," said Lucien under his voice. "He won't remember anything once he sleeps it off."

"Heard that!" said Hal indignantly. "I'm not—that is—maybe I'm a little—hic!—indish—indish—under the influe-whatsis."

"A little?" said Sally.

Lucien looked to Sally. "You should go."

"You'll be all right?"

"I've put drunks to bed before." His cousins in New Orleans were no strangers to overindulgence.

"I'm not—"

"I know," said Lucien. "I know. You're only a trifle indisposed. Let's get you to your room." Lucien hefted his cousin up, looping a limp arm around his shoulders. "What the devil have you been drinking?"

"Bl-blue ruin." Hal shook off Lucien's supporting arm, catching himself against the wall. "I'm ruined. Ruined with blue ruin." He looked at his cousin with sudden alarm. "Won't tell my father?"

"Your secret is safe with me." Lucien made a flapping gesture at Sally behind Hal's back.

"Here." Sally darted forward to lift the edge of the tapestry for him. "You can't manage both him and the door."

Hal's arm slid from the wall. He sprawled inelegantly on the stone floor. "God! If I could make it all just go away!"

"I rather expect it might, at that," said Lucien prosaically. Giving up all attempt to shoo Sally out of the way, he said, "There should be a basin to the right of the bed."

Hal caught at the hem of Sally's robe. He looked up with glittering eyes. "I need more gin."

"No, you don't," said Sally, giving her dressing gown a good, hard yank. "Gin is the last thing you need."

The basin, on the other hand, was looking increasingly necessary.

Lucien grabbed Hal beneath the arm, making an attempt to hoist him up, away from Sally. Hal's eyes rolled back in his head, showing an alarming amount of white.

"I keep seeing her—keep seeing—" A blast of gin hit Lucien full in the face. "I saw Sir Matthew Egerton at the Cockeyed Crow."

Lucien froze, letting his cousin's arm drop. "Here?"

Hal slid down along the wall. "He followed you. All the way from London."

"That's hardly a feat of tracking," said Sally acidly. "Following the Duke of Belliston all the way to his ancestral home."

Both men ignored her. Lucien turned to Hal. "Did he say anything to you?"

Pressing his hands against the rough stones of the wall, Hal clawed his way upright. "He thinks you did it." His words were slurred, but his intent was clear. "He thinks you killed Fanny."

"Of all the—," Sally began indignantly.

"Wait." Lucien's voice was too loud for the small landing. He could hear it echoing in his ears. He forced himself to focus on his cousin's face, the familiar Caldicott features, the fair hair dark with damp. So familiar, and yet so alien. "How did you know that?"

Hal's eyes shifted. "Shaw—I mean, saw—him in the Cock-eyed Crow. Told you that. Jusht now."

"No." Behind him, Lucien could hear Sally's sudden sharp intake of breath. He forced himself to go on, to ask his cousin the one question he didn't want to ask. "How did you know who she was?"

Chapter Nineteen

It felt suddenly cold in the passageway. Hideously, bone-jarringly cold. Sally felt a sick jolt in the pit of her stomach.

The cunning of the extremely drunk spread across Hal's face. "Saw her in the play, of course," he mumbled. "Who didn't know Fanny?"

Lucien's cousin was a remarkably poor liar.

"It was you," Lucien said. It was a statement, not a question. He stepped back, away. "You were her protector."

"That was you?" Sally gave up any effort to hide either her presence or her disgust. "You wrote those letters?"

Hal's head whipped around, his cheek scraping against the stone. "I—you—you've read them?"

"Every last, excruciating line." She hadn't, but Hal didn't

need to know that. The two she had perused had been more than enough. Sally drew herself up to her full height, an avenging angel in an embroidered nightdress. "You, sir, have some explaining to do."

Hal looked from one to the other, and evidently decided Lucien was the less alarming of the two. He grasped at Lucien's brocaded sleeve, his damp fingers scrabbling against the cloth. "I didn't do it. I didn't have anything to do with Fanny's death. You have to believe me, Lucien. I didn't do it!"

The duke's expression was carefully expressionless. Something about it made Sally ache. "Why didn't you come forward at the time?"

"Why—" Hal laughed wildly. "Do you think I'm mad? They would have blamed it on me! They would have thought—"

"Instead you let them blame it on Lucien." Sally's voice was sharp as a lash. "How terribly noble of you."

Hal looked again from one to the other, like a caged beast. "It wasn't like that! You don't understand." He made an effort to draw himself up. "Couldn't do that to old Clarissa, not at her ball. Couldn't let them think I—"

"Oh, but it was better to let suspicion be thrown on her brother?" Sally stalked forward. "That would enliven her party no end, having her brother hauled away in chains for murder. Not that you would care, would you?"

"I didn't mean—" Hal stumbled back as Sally advanced, her skirts rustling purposefully against the stone floor.

"How terribly fortunate for you, to have such a convenient

scapegoat on hand to take the blame for your crime." Sally held the candle high, letting the light shine full in Hal's face. "Did you kill her, Mr. Caldicott? Did you paint those fang marks on her neck?"

"Did I—fang marks—no! No!"

Lucien gently moved the candle out of the way. "Why should we believe you? What cause have you given us to trust you?"

"Because I wouldn't!" Hal looked desperately from Lucien to Sally and back again. He slumped down on the stairs, like a marionette with the strings cut. His voice was muffled as he said, "God knows I thought about it. That woman—you don't know how it was."

"We've read the letters," said Sally pointedly.

Lucien looked down at his cousin. "What happened, Hal?"

Hal pressed his hands against his temples. "She was like a disease, and once I'd caught her, I couldn't get free. God! She made me crazy." He looked up, his eyes glazed with gin and memory. "She'd smile and laugh and promise me everything— and then the next day she'd be cool as you please. I would have done anything to have her. Anything."

Lucien crouched on the stairs beside him. "How badly were you dipped?"

"Dipped? To my limit. Beyond. Couldn't go to Father—he wouldn't understand. Meant to hold up the name of the Caldicotts. Blasted family name." He cast a sly look at Lucien. "Not as though it ain't besmirched enough already."

Sally's hands itched with the desire to shake the smug look

off Hal Caldicott's slack-jawed face. "Those are rumors," she said coldly. "Rumors based on nothing more than boredom and sheer idiocy. What's your excuse?"

"Madness." Hal looked wildly at Lucien. "They say we're mad, don't they?"

"No," said the duke. "They say I'm mad."

He sounded impossibly tired. Sally resisted the urge to go to him and put her arm around his shoulders and draw his dark head to her breast.

Hal tugged at his caped greatcoat where it had become tangled around his shoulders. One of the many fobs on his waistcoat pulled off, falling to the floor with a discordant clang. "She claimed I'd promised to marry her. Can you imagine? An actress?"

Sally thought back to that poor woman, the one who had nursed the first baron back to health after Bosworth Field. "Did you?"

Hal's eyes shifted. "Not in so many words—I'm not that stupid!"

Sally's eyes met Lucien's. It didn't take much insight to tell what the duke was thinking.

Hal saw it too. His cheeks flushed. "It was just—she wouldn't have me any other way! There was nothing binding."

"No," said Lucien. He rose slowly to his feet, stepping away. "Just your word."

"Exactly!" Hal nodded enthusiastically. "I never put anything down on paper. But she was threatening to sh— to sh—

to take me to the courts. She wouldn't have. She wouldn't have. It was just a ploy. Get more money out of me."

Sally risked a glance at Lucien. His face was still and set.

Lucien reached out a hand to his cousin, hauling him none too gently to his feet. "Sleep it off, Hal."

"We were done," said Hal urgently, breathing gin fumes so strong that Sally could feel the impact from a yard away. "She knew that. Didn't need—didn't need—oh, God. I just wanted her to go away. That was all. Just go away. Not like that . . . Not like that . . ."

There were tears running down his wind-reddened cheeks. Sally found herself caught between disgust and pity.

Lucien slid an arm under his cousin's shoulders. "I'm going to put him in my bed," he said in an undertone. "Do you hear me, Hal? We're going to get you into bed."

"Bed," said Hal, and Sally watched as his eyes rolled slowly back in his head.

Lucien hadn't been lying. He did have experience seeing drunks to bed. He was gentler than Sally would have been about it. Left to herself, she would have dumped a pitcher of cold water over his upturned face and shaken him until he sput-tered. Hal Caldicott had seen Sir Matthew Egerton in the vil-lage, but had he bothered to tell him that he knew who the murdered woman was? Intimately?

Sally would be willing to wager not.

It was worse than craven. It was low and crawling and worm-like.

While Sally fumed, Lucien deftly stripped Hal of his cape and deposited him in the great bed, beneath the sigil of the broken sword.

Sally looked at Hal Caldicott, snoring away in the vastness of the ducal bed. Seeing him in Lucien's bed, tucked up comfortably among the embroidered bedsheets, added insult to injury.

Sally turned to Lucien, her hands on her hips. "That's all very well and good, but where are you going to sleep?"

Lucien shrugged. "There's a cot in the dressing room."

Sally pressed her lips together. Fifty-odd bedrooms and sundry feather beds, and the duke was sleeping on a cot in his own castle.

Sally glared at Hal's sleeping form. "Do you believe his story?"

Lucien drew the bed curtains closed around his cousin. Sally watched his hands on the cords, deft and sure. "I would prefer not to do otherwise."

"Words," said Sally belligerently, "are meant to convey meaning, not to obscure it."

"There's nothing about this business that isn't obscure," Lucien said bitterly. He dragged a hand through his hair. "Do you think I want to believe that Hal could— We were boys together!"

Yes, and Sally had been girls with some quite unmentionable creatures at Miss Climpson's.

The expression on Lucien's face was such that she decided not to mention that.

Sally put a hand on Lucien's crimson brocade sleeve. The fabric was warm beneath her fingers. "You do realize what this means? If your cousin killed Fanny Logan—then it's not about your parents at all."

If there wasn't a French spy on the rampage, it did beg the question of what she was doing here, enmeshed in a false betrothal, but she decided to deal with that later.

Lucien looked down. "No," he said. "It just means that my cousin killed his mistress and then tried to see me blamed for the murder."

When he put it that way . . . a French spy would be preferable.

Sally gave Lucien's arm a squeeze. "He might be telling the truth."

"He might." Lucien's face was bleak. He looked down at her. "I should see you to your room."

Sally wrinkled her brows. Did he really think she was going to leave him to brood nobly on his lonely cot?

"You've just had a shock. You shouldn't be alone."

Lucien thrust his hands into the pockets of his dressing gown. "I'm fine."

And she was Queen Charlotte. "No, you're not. Not that it's the least bit surprising," Sally said encouragingly. "You do have the most appalling family. Anyone would be distressed to discover his cousin might be a murderer."

Lucien's face twisted into a crooked smile. "Are you trying to make me feel better by telling me how miserable I am?"

"I—" Put that way, it did sound a little absurd. Sally shook her hair back behind her shoulders. "Well, it worked, didn't it?"

Lucien didn't mean to laugh. It came out as a cross between a hiccup and a snort. "Only you," he said, his voice rich with amusement. "Only you."

If Lucien hadn't meant to laugh, he most certainly didn't mean to kiss Sally. It just . . . happened.

She looked so delightfully smug, with her lips pursed in that smirk that was so entirely hers, and her hair tumbling down around her shoulders, that it was just impossible not to kiss her. His fingers, of their own volition, curved around her cheek, the strands of her hair brushing his wrist, catching on his sleeve, crimson and gold in the firelight.

Lucien was still shaking with laughter as his lips touched hers. But not for long. He could feel her brief, startled movement, and then her hands slid up around his shoulders, and her lips angled against his, and any laughter was lost, lost between their lips, behind the lids of his eyes, in a warm, velvet darkness where there was nothing but the feel of Sally in his arms, the silk of her hair forming a tangled net around his hands, the velvet of her robe soft and supple beneath his fingers.

Sally fit against him as though she had always belonged there, the lithe line of her body molding itself to his, her long skirts tangling around his legs, the lace ruffles on her sleeves tickling the back of his neck. She smelled of French soap and lilacs and the fresh green buds on trees in spring, or at least that was the image that came to Lucien's mind—a garden, in its first bloom, dappled in sunlight.

There was a groaning noise, followed by a thrashing, followed by a most unpleasant retching.

Lucien came back to earth with a thud. His lips parted from Sally's with a pop. They stared at each other, just a hand's breadth apart, so close that Lucien could feel Sally's breath against his cheek, feel her heart pounding wildly through the fabric of her robe. Or perhaps that was his heart pounding. He wasn't quite sure. He felt as though he'd run a mile across rough terrain, windburned and breathless, every muscle straining, including the unmentionable ones.

"Hal." Lucien's voice sounded scratchy. "That was Hal."

His arm was still around Sally's waist, her hair still tangled around his sleeve. Sally blinked several times, her blue eyes slowly focusing on his face.

"Well, then," she said. "Well, then."

Lucien knew exactly what she meant. He dug around in his muddled brain for something eloquent to say. "Well, then," he agreed.

The retching sound came again from behind the bed curtains, followed by a bout of coughing.

Lucien winced.

Sally shook herself free of Lucien's encircling arm, sweeping her hair back with an abrupt gesture and bundling it in a knot that promptly fell down again. There were still golden strands clinging to Lucien's arm. Somehow—Lucien wasn't taking responsibility for something he couldn't quite remember doing—her robe appeared to have come undone, revealing a white linen nightdress that had most certainly not been designed for a drafty castle in October.

Sally looked from Lucien's hands to his face and back again, pulling her robe more tightly around her.

"Goodness!" she said brightly. "That was quite an act!"

"An act?" The blood was thrumming in Lucien's temples. He was hot and cold and thoroughly confused.

Sally swallowed, hard. Lucien could see her throat working beneath the ruffles at her neck. "Keeping up our betrothal. Our false betrothal. That was *terribly* convincing."

"Terribly," Lucien echoed.

The word "false" reverberated through his brain.

Of course. That was all it was. A contrivance. A fiction.

Lucien's heated body protested that, quite to the contrary, the curve of her chest, her waist, her hip beneath his hands had been quite real; there had been no feigning in the answering pressure of her lips against his, the way she had stood on tiptoe to wrap her arms more firmly around his neck. He could still feel her against him, the slide of the silk of her hair between his fingers, the softness of her skin.

Some relic of self-preservation surged to the fore. Lucien stepped back, stuffing his hands in his pockets, preventing himself from reaching for her and drawing her back into the circle of his arms, proving that there had been nothing false about it.

That would be the act of a cad.

Sally was looking at him with wide, expectant eyes, waiting for him to take her cue. Lucien could see the uncertainty there, and it struck him to the core. One slippered toe stuck out beneath the hem of her robe, as though poised for flight.

Lucien gathered the shreds of his honor.

"We mustn't be too convincing," he said quietly. "Unless you want this betrothal to be more than a fiction."

Sally blinked rapidly, and then mustered an entirely unconvincing laugh. "Don't be foolish! The point is to keep you out of shackles, not to fit you with new ones." She moved rapidly towards the secret door. "I'll just be going now, shall I? No need to see me out. I know the way."

Before he could molest her again? Lucien's conscience smote him. Consciences could be extremely inconvenient items. "Don't be absurd," he said shortly. "I'll see you to your room."

"There's really no need." Sally fluttered her hands elegantly, moving with a speed that in anyone less graceful might have looked like flight. "I'm hardly going to run into anyone else on the secret staircase. Although your secret staircase isn't very secret, is it? You really must do something about that."

Lucien ducked under the tapestry after her. "I'll see to it at the first opportunity. Sally—"

"No, no, no need to look for bogeymen under my bed. I'm sure I'll be perfectly safe." Sally's slippers beat a rapid tattoo on the stone stairs.

Lucien fell back, feeling like the worst sort of cad. Did she really feel that she needed to run from him?

"Nothing has changed." That was a lie, if ever he'd heard one, but he didn't know what else to do, what else to say to make things right. "What just happened—it was a mistake. It won't happen again."

Already on the landing, Sally looked back over her shoulder. "Of course not." Even with her hair down around her shoulders and the sash of her robe tied crookedly, she held herself like a duchess. "As you say, we wouldn't want our betrothal to be too convincing."

And with that, Sally disappeared behind the secret door in the paneling, leaving Lucien alone in a windowless stairwell that felt darker and danker than it had a moment before.

Chapter Twenty

Sally collapsed with her back against the paneling.

That had not been part of the plan.

Not that she had had terribly much of a plan in mind when she went barreling down the secret staircase, but if she had had one, that would not have been part of it.

Sally lifted one hand tentatively to her lips. For a rather foolish moment, it had been all too easy to forget that this betrothal of theirs was meant to be a sham. She wasn't quite sure how it happened. One minute, they were talking, and the next . . .

She had felt sorry for him; that was all. His family was so awful to him and his cousin was in his bed and he had looked so broken up about Hal, and, really, wasn't it enough to melt the hardest of hearts? And she was nothing if not compassionate.

Compassion—that was all it was. Why, she was practically a Good Samaritan! It had nothing at all to do with the way his hair tumbled down across his brow or the triangle of his chest exposed by his open dressing gown or—

Lady Florence poked her narrow head out of her basket, fixing Sally with one beady eye.

"Don't you start," warned Sally.

A rapping on the paneling behind her back made her jump.

"Sally?" It was Lucien's voice, distorted by the wooden barrier between them. It sounded oddly hollow and echo-y.

Sally whirled around, making frantic attempts to tidy her hair. "Yes?"

Naturally, she would be dignified and distant. . . . Well, maybe not too dignified and distant. Just dignified and distant enough. She caught sight of herself in the mirror across the room. Was her hair really that much of a mess? No time to brush it now.

"It's Lucien," said Lucien, from the other side of the door.

"I know that." Sally snatched open the secret door.

Lucien stood on the other side, looking unfairly rakish with his dressing gown open over his loose linen shirt, his dark curls tousled. She knew what those curls felt like now beneath her fingers, the weight and texture of them, the short hairs at the back of his neck, the prickle of his chin against her palm.

"What?" Sally snapped. "What is it?"

She wasn't meant to be thinking of the feel of his skin or the way his fingers felt as they brushed her cheek, so carefully, so delicately. And she would tell him so if he asked. This was a false betrothal—that was all it was. *Good Samaritan*, she reminded herself. *Compassion*. Her halo was so shiny she could practically see her face in it.

"You forgot this." Lucien was holding something out to her, something mahogany, chased in silver. Sally stared at it, trying to make her scrambled brain do its work.

"A pistol," she said blankly. "You brought me a pistol?"

A faint smile crossed Lucien's lips. "I know they aren't much use against ghosts and ghouls," he said, and something about the way he said it made Sally cross her arms more firmly across her chest, because otherwise she might be tempted to fling her arms around him. "But just in case."

"Thank you," said Sally. She made no move to take the pistol. "But I have Lady Florence with me."

"The famed stoat defense?" Lucien set the pistol down on a low table, a good yard away from Sally. He made no move to come any closer. "I'll leave this with you all the same."

"Thank you," said Sally politely. And then, since something more seemed to be required: "Good night."

It seemed like an absurd conversation to be having with someone against whom she had been pressed intimately only five minutes before. Not that she was sure what sort of conversation one was meant to be having with someone against whom one had been pressed intimately.

"Good night," said the duke, just as correctly, and with a little bow for good measure. The formality of the gesture contrasted oddly with his dressing gown and the open neck of the shirt beneath. And then, without further ado, he pressed the mechanism that opened the door in the paneling.

He was, Sally realized incredulously, leaving. Just like that.

Lucien paused, one hand on the open panel. "Sally?"

"Yes?" Sally tried not to sound too eager.

Lucien nodded in the direction of the other entrance. "Lock your door. Both of them."

And with that, the panel clicked shut behind him.

"I was planning to," she protested, but Lucien wasn't there to hear. She was left talking to the empty air and one unapprecia-tive stoat.

Sally hugged the velvet folds of her dressing gown to her. That was it? That was all? No undying avowals of love? No at-tempted ravishment? She had a dozen cutting set-downs all pre-pared. She bit her lip, as her conscience uttered derisive noises that sounded a good deal like Miss Gwen. She would have used them, she told herself. Eventually.

But, no. Lucien, Sally realized with a growing sense of in-dignation, had evidently meant what he said.

It was a mistake. It won't happen again.

Of course, it wouldn't happen again. It shouldn't have hap-pened even once, but for the fact that she was so warmhearted and compassionate and charitable and all that sort of thing.

Sally locked the door and put a chair beneath it for good measure. Not that she thought she would need it, but just be-cause.

Did he think she wanted him to kiss her again? Had she somehow given that impression? If so, she thought indignantly, kicking the hem of her robe out of the way, she would soon put the matter straight. It wasn't as though she had invited his attentions. Her eyelashes hadn't been fluttering, not in the least.

It was very hard for one's eyelashes to flutter when one's eyes were closed.

That wasn't the point. The point was . . . What was the point? Oh, right. She remembered now. It wasn't as though she was the one who had initiated the embrace. She had been innocently minding her own business, tendering the benefit of her good advice, when, suddenly, out of the middle of nowhere, he had just *swooped*. She certainly hadn't asked him to sweep her up in his arms and kiss her dizzy.

Yes, yes, she knew she shouldn't have been in Lucien's room in her dressing gown, but, really, it wasn't as though she had intended to be in Lucien's room in her dressing gown. Much like everything else, it had just happened. Her dressing gown covered quite as much of her as any of her morning gowns or walking dresses and certainly more of her than most of her evening gowns.

Really, it was all quite respectable, or as respectable as it could be under the circumstances. It wasn't as though she had known that that stair led to his room. If she had—

Sally paused at this point in her musings, then shook her head. No. However much curiosity might have tempted her, she most certainly wouldn't have visited Lucien's room in the dead of night. At least, not while he was there. Even she knew that such behavior was beyond the pale.

But once there . . . Well, it really wouldn't have been polite just to barge out again, would it? It wasn't as though she had flung herself into his arms and begged to be ravished.

If she went downstairs and told him that, would it be construed as an invitation to ravish her again?

Sally squelched that thought before it could proceed further. She wasn't supposed to want to be ravished. She made a wrathful face at her own reflection in the windowpane. Maybe Lucien really was a vampire. That would explain how he'd sucked the sense out of her and turned her into one of those hideous simpering creatures who clogged the mirrors in the ladies' retiring room, sighing over this viscount and that baronet and who had attempted to kiss whom.

Sally drew herself up proudly. It wasn't as though no one had ever attempted to take liberties before; she wasn't such an antidote as that. She had learned how to deal patiently, scornfully, or crushingly with would-be Lotharios, depending on the extent of their daring and the degree of their offense.

But none of them had ever made her cheeks grow hot and her hands grow cold and her breath catch in her chest and—and—

"Don't say it!" she snapped at Lady Florence, who, being a stoat, hadn't said anything at all.

As soon as it was decently light, a sleepy and cranky Sally stalked down the corridors of Hullingden in search of Miss

Gwen. Miss Gwen had got them into this—Sally conveniently papered over her own part prior to Miss Gwen's involvement—and it was up to her to find the murderer so that Lucien's name could be cleared and they could all go home.

The end.

Sally spent a moment basking in the image of Lucien, reinstated to all the honors of which he hadn't yet been stripped, going down on one knee and vowing that he owed it all to her, while she very graciously acknowledged his acknowledgments and then freed him from their betrothal.

This highly satisfying image was, unfortunately, superseded by that of Lucien in his dressing gown, looking down at her with regret in his dark eyes, saying, "We mustn't be too convincing."

Sally tackled her task with renewed purpose. Charity and compassion went only so far.

She couldn't have the duke thinking she wanted to stay longer at Hullingden.

Even if she did.

It took her several false starts, one wrong turn down a service stair, and the help of a friendly under-housemaid (who, it turned out, also had an excellent recipe for freckle cream), but Sally eventually found her way to Miss Gwen's room, only an hour after she had left her own.

Really, guests should be given maps, she thought grumpily. She added that to her list of grievances as she knocked peremptorily at the door of Miss Gwen's room.

Miss Gwen's familiar dulcet tones issued forth from behind the closed door. "Go away."

Sally went in anyway.

The door to the dressing room clicked shut as Miss Gwen's maid whisked out of the way, carrying a pile of garments over one arm, her cap pulled down low over her brow.

"Did you know that Fanny Logan was Hal Caldicott's mistress?" Sally said without preamble.

"Now I do." Miss Gwen's room, unlike Sally's, was in the new wing. Instead of dark paneling, everything was light and airy, from the white woodwork to the cheerful birds and flowers embroidered on the counterpane. Miss Gwen was comfortably ensconced in a bed that looked as though it had been purchased within the past century, propped against a number of pillows, a tray on her lap. Her pince-nez were perched upon her nose and there was a pile of papers on the bed beside her.

Sally felt a surge of relief. Miss Gwen was on the case. They would find the real murderer, clear Lucien's name, improve the castle kitchens, and then retire to London in a blaze of glory.

Then everything could go back to just the way it was.

Somehow, that wasn't quite as satisfying a prospect as it ought to have been.

"What did you find? Correspondence? A journal?" Sally plunked herself down on the bed, making the chocolate cup rock on its saucer. She snatched eagerly at the nearest page. "*Sir Magnifico bent his knee. 'It would be selfish in me to keep you by my side when such evil stalks the land.' With one noble tear—* You're working on your book?"

Miss Gwen snatched the page away. "Manuscripts don't just write themselves."

Sally wiggled off the bed, waving her arms for emphasis. "Yes, and murders don't just solve themselves either! There are *lives* at stake."

Not to mention her pride, which was currently sporting a duke-shaped dent.

"You have lives to save; I have a deadline." Miss Gwen permitted herself a small smirk. "Many people are waiting for the sequel to *The Convent of Orsino*."

Sally's nails dug into her palms. "Is this the sequel in which a duke is unfairly charged with murder because someone spread ridiculous rumors about vampires?"

"Who would want to read that?" Miss Gwen regarded her manuscript pages fondly. "Plumeria must leave her child with Sir Magnifico and go to battle the dread Goblin King, who has risen from the dead to menace the kingdom."

This was beginning to sound far less fictional. Miss Gwen had left her own infant daughter, Plumeria, at home with her husband, Colonel Reid. Colonel Reid, who had five previous offspring from various relationships, was something of an expert when it came to infant wrangling.

Sally didn't bother to keep the edge out of her voice. "Is there also an old castle in the countryside all covered in vines?"

"Guarded by ten fearsome ghouls in two straight lines." Assuming a soulful expression, Miss Gwen intoned, "In two straight lines they shook their spears, bared their teeth and pulled their ears."

They didn't sound particularly fearsome to Sally. "Is there also an intrepid golden-haired heroine?"

Miss Gwen looked at Sally over her spectacles. "No," she said succinctly.

Well, then. Sally paced restlessly alongside the bed. "Fiction is all very well and good, but we have a real murderer stalking the night. Are we going to wait until he kills again?"

"Certainly not. Corpses are so untidy." Miss Gwen squinted at her manuscript, crossed something out, thought better of it, and crossed out the cross-out. "There's no need for these histrionics. I have it all in hand."

All she appeared to have in hand was her manuscript. "Not to sound critical, but . . ."

"That's the problem with your generation. None of you have a particle of patience." With a martyred air, Miss Gwen set her manuscript aside. "I made good use of my time last night. While *you* were gadding about."

Gadding. That was one way to put it.

Sally tried not to squirm under the scrutiny of those beady black eyes. Miss Gwen couldn't possibly know. . . . No. Not even Miss Gwen was that omniscient.

Sally hoped.

She took refuge in a barrage of questions. "Did you contact the Pink Carnation? Is the Carnation on the case?"

Or on the premises. Sally had her suspicions about her new maid.

Miss Gwen regarded her with displeasure. "Don't you think the Carnation has better things to do?"

Better than tracking down a maimed and homicidal French spy?

"Such as?" Sally challenged.

"That," said Miss Gwen pointedly, "is privileged information. All you need know is that the Carnation has been informed. In the meantime, *I*"—she stressed the pronoun—"made certain discoveries while you were carousing."

Dinner with Lucien's Aunt Winifred hardly counted as a carouse. Sally wasn't satisfied, but since Miss Gwen appeared determined to stay mum on the topic of the Carnation, she demanded instead, "What did you find? Are the duke's and duchess's papers still here? Was there anything in them about the Black Tulip?"

"Only if you're interested in rare plants." Once she was sure that Sally was properly squelched, Miss Gwen folded her pince-nez and said, "In the weeks preceding the duke's and duchess's deaths, each made a number of unscheduled trips to London. The duchess for 'meetings of a horticultural society.'"

Sally couldn't keep the disappointment out of her voice. "Was that all?"

Miss Gwen looked deeply affronted. "What did you expect? A pile of correspondence labeled 'Secret Correspondence'?"

Yes.

"Of course not," said Sally with great dignity. "But that's hardly conclusive."

"Do you expect me to do all of your thinking for you?" Miss Gwen took a sip of her chocolate and made a hideous face. "Paugh! Stone-cold."

Sally frowned. "Wasn't the duchess a botanist? Surely, a horticultural society wouldn't be out of the way."

"The duchess wrote her husband that she was delayed in town due to new information about a *rare species*." Miss Gwen fixed Sally with an unblinking charcoal stare. "The black tulip is a botanical impossibility."

One didn't say such things to Miss Gwen, but it all sounded just a little far-fetched.

On the other hand, one might have argued the same thing about the mysterious messages being left in Christmas puddings at Miss Climpson's Select Seminary. And Miss Gwen was the expert.

"And what about the old duke?" Sally plucked at the French knots on the counterpane. "Do you think he was following her?"

"Possibly. The record is unclear." Miss Gwen looked distinctly dissatisfied. "The last duke spent a great deal of time in London as a rule. On those weeks, however, he appeared to have a series of meetings with his solicitor. They met six times over the space of two weeks. The matter appears to have been one of some delicacy. The duke made no record of it in his papers, only the meetings themselves."

Sally wasn't sure she liked the shape this was taking. The

duke had been a member of the government; if he had discovered his wife was funneling information to the enemy . . .

At what point did honor trump affection?

Beneath her indignation, Sally felt a little flicker of unease. Lucien spoke of his parents with such affection, such regret. She did not think that he would react well to discovering that his father had been planning to have his mother clapped in irons. Even if they were very well-padded irons in a very comfortable cell.

"Do you think the duke was looking into bringing proceedings against his wife?"

Miss Gwen settled back against her pillows. "That would certainly provide the Tulip with motive to kill."

"It's all such a waste," said Sally passionately. "Two lives lost, and for what?"

"Three lives," Miss Gwen corrected her. "Some would consider that a small cost."

Whoever those people were, they hadn't seen the aftermath. Sally thought of Lucien, a stranger in the home that ought to have been his.

"But what about Hal Caldicott? It can't be a coincidence that the murdered woman was his—" Sally waved her hand.

"Mistress? Paramour? Light of love?"

"Yes," said Sally hastily, before Miss Gwen could go on spouting synonyms.

"Did it ever occur to you that someone might deliberately have put Miss Logan in Mr. Caldicott's way?" With a long-suffering sigh, Miss Gwen lifted her cup of chocolate, contemplating the delicate spray of flowers interlaced with vines that adorned the sides. "The Tulip only employed female agents. He called them his petals."

"Yes. So you've said." Sally tried to untangle Miss Gwen's logic. "The Black Tulip hired Miss Logan to seduce Hal Caldicott, and then used that relationship to lure her to Clarissa Caldicott's ball, where he knew Lucien would be present. Then he killed his own agent and sent Lucien that note, all to see Lucien convicted of murder."

"Precisely," said Miss Gwen, and took a hefty swig of the despised chocolate.

Sally frowned at Miss Gwen. "Don't you think that sounds unnecessarily convoluted? If the Black Tulip wants Lucien—" She saw Miss Gwen's expression, and caught herself. "I mean, the duke—out of the way, why not just shoot him and have done with it?"

"That," said Miss Gwen succinctly, "would be far too easy. You make the mistake of believing you are dealing with a rational mind. The Black Tulip is a creature of twisted cunning. He couldn't take a straight path if someone measured it for him with a ruler. It would be just like him to go to the trouble of spreading elaborate rumors, just to catch your duke in a web of his own devising. Like a spider, the Black Tulip enjoys playing with his prey."

"How charming." Sally sat down on the edge of the bed. "What do we do?"

"I," said Miss Gwen, prodding at Sally with the blunt end of her teaspoon, "am going to finish my chapter. As for you, you can go do whatever you like. Go to the village and buy new ribbons. Annoy your hostess. Take your stoat for a walk."

Lady Florence preferred to be carried. But that was beside the point. Sally slid off the side of the bed. "I meant something useful."

And, more importantly, something that would keep her well out of Lucien's way.

"You aren't here to be useful. You are here to provide the experts with an entrée. Which you have done very nicely," said Miss Gwen, in the tones of one making a great concession. She waved a hand at Sally. "Now run along and entertain yourself—there's a good girl."

"Entertain myself," Sally repeated flatly. She wasn't here to entertain herself. She was here to uncover a spy and cover herself with glory. Or something along those lines. "We only have three days. Shouldn't I be—oh, I don't know—questioning the servants? Looking for secret papers?"

"No," said Miss Gwen.

"But—" Sally felt increasingly frantic. Surely, there had to be something she could do, something useful.

"No." Miss Gwen snapped open her pince-nez and propped them back onto the bridge of her nose. "If you truly want to be useful—"

"Yes?"

"You can tell the maid to send up a fresh pot of chocolate."

Miss Gwen regarded her cup with displeasure. "This is undrinkable."

"That didn't stop you from drinking it," said Sally, but only once the door was closed behind her.

Miss Gwen wasn't quite as deadly with a teaspoon as she was with a parasol, but that didn't mean she couldn't bruise.

Sally stomped her way down to the inconveniently located dining room. If this were her house—but it wasn't, and she didn't have any business redesigning it. She didn't have any business doing anything, apparently. She might as well just collect her stoat and go home. Never mind the fact that if it weren't for her, Lucien would have gone off onto that balcony by himself and been found with the girl's body and no one would have the least notion that the Black Tulip had risen from the dead, but, really, why let that weigh with anyone? She was just a pretty face—that was all. Buy herself new ribbons, indeed!

Although, to be fair, there had been some rather pretty primrose silk ribbons in that shop in the village that would go perfectly with her jonquil morning dress . . .

Sally spent an engrossing moment in sartorial calculations before remembering that she was meant to be above such shallow pursuits.

And the ribbons hadn't been that pretty.

Dabney, who appeared to have a habit of omniscience as well as several useful tips on the care and feeding of stoats, opened the dining room door for her.

Sally nodded graciously to the butler as she passed through the doorway. "Thank you, Dab—"

She caught sight of Lucien at the sideboard, spearing a kipper, and her tongue froze.

"—ney," she finished numbly.

Dabney closed the door behind her before she could bolt back towards the hall. She wasn't entirely sure it was unintentional. For a split second, she contemplated escape. She needed a shawl—no, she had a shawl. A warmer shawl! Extra hairpins?

It was too late. Lucien had seen her. At least, Sally noticed with a certain grim satisfaction, there were dark circles under his eyes that matched the ones beneath hers.

Although that might be because he had spent the night on a cot while his cousin snored on his bed.

Lucien opened his mouth to say something. It might just have been "Good morning," but Sally wasn't taking any chances. It was best to set the tone early, before he could accuse her of attempting to ravish him.

"What have you done about your cousin?" Sally demanded, before he could say anything.

If he was at all affronted by her lack of a greeting, Lucien didn't show it. "I left a basin by the side of the bed and a pitcher of water on the bedside table," he said mildly. "Beyond that . . ."

It was entirely unfair that he should be so pleasant when Sally had spent the night trying very hard not to remember their kiss, which meant that she had remembered it every time she had tried not to remember it. "That's not what I meant."

Lucien lifted his plate, regarded a kipper with disfavor, and set it down again. "I'd forgotten how grisly these English breakfasts could be." As Sally began to fidget with impatience, he added, in a conciliatory tone, "I intend to speak to my uncle about him."

Sally looked at him sharply. "Not to Sir Matthew Egerton?"

Lucien busied himself in choosing a sausage, a matter which apparently required his full concentration. "Sir Matthew Egerton believes I'm all four horsemen of the apocalypse rolled into one. It would be a wasted interview."

Sally boiled with frustration. "You mean you don't want to expose your cousin to the full force of the law."

"I didn't say that." Lucien carefully transferred a sausage onto his plate, but the extreme precision of his movements told Sally she had hit home. "If my uncle chooses to do so, he can go to Sir Matthew."

It would have been better if he hadn't sounded so entirely reasonable. When, in fact, nothing could have made less sense.

"In other words," said Sally succinctly, "you're not going to do anything at all."

A flush rose in the duke's cheeks. "I told you. I'm going to—"

"I know. Talk to your uncle. Your uncle isn't the one being charged with murder."

Lucien moved abruptly away from the sideboard. "No one has charged me with anything."

"Yet." Sally followed him, spoiling for a fight. "What happens when Sir Matthew Egerton shows up with his Bow Street Runners and a warrant for your arrest? Will you say anything then? Or will you just say 'thank you very much' as they clasp the manacles around your wrists?"

Lucien set his plate down with a clink. "That's ridiculous."

"Is it?" It was sunny outside, but the dining room was in gloom because Lady Henry didn't like the curtains opened. It all made Sally want to stamp her feet with frustration. "You're the duke. Act like one."

Lucien straightened, looking Sally full in the face. "What," he asked, with ominous calm, "is that supposed to mean?"

Chapter Twenty-one

*L*ucien gave Sally his most ducal glare, but Sally wasn't the least bit daunted.

She set her hands on her hips. "All of this. You act like a guest in your own house. You sleep in a cot in your own room."

"Was I meant to leave Hal on the floor?" Lucien's words dripped with sarcasm.

"Yes! On the floor, on the cot, on the settee—"

The landscape conjured up by her words brought with it a host of illicit imaginings that did nothing to improve Lucien's mood.

Sally waved her hands in the air. "It doesn't matter where he slept. The point is that all this is yours. It's your responsibility. And you behave as though you're just passing through."

332 🌿 Lauren Willig

"I have had other matters on my mind," said Lucien, with dangerous civility. "I had my reasons for staying away."

"Yes," said Sally, throwing caution to the winds. "And it's all quite dreadful, but you've been so busy brooding over the past—"

Lucien looked at her with smoldering eyes. "I do not brood!"

"What do you call that, then?" Sally's voice rose with every word. "*As* I was saying, you're so busy brooding over the past that you've entirely neglected the present! What did you plan to do when you solved your parents' murders? Slink back off into the shadows? Do you know what I think?"

"No," said Lucien in clipped tones. "But I am reasonably sure you intend to tell me."

Sally glared at him, her blue eyes as bright and merciless as a cloudless summer sky. "I think that the real reason you stayed away so long had nothing to do with your parents at all. It was because you were afraid that if you came back, you might actually have to take responsibility for all this, and that—*this*—scares you silly."

The sheer injustice of it took Lucien's breath away. Scared? What in the devil was she talking about? What did she know about it? Just because there were hundreds of tenants—thousands of acres—a million decisions he knew nothing about—that had nothing at all to do with any of his actions. Nothing.

And what did Miss Sally Fitzhugh know about it? She hadn't had her family ripped away from her, first, in their deaths, and then again, in the massacre of their reputations. No. She was the center of a loving family circle who protected and cosseted and teased her.

With a flash of disgust, Lucien realized that he was jealous. Sickeningly, indefensibly jealous of the warm circle of affection that surrounded Sally, the affection she bestowed so generously on those around her. He wanted a drawing room that smelled of cinnamon and a child with her pudgy hands smeared with raspberry jam. He wanted, as he had so long ago, to be part of a family, a real family.

What was the point of it? Bile rose at the back of Lucien's throat. He didn't have that sort of family. He had a sister who despised him, a cousin willing to stand back and see him hang, an aunt who wanted him dead, and parents who might not have been at all what he believed them to be.

It was, he decided, all Sally's fault for filling him with these foolish wishes, for making him see Hullingden as the home it could be. Lucien dragged one of the drapes defiantly open, yanking the rope into place on its gilded hook. "It might be better for everyone if you took a little less responsibility."

Sally blinked in the sudden onslaught of light. "I don't—"

"You do," said Lucien shortly. "Whatever it is, you do. You're like—you're like a puppy."

"A puppy?" Sally regarded him incredulously, looking entirely unlike a canine of any species and very much like an irate young lady of considerable good looks.

"Yes." Perhaps it wasn't the best simile, but he certainly

wasn't backing down now. "Constantly bounding around and getting underfoot and snarling up the carpets. Do you ever stop to think before you go charging in?"

"I—," began Sally.

Lucien wasn't prepared to stop. "You're a one-woman cavalry charge! It doesn't matter if it's a windmill at the other end. You'll tilt at it anyway, because: You. Don't. Stop. To. Look. Everyone else's troubles are just so much fodder for your entertainment. Never mind the toes you might tread on in the process."

Sally bristled. "If I'm asked for help—"

"Are you?" Lucien retorted. "Are you? Or do you offer it regardless of whether it's wanted or not? When was the last time you left well enough alone?"

There were two bright spots of color in Sally's cheeks. "That," she said, "is entirely unfair."

"Is it?" said Lucien sharply. "How did you end up on that bloody balcony with me?"

"I was *trying* to save you from fortune hunters." Sally bit down hard on her lower lip. "And you should be grateful that I did! What would have happened if I hadn't been out there with you? If I hadn't, you—"

"Would have dealt with it myself, with a great deal less fuss and bother." The thought that she saw him as that weak, that ineffectual, filled Lucien with gall. "Did you ever stop to think, just once, that perhaps the world might not be in need of your expert advice?"

Sally flinched at the acid in those last two words. She breathed in deeply through her nose. "You seemed to like my advice well enough before."

"I was being polite!" All the frustration of the past night found an outlet in Lucien's voice. "Do you think I enjoy being embroiled in this—this farce?"

The words cracked off the walls.

Sally's face went as pale as porcelain. As abruptly as it had risen, Lucien's anger bubbled away. He ought to feel smug that he had made a dent in that boundless self-confidence of hers. Instead, he felt as though he'd taken a bat to a priceless porcelain ornament just to hear it crack.

There was no triumph in it, only the shards of something precious that used to be whole, but wasn't anymore.

"Well, then," said Sally. "Well, then."

With a pang, Lucien recognized it as what she said when she didn't know what to say, because, being Sally, she couldn't bear to say nothing at all.

He was worse than a cad. He was an idiot.

He took a step towards her. "Sally—"

Sally moved hastily out of his path, her skirt swishing around her legs, speaking rapidly all the while. "You needn't worry. I shan't embroil you any longer. Would you like me to release you from your obligations? There. It's done."

Being beaten around the head with a bat was too good for him. "Don't be hasty."

"But I am. Isn't that what you told me? That I don't think?" Sally's eyes were suspiciously bright. "Besides, it's hardly hasty when we always knew this had to end anyway."

Lucien felt as though he was sinking in a swamp of his own devising. "I didn't mean—"

"We have our betrothal ball tomorrow night. It will be the perfect time to announce our disengagement. It will be our un-betrothal ball." One hand on the doorknob, she paused only long enough to look regally over her shoulder. "Who knows? Perhaps we'll start a fashion."

And with that, she sailed out the door, nearly colliding with Dabney, who managed to scrabble out of the way just in time to escape a doorknob to the nose.

"Sally!" said Lucien, starting after her, only to be thwarted by Dabney, who planted himself smack in the center of his path.

For a slender man, Dabney could take up a great deal of space when he chose.

Behind him, Sally was disappearing through the arch that led into the Great Hall. Lucien could hear the furious slap of her slippers against the marble floor. Her lilac scent still lingered in the air, an olfactory reproach.

He'd been an idiot and he needed to make it right, but for the fact that there was a butler in his path.

"Not now, Dabney," Lucien ground out.

The fact that Dabney had clearly been listening at the keyhole did nothing to improve Lucien's mood.

Dabney neatly blocked him, all without appearing to move. "Lord Henry wishes to see you, your grace."

The last flounce of Sally's jonquil yellow skirt swished through the arch, like sunshine disappearing behind a cloud.

What in the devil was it that Dabney was saying? Oh, yes. Uncle Henry. Lucien bounced from one foot to the other, trying to get a glimpse of Sally over Dabney's shoulder. "Tell Lord Henry that I will be with him presently."

Despite an entirely bland countenance, Dabney still managed to convey an air of extreme reproach. This, after all, was the man who had fished Lucien out of the frog pond when he was a five-year-old. "I had the impression it was quite urgent, your grace."

The very fact that Dabney was calling him "your grace" rather than "Master Lucien" was a clear indication that Lucien was out of favor.

Brilliant. He'd alienated not only his betrothed, but his servants as well. It might have something to do with the fact that Dabney was a font of information on the care and feeding of stoats, a fact of which Lucien, despite a childhood at Hullingden, had been ignorant. It had taken Sally all of fifteen minutes to ferret it out, and to win Dabney's undying devotion by soliciting his advice on all matters stoat.

According to Patrice, who heard such things in the servants' hall, Sally had also, in that brief space, managed to recommend a poultice for the gamekeeper's daughter's sore leg, and warmed the cockles of Cook's heart by asking for her recipe for raspberry jam.

Sally, thought Lucien grimly, would make a brilliant Duchess of Belliston. Not the "go to London and sparkle at parties" sort of duchess, but the "organize the county gentry and bring all the tenants soup" sort of duchess. The sort of duchess his mother had never tried to be. The sort of duchess that his Aunt Winifred so desperately wanted to be, but wasn't, even aside from the small fact of her not being the duchess.

Sally would be a brilliant duchess. But he wasn't that duke.

That was the devil of it. Sally was right. Completely, undeniably right. Lucien didn't know the first thing about being the Duke of Belliston. In addition to Hullingden, there were three other, lesser estates, at least one of which had been deeded to Clarissa upon his parents' deaths. Lucien was sketchy as to the details of what fell within the entail and what didn't; he had never bothered to find out.

First he had been too young, and then—it had been easier to be indignant and alienated than to come home and face his responsibilities.

The realization struck Lucien like a cannonade. All of those years, wandering the world, feeling sorry for himself, being cosseted by Tante Berthe. He ought to have been here, learning how to care for his tenants, doing his duty by Clarissa. There he was, envying Sally the warmth of her relations with her family, her easy camaraderie with her friends, as though one were either blessed with such things or one weren't. Maybe it wasn't a matter of blessing. Maybe it was a matter of working at it.

He was the one who had run away all those years ago; he was the one who had made himself a stranger to his lands, a stranger to his family. No one had done that to him; he had made those choices for himself. And he didn't know how to fix that any more than he knew what to say to Sally to make that light behind her eyes come back, that boundless self-confidence that was so much a part of her, that made her sparkle like a royal firework display.

He'd certainly fouled that up, hadn't he? Maybe Clarissa was right. Maybe they were a cursed race. Maybe the wrong ancestor had sacrificed the wrong chicken at the wrong time.

Except that sacrificing chickens made him think of Sally, and her odd grudge against poultry.

What did she have against chickens? Lucien wondered irrelevantly. As matters stood, it was unlikely he would ever find out.

Dabney pointedly cleared his throat. "Lord Henry is in his office, your grace."

"Yes, yes, I know." The last thing Lucien wanted was an interview with Uncle Henry, but the alternative, seeking out Sally and trying to figure out what to say, was even more alarming.

With chilling formality, Dabney said, "The office is—"

Apparently Lucien was still being punished. "I know the way. It hasn't been that long."

"Your grace," Dabney said gravely, and melted away into the dark recesses of the hall.

It was amazing how much reproach could be packed into

two little words, uttered with the utmost deference and respect. Lucien wondered if it was something that was taught to good butlers along with how to sneak up on one's employer and terrorize footmen with a single curl of the lip.

Lucien took himself off to his uncle's office, a nook in the old wing in between the formal part of the house and the servants' domain. It had its own exit and entrance, so that tenants and tradesmen could come and go without traipsing through the convoluted corridors of the house. Anything that happened at Hullingden passed through Uncle Henry's office.

It looked just as Lucien remembered. Unlike Uncle Henry's richly appointed study in his house at Richmond, a gentleman's retreat, the office at Hullingden had been designed for use. Shelves along the walls were crammed full of decades of ledgers detailing expenditures on everything from the servants' tallow candles to seed for planting. The large oak table at the center of the room was all but eclipsed beneath piles of invoices, correspondence, and, for some reason that probably made sense to Uncle Henry, a fowling gun.

"Lucien!" Uncle Henry looked up from his notations as Lucien entered. He plunked his pen back in its stand, pushed aside a fat ledger, and stood up, leaning his palms on the tabletop. "Dabney found you, then?"

Lucien inclined his head. "As you see."

If Uncle Henry noticed the edge in Lucien's voice, he didn't comment on it. "I just had a very unpleasant interview with Sir Matthew Egerton."

The day only improved as it went on. Lucien mustered a weary smile. "I wish I could say that surprises me."

Uncle Henry looked grave. "Sir Matthew refuses to be disabused of the notion that you had something to do with the death of that unfortunate woman. He believes you have, as he put it, 'an insatiable craving for blood.'"

That was all the situation needed. Lucien rubbed the heels of his hands against his eyes. "I wouldn't have thought that Sir Matthew would be a reader of *The Convent of Orsino*."

"No, no, not like that." A network of furrows appeared between Uncle Henry's eyes. "The phrase he used was 'like mother, like son.' He believes—"

"That we have the seeds of evil within us." Lucien meant the phrase ironically, but Uncle Henry nodded.

"Just so."

Lucien buried his head in his hands. "Good God."

"There are higher powers to which you might appeal," Uncle Henry suggested.

Lucien lifted his head. "The Almighty?"

"I was thinking more of the Lord Chancellor," said Uncle Henry. "He was well acquainted with your father."

Everyone had been well acquainted with Lucien's father— everyone who was anyone, that is. Lucien's father hadn't been very good at charming the tenantry, but he had been brilliant at dominating the ballrooms and back rooms of both London and Paris.

The thought rose, unbidden, that if he were to face up to his responsibilities—*stop brooding about the past,* whispered Sally's voice—he would be a very different sort of duke than his father had been.

Maybe, thought Lucien, looking at the daunting piles and piles of papers and ledgers, it was time to try.

And not just because he wanted Miss Sally Fitzhugh to look at him with something other than scorn in her bright blue eyes.

"Before we get to that," said Lucien, hating himself for the news he was about to deliver, "I have something I need to tell you."

"Not a confession, I hope," said Uncle Henry, smiling to show that he was joking.

"No." Not his, at any rate. Lucien couldn't think of any way to sugarcoat it, so he just got straight to the point. "The woman who was found dead—Hal was her protector."

"Hal?" Uncle Henry echoed the name, as though it was foreign to the tongue. "My Hal?"

Lucien felt like the embodiment of all evil. It was cruel, doing this to Uncle Henry—Uncle Henry, who had never been anything but diligent and honest. "I'm afraid so."

Uncle Henry sat down, hard.

When he looked up at Lucien, his face was pale, but composed. "Is there any chance that you might be—mistaken?"

Lucien hated to ruin his hopes. "No. I had it from Hal's own lips."

Considerably soaked in gin, but if vino brought *veritas,* then gin was a veritable fountain of truth.

"I see." Uncle Henry's face looked as gray as his hair. "I had suspected—guessed—that he was embroiled with an actress—the signs were there—but I hadn't realized—I hadn't known—that it was this particular one."

"It may be just an unhappy coincidence." Even as he said it, Lucien realized how absurd the words sounded. Gruffly, he added, "I can't believe that Hal is a murderer."

"Thank you." Uncle Henry mustered a faint smile. "You always were a good lad."

Lucien looked around Uncle Henry's office, so familiar and so foreign.

The point is that all this is yours. It's your responsibility. And you behave as though you're just passing through.

Which made Hal his responsibility too.

Lucien took a deep breath. "I'm not going to throw Hal to the wolves."

Whatever Hal might have been prepared to do to him. But Hal was young, untried. He had seen less of the world than Lucien had. He was so painfully young, not just in years but in experience as well.

And, as Sally had pointed out, Hal wasn't the duke.

"We'll see this through as a family."

Uncle Henry rose, stiffly, as though his joints pained him. "Would you mind if I spoke to Sir Matthew myself?"

Lucien hurried to clear a path for him. "I would be grateful for it. As you may have noticed, Sir Matthew has no great love for me. My intervention could hardly improve Hal's case."

Uncle Henry stared blindly over Lucien's shoulder. "This

was meant to be a time of celebration. Your return home after all these years. And we had hoped—" Uncle Henry checked himself. "It was your aunt Winifred's fondest wish that Hal and Clarissa would provide us another reason to rejoice."

Lucien looked at him blankly.

Uncle Henry elaborated. "Your aunt hoped that the betrothal ball might mark not one but two betrothals."

That explained Aunt Winifred's sudden largesse. He ought, thought Lucien wryly, to have realized that Aunt Winifred would never have gone to so much trouble for the small matter of his nuptials. It had just never occurred to him that she might have an ulterior motive. Particularly since neither Hal nor Clarissa appeared to have the least desire to be betrothed. At least, not to each other.

But Lucien wasn't going to say that to Uncle Henry, not when he looked like an old chair that had lost its stuffing.

"There is no reason any of this needs to be made public," Lucien said quickly. "I'm sure once Sir Matthew investigates, he'll realize that Hal's involvement is purely incidental."

It would have been better if Lucien had believed what he said. Right now, he wasn't sure what to believe.

"Yes," said Uncle Henry heavily. Coming around the table, he rested a hand on Lucien's shoulder, saying with false heartiness, "Let's not allow this to overshadow the occasion, shall we? It's not every day that the duke takes a duchess."

Oh, hell. On top of everything else, how was he meant to explain the sudden dissolution of his betrothal?

Sally not speaking to him would probably be a clue.

He should have gone after her. He should have bowled Dabney over and apologized to her right there and then. He should have told her he was an idiot and begged her to stay.

Not just for the ball.

Forever.

"I can't tell you how delighted I am." Uncle Henry walked with Lucien to the door, his hand as heavy as a shackle on Lucien's arm. Lucien only halfway heard him. "It's time to put the past behind us and focus on the future. Your Miss Fitzhugh may not be quite what I would have chosen for you—"

Why the devil not?

"Oh?"

"But she'll do very well, very well, indeed. She, er, seems to have a natural talent for the role. Whatever her plans for the kitchen."

Lucien felt like he was sinking deeper with every word. "As to that—"

"No, no, you needn't explain. It's natural a bride would wish to set her mark on her own home. And," Uncle Henry added damningly, "it is quite clear that she cares for you a great deal."

She did? Illogically, Lucien felt his spirits lift, before he remembered that, in fact, she was only going to care for him until roughly midnight tomorrow.

All Hallows' Eve.

Would she have maintained the pretense of the betrothal longer if he hadn't made such an ass of himself? And why did it matter one way or another?

Unless, of course, he held on to the fantasy that the pretense wasn't just a pretense.

That had never been part of the plan. He'd had no intention of staying at Hullingden, no intention of making a life for himself here.

No intention of falling in love.

"Ergh," said Lucien eloquently. Struggling to gain control of the situation, he said rapidly, "Thank you. That's very kind. As to Sir Matthew—"

"Don't let it bother you," said Uncle Henry. "At a time like this, you should be thinking of poetry and roses, not . . . unpleasantness. You just concentrate on that pretty fiancée of yours, and I'll take care of the rest."

There was a special circle of hell reserved for those who entered into false betrothals. "Thank you. That's more than generous. But—"

"You deserve your happiness," said Uncle Henry, adding coals of fire to Lucien's nicely sizzling infernal pit. "It will be nice to see Hullingden become a home again. Your marriage is a source of joy, not just to the family, but to everyone on the estate. The tenants look forward to these things, you know."

"Er—" Lucien didn't know what to say. "This betrothal ball will certainly be an occasion they'll remember."

Chapter Twenty-two

Cambridge, 2004

I wasn't feeling all that festive by the time we arrived at the
Dudley House Halloween Party.

I was freezing in my puff-sleeved "Regency" gown, which
had started life as a thrift shop nightgown, before being embellished into Austenian splendor with a ribbon around the Empire
waist. Long leather gloves completed the look, making it hard for
me to grasp anything with my fingers, a fact I was rapidly discovering as I tried to get a grip on a plastic glass of white wine.

I had a newfound respect for those intrepid ladies of the
early nineteenth century, who had managed to wield sword
parasols in gloved fingers and wear scoop-necked dresses in En-

gland in October. Their constitutions—and coordination—
were clearly far superior to mine.

"So," Colin said. "This is your Halloween party."

I couldn't blame him for making it sound like a question.
The dining hall tables and chairs had been shoved to the side to
make room for the festivities. The room was high-ceilinged,
classical in style with the woodwork painted white, but nothing
could quite disguise the fact that it was still a dining hall, or that
the other partygoers looked, from a distance of five years, quite
painfully young.

This was really an event for first- and second-years, people
still living in their grad school cliques. I hadn't been to any Dudley House events since . . . Well, I forgot when. Before England,
at any rate. I'd forgotten just how college-like it all was.

I'd brought Colin because I wanted to show him what my
grad school life was all about. But it wasn't my grad school life
anymore. It hadn't been for a very long time. I didn't know these
new people. I'd gone to this party my first year of grad school
and had a riotous time with my clique. Of that bunch, Megan
and I were the only ones left on campus. My friends were almost
all gone, away doing research, writing up elsewhere, in junior
faculty jobs at far-flung campuses. Or they had taken their interim master's degree and run, off to the real world, to non-
academic jobs. One was a lawyer now, another a middle-school
history teacher.

Somehow, when I wasn't looking, the world had changed
around me. I didn't belong here anymore.

I just wished I knew where I did belong.

Colin rested his own glass on the edge of the bar. "Would you excuse me for a moment?"

I looked up at him, one of my hairpins slipping. "Isn't that usually my line?"

The touch of his hand against the two-inch gap between glove and sleeve was warm, but his smile was perfunctory. "I'll find you here?"

By the bar? It seemed the most appropriate place. I wasn't quite sure what else to do with myself. I didn't know anyone in any of the chattering, squealing groups.

"You'll find me here," I confirmed, and managed to down my glass without spilling more than a few drops down my cleavage.

Colin had come in black tie. I wasn't sure if he was meant to be James Bond, or if it was just that he didn't have anything costume-y, but, either way, he looked unfairly handsome in evening dress with his bow tie rakishly askew. For a moment, I could imagine him as an undergrad at Cambridge, before his life became complicated, happily boozing it up at the May Balls.

I wished I had been there for that.

Or maybe not. If I'd known him then, we wouldn't be who we were now. I liked this Colin, even with his maddening reticence. I just wished he would tell me what was bothering him. It was there, between us, whatever it was, like an elephant in the room. And there was no space in my studio apartment for the two of us, much less a metaphorical pachyderm.

Not that I should talk. I was just as bad. When Colin had

asked me how my meeting with my advisor had gone, I'd gushed, "Not bad. Great!" and dragged him off to Casablanca for drinks, where I'd downed too many grasshoppers and talked brightly about movies I hadn't seen.

Telling Colin—telling anyone—would make that conversation too real. As it was, if I kept it to myself, I could pretend it hadn't happened, that I was still on track to graduate in June, or, at worst, next September. Theoretically, I could still graduate in June. I could hand in my dissertation as it was, and my committee would, probably, pass it. There were the requisite number of footnotes, after all. I'd have the letters behind my name, but my job prospects would be next to nil. Professor Tompkins wouldn't put his clout behind a product he considered subpar.

The alternative? Tear it up and rewrite it from scratch. "Fundamentally reconceiving the project"—that was the phrase Professor Tompkins had used.

Which meant, by extension, fundamentally reconceiving my future. I could take another three years to write a completely new dissertation and make Professor Tompkins happy. Or I could step back and ask myself some hard questions about what I was doing and what I wanted. How much was it worth to me to finish the PhD? Did I really want to be a professor?

And what would Colin think when he found out that my career had broken up with me?

"I'll take another of those, please," I said to the student bartender, who obligingly filled my glass back up and took my little yellow ticket.

If the night went on as it had begun, I was going to need a whole roll of those yellow tickets.

I waved to Megan, who was there in her capacity as a Conant Hall RA, mothering the little first-year grad students. She'd come dressed as a cat, in a black leotard and paper ears.

"Not a vampire?" I shouted over the din of "Monster Mash," pathetically grateful to see someone I knew.

"I'm off duty," she bellowed back. She looked over my shoulder. "Is Colin here?"

"Bathroom," I mouthed.

Megan said something incomprehensible.

"Huh?"

She made a frustrated face, gesturing in wordless annoyance at the student DJ, who appeared to have turned the sound system up to eleven. "Introduce me later."

I stuck two thumbs in the air to indicate consent. "Will do."

Assuming Colin reappeared sometime in this century. The puffed sleeves of my Regency gown were beginning to itch and my hands were sweaty inside the long leather gloves.

I fidgeted, looking at the place where my watch would have been, had I been wearing one.

The student bartender poured me another drink, this time without being asked, and without a yellow ticket.

I decided it was time to move away from the bar. Blotto was not the way I wanted to end the evening.

Wasn't this supposed to be the night of my birthday surprise?

Surprise! My boyfriend had disappeared on me.

My imagination began to run rampant. Maybe Colin had planned the sort of big, embarrassing scene one always sees at the end of Rom Coms. The DJ would stop the music, and Colin would take the microphone, singing—

No, wait. That had been Heath Ledger in *10 Things I Hate About You.*

If I was going to model my life on a movie, I should at least try not to pick a teen one. Not to mention that that sort of grand scene was entirely alien to Colin's character.

But all the same . . .

I wandered out into the crowd, keeping an eye out for Colin. The run of costumes included the usual vampires, pirates, and witches, mingling with the more abstruse. I spotted two Beethovens, an Adam Smith (minus his invisible hand), and a very boozy Heidegger. But no Colin.

Gathering my skirts in one hand, I forged towards the dining hall doors, only to come up short as someone called my name.

It was a voice I hadn't heard in a very long time.

For a moment, I was caught in an odd sort of temporal limbo. It was 1999 and I was a first-year grad student again, here in Dudley Dining Hall, with that cute Gov professor calling my name.

It had never occurred to me at the time to ask what a junior professor was doing hanging out with the twenty-two-year-olds.

I turned, trying not to trip on my hem. It wasn't 1999. And

I wasn't that twenty-two-year-old anymore. "Grant! How nice to see you!"

My ex-boyfriend appeared to be dressed as junior faculty circa 1970, complete with tweed jacket with leather elbow patches, an ascot at his throat, and a pipe in one hand. The other hand was wrapped firmly around the waist of Amy-the-Art-Historian, the infant for whom he had dumped me nearly two years ago.

It felt like much longer.

"Eloise." Grant's voice was like Betty Crocker Devil's Food Cake, just a little too rich. "What a charming surprise. You remember Amy?"

Hell, yes, I remembered Amy. The last time I'd seen her, she had been making out with my boyfriend at my department's Christmas party. It was hard to forget something like that.

This time, she was dressed as La Primavera, in a skimpy white dress, a garland of plastic flowers, and an exuberant blond wig, which seemed appropriate, given that she had to be a good decade younger than her boyfriend.

"Hi," I said.

"Hi." Amy shot me a decidedly hostile look from under her long blond wig. I guess no one ever likes to see the ex. And goodness only knew what Grant had told her about me. My guess was that it was along the standard "she doesn't understand me" lines.

Which usually means that the other person understood you all too well.

In retrospect, I owed a huge debt of gratitude to Amy. She had kept me from wasting more time on Grant. Because, with Grant, it had always been all about Grant.

"I'm surprised to see you here." Grant removed the stem of his pipe from his lips. "Haven't you finished yet?"

If Colin was going to stage a grand romantic gesture, now would be the time. Anyone? Anyone? Bueller?

I managed to keep my fixed smile on my face. "I'm planning to finish up this spring. Are you still in the Gov department?"

He looked mildly annoyed. "I'm on sabbatical this year."

"He's working on a book," piped up Amy-the-Art-Historian, sidling a little closer to her man in an attempt to shield him from predatory exes.

"Great to see you both, but"—I lifted the glass of wine I still held in one hand—"I promised my boyfriend a drink."

"Oh?" Grant made a point of looking for my imaginary boyfriend.

"He's visiting from England," I added, to add verisimilitude to what was otherwise a bald and unconvincing lack of boyfriend. "We met over there."

I really needed to make my lips stop moving. Who cared what Grant thought? I didn't. Not anymore.

Well, mostly not. No one wants to look pathetic in front of an ex, even one of the pond scum variety.

"There was an Englishman on the phone in the foyer." Grant gave a little smirk. "Is that one yours?"

A phone call?

Admittedly, it wasn't the most scintillating of parties, but that was no reason to abandon me. I struggled with a little flare of annoyance. If Colin had run off to make a phone call, he must have a good and sufficient reason for doing so.

At least, he had better have a good and sufficient reason.

"He's been planning some sort of mysterious birthday surprise for me." I smiled a phony woman-to-woman smile at Amy-the-Art-Historian. "He's gone all Double-O-Seven about it. Anyway." I waved the glass of wine about, sloshing some on the worn floorboards. "I should be going. Good to see you both."

"You too, Eloise." The sound of my name on Grant's lips felt uncomfortably overfamiliar.

I waggled my fingers and hightailed it out the double doors into the foyer. Sure enough, there was Colin, cell phone to his ear, one shoulder turned to the wall to create a little zone of privacy.

Not jumping out of a cake.

Okay, that was it. I was officially cutting myself off. No more wine for me.

Although the idea of a Colin-sized cake really was pretty funny.

"Mm-hmm," said Colin, looking grave. "Right."

Concern replaced annoyance. Colin's great-aunt, ageless as she always seemed, was getting on in years. And then there was his sister, who seemed to lurch from meltdown to meltdown. Had we ever been to a party that hadn't been interrupted by a Serena meltdown? I would be hard-pressed to name one.

They do say that when you marry someone, you marry their

family as well. Dating Colin was a bit like dating the Addams Family. They were ookey and kooky and you couldn't take one without the others.

I was mostly okay with that. Mostly.

I marched up and tapped Colin on the shoulder. "Hey!"

With an "Mm-hmm. Right. Cheers," Colin clicked END on the call. He tucked his phone away in his pocket and turned to me with a big, phony smile on his face. "Sorry to keep you waiting. Shall we go back to the party?"

"Is everything okay?"

"Fine," said Colin. "Just fine."

There had been a lot of "just fine" over the past few days. It was beginning to wear on my nerves.

If there was family drama, why not tell me? I'd been there with him for all levels of familial crazy, from his sister puking out her guts to his stepfather blandly renting out Colin's home to a film crew.

Unless, of course, it wasn't anything to do with his family at all. It wasn't the right time for calling England unless he was speaking to an insomniac.

But, then, what? And why hide it from me?

Despite my smug words to Grant, it didn't sound like a birthday surprise in the making.

"Who was that?" I asked, automatically taking a sip from the glass in my hand. It tasted like battery acid.

"No one."

Right. That was no one like I was Mother Teresa. I tugged on Colin's sleeve. "What's going on?"

"Nothing." Colin rested a hand against the small of my back, steering me back towards the dining hall. "Would you like another drink?"

"I've had enough." The wine tasted sour in the back of my mouth. I resisted the pressure of Colin's hand. "And it's not nothing. Something's going on. What aren't you telling me?"

"It's nothing like that," Colin said reassuringly, which would have been more reassuring if I'd had any idea what "like that" was meant to mean. "Let's rejoin your party."

I took a deep breath, which did interesting things to the bodice of my Regency gown. (Thank you, ahistorical Wonder Bra!) "Let's go somewhere else." There had been too much weirdness over the past two days. "I think we need to talk."

Words that tend to act like Kryptonite on the average red-blooded male.

Colin didn't argue. "I'll get your coat."

The October night was cold and dark, broken by the sounds of revelry. I'd planned for us to go to Finale, the dessert place in the Square, for post-party drinks, but, by unspoken agreement, we headed back to my place instead. Some discussions are best held in private.

I dumped my coat on the blanket chest and scooped up the battered old plastic pumpkin that sat in the middle of my kitchen table. "Halloween candy?"

"Please." My sofa squeaked as Colin lowered himself onto the sagging cushions.

I'd bought that sofa—used—my second year of grad school, when I had moved from the dorms into my studio apartment, the very first place I had ever lived on my own. At the time, it had been just right. Now, like the rest of my apartment, it seemed too small, too small and vaguely shabby.

I lowered the plastic pumpkin to Colin, who gravely passed over Reese's Peanut Butter Cups and Twix Minis with bats on the wrappers, selecting a miniature candy pumpkin.

"So," I said, perching next to him on the edge of a frayed sofa cushion.

"So," Colin agreed, and turned the pumpkin around between his fingers, while I tried not to squirm too visibly.

I dug into the pumpkin, pulling out a chocolate at random. Mr. Goodbar. Fine. I could eat Mr. Goodbar. "Is something on your mind? You've been a little . . . abstracted."

Colin looked up at me. "Good word," he commented, with a shadow of a smile.

"I try." I felt a chill at the elegiac tone of his words, as though they were already a testament to things past. "What's up?"

Colin lowered his head, examining that blasted candy pumpkin as though it were the Rosetta Stone. My heart clenched a little. I knew the top of his head so well, the streaks where the sun had turned his dirty-blond hair to straw, the cowlick at the back.

"Since we've been apart—I've been doing some thinking."

"Mmm?" I said encouragingly.

The bright bulb of the overhead light picked out the hollows below Colin's cheekbones. "You here, me there—it's not the same, is it?"

"Well, no. But it's just—" Just for now? That wasn't true. I peeled the wrapper off a Twix Mini. Inside, the halves had already broken in two. The sight fueled a growing sense of panic. I didn't want to be a lone Twix. "I'll try to come out to England again this spring."

"For how long? Three days? A week?" It would have been easier if Colin had sounded angry. Instead, he just sounded resigned. And that made me very, very afraid.

The Twix was melting in my hand, leaving chocolate streaks on my palm. I didn't want it anymore, but I shoved it into my mouth anyway. "There might be some changes to my schedule. I haven't signed up for any teaching yet next term."

Colin rested his palms on his knees. "That's not a solution," he said firmly. "I won't see you scuttle your career for me."

What if I didn't have a career left to scuttle? But now wasn't the time to tell him. Not when I had the uneasy feeling that we might, inexplicably, be heading towards "It's not you."

I crumpled the Twix wrapper between my fingers.

"It's hardly scuttling," I hedged. "I don't mind."

"But I do," Colin said gently. He took my sticky hand in his, and I tried not to remember alternative versions of this scene that had played in my head, versions that involved a ring and one knee. "This isn't working, is it?"

"No," I said, my throat dry. "But that doesn't mean we shouldn't try."

"On five minutes a day?" Put that way, it did sound absurd. Colin shook his head. "You here, me there—it's just not on."

There was a lump in my throat the size of Sussex. I couldn't think of anything to say. "So what do we do?"

"That's what I've been trying to figure out." Colin squeezed my hands. He looked down at my fingers, giving me a good view of that cowlick of his. "If we're to have a proper chance, we need to be in the same place for more than three days at a time. Which is why—"

"Yes?" My lips hardly moved.

Colin squared his shoulders. "I'm leaving Selwick Hall."

Chapter Twenty-three

Hullingden, 1806

"Am I truly meddlesome and officious?" Sally demanded of her two best friends.

Finally freed from the receiving line, Sally had bolted like a champagne cork from a bottle in the direction of Lizzy and Agnes, both of whom had arrived for the masquerade ball, along with what seemed like the rest of London.

Lizzy and Agnes were among the first group of guests, along with Lizzy's father, Colonel Reid, and her nine-month-old half sister, Plumeria. There really weren't meant to be children at the masquerade, but Colonel Reid had blandly explained that she was part of his costume. Plumeria was currently perched on her father's shoulder, doing her best to live up to her monkey costume by grabbing at footmen's wigs as they passed by.

Turnip, disguised as a giant carnation, was browsing among the comestibles, assisted in this task by Miles Dorrington, who was dressed as a cavalier, complete with a long feather that kept flopping down over his brow. Their wives were a few yards away, deep in conversation with Letty Pinchingdale, who, from what Sally was overhearing, was expecting a fourth addition to the Pinchingdale nursery.

All around them, revelers were reveling, the Vaughns were sneering, and Percy Ponsonby appeared to have got himself tangled up in the train of someone's costume.

In short, it was life as usual.

Except that it wasn't. It had been sheer torture standing there beside Lucien, accepting the congratulations of their guests, when, of course, there was no "their." Their betrothal was about as convincing as Turnip's costume, a trumpery thing, designed only to fool the severely credulous or madly myopic. Sally had pasted a fake smile on her face and smiled and smiled and smiled, when all the while she was stewing inside, fuming and fulminating and altogether too aware of the man standing beside her. The man who didn't want to be beside her.

Fine. If Lucien didn't want her help, he didn't have to have her help. It wasn't as though it made any difference to her, Sally told herself, and bared her teeth in the direction of a new group of guests. She wasn't the one headed for the gallows.

Meddlesome? He should be grateful—grateful!—that she had stepped in out of the goodness of her heart to help him out of his difficulties.

Except that it wasn't all goodness, was it?

Everyone else's troubles are just so much fodder for your entertainment.

Sally couldn't quite shake the guilty, squirmy feeling that there might be the tiniest little grain of truth to what Lucien had said. That did nothing to improve her disposition.

Lucien thought he could manage without her? Sally would just like to see him try. He needed her. He might not see it, but he needed her. Left to himself, he would let his family take over his home and Sir Matthew hang him for a crime he didn't commit—all right, behead him for a crime he didn't commit—and if that was the way he wanted it, that was just fine with Sally.

She had her own life to get back to.

She had her own comfortable bed in her own comfortable room, in a house where the food was served warm and the company was pleasant and there were no ghosts or Haunted Chambers or secret passageways or brooding dukes. There would be raspberry jam with Parsnip in the mornings and ratafia with Lizzy and Agnes in the evenings and balls and routs and Venetian breakfasts and shopping in Bond Street and then more shopping in Bond Street.

For some reason, that prospect, instead of lifting her spirits, made Sally feel distinctly blue-deviled. Which was ridiculous.

She *liked* her life. She liked her niece, she liked her friends, and she certainly liked shopping.

There was a particular hat she had her eye on at the moment, blue velvet, with the most cunning little feather. It made her eyes ridiculously blue, or would do, as soon as she acquired it.

Sally indulged in a brief, vengeful fantasy of Lucien encountering her in Hyde Park. "How blue your eyes are," he would say—only he wouldn't say nonsense like that, and why was she even bothering herself trying to impress him, when it was obvious that he was an ungrateful boor and she certainly didn't care in the slightest and, besides, she had only kissed him out of pity anyway, if she was thinking about that kiss, which she wasn't. And, even if she was, the nasty things he had said that morning ought to have made it quite clear that there were no tender feelings between them.

Goodness, it was exhausting living in her head.

Sally turned on her two friends. "Well?" she asked ferociously. "Am I meddlesome and officious?"

Her two closest friends exchanged a look. Lizzy was dressed as her namesake, Elizabeth I, complete with orb, scepter, and long rope of pearls. Agnes, going back to her rural roots, had come as a shepherdess, with a stuffed sheep under one arm.

Agnes nervously fingered the ears of her sheep. "Only in the nicest possible way," she said earnestly. She turned to Lizzy. "Don't you agree?"

Lizzy tapped Sally's arm with her scepter. "We wouldn't love you so much if you weren't."

"But— But I—" Sally looked from one to the other, her words sputtering to a halt. There was concern on Agnes's face, wry understanding on Lizzy's. Neither was a comforting response. "But I thought you wanted my help."

"Always," said Lizzy, and squeezed her hand.

"Sometimes it's even helpful," piped up Agnes.

Lizzy whacked Agnes with her scepter. "Hush," she said imperiously. "You're meant to be making her feel better, not worse."

"I—" Sally didn't even know what to say. She felt bare and cold in her Diana the Huntress costume. The white tunic wasn't particularly skimpy, but she felt exposed all the same. Her arrows were flimsy, trumpery things, mere straws against the monumental sense of hurt that enveloped her.

Sally lifted Lady Florence out of her specially designed quiver and buried her fingers in the animal's sleek fur. Lady Florence squirmed irritably, twisting out of Sally's grasp.

Wonderful. Even her stoat didn't want her company.

"You might have told me," Sally said stiffly. "I had no idea I was such a burden."

"Don't be silly." Lizzy scooped up Lady Florence and dumped her back in Sally's quiver. "You have brilliant plans. And anyone who tells you otherwise isn't worth your time. Just think about all the scrapes we've been in together. Would anyone else have thought of immobilizing a spy by sitting on him?"

"You were the one who did the sitting." Sally's voice felt scratchy. "And he wasn't a spy."

"Yes, but he might have been," argued Lizzy. "And you were the one who secured him with your sash. You led the way. Just as you always do."

The faux jewels dotting Lizzy's bodice sparkled just a little too brightly. It was the candlelight—that was all. Sally blinked the inexplicable moisture from her eyes.

"Thank you," she said gruffly. She felt suddenly, deeply ashamed of how much she had resented Lizzy's success. Her friend was truer than she had been. "Thank you for being here."

"Each for each, that's what we teach," Agnes solemnly intoned the motto of Miss Climpson's Select Seminary.

Lizzy rolled her eyes. "Did you really think we would miss your betrothal ball?"

"Don't you mean my un-betrothal ball?" said Sally bitterly.

"I didn't know there were such things," said Agnes.

"Well, this one is." Sally had never discussed with Lucien how they would end it. Should she storm off the dance floor? Cause a scene in the conservatory? She had promised to free him and free him she would.

"You do realize," Lizzy said craftily, "that when you cry off, it's going to make the rumors about the duke that much worse."

Sally felt a momentary twinge of guilt. What was it Lucien had said? That she played with people's lives like toys? If she hadn't meddled, they wouldn't be betrothed. And if they weren't betrothed—they wouldn't have to become unbetrothed.

"It can't be helped," said Sally shortly. She rubbed her gloved hands along her bare arms. "It was going to end sooner or later. You know it's only a pretense."

Even if that kiss last night hadn't felt like a pretense at all. It had felt—well, rather as though Lucien wanted to be kissing her.

Before he had announced that it was a mistake.

"Mmm," said Lizzy.

No one could be quite so loving or quite so maddening as Lizzy. *Mmm?* What was "Mmm" supposed to mean? Sally glowered at her friend.

Lizzy hefted her orb. "Don't look at me. Your pretense is coming this way."

And he was. Sally watched the crowd part as the Duke of Belliston crossed the Great Hall, darkly handsome in a crimson doublet and tights and floppy shoes that ought to have looked silly, but, on Lucien, didn't look silly at all.

Maybe it was the tension that seemed to hover in the air around him; maybe it was the dark hair tumbling around his brow, giving him the look of a Renaissance grandee; maybe it was the effect of those tights, but no one was laughing. Far from it. Georgiana Thynne was eyeing the duke with unabashed admiration, and Delia Cartwright was batting her lashes hard enough to create a gale a county away.

Sally felt a surge of indignation. That was her duke.

Only, he wasn't. Sally grasped at the embers of her anger. He didn't want her here and she didn't want to be here, so there.

Or something along those lines.

"Ladies." Lucien's voice matched his doublet, rich and velvet-smooth. He made an elegant leg, the tight fabric of his tights lovingly displaying every ripple of muscle.

"Duke," said Sally, drawing herself up to her full height. Her hair fell in a ripple of carefully contrived golden curls from a knot at the back of her head. She took comfort in the knowledge that her silk tunic glittered with hidden silver threads and the pearls at her ears and throat were the equal of anything the Belliston coffers had to offer.

"So formal?" said her betrothed. His dark eyes met hers, and Sally felt a flush begin to creep up her throat.

Sally fumed and smarted. He wasn't meant to be acting all—all betrothed when they were about to be unbetrothed.

"With reason," Sally said tartly. And then, because she couldn't just keep on staring at him, however tempting an option that might be, "You remember Miss Reid and Miss Wooliston, don't you? You met them at my brother's house."

"How could I forget?" Lucien favored her friends with a smile nicely calculated to indicate a certain intimacy.

"May we be among the first to wish you happy?" said Lizzy, and Sally shot her a warning look.

"Thank you," said Lucien, and glanced sideways at Sally.

Sally's teeth dug into her lower lip. She wasn't sure why he was looking at her like that, not when he had made his feelings quite clear this morning. Had he forgotten that she was meddlesome and their kiss was a mistake?

Even if he had, she hadn't.

"Did you want something?" she said ungraciously.

"Yes," Lucien said, and something about the way he said it, the way he was looking at her, as though she were the only woman in the room, made Sally's heart lurch, just a little. He held out a hand to her. "You."

"Me?" Sally's chest was tight beneath her sparkling bodice.

Lucien looked at her quizzically. "We are expected to open the dancing."

"Of course. Naturally. I knew that." Sally hoisted her quiver higher on her shoulder. "If you think you can stomach my company for the length of a quadrille."

"I would be honored if you would favor me with one," Lucien said, and if Sally hadn't known better, she would even think that he meant it.

"Hmph," said Sally.

Why did he have to be so nice? So thoroughly decent? It would be much more pleasant if he would behave like a cad so she could continue to warm herself at the altar of her anger, stewing in a pleasant glow of self-righteousness.

Blast it all, couldn't he even leave her that?

"Don't let us keep you!" Lizzy wielded her scepter with a dexterity worthy of her stepmother's parasol.

Lucien stepped hastily out of the way. "Thank you, we shan't." He held out an arm to Sally. "Shall we?"

Sally took his arm, smiling and smiling and smiling. The faces around them whirled and blurred, a nightmare panoply of grotesques, all teeth and eyes. "You don't have to pretend for Lizzy and Agnes," she said bluntly.

"I'm not pretending." They took their place at the front of the set. Lucien knew he ought to relinquish her hand, but he held on to it all the same, just a moment longer than propriety allowed. They were betrothed, after all.

For the moment.

"You look beautiful," Lucien said softly. There might be other women in the room, women with larger jewels and more elaborate gowns, but none could hold a candle to Sally. Her gown was made of some sort of sparkly fabric, but it was nothing against the bright curls of her hair, the graceful line of her neck, the bright blue of her eyes.

Those eyes were currently regarding him with more than a little hostility. "You're very kind."

"No, I'm not." He was anything but kind. Which brought him to the subject both of them were avoiding. "About this morning—"

"Think nothing of it." Sally sank into a curtsy, her draperies drifting around her. "I'll be gone by tomorrow. You won't have to put up with my meddling any longer. Our association has served its purpose."

"Has it?" Lucien lifted her from her curtsy, moving her into the first figure of the dance. Sally twitched her fingers away from his. "I owe you an apology."

"Apology accepted," said Sally curtly.

"A real apology." They circled away and back again. Lucien found himself thinking unkind thoughts about whichever person had invented these absurd dances, where a couple was apart as much as they were together. How was a man meant to grovel in three-second intervals? "I don't want you to think I'm not grateful for everything you've done."

"There's no need for you to be." A touch of bitterness crept into Sally's voice. "I haven't done anything at all."

"You've done a great deal." Lucien didn't know how to make her see just how much she had done for him. Yes, some of it might have been rather ill-advised, but that was part of what made it so magnificent. So gallant. "You endangered your own reputation to try to save mine."

Sally cast him a sideways look. "I thought I merely played with people for my own sport."

"If I could take back those words, I would."

They came together, their hands pressed palm to palm.

Lucien forced himself to say the words. "Everything you said this morning was true." They circled and came together again. "You were right. About all of it. I have been living too much in the past. I haven't acknowledged my responsibilities."

Sally bit her lip, looking back at him over her shoulder as they circled. "You had your reasons."

It was, Lucien thought, just like her to make excuses for him. "I had a twelve-year sulk," he said bluntly. "You've made me realize just what a self-indulgent fool I've been."

"Well, then," Sally said, and Lucien felt some of the tight knot of tension in the small of his back release, because if Sally was saying "well, then," it meant that all wasn't lost.

All around them, women were sinking into curtsies. Lucien hadn't even noticed that the music had stopped.

It was time to press his advantage. "Can we go somewhere? Somewhere we can talk?" Lucien raised a brow. "Or I can just prostrate myself at your feet?"

"And have someone trip over you? Don't be silly. I can spare you a moment," Sally said magnanimously.

Lucien let out the breath he hadn't realized he had been holding. "How very generous of you."

"I try," Sally said regally. Her rodent—er, stoat—peeped over the edge of her quiver at Lucien, yawned, and went back to sleep. "We shouldn't go far."

"We are still betrothed," Lucien reminded her, steering her out of the ballroom.

"For the moment," Sally reminded him.

Lucien looked down at her, his expression inscrutable. "Are you counting the minutes?"

"I thought you were."

Lucien put a hand under her arm. "Not in the way you think."

Somewhere, a clock chimed eleven. Like Cinderella, her deception would be over by midnight.

They turned down a corridor, and then another one. Sally assumed that Lucien knew where he was, because she hadn't the slightest idea. Hullingden hadn't been designed with logic in mind.

Sally chose a door at random. "Here," she said. Before they wandered any farther from the Great Hall.

She pushed open the panel and stumbled into a tropical paradise.

Braziers burned in the corners of the room, creating a sultry warmth. Sally could practically see the heat shimmer in the air. Flowers bloomed everywhere, flowers she had never seen before, flowers for which she had no name. Some were ghost pale. Others flamed with color. Together, they filled the room with their heavy exotic perfume.

Through the glass walls, Sally could see the lanterns that had been hung all about the gardens, shimmering like stars against the dark hedges.

Sally turned in a slow circle, the floating edges of her Grecian tunic brushing the corners of the flower pots. "What is this place?"

There were no lights lit, but the braziers created their own sultry light, lending a warm glow to the haze of heat.

"It was my mother's workroom." Lucien ducked beneath the hanging branch of a richly flowering tree. The white petals clung to his red velvet shoulder, releasing a heady scent. "I hadn't realized Uncle Henry had preserved it."

Impulsively, Sally set a hand on his arm. "Are you all right?" Belatedly, she remembered that he didn't want or need her help. "I mean—"

"I know." Lucien captured her hand before she could retrieve it. "And, yes. Thanks to you."

"Me?" Outside, the lanterns twinkled in the cold, but inside it was all warmth and gentle darkness. The faint glow of the braziers limned Lucien's familiar features and made the gold embroidery on his doublet burn with hidden fire.

"I did a great deal of thinking this morning." Lucien's fingers twined through hers. "Some of it wasn't particularly pleasant."

"Oh?" Sally was having a hard time concentrating on what he was saying, what with all the hand-holding.

"Yes," said Lucien. "I've been a self-indulgent idiot."

"I wouldn't say idiot. . . ."

"But definitely self-indulgent." Lucien released her hand, folding his arms across his chest, and Sally tried to tell herself that she didn't mind. "I sentenced myself to exile, telling myself I wasn't worthy to return until I avenged my parents' deaths. I thought that I was honoring their memory by staying away."

"No one can blame you for wanting vengeance," said Sally encouragingly. "Who wouldn't want an eye for an eye?"

"It wasn't vengeance," said Lucien firmly. "It was a waste. A waste of my life and their legacy. Whatever one might say about my parents, they both lived. They pursued their own passions."

The word seemed to linger in the air between them, charged with all the sweetness of the tropical night.

Aside from the fact that they were in Leicestershire in October.

"Like these flowers?" said Sally, turning hastily away before she could do something foolish. Correction: something more foolish than she had done already.

"Like these flowers," Lucien agreed.

Maybe looking away hadn't been the wisest idea. Sally could feel Lucien's presence behind her, so close that his breath ruffled her intricately arranged curls.

"This was my mother's greatest achievement. She catalogued plants no one had ever seen before."

Lucien's velvet sleeve brushed Sally's bare shoulder as he reached around her to finger the purple leaves of a plant with tiny white flowers.

"They're lovely," said Sally breathlessly. "Truly lovely. It feels as though we aren't in England at all."

All the way in this odd nook of the castle, they might have been on a tropical island, a million miles away, lost in a soundless sea, the lanterns in the garden mere phosphorescence on the foam. Someplace without all of the rules and strictures of society. Someplace where nothing mattered but the two of them.

"Most of the plants are from Martinique." With a twist of his fingers, Lucien broke off a pink flower with a profusion of petals. "They call it the Isle of Flowers."

Leaning forward, he tucked it into the pearl diadem that held the hair back from her brow. The petals brushed her temple, their scent a heady promise of pleasure to come.

"Do they?" Sally ducked around Lucien's arm, walking rapidly down the long aisle between plants.

Before she made any more mistakes.

They had agreed their kiss was a mistake, hadn't they?

Sally's flat slippers slapped against the flagstones of the floor. It was common sense, she told herself, common sense rather than flight. She came to a halt by a large pot holding a tree adorned with unimpressive greenish-white flowers. There was something rather familiar about those shiny green leaves.

"Lucien?" Sally used his name without meaning to. It just slipped out. Sally gestured towards the plant. "Are those the same leaves someone left in your carriage?"

"Don't touch that!" Lucien leapt between Sally and the manzanilla.

"I wasn't planning to," said Sally. Although it was, really, rather sweet that he'd felt the need to defend her from a plant. "It's a manzanilla, isn't it?"

Lucien circled the tree, which looked deeply innocuous for something with the potential to wreak so much havoc. "I hadn't realized it was still here. I had assumed—" He rubbed a hand against his brow. "Foolish of me. It's not as though it was the tree's fault."

"It was this tree?" The plant took on a sinister aspect.

Lucien nodded. "There aren't many of them in England. In fact, I'm not sure there are any. . . ."

His eyes met Sally's as the impact of his words hit them both.

"There might be others," said Sally doubtfully. If there weren't, that meant that whoever had left the manzanilla leaves in Lucien's carriage had come from the castle. She seized on an alternative. "The castle isn't precisely fortified. Anyone might have snuck in here."

"The same person who snuck in and found my father's snuffbox?" Lucien's face was hard in the light of the braziers. "I should have known. I just didn't want to see it. Hal had both the motive and the means."

And a convenient scapegoat in the person of his cousin.

It seemed like a very unsatisfying ending to their investigations. Hal was just so . . . ordinary. It was rather lowering to chase a legendary spy and end up with Hal. But if Hal had, indeed, killed Fanny Logan—which, as Lucien had so reasonably pointed out, he had every reason to do—then it seemed highly unlikely that there was a spy in the mix.

Which meant that they still had no idea who had killed Lucien's parents.

And there was one other slight problem.

Sally dragged her shining skirts slowly down the path between the flowers. "You do realize what this means?"

"Yes," said Lucien heavily. "It means my cousin is a murderer."

Sally waved an impatient hand. "Yes, that too." That wasn't the worst of it. "It means that Miss Gwen was wrong. There is no spy. It means that our betrothal—all of this"—Sally's gesture encompassed the lanterns in the garden, festive decorations for a celebration that wasn't—"was for nothing."

Lucien's head snapped up. "Don't say that." His eyes burned

brighter than the coals on the brazier, smoldering from within. "It wasn't for nothing. You've given me my home back." A hint of amusement quirked the corner of his lips. "You've brought me back from the realms of the undead."

Sally wrapped her hands in the cool silk of her tunic. "I thought you didn't believe in vampires."

"I don't. But there's more than one kind of tomb." Lucien touched her cheek, as gently as the brush of a flower petal. "You rescued me from a mausoleum of my own making. Even if I wasn't terribly gracious about it."

It was rather gratifying to be appreciated, even if it had taken him a while. "You would have done it yourself eventually. I didn't do anything except ambush you in a ballroom."

"And my garden," Lucien pointed out, smiling in a way that did dangerous things to Sally's insides. "Don't forget my garden."

Sally tossed her curls back over her shoulder, striving for normalcy. "How could I? You were absolutely infuriating."

"And you were trespassing," Lucien reminded her. There was a glint in his eye that Sally found deeply unsettling. "Isn't there generally a forfeit in that sort of situation?"

Lucien reached out, twining one of her bright curls around his finger. Sally couldn't take her eyes off it. "If so, you should have taken it at the time," she croaked.

Lucien followed the length of the curl up to her cheek. "I didn't know you then."

"But you do now?" There was something deeply unsettling and exhilarating about that thought.

"Oh, yes," he said, and Sally could feel his breath soft against her lips. "If I had known then . . ."

It was rather close in the greenhouse. Sally was finding it more than a little bit difficult to breathe. "Then what?" she demanded.

"Then this," he said, and kissed her.

Chapter Twenty-four

*H*e kissed her because she looked so damned kissable in the low light of the braziers. He kissed her because he couldn't help kissing her. He kissed her because it was easier than trying to tell her all the confused thoughts that were bumping around in his head, all of which began with "stay," and ended, frighteningly, dangerously, with "love."

He didn't want to think of love. Love was terrifying. Love made you vulnerable. Love hurt. So he kissed her instead, long and hard and desperately, with all the feelings he didn't have the words to express, his hands spreading across the warm silk of her back, her curls tickling his cheek and neck.

"You are so lovely," Lucien said tenderly. "Inside and out."

Sally drew an uneven breath, her breasts rising above the low neckline of her tunic. "What about meddlesome?" she demanded.

"That too," said Lucien. He couldn't stop the foolish smile that was spreading across his face. Her indomitable will was part of what made her Sally, and he wouldn't have her any other way. "Especially that."

"But—," Sally began, which promptly turned to "mmrph" as Lucien leaned forward and kissed her again, more thoroughly this time, the crushed petals releasing their exotic fragrance in the air around them, and then to a very different sort of "mrrph" as her fingernails rasped against the velvet of his tunic and her rings caught in his hair and she kissed him back as though her very survival depended upon it.

Which it might, given that he seemed to be holding her at a rather gravity-defying angle.

Dragging his lips from hers, Lucien flicked aside one long golden curl and kissed the base of Sally's ear, just below a dangling pearl that teased his nose; he kissed the side of her neck, the slope of her shoulder; he kissed the skin exposed by the embroidered straps that held up the bodice of her tunic, the gold of the embroidery dark and dull next to the bright color of her hair.

"Sally," he said raggedly, but the response came not from Sally, but from behind him, as someone cleared a throat.

Sally let out a squeak and pulled back, yanking at the strap of her tunic. Her cheeks were flushed, her hair rumpled, her carefully arranged curls falling the wrong way forward over a diadem that was distinctly askew.

Her eyes darted from Lucien—to someone just over his shoulder—and back to Lucien again.

"Well," she said faintly. "Well, then."

Lady Florence lifted her head from her quiver and subjected Lucien to a frankly appraising stare.

"Go away," Lucien snapped, his eyes intent on Sally. There was so much that needed to be said, if only he could think of the way to say it. And who the hell's business was it but their own? They were betrothed, after all. Anyone with any decency would turn around and scurry away, not stand there harrumphing like a dowager with a chest infection. "This room is occupied."

"I see that," came the apologetic voice of Lucien's former tutor. "I hate to intrude, but it really is rather urgent."

Sally whisked around Lucien so quickly that Lady Florence gave an indignant squeak from the depths of her quiver. "Mr. Quentin! What are you doing here?"

"Intruding," said Lucien flatly, fighting a wave of irritation mingled with more than a little fear that, once broken, the moment would never come again, that Sally would whisk away out of his life, leaving him darkling.

Love. He hadn't mentioned love. Perhaps he ought to have done so before he swooped. But she was looking so kissable that swooping had felt absolutely imperative at that particular moment.

Sherry stepped into the room, a cloak still draped around his shoulders, spattered with mud or a very convincing facsimile thereof. "With good cause, I promise."

"It had better be very good cause," Lucien said grimly.

His eyes slid towards Sally, who had drawn herself up with her usual aplomb, as if she were at St. James and ready to be presented. Even ruffled and befuddled, she looked like a queen. No, a duchess.

His duchess.

Lucien could imagine a dozen Sallys throughout the years: Sally wrangling the tenantry and making them drink soup, whether they wanted it or not; Sally feeding raspberry jam to a child with his dark eyes and her bright gold curls; Sally cream and rose and gold against the crimson sheets of that ducal bed that was far too large for one.

Lucien felt a powerful surge of possessiveness. He hadn't been lying when he said she'd given him his home back; what he hadn't realized was that it was a home only if she was in it with him.

It was a distinctly terrifying thought.

Sally sidled in the direction of the door. "I'll just leave you to it," she said, with a bright social smile. "I'm sure you both have a great deal to speak about."

"No," said Lucien, just as Sherry said, "Yes."

Sally's eyes met Lucien's and then flicked away again. "I'll be in the ballroom," she said quickly. "Dancing. And . . . dancing."

Lucien moved to intercept her. "Wait for me. I'll see you back." With a pointed look at Sherry, he added, "I'm sure this won't take long. And I don't want you roaming the corridors by yourself."

Better to sound overprotective than lovelorn? Lucien quietly gnashed his teeth. All they needed were five more minutes alone. Just five more minutes.

Or maybe ten.

"No, really, it's all right." Sally made an airy gesture with one hand. "I'm in no danger from your cousin."

Lucien grasped at straws. "Are you sure? That note in the carriage—"

"Was pure pretense," said Sally confidently. With splendid illogic, she added, "Hal Caldicott belongs to my brother's club. He wouldn't dare to hurt ME."

And with that, she disappeared out the door in a swish of spangled silk, leaving Lucien torn between affection and frustration.

"I understand you're betrothed?" said Sherry mildly, from somewhere behind him.

"For the moment," Lucien said shortly. He turned reluctantly away from the door. Sally was right; Hal had no reason to hurt her. And if Hal tried, she didn't need those arrows to skewer him. She could do it with one or two well-chosen words. "I assume you didn't come all this way merely to offer your felicitations."

If Sherry was put off by his ungracious tone, he didn't show it. "No—although I assume felicitations are in order?"

For a moment, the urge to pour out his troubles to the man who had once been his confidant was overwhelming. Sherry had always been a good listener. But that had been a long time ago, and the moments were ticking away.

There was the small matter of Hal to be dealt with, but, more importantly, he needed to make sure that Sally didn't break off their betrothal before he had a chance to persuade her otherwise.

He was rather looking forward to the persuading.

"They will be," Lucien said brusquely. "What brings you here?"

Sherry subjected Lucien to a long, searching look, but he didn't press the topic. "We cleaned out Fanny's dressing room this week."

Lucien remembered being there with Sally, in that close, crowded dressing room, back when they scarcely knew each other, when she was Miss Fitzhugh, and he—he had been wrapped in his own despair still.

But not too wrapped in his despair not to notice how infinitely alluring Sally was. Even when she was ordering him about.

"Yes?" said Lucien gruffly.

"I found this beneath Fanny's dressing table." From the folds of his cloak, Sherry brought out a grimy piece of paper. He handed it to Lucien. "I thought you should see it."

Automatically, Lucien took it from him, smoothing out the crumpled page. It was good, cream-colored paper, but it had been crushed and crumpled, the ink on the letters running together, as though the note had been stuffed down a damp bodice in some haste, or crushed in a warm hand.

The words were blurry, but still legible, written in a strong, clear hand. "If you come to Richmond on the evening of the tenth of October, I am sure we can reach an arrangement to our mutual satisfaction."

The tenth of October. The night of Clarissa's ball. The night Fanny Logan had been killed.

Someone had summoned Fanny Logan to her death. The same someone who had drawn fang marks on her neck. The same someone who had planted Lucien's father's snuffbox by her body.

"I had thought this might be of interest to you," said Sherry quietly. "I assume you didn't write it."

"No." Lucien stared unseeingly at the blurred words. "I didn't even know she existed."

Hal had. Hal had motive. Hal had means.

But this wasn't Hal's handwriting.

Lucien should have realized. He should have realized before, when he received the note in the ballroom, the note in his carriage. All had been on the same cream paper, all written in the same bold, black ink.

None of them in Hal's hand.

Lucien looked up abruptly at his old tutor. "You have no idea who sent it?"

Sherry shook his head. "I know only what I told you—Fanny said that she was moving on to better things. I suspect," he added delicately, "that she might have been blackmailing someone."

Not Hal. Fanny Logan had already drained him dry. What if Mrs. Reid were right? What if a half-mad, scarred French spy were intent on preventing him from accessing his mother's papers? They hadn't found anything particularly damning yet, but that didn't mean that the damning document didn't exist, a document so damning that a man would contemplate murder.

Again.

And again.

Lucien had a fleeting memory of a scattering of manzanilla leaves, and a note, a note on the same cream-colored paper, in the same hand.

Stay away. Or she'll be next.

If Hal hadn't killed Fanny Logan, someone else had. And that someone was still out there, in the writhing, dancing, whirling mob of revelers.

Just waiting for an opportunity to strike.

Lucien thrust the note into his pocket. "Excuse me," he said to his old tutor, his voice hoarse. "I need to find Miss Fitzhugh."

Before someone else found her first.

What had happened to *This is a mistake*? What had happened to *It won't happen again*?

Sally blundered down the corridors of Hullingden Castle, her quiver banging against her back as she passed through a long gallery filled with portraits of long-dead dukes of Belliston. Theoretically, she was in search of the ballroom. In reality, she wasn't in much of a hurry to find it. At the moment, she was grateful for the maze of passageways that separated her from the other partygoers, that provided time for her hot cheeks to cool, and, hopefully, for the marks to fade from her neck.

If Delia Cartwright saw the red blotches, she would start screaming about the vampire's bite. There would most likely be swooning involved.

Maybe there was something to that. It would certainly explain her otherwise inexplicable behavior. Sally's cheeks burned with shame and wounded pride. All it had taken was one little *I'm sorry*, one little *You're so lovely*, and there she was, behaving like—like Lucy Ponsonby. Like one of those silly, simpering creatures out there in the ballroom.

Now, now that she was away from Lucien, surrounded by the censorious stares of some rather grim-looking sixteenth-century Caldicotts, Sally knew exactly what she ought to have said. She ought to have reminded him that he had said their kiss was a mistake; she ought to have pointed out, kindly but firmly, that there was still his cousin Hal to be dealt with. She ought to have told him that she was flattered by his attention, but it would only lead to unnecessary complications should they indulge in such behavior.

The words rolled so glibly off her tongue now. Where had they been then? Where had they been when Lucien was brushing her hair back from her face? Where had they been when his breath was warm on her lips? Where had they been when he had trailed kisses straight down to her shoulder?

Had she slapped him? No. Instead, she'd arched her neck to give him better access.

It was too, too shaming. Where was her pride? She had slapped men for less.

But this wasn't men. This was Lucien. Somehow, while she wasn't looking, he had slipped into a category all his own. When he bantered with her, there was never an edge to it. His teasing had no bite. She felt comfortable with him, comfortable and safe and free to be as outrageous as she liked, knowing that he wouldn't be appalled or disapproving or try to rein her in as so many others had. He liked her as she was. And there was something terribly heady about that.

Not to mention that the man needed her, Sally reminded herself. Had she mentioned that he needed her? Lucien might be a duke, but he was too softhearted to be left to himself. He needed her. He needed her to take that troubled line away from between his eyes and make him laugh. He needed her to teach him the intrinsic value of stoats. He needed—

In her quiver, Lady Florence yawned.

"It's true," Sally insisted, and then felt even worse, because she was arguing with a stoat, for heaven's sake. And everyone knew that stoats were just a whisper away from weasels, and you could never win an argument with a weasel, because they were just too slippery.

All right, she would admit it. She liked the man. She liked him tremendously. She liked the wicked sense of humor that lurked behind that air of reserve, she liked his quiet good manners, she liked his instinctive gentlemanliness.

And she felt obligated to him. That's what it was. Obligation. After all, she had promised him that she would help him out of a coil, and, in doing so, she had created an even more coiled coil. Let it never be said that a Fitzhugh was one to turn her back on her debts.

Sally fought a strange sensation of panic, as if she were clutching a rope that was slipping from her grasp, tearing her palms the harder she tried to hold on to it.

Just because she liked the man, just because she owed him a duty—wasn't "duty" such a nice, noble-sounding sentiment?— just because she owed him a duty didn't mean that there was anything more to it.

Sally decided to focus on duty. Because, otherwise, she might have to admit that she cared. That she cared very much indeed. And that the thought of walking away from Hullingden, walking away from Lucien, leaving things just as they were, made her feel like a shriveled leaf that had lost its tree.

Sally paused at the end of the gallery, just outside the bright circle of light streaming in from the ballroom, watching, unseeing, as the dancers danced and the players played and the gossipers gossiped, all frozen in place as the true horror of her situation dawned upon her.

She could tell herself whatever she wanted, but the fact of the matter was that when she was in Lucien's arms she wanted never to be anywhere else, ever again. It didn't matter if they were in a moonlit greenhouse, or a frosty tundra. His embrace felt like home, as nothing else ever had.

It was insupportable, unthinkable and entirely unacceptable, but there it was.

How on earth had she been so careless as to allow herself to fall in love?

It was all Lucien's fault. It was his fault for being so—so himself.

"Argh!" Sally jumped as a skeletal hand closed over her arm. The hand was attached to a dark sleeve of some rough fabric, which, in turn, was attached to a hideous specter, faceless in the shadows.

"Miss Fitzhugh?" intoned the specter.

"What the— Oh. It's you." Those weren't skeleton fingers; they were white gloves.

Sally's breathing slowly returned to normal as the figure resolved itself into a man in a cassock, the hood pulled up over his head. Jangling metal implements hung from the leather cord around his waist.

Trust Sir Matthew Egerton to come to the ball as the Grand Inquisitor.

"Did you want something?" Sally asked ungraciously. She really wasn't in the mood for Sir Matthew at the moment. She wasn't in the mood for anyone, including herself.

In love. With Lucien. How had that happened?

More importantly, how did she make it stop? Was there a cure? Cold tea? Hot baths? Eye of newt and toe of stoat?

"A word." Sir Matthew pushed the cowl back from his jowls. "In private."

"This really isn't a good time." Really, it was too annoying to be interrupted in the middle of an epiphany. It was her betrothal ball and she could brood if she wanted to. "Perhaps later?"

"Oh, no," said Sir Matthew. The torchlight glinted off his pale eyes, making them glow an uncanny red. "This is precisely the time."

Chapter Twenty-five

"Have you seen Sally?" Lucien caught up with Turnip Fitzhugh just in front of the refreshment table.

Sally wasn't in the gallery, she wasn't in the music room, and, as far as he could tell, she wasn't in the ballroom.

Lucien felt a chill that cut right through the velvet of his tunic. He should never have let her leave that conservatory by herself.

He tried to take comfort in the fact that Sally was the very opposite of a wilting violet. And she was armed, in a fashion.

But even Sally could be taken by surprise.

Lucien's imagination presented him with a hundred horrible possibilities. A hand, reaching out of the darkness, grabbing Sally's golden curls, bending her head back, setting a knife against her neck.

Leaving her pale and cold on a bench in the garden.

"I say, don't want to ruffle the petals, don't you know," said Turnip, and Lucien realized that he was clutching the front of the other man's costume with both hands.

Lucien abruptly let go. "Sally? Have you seen her?"

"Thought she was with you," said Mr. Fitzhugh, with, Lucien decided, a criminal lack of concern. "Busy being betrothed and all that sort of thing."

"She's not." Bile rose in the back of Lucien's throat. "I was hoping she might be with you."

"Misplaced her, have you?" said Mr. Fitzhugh genially.

"Something like that." Why hadn't he shoved Sherry out of the room and wrapped her in his arms and held her tight? Yes, a French spy would still be out there, but he and Sally would be together.

If he found her—no, *when* he found her—he wasn't going to make that mistake again.

"Your grace?"

It was one of the footmen, clad like all the others in the Belliston livery of crimson and gold. But all Lucien saw was the silver tray in his hands.

A silver tray bearing a single sheet of cream-colored paper.

Inside, there was only one line, written in a bold, black hand:

Miss Fitzhugh awaits you in the Folly.

———

"Is this entirely necessary?" Sally demanded, as Sir Matthew led her into the mirrored gallery through which Lucien had taken her two days before.

Then, the mirrors had sparkled with late-afternoon sunlight. Tonight, theirs was a chill brilliance, lit by sparse clusters of candles in branched holders. The only furniture in the long, narrow room was backless benches set at intervals along the walls, upholstered in a pale blue that seemed tinged with frost.

Sally could see her own form, tall and pale in her spangled gown, reflected back at her again and again from the tall mirrors.

Lady Florence stuck her narrow head up, favoring Sir Matthew with a distinctly inimical stare.

"This is only necessary because you have made it so." Sir Matthew closed the door behind them with a distinct click.

The sound seemed to reverberate down the corridor, like a coin dropped into a deep well.

Sir Matthew stalked forward, the folds of his robe hissing against the parquet floor. "When you gave your evidence to me, you neglected to mention that you were affianced to the Duke of Belliston."

Sally flicked a long curl back behind her shoulder. "I wasn't. Not then."

"Is this the way the duke repays you for your perjury?" Despite herself, Sally felt a frisson of unease. In his dark robes, there was something decidedly sinister about the magistrate. "Is a coronet sufficient to pervert the course of justice?"

"Justice?" That was rich. Lady Florence bared her teeth. Sally patted her stoat on the head. "Is it just to hound an innocent man? Is it just to condemn someone based on mere rumor and speculation? I don't call that justice. I call it laziness."

Sir Matthew fingered the jangling chain hanging around his waist. "You aren't going to make this easy, are you?"

"If by easy, you mean am I going to tell you what you want to hear, then no." If Sir Matthew thought she was that easily intimidated, he had another think coming. Sally lifted her chin, her nostrils flaring. "If you had bothered to do your job, you would know that the woman in question was the paramour of Mr. Caldicott. But are you hounding him? No. Instead, you let yourself be distracted by a ridiculous rumor about vampires."

If Sir Matthew was taken aback by the news about Hal, he recovered himself quickly. "There's no need to continue your act with me, Miss Fitzhugh."

"It's not an act," Sally said shortly. "The duke is the best and the kindest of men and I would count myself fortunate to be his bride under any circumstances. I would count myself fortunate if Hullingden were a hovel and the duke were a tenant on his own estate. I would count myself fortunate if he were one of those annoying dancers with the bells and the little bits of cloth. I would—"

"Yes, yes." Sir Matthew hastily held up a hand to ward off further examples, which was a good thing, since Sally was rapidly running out of odd occupations. "You are determined, aren't you?"

Sally bared her teeth at him. "You have no idea."

"I am aware"—Sir Matthew's robe whispered against the floor—"that many ladies view a coronet as something to which to aspire, but, in the interest of your own safety, I implore you to reconsider your decision."

She hadn't felt unsafe until now.

Sally's hand snuck back towards her quiver, where she had stowed, in addition to Lady Florence, a few ornamental arrows. Her little golden bow was primarily for show, but it was strung, and the arrows did have pointy tips. They probably wouldn't do more than scratch, but the surprise of it might give her time to bolt.

"You are very kind to take an interest in my matrimonial matters, Sir Matthew," Sally said coolly, "but, as this is my betrothal ball, I really ought to be getting back. Before I'm missed. Because this is my betrothal ball. Where people will be looking for me."

"A betrothal to a villain? To a murderer?" Sir Matthew's eyes burned like the fires of a dozen autos-da-fé. "You are playing with fire, Miss Fitzhugh. And those who play with fire—"

"Generally get burned. I know." The oddity of it was that Sir Matthew appeared entirely sincere.

Much in the way that Tomás de Torquemada had been sincere. Sincerity and torture weren't necessarily mutually exclusive.

"No. You don't know." The metal tips of Sir Matthew's belt jangled as he stalked forward. "What would you say if I told you that madness ran in the duke's blood? What would you say if I told you that the man was a danger to himself and to society?"

"I would tell you," said Sally smartly, "that you ought to look in a mirror."

Sir Matthew stopped short, his expression one of outrage. "You think I— You believe that I am—"

"Deranged," Sally provided helpfully. "Delusional. Consumed by your own dark fancies."

Sir Matthew was between Sally and the door, but there was the other door, the one that led out into the gardens. If she could just back along that way . . .

"There is nothing fanciful about that woman's death." Sir Matthew's hands clenched into fists. "Miss Fitzhugh, the duke believes himself to be a doomed creature of the night. He lurks in shadows. He lusts for blood. He has fallen prey to his own fancies. Can you still defend him after you have seen, with your own eyes, the destruction of which he is capable?"

"The destruction of which you think he is capable," Sally hedged.

When it came to falling prey to fancies, she began to wonder if Sir Matthew hadn't tumbled into his.

Was the magistrate mad enough to have murdered Fanny Logan to provide his own proof of Lucien's guilt?

It had an insane sort of logic.

Sir Matthew stalked forward. "The late duchess killed her husband in cold blood. Her son inherited her taste for blood. You can see it in his eyes."

All Sally saw in Lucien's eyes were eyes. They were very nice eyes. She was very fond of them. But eyes were eyes.

It would have been funny if it weren't so awful. Sally's urge to laugh faded. "The duke's mother was murdered. Which you would know if you had bothered to do any investigating."

"Is that what he told you?" Sir Matthew looked at her with something very like pity. "Lies, Miss Fitzhugh. All lies. The truth is that madness runs in that line, madness, and a bloodlust so strong, so dangerous, that the duke's own family has found it necessary, for the past decade, to keep him in restraints in his own castle. Only shackles, Miss Fitzhugh, have kept the duke from enacting his dread fancies."

Sir Matthew uttered the words with such conviction that Sally stopped sidling backwards long enough to stare at him.

"He hasn't been in shackles; he's been in the colonies." Which some people might regard as the same thing, but that was another matter.

"Are you so sure, Miss Fitzhugh? I have it on the most reliable authority that the duke has spent the past decade in strict confinement."

"Reliable authority?" Sally repeated incredulously. "What reliable authority?"

Sir Matthew's eyes shifted. "That is a matter of strictest confidence."

"It isn't strictest confidence—it's slander. Next you're going to tell me Lucien has been sacrificing chickens," said Sally in disgust. "Not that they wouldn't deserve it, nasty, clucking things."

Sir Matthew fixed her with a stern gaze. "Do you dare to joke of this matter?"

Sally met him eye to eye. She wasn't afraid anymore. She was too angry to be afraid. "I never joke about chickens."

"Do you think this is pleasant for me?" Sir Matthew appeared to be at the end of his patience. "Do you think I enjoy arguing with an impudent chit of a girl who doesn't know what is good for her? It would be your own just deserts if I left you to that monster!"

"Yes," said Sally, edging away towards the door. "You do that."

Sir Matthew thrust his hands into his sleeves. "If you are harmed, it will be, in some respect, on my own head. If I had spoken, all those years ago, instead of keeping the matter silent, as the duke's family wished . . . then the unfortunate who was murdered on that balcony might yet live."

Sally stopped edging away and stared at the magistrate. He didn't sound mad. He sounded exhausted. And entirely sincere. "You really believe it. Good heavens, you really believe it."

"I believe it because it is true," said Sir Matthew simply.

There was such a world of wrong in that statement that Sally didn't even know where to begin. Other than, possibly, informing the Prime Minister, Lord Grenville, that there was something terribly wrong with the state of law enforcement in England.

Really, someone ought to do something to fix that. But, first, she needed to set Sir Matthew straight.

"I don't know who has been giving you this information—

this misinformation—but there isn't a word of truth in any of it. The duke wouldn't hurt"—Lady Florence provided Sally with inspiration—"he wouldn't hurt a stoat! And that isn't to say he hasn't been provoked. As for his mother," Sally continued sternly, "what about the Black Tulip?"

"The black what?"

"The Black Tulip. The spy. Good heavens, didn't you do *anything* all those years ago? The spy to whom the duchess was passing information."

"A spy," repeated Sir Matthew.

"Yes," said Sally, in fine form. "The duchess's contact. The deadliest spy in all of France. Why didn't you bother to do anything about him?"

"We aren't in France," Sir Matthew pointed out.

Sally rolled her eyes. "The deadliest spy *from* France. They do move around, you know. It wouldn't make much sense for a French spy to be in France, now, would it? There's much more dastardly work for them to do over here. As in the case of the duke's parents," she finished triumphantly.

Sir Matthew sat down heavily on one of the narrow ice blue benches. "Miss Fitzhugh, if the duke spun you such a tale—"

Sally folded her arms across her chest. "What makes you think it's a tale?"

"—that can only be further proof of his instability of mind. I investigated his parents' murders. There were no . . . spies."

Sally pressed her lips together. "Maybe you just didn't look hard enough."

"My dear girl, I assure you, if there had been"—Sir Matthew seemed to choke on the word—"spies, I am sure they would not have escaped my notice."

"Spies, by their very nature, are designed to escape notice." Sir Matthew did not appear impressed by that argument, so Sally tried another tack. "Ask Lord Henry Caldicott. He'll tell you."

Ha! That should do it. Lord Henry was, after all, the one who had told Lucien of his mother's illicit activities. He was an unimpeachable witness, solid, respectable. Sir Matthew might believe that Lucien was mad and Sally was most likely stupid and quite definitely venal, but he would listen to Lord Henry.

Sir Matthew blinked at her. "Lord Henry?"

Sally couldn't resist a bit of sarcasm. "A tall man with graying hair. He lives here at Hullingden. I believe you have met before."

"We have." Sir Matthew's brows drew together. "It was Lord Henry who told me of his nephew's dangerous delusions."

Chapter Twenty-six

"Lord Henry," Sally repeated. "Lord Henry told you that Lucien was mad?"

Sir Matthew eyed her warily. "It was quite painful for him," he said repressively. "As you can imagine."

"Oh, I'm sure it was."

Who had told Lucien about the spies? Lord Henry. Who had access to the snuffbox and the manzanilla plant? Lord Henry.

Who benefited from Lucien's death? Lord Henry, that was who.

"Didn't you stop to ask anyone else?" demanded Sally in disgust. "Or were you willing to condemn the duke on one man's word?"

Sir Matthew looked down his nose at her. "Lord Henry," he said severely, "is a highly respected—"

"Yes, yes," interrupted Sally impatiently. Really, Sir Matthew was entirely without imagination. It was all as plain as the muzzle on Lady Florence's face. If Lucien were executed, Lord Henry would have not only Hullingden but the title as well. Lord Henry could play the bereaved uncle—he could even defend Lucien and claim that he would never have believed it of him—and everyone would say how noble he was and feel terribly sorry for him. It wasn't Lord Henry's fault that his nephew was a vampire.

Only it was. Sally wondered whether he had got the idea for the vampire rumor from *The Convent of Orsino*. The bit about Lucien being chained in the attic was a nice touch. She had assumed that charming bit of slander had come from the fertile imagination of Delia Cartwright, but apparently not. It was Lord Henry Caldicott who had spread the rumors, setting the scene.

Lord Henry was probably to blame for the sacrificial chickens as well.

He also, Sally realized grimly, was the one with the strongest motive for doing away with Fanny Logan. A future duke couldn't be embroiled in a breach-of-promise suit with an actress—not when his father was determined that he marry a duke's daughter.

In one fell swoop, Lord Henry had removed his son's inconvenient mistress and incriminated the man who stood between him and his title.

It really was incredibly clever, not to mention quite economical.

There was just one flaw. Lord Henry Caldicott had failed to reckon with Miss Sally Fitzhugh.

"Miss Fitzhugh." Sally looked at Sir Matthew in surprise. She had nearly forgotten he was there. "Miss Fitzhugh, I implore you, have a care. Tonight of all nights . . ."

"Tonight? Oh." Another piece of Lord Henry's diabolical plan snapped into place. "All Hallows' Eve." The night ghosts walked.

Sally had thought it was an odd choice for a betrothal ball.

"Precisely," said Sir Matthew, his face a map of worried wrinkles. He no longer looked sinister; he put Sally in mind of an ancient mastiff, chewing the wrong bone. "Given the nature of the duke's delusions . . ."

It really was quite diabolical and rather brilliant. Everyone in costume, everyone flirting with the idea of being just a little bit afraid. None of them knew that there was a real monster roaming the grounds, and that his name was Lord Henry Caldicott.

What did he mean to do? Would there be another woman killed and Lucien framed? If another woman was found dead with fang marks on her neck, the hysteria alone might be enough to carry Lucien to the block.

Possibly. But, the first attempt having failed, Lord Henry might not be willing to trust that a second attempt would succeed. He had already seen Lucien slip through his net once—with, Sally thought smugly, more than a little help from her.

Sally's smugness faded as the necessary corollary of that struck her. Indirect means having failed, Lord Henry might be moved to more direct measures. Her imagination supplied her with an image of Lucien, sprawled on the ground, a stake through the heart.

Or would a silver bullet suffice?

Either way, no one would ask too many questions about the death of the vampire duke. No one would look too hard for his killer. Lord Henry would quietly assume his title and dignities.

"Pardon me," said Sally, and barged past the startled magistrate. "I need to stop a killer."

If she could find him.

The ballroom bustled with people. Too many people. All masked, all disguised, all taking advantage of the chance to be someone else for an evening, to behave just a little bit too scandalously, to laugh just a little too loudly. Sally dodged an inebriated Roman centurion who appeared to be chasing a water nymph. Or she might simply have been a nymph who had spilled water over herself.

Sally searched desperately for a glimpse of a red velvet tunic embroidered with gold, brushing away the well wishes of some and the thinly veiled sneers of others.

There was no sign of Lucien, or of Lord Henry. Sally spotted Lady Winifred presiding over a table in the card room, but her husband wasn't by her side.

Sally had always heard that dread was cold. It wasn't. Her

hands and cheeks burned, her breath rasped in her chest, her stomach jittered with anxiety. She was everywhere at once, but nowhere that she needed to be. She was like a child's top spinning in circles, around and around and around.

Think, she told herself. *Think*. If she were Lord Henry, where would she stage her scene? The last one had been on the balcony. Would he do the same here?

Sally made a run for the balcony, bursting through the long glass doors, but there was no one on the other side but Clarissa Caldicott, whose hands were being clasped by a young redhaired man in a considerable state of agitation.

"—but I would never have said such a thing! They told me that you broke it off with me. They said you could look higher than a mere squire."

There was color in Lady Clarissa's pale cheeks. "I never wanted to look higher. All I wanted was—"

"Excuse me," chirped Sally. Both twisted to stare at her with identical expressions of indignation. "So sorry! I really wouldn't have interrupted if it weren't entirely necessary. Have you seen your brother?"

Lady Clarissa regarded her with equal parts confusion and hostility.

Sally tried again. "Your uncle?"

Lady Clarissa looked at her blankly.

Sally waved an impatient hand. "Oh, never mind. I'll find them myself. You can go back to telling him that you love him."

Lady Clarissa made a stuttering sound in the back of her throat that would have probably been unprintable if she could have found the words.

"Miss Fitzhugh?" The redheaded man managed to shake himself out of love's young dream long enough to glance up at Sally. "I'm not sure where the duke is, but I did see Lord Henry leave the ballroom some time ago."

"Some time? Some time a little time or some time a lot of time?"

The red-haired man looked at her apologetically. "Before the dancing began." He looked at Lady Clarissa with warm eyes. "I didn't have my eye on the clock."

Before the dancing. An hour, at least.

"Thank you." Sally was halfway through the door before she stopped and turned around again. "You should really keep this one," she informed a startled Lady Clarissa. "Run off with him if you have to. It will do wonders for your disposition."

And with that, she was back in the overheated ballroom, her nails digging into her palms, her teeth sinking into her lower lip. No Lucien. No Lord Henry.

Sally spotted Elizabeth I holding court to a motley group of courtiers in between two potted plants.

"Excuse me. Pardon me." Sally elbowed her way between an offended cavalier and a tipsy Harlequin. Breathlessly, she demanded, "Have you seen Lucien? I mean, the duke?"

"Am I your duke's keeper?" demanded Lizzy. "I thought he was with you. Don't tell me you've lost him already."

"He isn't a pair of gloves," said Sally with some asperity.

"Oh, hullo, Sal." Her brother ambled over. "If you're meant to be Saint Francis, I'd think you'd need a few more animals."

"I'm not Saint Francis; I'm Diana the Huntress. You haven't seen Lucien, have you?" Sally was in the last stages of desperation.

To her amazement, Turnip nodded, petals wagging. "Not ten minutes ago. Come to think of it, he was looking for you."

Every nerve in Sally's body went on alert. She clutched her brother's arm. "Where did he go?"

With a reproachful look, Turnip smoothed out the wrinkle in his sleeve. "Someone brought him a note. He muttered something about folly and bolted off into the night." He peered closely at his sister. "I say, Sal, are you quite the thing? You look a bit flushed in the cheeks."

Sally ignored Turnip's editorial additions. "Folly—the folly?"

Why hadn't she thought of it before? Where better to kill this duke than in the place where his father had perished before him. Sally hadn't thought blood could run cold, but hers was feeling distinctly icy just about now.

"Seemed pretty foolish to me," agreed Turnip, "but one doesn't like to judge and all that. Many a man's been made a fool by love."

"Not this one," said Sally grimly. To Lizzy she said rapidly, "Find Miss Gwen. Tell her to gather her forces and meet me in the folly."

Lizzy perked up. "Where are you going?"

Ten minutes, Turnip had said. There was no counting on the cavalry arriving in time.

Sally strung her golden bow over her shoulder. "I am going to rescue my duke."

There were lights blazing in the folly.

Fear quickened Lucien's pace. Mist rose from the ground, creating an odd reddish haze. Ahead of him, the folly loomed, curiously insubstantial in the mist. It flickered in front of him, the lights playing tricks, showing it to him as it once had been, in summer rather than fall, by day rather than night. Fallen teacups and crumpled linen and his father's wig lying abandoned on the floor.

Lucien wrenched himself back to the present. He might not have been able to save his parents, but he'd be damned if he'd let anything happen to Sally.

Fang marks on her neck. White skirts floating around her.

Lucien slid around the side of the building, listening with every fiber of his being for any sound of life within.

There was nothing. Nothing but the dry scratch of the bare tree branches, the creak of rusted metal as the lanterns swung on their hooks.

This spy, this Black Tulip—he didn't want Sally. She was just the bait. Lucien clung to that thought as he moved cautiously beneath the pillared portico, towards the arch that led to the interior of the folly. There was no point in killing her until she had served her purpose.

Lucien ignored the thought that a dead Sally would serve the Black Tulip's purpose just as well as a live one.

A heavy brocade curtain, now in faded tatters, hung from the arch. The long strips of decaying fabric floated eerily in the breeze, creating the illusion of movement, playing tricks with Lucien's eyes. The floating fabric reached out to him, stretching towards him, like a pair of pleading arms.

His Sally wouldn't go meekly. She was indomitable. She was—

Lucien barreled through the curtain, stopping short as the light of a dozen candelabras assaulted his eyes.

Not there.

The only sound in the room was his own hurried breathing, painfully loud. The silence was so complete that it hurt Lucien's ears. He could feel the coiled tension in that silence, like a bubble about to pop.

Someone had refilled the pool. The candlelight danced off the clear water, making the little room bright as day, creating an illusion of summer but for the chill wind that made the candle flames dance on their wax tapers.

The furniture had been replaced, replaced with exact copies of the red-and-cream-striped settee and chairs that had been here twelve years before.

There was no sign of Sally.

Not on the settee, not on the chairs, not between the arches where marble nymphs posed gracefully on their assigned pedestals.

But someone had been here. There was a sumptuous repast set out on a low table between two nymphs. Green grapes glistened in perfect clusters on silver platters. Peaches of marzipan, cunningly colored to replicate the bloom of ripe fruit, mingled with equally false apricots and pears, all spilling from a cornucopia in an illusion of the harvest's bounty. There were pastries laden with smooth-whipped custards and berries fresh from the hothouse, and, in the center of it all, an apple, cut into quarters, on a delicate porcelain plate, a paring knife beside it, the mother-of-pearl handle glimmering in the candlelight.

Something about that apple sent a chill down Lucien's spine.

The death apple. That was what they called the fruit of the manzanilla tree. One bite. That was all it took. One bite, and then a horrible, lingering death.

Despite himself, Lucien let himself entertain a furtive, fugitive trickle of hope. The apple was still whole. The apple might be just an apple. What if he had arrived in time? What if the scene had been set, but the principal actress had never arrived?

Pride flared deep in Lucien's chest. The Black Tulip hadn't reckoned with his Sally. He would wager that Sally had eluded whatever trap had been set for her. The Tulip might, even now, be trussed and bound with Sally sitting on his chest, giving him her firm opinion of his activities and morals.

The thought made Lucien smile, just a little.

"Sally?" Lucien called again, his voice echoing eerily off the domed ceiling of the pavilion.

He never expected anyone to answer.

"She'll be along presently." A man stepped through the arch, the tattered drapery catching on the shoulders of his toga and the laurel crown that circled his brow. Uncle Henry brushed the strips aside. "I really must remember to replace that curtain."

"Uncle Henry?" Relief warred with confusion. "What are you doing here?"

Uncle Henry cocked his head, smiling his usual kindly smile. "I know, I know, I should have left you and your bride to enjoy your surprise, but I couldn't resist coming along to see how you liked it."

"Our surprise."

"Your betrothal feast," said Uncle Henry easily, regarding the platters of food complacently. "I know this homecoming hasn't been without its difficulties. And your betrothal—I hope you won't be offended if I say that it all happened rather quickly?"

Lucien nodded numbly.

There was a silver cooler on the far end of the table, adorned with two snarling lions, one on either side. Uncle Henry reached inside, retrieving a bottle of champagne. "I wanted the two of you to have some time away from the throng." He wrestled the cork free from the bottle, pouring the bubbling liquid into one tall glass.

"That's very kind of you." Lucien watched the liquid, transfixed, as it bubbled into the glass, like sunshine seen through a frosted window. "There was a note. . . ."

"I hope you don't mind the mystery," said Uncle Henry jovially. "All part of the surprise." He held out the champagne flute. "Have a glass of champagne."

Lucien reached automatically for the glass, fighting a sense of something terribly, jarringly wrong, something so wrong that he was afraid to even try to put it into words. "You sent that note?"

"Well, yes." Uncle Henry looked at him in surprise. "Your aunt thought it would be more dramatic if we had a liveried page lead the way, but a note seemed more subtle. Go on! Sit down. Drink up."

Lucien set the glass down on the edge of the table. "I'll just wait for Sally." There was an acid taste at the back of his mouth. "I wouldn't want to spoil the . . . surprise."

"I'm sure she'll be along." Uncle Henry's smile had acquired a fixed look, as false and waxen as the marzipan peaches on the platters. He nudged the glass towards Lucien. "You have your champagne. I'm sure Miss Fitzhugh won't mind your starting without her."

Standing over the body of Fanny Logan, all those weeks ago, Sally had quoted Hamlet. Now another line from the play rose unbidden in Lucien's mind.

Give me the cup. . . . There's yet some liquor left.

That had been an uncle too. An uncle who had dropped

poison in the king's ear. An uncle who had usurped the kingdom.

No. Every instinct in Lucien's body warred with what his brain already knew, old affection pitted in a losing battle against cold logic. Not Uncle Henry. Not the man who had—tried to—raise him. Lucien would never have said that Uncle Henry loved him as his own, but he'd always believed that he cared for him, in his own casual way.

But Uncle Henry had never cared for any human being as much as he did for Hullingden.

The realization reverberated to the depths of Lucien's soul. He felt like a crystal ball, about to shatter. Or like a hunted animal, pinned in its covert.

"I've never much liked champagne," said Lucien casually. "I've always preferred brandy. You have it, Uncle."

"Oh, no," said Uncle Henry, and there was that fixed smile on his face as he held out the glass of champagne, smiling, smiling, pushing the glass forward. "This is yours."

"Don't drink that!" A voice rang out behind them. "It's poisoned."

Uncle Henry whirled, champagne sloshing over the rim of the glass, down the folds of his toga, onto the stone flags of the floor. "Miss Fitzhugh!"

Sally stood in the archway, her spangled silk tunic glittering in the candlelight. In her hands, she held a miniature gilt bow, one gilded arrow trained on Uncle Henry.

Lucien felt a crazy smile spreading across his face. "Sally."

Sally acknowledged his presence with a sharp nod, all her attention focused on Uncle Henry. "Drop that glass and step away from my duke."

"Very amusing, Miss Fitzhugh," said Uncle Henry with a forced smile. "That is quite a cunning little accessory to your costume. If you're quite finished playing with it, why don't you come in and join us?"

Sally narrowed her eyes at Lucien's uncle. "I'm a crack archer. I can hit a bonnet at fifty paces."

"Then," said Uncle Henry, "it is fortunate that I'm not wearing one." He winked at Lucien, in a conspiracy of men.

Sally held the bow steady, but her eyes shifted desperately towards Lucien. "It was your uncle all along," she said rapidly. "He spread those rumors. He killed Fanny Logan. He's told everyone that you're mad—dangerous. This is his final attempt to finish you off."

Uncle Henry made a choking noise. "My dear Miss Fitzhugh! I don't know what to say."

"You've said enough already," said Sally fiercely. "He told everyone that you were a vampire. He was the one who spread the rumor about your being kept in an attic. I shouldn't be surprised if he was the one who killed your parents."

Uncle Henry's smile slipped. "Really, Miss Fitzhugh. You have been spending far too much time with Mrs. Reid."

Sally's teeth dug into her lower lip. She looked to Lucien, her expression imploring. "He wanted us off on a wild-goose chase, running after imaginary spies. But it was him all along."

"And you've come to rescue me." Lucien didn't know whether to laugh or weep or go down on one knee.

"It's absurd," said Uncle Henry firmly, and part of Lucien wanted to believe him, to believe that Sally was mistaken, that the man who had raised him couldn't contemplate his death.

"Lucien?" said Sally, and he saw her arm start to quiver, just a little.

"Lucien," said Uncle Henry sharply. "*Lucien*. Who are you going to believe? Your own uncle or the sister of a known idiot?"

Sally bristled. "Turnip is hardly an idiot." She turned to Lucien. "He's occasionally a little . . . literal. That's all."

Uncle Henry raised a brow. "Do you see what I mean?"

"Yes," Lucien said slowly.

Sally's arm faltered.

"What's in the champagne, Uncle Henry?" Lucien demanded, his voice hard, and he saw relief blaze across Sally's face, relief and an expression of joy so bright it made him dizzy. "Is it manzanilla extract? Or did you have the decency to at least choose something a little less painful?"

"You're as mad as she is!" Looking from one to the other, Uncle Henry gave a gusty laugh. "Lucien! Do you really think I would do anything to hurt you?"

"Yes," Sally answered for him.

Lucien kept his eyes trained on his uncle, on the man who had put him on his first pony, the man who had taught him to use a gun.

It would have been easier had Uncle Henry leered or jeered, had he twirled his cloak, or suddenly developed a squint; instead, he looked and sounded just as he always had—the same frank voice, the same fond smile.

There was a pain in the pit of Lucien's stomach, betrayal and confusion and a horrible fear he couldn't quite name.

"Did you kill my father?"

Uncle Henry stood his ground. His hand slipped between the folds of his toga. "I loved your father."

"Did you kill my father?" Lucien's voice rang off the dome of the folly, clashing against the crystal of the glasses, waking the echoes in the still depths of the pool beside which his parents had died.

Uncle Henry looked away. There were lines that Lucien had never noticed before at the corners of his mouth. "Your father treated me like a lapdog," he said shortly. Lucien must have made some movement, because Uncle Henry looked up quickly, his expression bitter. "You think I didn't know that that was what he called me? He made no secret of it. But I didn't mind," he added hastily. "We had our arrangement."

Uncle Henry looked at Lucien, and behind his uncle's eyes, Lucien saw a man he didn't recognize. "Your father was never meant to marry."

As if from very far away, Lucien heard the whisper of Sally's tunic against the floor, felt her hand on his arm, steadying him.

Without looking, he groped for her hand, grasping it like a lifeline. "Have you always hated me?"

Uncle Henry looked at him in surprise. "I never hated you. You always were a good boy." The words sounded like an elegy.

Sally tugged on Lucien's arm, drawing him back with her. "I think it's time for us to go."

"Oh, no," said Uncle Henry kindly. "I'm afraid you won't be going anywhere at all."

He drew his hand from the folds of his Roman costume, revealing a pistol that was anything but antique.

"You see, I have other plans for you."

Chapter Twenty-seven

S ally grabbed for her bow, loosing her golden arrow.

It plunked harmlessly into the silver champagne cooler.

"Really, Miss Fitzhugh." Lord Henry looked at her reproachfully. "There's no need for such histrionics."

"I would say that being murdered is every need," retorted Sally indignantly.

"'Murder' is such a strong word," said Lord Henry conversationally, his pistol trained on Sally's chest with an easy competence that suggested his aim might be somewhat better than Sally's.

Sally knew she ought to have paid more attention to the archery at their archery lessons rather than hiding behind a tree with the latest *Cosmopolitan Ladies' Book*.

"I'm sure this is all a misunderstanding," Lucien said soothingly, moving carefully forward.

Sally, with a twist of the heart, realized exactly what he was trying to do. He was trying to step in front of her, to shield her with his body.

"Yes," agreed Uncle Henry, moving to keep his pistol trained on Sally. "Miss Fitzhugh was never meant to be here. However," he added, with a cheerfulness that Sally found highly unnerving, "this might just be even better. It will make a very affecting scene. The duke, having, in a fit of mania, poisoned his betrothed, slays himself in remorse. Shakespeare couldn't do better."

"I've never liked those plays where everyone dies in the end," said Lucien. From the corner of her eye, Sally saw him flick his wrist, such a tiny movement that she thought she had imagined it, until he did it again.

"Yes, it clutters up the stage awfully." Sally's eyes met Lucien's, and what she saw there warmed her to the core. Whatever happened, they were a team, working in concert.

She would just prefer to be a team in life, rather than death.

"Like *Romeo and Juliet*," Sally said at random, edging slightly towards the right, as Lucien had indicated. "I've never understood why everyone loves that play so. The hero and heroine are annoying and the ending is depressing."

Lord Henry swung the pistol in her direction. "Stop right there, Miss Fitzhugh."

Sally stopped. She opened her eyes wide. "You wouldn't

want to spoil your affecting scene by shooting me. Bullet holes are *so* uncouth."

"At this point," said Lord Henry, "I am prepared to take that risk."

There was something in his expression that said he meant it.

"I imagine," said Sally kindly, attempting to keep his attention away from Lucien, "that it must be very provoking to have quite so many of your plans go awry."

"I understand that I have you to thank for that." Lord Henry didn't sound at all thankful.

Sally felt for an arrow in what she hoped was a subtle fashion. "One does what one can."

"Not any longer," said Lord Henry, and cocked his pistol. "I have a new plan. Duke shoots his betrothed and then shoots himself in a fit of remorse. It's not as tidy as poison, but it will serve."

"Let her go." Lucien's voice rang out from two yards to Sally's left. He held up his empty hands. "Take me. That's what you want. She's nothing to do with anything."

Lord Henry's pistol swung away from Sally. "I might just," said Lord Henry, and took aim.

There was no time to notch an arrow. Sally grabbed for the first thing she found in her quiver.

"Kill, Lady Florence!" she shouted, and flung the outraged stoat at Lord Henry's head.

It worked rather better than Sally had expected. Lord Henry dropped to his knees, flinging up his arms to shield his head as ten pounds of furious fur and muscle landed on his shoulder, claws scrabbling for purchase in the fabric of his toga.

The pistol clattered to the ground, going off with an explosion that filled the room with acrid black smoke. The pistol ball ricocheted off the silver wine cooler. Sally didn't wait to see where it went. She flung herself on the floor, only to be mashed to the ground by a heavy male form as Lucien flung himself on top of her.

"Down!" he barked, holding out his arms to shield her.

"Umph," said Sally, which, if she was thinking about it, translated a little to "I love you" and a lot to "Ouch, you're squishing me."

An uncanny howl rose from Lord Henry, spiraling to a soprano shriek as Lady Florence bit down hard on the back of his neck.

In the middle of it all, there was the sound of feet pounding against the flagstones and shouting and jostling and someone yelling, "Sit on him! Sit on him! Before he gets away!" followed by an indignant "Agnes! That was my foot!"

"Sorry," said Agnes's familiar voice.

"I say," came Sally's brother's voice, sounding rather more cheerful than the situation warranted. "Are those puddings?"

"Don't eat anything!" Sally attempted to lift her smoke-grimed face from the floor and encountered an expanse of scratchy red velvet blocking her view. "I think the cavalry has arrived," she croaked into Lucien's chest.

Lucien rolled off her. "I think it has," he agreed.

Struggling to a sitting position, Sally saw a series of scratches on Lucien's face, including a rather nasty one above his right eye, which was oozing blood in a piratical fashion.

Sally touched a finger to the corner of the scratch. "Are you all right?" she asked.

She wasn't referring to his wounds. Not those wounds, at any rate.

Lucien glanced back over his shoulder, where his uncle was curled in an unhappy ball on the floor, Agnes sitting on his chest, Lizzy standing guard over him with her scepter at the ready, as Lady Florence complacently licked her own tail.

"I will be," he said, and Sally opened her mouth to tell him not to be stoic, when he silenced her by adding, with a look that made her go warm down to her toes, "Thanks to you."

Sally did her best to shrug, which wasn't as easy as one would think when one was partially prone, in a dress that showed an alarming tendency to slip off her shoulder, one strap having been ruptured in the fray.

"Well. You know," said Sally, looking up at him with her heart in her eyes, "anyone would have done the same."

"You say that," said Lucien, holding out a hand to help her up. "I do not think it means what you think it means."

His hand closed over hers, large and firm and safe. He was safe now, Sally realized. It was all over. The villain had been apprehended. The mystery was solved.

"What do you think it means?" she asked, her hem getting

all tangled underfoot because her eyes were on his face rather than her feet.

"I think," said Lucien, his eyes very bright in his powder-grimed face, "that it means that you are magnificent."

Someone let out a loud harrumph behind them.

"Don't let us interrupt you," said Miss Gwen loudly. She slapped her purple parasol impatiently against her palm. "Just because we have the villain in custody."

"You mean, Sally has the villain in custody," said Lucien. Sally tried to tug her hand away, but Lucien held it fast. "She was the one who figured it all out."

That reminded Sally. . . . "Spies?" said Sally, looking pointedly at Miss Gwen.

"You were the ones who came along prattling about spies," said Miss Gwen loftily. "I only drew the obvious conclusions. How was I to know it was all a petty matter of inheritance?"

"Petty?" Sally sputtered. Her eyes flew to Lucien, magnificent and bedraggled, his face scarred, his doublet charred. But alive. Wonderfully, gloriously alive. "Petty?"

"Ah, well," said Miss Gwen, with magnificent condescension. "At least we need waste no more time on this matter."

"What about the puddings?" inquired Turnip, browsing among the comestibles. "What? Nothing like a rescue to raise the appetite, and all that."

"Fourteen lobster patties weren't enough?" said Miss Gwen. She poked her parasol in Sally's general direction. "Go on. Say your good-byes." She consulted the watch pinned to her bodice. "If you cry off, we can go home and I can finish another chapter before Tuesday."

What if she didn't want to cry off? But that wasn't her decision to make. Sally looked at her duke, and knew that wherever he went and whatever he did, he would always be her duke. Even if he didn't know it.

"Well, then," Sally said, playing for time.

"Don't," Lucien said. His voice was hoarse with smoke; the words came out in a croak. It still sounded like music to Sally. "Don't cry off."

Sally cocked her head, trying not to let the hope show in her eyes. "Tonight?"

"Ever." The word seemed to echo in the air between them. Lucien took a deep breath, taking his heart in his hands. "Stay here. With me."

"Was that a proposal?" whispered Agnes.

"It did seem to be missing certain key words," commented Lizzy. "Like 'will you' and 'marry me.' "

Lucien wished all of them to perdition. He held out his hands to Sally, twining his fingers through hers.

"Don't go. I meant what I said before. I don't have much to offer—"

Miss Gwen emitted a loud snort.

Lucien ignored her. "—but what I do have is yours." He used their joined hands to draw her closer, trying to keep his voice light as he wheedled, "You know you'll make a brilliant duchess."

Sally looked up at him, her blond brows drawing together. "Is that the only reason you want me to stay? Because you need a duchess? To go with all this?"

It would be easy to pretend that that was all it was. A dynastic alliance. An attempt to prevent scandal or save her reputation. But that would be a lie.

"I don't need a duchess. I need *you*. I need you hectoring and meddling—"

"Really!" Sally tried to pull her hands away, but Lucien held them fast.

"—and bedeviling my relatives and bewitching my servants and making the room brighter simply by being in it." Once started, Lucien couldn't stop. "That night you blundered into my garden was the luckiest night of my life."

"Oh," sighed Agnes, hugging her sheep.

"If I were you," commented Lizzy, "I would say yes."

"He hasn't asked me anything yet," said Sally.

Lucien couldn't stop the smile that tugged on one corner of his mouth. "Oh, is that what you were waiting for?" He dropped down on one knee, trying not to wince as his knee struck the flagstones. "Miss Sally Fitz—"

"Her real name is Sarah," provided Turnip helpfully. "Sarah Claribelle Dulcinea Fitzhugh. Shouldn't want to plight the troth in a shoddy way."

Sally rolled her eyes to the ceiling in an extremity of annoyance.

"Claribelle?" repeated Lucien.

"Have you met my family?" said Sally, through gritted teeth. "I count myself fortunate it wasn't Aubergine."

Lucien felt a bubble of laughter swell in his chest, and with it, a sense of well-being so powerful that it seemed to bathe the whole room in sunshine.

When he thought of this place in the future, it wouldn't be with sorrow or fear, but with the memory of this moment, the moment when he asked the most important question of his life.

"Miss Sarah Aubergine Fitzhugh, will you do me the honor of not breaking our betrothal? If it helps," he added, as an aside, "I'll even pretend to admire your weasel."

"Stoat," Sally corrected him, looking down her nose. "She's a stoat. And Dabney will be very cross with you if you're unkind to Lady Florence."

"It's not Dabney I'm worried about," said Lucien, whose knees were beginning to feel just a little uncomfortable. "Besides, I owe a debt to Lady Florence. And her owner."

Sally looked down at him, and a shadow passed across the clear blue of her eyes. "I don't want you to marry me to cancel a debt."

This whole kneeling thing didn't seem to be working very well. He would prefer to speak to Sally as they did best: eye to eye. As equals.

Lucien hauled himself to his feet. "I want to marry you because I love you," he said bluntly.

"Oh," said Sally, and, for a moment, there wasn't anything imperious about her at all. Her hands tightened on his. She made an attempt to reclaim her dignity. "Well, if *that's* the way you feel . . ."

Miss Gwen murmured something that sounded like "Ha! I knew it."

"I love a love match," said Turnip happily.

From the floor, Uncle Henry emitted a loud groan. That was followed by a *thunk*, into which Lucien decided not to inquire too closely, although he suspected that it might have had something to do with Lizzy's scepter.

Lucien turned so that his back blocked the lot of them. "Well?" he asked, settling Sally's dangling diadem straight on her head. "Will you have me?"

Sally lifted her head proudly. For the benefit of their audience, she said, loudly, "Only because Lizzy tells me that crying off will do terrible things to your reputation."

Lucien raised a brow. "Oh?" he said gently.

Biting her lip, Sally lifted her eyes to his. Lucien could see the laughter in them, and the resignation. And the love. "And because I can't imagine living without you," she said ruefully. "It's very vex—"

Lucien couldn't help it. He had to kiss her. It didn't matter if she was in the middle of a word. A kiss was absolutely imperative.

From the way Sally's arms twisted around his neck, she seemed to agree.

It was some time before they pulled apart to arm's length, Sally's cheeks rosy, her hair tousled, and her eyes glowing.

"—very vexing," she finished triumphantly, if somewhat breathlessly. "I didn't mean to go falling in love with you, you know."

"I know," Lucien agreed. "I know."

He rested the tip of his nose against hers, thinking of the strange and tortuous paths by which they had arrived at this moment. He lifted his head, looking into the bright blue eyes that were all the seas he needed to sail and all the sky he needed to see.

From now on, his future was here, with Sally.

There was just one thing. Lucien rested his hands on his betrothed's shoulders. "There's something I've been meaning to ask you," he said solemnly.

Sally drew a deep breath that did further damage to her ruined tunic. "Anything," she said recklessly.

"My dearest love . . ." Lucien cradled her face tenderly in his hands. "Just what do you have against chickens?"

Chapter Twenty-eight

Cambridge, 2004

*T*he plastic pumpkin rocked on its dented base. I hastily steadied it before it could spill candy out across the floor.

"Did you say you're leaving Selwick Hall?"

Colin spoke through a mouthful of candy pumpkin. "Leasing." He swallowed the orange goop and tried again. "I'm leasing Selwick Hall."

I stared at him. "I thought you were breaking up with me," I said numbly.

"Would I be here if I were breaking up with you?" Colin grimaced, wiping his sticky lips with the back of his hand. "This stuff is vile."

"Here." I thrust the plastic pumpkin at him. "Have a Snickers to clear your palate. Leasing Selwick Hall. Why are you leasing Selwick Hall?"

Colin had moved heaven and earth to hold on to Selwick Hall. Since his father died, it had been his home, his project, his world.

A dark suspicion entered my mind. "Has Jeremy—"

"No." Colin held up his hands. "Jeremy hasn't done anything. He's been quite helpful, really."

"Then—why?" I looked helplessly at Colin. "I don't get it. You love Selwick Hall."

Or, at least, I'd always assumed he did. But maybe love didn't translate to wanting to stay there.

I'd always said I loved grad school, and look at me.

"You here. Me there," Colin said patiently. "If Mohammed won't come to the mountain . . . Unless you don't want me to, that is."

"I'm not sure I like being compared to a mountain," I said numbly. This was so beyond anything I had expected. Colin leave Selwick Hall?

"You're not the mountain; I'm the mountain." Colin tugged at his tie. "Nothing is definite yet. It's all still in the planning stages, but there are some Americans who are interested." When I didn't say anything, he added, "They're friends of Jeremy's."

Of course. They would be. Colin's stepfather/cousin lived a very transatlantic life.

Colin squirmed himself out of the dent in the center of the

cushion where the springs had long since expired. "Look, I realize it's a bit of cheek inviting myself into your life. If you don't like the idea—"

He was, I realized, nervous. Palm-sweating, tie-tugging nervous.

And I? Was beyond words. "*Like* the idea? I *love* the idea. I— Wow!"

The idea of Colin without Selwick Hall was mind-boggling. Colin giving up Selwick Hall for me—I didn't even know how to react to that. A proposal would have been easy. This—this meant so much more.

It meant so much more and it made the stakes so much higher. "Are you sure you want to do that?" I said awkwardly. "For me?"

"For us," Colin pointed out. "There's a difference."

I took a deep breath. "True, O King. I just—I don't want you to wake up six months from now hating me because I've made you give your home away."

Colin took my hands in his. "Three things," he said gravely. "One, I'm not giving it away. I'm only leasing it. I'll get it back."

"Yes, but—" I knew how batty it would drive Colin to have strangers at the Hall, wrinkling the pages of his father's paperbacks and ruining the perfect dent in his favorite chair in the library.

Colin squeezed my hands. "Two, I wouldn't have offered if I weren't prepared to go through with it."

I shifted uncomfortably on my perch on the arm of the

couch. Prepared wasn't the same thing as ready. I didn't want my boyfriend to martyr himself for me. "I know that, but—"

"And, three"—Colin gave a little tug, and I plopped down inelegantly onto his lap—"it's just a house."

"It's your house," I pointed out, struggling to sit upright, much hampered by my flowing skirts. I managed to claw my way up his chest into something resembling a sitting position, shaking my tousled hair out of my face. "You love it there."

"I love you," said Colin, sliding his fingers under my chin. A hint of a smile touched his lips. "The house never comes to the pub with me. It rarely makes me burned toasted cheese—"

"Hey!" I protested. "Those sandwiches were hardly singed."

"—and if it tried to sit on my lap, that would be the end of it for me." More seriously, he said, "I've had a lot of time to think since you've gone. More time than I would have liked. I don't want to live for a house, no matter how fine a house it is."

"What about your old life in London?" Before I had known him, Colin had been an I-banker with a trendy flat in one of the gentrifying areas of London. He had thrown it all in when his father died and his mother remarried.

I had always wondered, in the back of my head, if the Colin I knew wasn't still in a prolonged phase of grief, his Selwick Hall life just a stage.

His relationship with me just a stage.

Colin shook his head. "What is it you say? Been there, done that. Besides," he added, more practically, "when I left, I cut all ties. I couldn't go back if I wanted to. And I don't want to."

"What do you want?" I asked, my eyes searching his familiar face.

He cupped my face in his hands. "You," he said. A hint of a smile touched his lips. "And, eventually, some singed toasted cheese."

I knew I ought to protest, to argue, to try to make him see reason for his own good, but my heart was too full. "Was this my birthday surprise?"

"No," said Colin frankly. "Your birthday surprise is a desk chair. It was supposed to arrive today, but it appears to have gone astray. Which is just as well. I'm not sure there's room for it in here."

"We'll have to find a bigger place," I said, testing it out on my tongue. We. Us. Our place. The magnitude of Colin's sacrifice humbled me. "Are you sure you'll be okay with a one-bedroom apartment after the Hall?"

"As long as you're in it with me," Colin said gallantly. He eyed my bed askance. "Preferably in a larger bed."

"I think that can be arranged." I stopped, biting my lip, as the weight of reality bore down upon me. "Except—?"

Colin thought we were talking one more semester, maybe a year on top of that if I got a fellowship in Hist and Lit. I hadn't told him that my career plans had exploded around me.

"Except?" Colin repeated. He struggled to sit up straighter, which wasn't easy given that his legs were entirely smothered by my gown. "If you don't like the idea, just say so."

"No!" I said quickly. "No. It's not that. It's just—" I pressed my lips together, trying to think of the best way to tell him. I stared at my own hands, so incongruously tan and calloused against the pale stuff of my dress. "That meeting with my advisor. It didn't go as well as I told you. In fact, it didn't go well at all." I smiled crookedly. "'Catastrophic disaster' would be a more accurate summary."

"How catastrophic?" Colin's voice was gentle, undemanding.

I took a deep breath. "He thinks I need to rewrite my dissertation from scratch. That means I won't be on the job market this year. Or next year. Basically, my career is in limbo."

I had never realized before just how accurate that word was. "Limbo," where souls were left wandering between heaven and hell, neither here nor there.

"What's wrong with it?" Colin demanded, offended on my behalf, and, in the midst of my misery, I felt a little glow of warmth, because, if nothing else, Colin believed in me. Even if he didn't trust my sandwich-making skills.

I snuggled down into the comfortable crook of his arm. "He thinks it reads too much like fiction."

Colin's lip curled. "Maybe fiction is too much like life," he said dismissively. "You can't help it if my ancestors tended to be . . ."

"Somewhat flamboyant?" I offered. "That's another problem. He thinks I'm relying too heavily on one source base. I'd have to go and try to drum up other documents."

Other archives. Other spies. Once, I might have felt excited about that. Now—

I was done.

I could go through the motions, but my heart just wasn't in it. I cared about the Pink Carnation. I wasn't sure I cared about spies in the abstract.

"What are you going to do?" Colin asked quietly.

"I don't know," I said wretchedly. "I could probably graduate this year anyway. I wouldn't be eligible for any of the big jobs, but I might be able to find a teaching position somewhere."

I felt Colin's lips against my hair. "You don't sound thrilled about that."

More horrible truths. "I don't really like teaching. I'm okay at lecturing, but I'm horrible at leading a seminar. And I hate grading. If I get one more complaint just because I gave someone a B minus . . ." I buried my face in Colin's chest. "But the thought of going back to the archives and starting all over makes me want to curl up in a little ball and cry."

Colin leaned back, peering down at me. "If you don't like the teaching and you don't like the research—why are you doing this?"

"Because it's what I thought I wanted six years ago."

"Six years ago," said Colin, "I thought I wanted a posh flat and an office with a glass door."

Point taken.

I rested my elbows on his chest and pushed my hair back behind my ears. Behind him, I could see my bookshelves, crammed with monographs and reference works, all the effluvia of the last six years.

"If I don't do this, what do I do?" I transformed my face into a comical grimace. "I don't want to go to law school."

Only it wasn't funny. Two of my advisor's other students had already gone that route. A third had become personal trainer to the Duchess of York, but I didn't think that was an option for me. I wasn't any good at making myself exercise, much less someone else.

Colin just barely managed not to smile. "There have to be other options."

Were there? I had a hard time thinking of any. That was, I realized, a large part of why I had gone to grad school in the first place. It gave me something to do. And it wasn't law school.

Which, in retrospect, wasn't a great reason for choosing a career.

"I really do love history," I said wistfully. "I just don't love the practice of it. All this"—I waved a hand in the direction of the bookshelves, all those weighty tomes bristling with footnotes—"it sucks all the life out of it."

Colin stroked my hair. I resisted the urge to purr. "Your advisor said your dissertation sounded too much like fiction?"

I nodded.

"Then write it as fiction."

I blinked up at my boyfriend. I could still see only one of him, so I couldn't be that sloshed. "That's crazy."

"Is it? You have the material. All you have to do"—Colin's lips lifted at the corners—"is add dialogue."

I didn't think it was really quite that easy, but Colin's smile was so irresistible that I couldn't help but smile back. I struggled out of his lap, sitting back so I could see him better. "You wouldn't mind? Your family history being on display like that?"

"It was going to be on display in your dissertation," he pointed out.

"Yes, with a circulation of three." In other words, my dissertation committee. "If I wrote it as popular fiction, you run the risk that it might be—"

"Popular?" Colin raised a brow.

"Yes," I said, with dignity. "I mean, I realize how hard it is to get a book published. It might be a complete flop. But just on the off chance—do you really want all of this out there?"

When I'd first met him, Colin had had firm feelings about guarding the integrity of the family archives. The Pink Carnation had stayed a secret for a very long time.

To my surprise, Colin considered my question seriously. "I'd rather you do it than someone else. Besides," he added, "it would be fiction."

This crazy idea was beginning to seem less and less crazy. "But it's not."

Colin stretched his arms over his head. "Your readers wouldn't know that. Isn't there an old adage about hiding in plain sight?"

"I think it was an Edgar Allan Poe story."

What if Colin's crazy idea weren't so crazy after all? My mind was spinning with possibilities. People had been hunting for the identity of the Pink Carnation for years. As nonfiction, it might make a stir in certain communities.

As fiction . . . Look at the Scarlet Pimpernel. Ask nine out of ten people, and they'd say that Sir Percy Blakeney was a figment of Baroness Orczy's imagination.

I looked up at Colin with wide, startled eyes. "You know, that's not entirely crazy."

"You say the sweetest things," said Colin drily. "I wouldn't run to say anything to your advisor yet."

"No," I agreed. I didn't need to submit this spring. I could hold off another year, give this fiction-writing thing a try.

"And," said Colin cannily, "there is an additional benefit to this plan."

"Oh?" I was still busy dealing with the revised road map of my life.

Colin innocently straightened his cuff links. "If you need somewhere to write, I hear there's a house in Sussex for lease."

I narrowed my eyes at my boyfriend. "Really? What about Jeremy's Americans?"

"Nothing has been signed yet. We were still negotiating the rent. But, for you," Colin said encouragingly, "I'm sure we could come to a special arrangement."

"Oh?" It would, I realized, be a rather perfect solution. Why make Colin leave his home if he didn't have to? "The Gift of the Magi" always made me cry. I wanted that poor woman to have her hair back.

Not to mention that I rather liked Selwick Hall. I wasn't sure I'd be up for staying there for the rest of my life—I'd been born and raised a city girl—but if Colin could give the U.S. a go for a year, I could certainly do the same with Selwick Hall. Particularly if the rent were right.

"Just what is this special rate?"

"One pint once a week," said Colin promptly. "Of course, you have to put up with the landlord. I hear he can get a bit cheeky."

"That's a chance I'm willing to take." I could feel a smile beginning to spread across my face, a smile that came from deep in my chest. "Is there room for a large desk chair?"

"I'm sure we can find a corner somewhere. Does that mean—is that a yes?"

It wasn't exactly the question I had imagined he would be asking me this weekend. But, then, as the Duke of Belliston had pointed out, the best things sometimes happened by accident. I had expected a proposal and a PhD, not so much because I wanted them, but because that was what I was supposed to have. The ring and the degree. The outward symbols of success.

What Colin was offering me was something more than symbol. It was the day-to-day reality of being together, of seeing if we could mesh our lives into one.

The ring could come later.

As for the degree—well, we would see. I hadn't entirely processed it all yet, but I rather liked the idea of writing with dialogue rather than footnotes. I could see the story unrolling before me. Amy Balcourt, and the Purple Gentian, and her fearful chaperone, Miss Gwen, and, perhaps, eventually, even a vampire duke.

There was just one mystery remaining: what had happened to the Carnation after she had dismantled her League?

I had a sneaking suspicion that the answer lay at Selwick Hall.

With Colin.

"Yes," I said. I didn't remember standing, but there I was, my Regency gown light as gossamer, as though I'd been freed of a terrible weight. And Colin was standing too, his arms around me, swinging me around in a dizzying circle. "Yes."

Colin set me back on my feet. "I almost forgot. . . . Stay there. And cover your eyes."

I obediently put my hands over my eyes. "I thought I already had my birthday surprise." A dark suspicion struck me. "You didn't hide the desk chair in the shower?"

I didn't think that would do much for the desk chair. Or the shower.

"Hush," said Colin. "Oh, for the love of— There." There was a rustling noise, some cursing, and the sound of a match hissing.

"Are you all right over there?" I asked, from behind my fingers.

"Bloody icing," muttered Colin. "Right. You can look now."

I took my hands away. There, on my kitchen table, was a cupcake in the shape of a carnation, one pink candle burning in the center.

There was a shiny decoration at the base of the candle, like a glistening drop of dew at the heart of the flower.

It appeared to be attached to a ring.

I looked up at my boyfriend. His tie was askew, and there was a smudge of pink icing on his sleeve.

He smiled, a little self-consciously. "I hope you don't mind. . . . I couldn't find twenty-nine candles."

I looked from the candle, to Colin, and back again. "This one will do just fine." My voice sounded high and strange. "Is that what I think it is?"

The corners of Colin's eyes crinkled. "Why don't you blow it out and see?"

He leaned across the table for a kiss that tasted a little bit like candy corn pumpkin and a lot like love.

"Happy birthday, Eloise."

Acknowledgments

Writing a book with a newborn is the hardest thing I've ever done. I owe a big debt of gratitude to many people for making this book possible in the midst of all the confusion that comes of learning how to care for a new little person.

This book would never have happened without my mother, who trekked over day after day, rain and shine, to cradle the little one so I could slip away to write (and, occasionally, nap, eat, and shower). She also taught me everything I know about the Itsy Bitsy Spider, the Muffin Man (did you know that he lives on Drury Lane?), and the art of coaxing baby giggles. Thanks, Mom!

I am so grateful for the patience of my editor, Danielle Perez, who okayed first one extension . . . and then another . . . and then another. Many thanks to the whole team at Penguin for their support, generosity, and a very cute baby gift.

Thanks also to my husband, who diapers and sings "Hush Little Baby" with the best of them—and who took a day off work so I could write when the deadline got tight.

Thank you to Connie at my favorite Starbucks, who cheered me on from the beginning all the way to the last line and primed the pump with an endless supply of decaf skim venti peppermint mochas.

Huge thanks go to my two plot doctors, Claudia Brittenham and Brooke Willig, who spent endless hours trying to help me wrap my sleep-deprived brain around what made these characters tick.

When I was at my most tired and grungy, nothing cheered me up like a visit to my Web site or Facebook. Thank you, so very much, to the whole extended Pink family, for reminding me of why I love my characters, and why writing about them is worth all those lost nap opportunities. Your enthusiasm kept me going in those long, caffeine-less days.

Lady Florence owes her existence to Justin Zaremby, who, in circumstances I cannot perfectly recall, dared me to put a stoat in the next book. Justin, this stoat is for you.

Last but not least, thank you to my daughter for becoming more adorable every day. I have created many characters over the past few years, but none nearly so fascinating as you.

Historical Note

As I was writing it, I jokingly referred to *The Mark of the Midnight Manzanilla* as my Halloween book. You may have noticed, however, that Halloween, as such, does not make an appearance in the historical part of the story.

The origins of Halloween as we know it are murky. One version has it that Halloween originated in the Celtic festival of Samhain, a time when the dead wandered among the living. Later, in the ninth century, Pope Gregory IV transformed the celebration into a Christian holiday, Hallowmas. The name "Halloween," or "Hallowe'en," comes from the festival of Hallowmas: All Hallows' Eve, All Hallows' (or All Saints') Day, and All Souls' Day, in which the dead are remembered.

Either way, the tradition of the evening of October 31 as a

night on which ghosts walk goes back a very long time. As for the other practices we associate with Halloween . . . sources have it that "mumming and guising" were popular in the Celtic fringe (Ireland, Scotland, and Wales), but they don't seem to have taken much of a hold in England. There was also a form of trick-or-treating: going door-to-door collecting "soul cakes" to pray for those in purgatory. Bonfires were lit as well, either to guide the souls to heaven or to scare them away from the living (depending on whom you ask).

The Reformation appears to have put paid to many of these practices in England. In the seventeenth century, the introduction of Guy Fawkes Day—a commemoration of the 1605 plot to blow up king and Parliament—meant that the bonfires moved a few days, to November 5. Elements of the older holiday remained in rural communities in England, with bonfires, carved turnip lanterns, bobbing for apples, and other traditions that varied by locale, but the gentry did not observe these rituals. Halloween, as we understand it, would have been unknown to Miss Sally Fitzhugh or the Duke of Belliston, although they might have been aware of the superstitions attached to the night as practiced by the tenants on their estates.

The modern holiday of Halloween, with its costumes, jack-o'-lanterns, and trick-or-treating, is generally held to be a mid-nineteenth-century Irish export to America. For those wishing to know more about the history of Halloween, I recommend Lisa Morton's *Trick or Treat: A History of Halloween.*

The vampire, however, would not have been unknown in

early-nineteenth-century London. While we associate the vampire myth with Bram Stoker's 1897 novel, *Dracula*, the legend of these bloodsucking creatures of the night goes back much further. The eighteenth century saw vampire panic in various outposts of the Austrian empire. In his *Dictionnaire Philosophique* of 1764, Voltaire includes this précis of the vampire: "These vampires were corpses, who went out of their graves at night to suck the blood of the living, either at their throats or stomachs, after which they returned to their cemeteries. The persons so sucked waned, grew pale, and fell into consumption; while the sucking corpses grew fat, got rosy, and enjoyed an excellent appetite." Sounds pretty familiar, doesn't it?

The vampire legend pops up in English literature at the beginning of the nineteenth century. Although many refer to Byron's 1813 *The Giaour* as the beginning of the vampire in popular literature in England, his is not the first bloodsucker on the page. Robert Southey's 1801 epic poem *Thalaba the Destroyer* includes a vampire, followed, in 1810, by John Stagg's *The Vampyre*. In his introduction to his poem, Stagg explains that his work "is founded on an opinion or report which prevailed in Hungary, and several parts of Germany, towards the beginning of the last century: It was then asserted, that, in several places, dead persons had been known to leave their graves, and, by night, to revisit the habitations of their friends; whom, by suckosity, they drained of their blood as they slept. The person thus phlebotomised was sure to become a Vampyre in their turn; and if it had not been for a lucky thought of the clergy, who ingeniously recommended staking them in their graves, we should by this time have had a greater swarm of blood-suckers than we have at present, numerous as they are." But the vampire (and his "suckosity") really came into his own in England in 1819, when Lord Byron's physician, Polidori, made waves with the first vampire novel, named—wait for it—*The Vampyre*.

Miss Gwen, of course, is highly indignant that Polidori gets the credit for the first vampire novel when her *Convent of Orsino* came out thirteen years earlier. She attributes this to the male bias in critical literary studies.

Moving away from the occult, I owe one last historical mea culpa. On the back cover of the novel, the autumnal social whirl is referred to as "the Little Season." That term came into use only later on in the century, as a means of differentiating the September to November social season from the Season proper in the spring. However, since it has become a commonplace in novels set during the period that the Season takes place during the spring, I was afraid that if I didn't make clear that we were in the social subseason, there would be pointing of fingers and cries of "But that's not the right time for the Season!"

In fact, the Season was something of a moving target. The Season developed as a means of entertaining those eminences who came to town to do their duty in Parliament, which meant that the Season tended to overlap with the parliamentary sessions. From the eighteenth century through the early nineteenth century, this meant that there was just one Season that ran from roughly October to May. Starting around about 1806, the Season began to gradually shift later and later, with the opening of Parliament pushing back from November to December to January, until, by 1822, the opening of Parliament and, with it, the Season had settled into the stretch between February and July. By the middle of the nineteenth century, one had two official social loci: the Season, which took place during the spring and summer, and the Little Season in the autumn.

One final note: Despite what Eloise may have said in that last chapter, Sir Percy Blakeney, aka the Scarlet Pimpernel, was not, in fact, a genuine historical character.

I'll leave you to draw your own conclusions about the veracity of the Pink Carnation (whose book is coming up next).

Photo © Sigrid Estrada

The author of ten previous Pink Carnation novels, **Lauren Willig** received a graduate degree in English history from Harvard University and a JD from Harvard Law School, though she now writes full-time. Willig lives in New York City.

CONNECT ONLINE

laurenwillig.com
facebook.com/laurenwillig

The Mark of the Midnight Manzanilla

A PINK CARNATION NOVEL

LAUREN WILLIG

A CONVERSATION WITH LAUREN WILLIG

Q. Wasn't this book supposed to be about the Pink Carnation?

A. As those of you who follow me on my Web site know, Pink XI was originally meant to be about the Pink Carnation. It seemed like such a tidy end to the series: Miss Gwen's book followed by Jane's.

And then circumstances intervened.

Part of it was Sally's fault. I had always intended to write a book about Sally Fitzhugh. If Turnip had a book, Sally had to have one too. It was, Miss Fitzhugh informed me, non-negotiable. But I had meant for Sally's book, like Turnip's, to be a Christmas book, out of the structure of the official series. There were just a few problems with this. Turnip went with Christmas like mistletoe with pudding. But Sally . . . didn't. I plotted and I planned, but that Christmas book just wouldn't come together. I tried to set her up with a relation of Lord Vaughn. I threw in pipers piping and geese a-laying.

I should have remembered Sally's feelings about poultry. . . .

Any holiday that included multiple species of birds was not for her. She flatly refused the partridge and became quite rude about the French hens.

Halloween, on the other hand, suited Sally beautifully. Counting my two stand-alone novels, *The Mark of the Midnight Manzanilla* is my thirteenth book. I couldn't resist the idea of writing a Halloween book for number thirteen. (Black cat sold separately.) And, ever so conveniently, by the end of *The Passion of the Purple Plumeria*, Miss Gwen had just written the best seller of 1806, *The Convent of Orsino*. For a very long time (we're talking circa 2006), I had been itching to write a vampire spoof, transposed to the early nineteenth century. Having Miss Gwen as the author of the 1806 equivalent of *Twilight* provided me with the perfect opportunity to get in a little vampire mockery.

Also, if I ended the series on Pink XI, it would be an odd number, which would make the display of covers on my website uneven. Twelve was a much more symmetrical number. Twelve Pink books. It had a nice ring to it.

There were also some less-frivolous reasons. The Pink Carnation's book needs to take place, for various historical reasons, in late 1807. *The Passion of the Purple Plumeria* is set in the spring of 1805. That's a big gap. I also wanted us, before the series ends, to get a last visit with some of our old characters. Jane's book, for the same historical reasons mentioned above, takes place in Portugal, a long way from London, the Vaughns, Turnip, and the rest of the gang. It seemed hard to end the series without getting to see a little bit more of them. Meanwhile, in the modern part of the story, Eloise and Colin needed a little more time to get their affairs in order.

All of these were factors in the balance. The final decider? Real life took its toll. I knew that I was going to be writing Pink XI on a tight deadline, with a newborn. I hadn't had much experience with newborns, but I knew enough to realize that they generally involve a lack of sleep and something called "baby brain." I did not want to tackle Jane Wooliston's book with baby brain. Thirteenth book plus baby brain sounded like very bad luck, indeed. . . .

And that, my friends, is how Sally Fitzhugh got her book.

Q. When will we finally have the Pink Carnation's story?

A. This is it, folks. The end of the line. Pink XII, aka The Next Book, aka The Something Something Moonflower, will be Jane's book and the last book in the series. It's been a much longer run than I had ever imagined—at one point, the idea that the series would stretch to six books would have boggled my brain—but it's time to wrap things up.

The nice thing about taking the time to write Sally's story in between is that it gave me an extra year for the details of Jane's story to percolate and mull. The series has been building to this book for a long time, so I want us to go out with a bang!

Q. Does that mean no more Pink books after Pink XII?

A. I'm not ruling out the prospect of Pink spin-offs. I still have a number of characters, like Kat and Tommy, whom I'd like to see settled, and I've wanted, for a very long time, to write a mystery novel featuring Colin and Eloise. I'm also itching to do a novella about Jane in that missing time between the end of *Purple Plumeria* and the beginning of her book. On the other hand, I'm committed to writing two more stand-alone novels (the next one, set in the 1920s, will be coming out in 2015), so it all depends on how quickly the prose flows and how much extra time I can carve out to play with my old Pink friends.

Q. Did what I think happened with Eloise and Colin happen with Eloise and Colin?

A. You'll just have to wait for the next book to find out! But I will say this: that was not how I intended the last chapter of this book to end. There I was, pounding away at the keyboard, swigging my second decaf venti skim peppermint mocha of the morning, convinced that I knew where that scene was going—when Colin surprised me as well as Eloise.

You will, however, be relieved to know that Colin isn't renting out Selwick Hall after all. We'll see him and Eloise back there in Pink XII. . . .

QUESTIONS FOR DISCUSSION

1. The Duke of Belliston's introduction in the novel is shrouded in mystery and distorted by fantastical gossip about him being a vampire. Did this color your initial perception of him? Or do you think the mysteriousness of his character made him more intriguing?

2. "Just because the man scorns society doesn't mean that he's an unholy creature of the night." Even before Sally has met the duke, she defends him from the slanderous gossip of the *ton*. What do you think this says about the type of person she is?

3. How do you think the deaths of Lucien's parents and his strained relations with the surviving members of his family shaped his character? How does his family situation impact his relationship with Sally?

4. Lucien and Sally are both very strong-willed individuals who prefer to be in control of various situations that arise. Do you think that either of them has the upper hand in their relation-

ship at the beginning? Do you feel that the power dynamic between them changes over the course of the story? How do you think this will this affect their relationship going forward?

5. Do you think Sally and Lucien make a good couple? What about each of them makes them perfectly suited for each other? What makes them perhaps not perfectly suited?

6. Discuss Lucien's motivations for running away to the Americas in the aftermath of his parents' deaths. Do you think his fears were justifiable? If he had stayed (and tried to avenge his parents' deaths), do you think he would have grown up to be the same man? How do you think he will make amends for his actions moving forward with Sally by his side?

7. Initially, who did you think was actually responsible for the murder of Lucien's parents? Were you surprised when the real villain was revealed at the end? What were some of the clues that might have pointed to the real villain?

8. Why do you think Colin was initially so distant toward Eloise when he came to visit her? If you were her friend, what advice would you have given her? Were you caught off guard when he proposed to her at the end?

9. Why do you think Miss Gwen suggested that Lucien and Sally enter into a false engagement? Do you think she perceived

their budding feelings for each other and was trying to "help things along"?

10. "You're a one-woman cavalry charge! It doesn't matter if it's a windmill at the other end. You'll tilt at it anyway, because: You. Don't. Stop. To. Look. Everyone else's troubles are just so much fodder for your entertainment. Never mind the toes you might tread on in the process." Do you think Lucien's accusations are true? Would you like Sally's character as much if she were less meddlesome and officious? Or do you think that's part of what makes Sally so endearing and lovable?

11. Just what do you think Sally has against chickens?

12. What do you think Sally gains from her relationship with her pet, Lady Florence? Does the stoat provide some sort of emotional support?

13. What do you think of Sally's relationship with Lizzy and Agnes? At the beginning of the book, their friendship is undergoing a change as they move from their school days to their new positions in the outside world. Do you think those bonds will stand the test of their changing circumstances?

14. Even though the Pink Carnation is offstage in this book, what do you think she might be up to? Do you think she and Miss Gwen are still working together in some capacity?

15. At the end of the book, Eloise thinks to herself that "the best things sometimes happened by accident." Do you think this is generally true of life, or do you think things turn out better when they're planned?

Don't miss the last novel in the bestselling
Pink Carnation series by Lauren Willig

The Lure of
the Moonflower

Available from New American Library in Summer 2015.

Lisbon, 1807

The mood in the Rossio Square was nasty.

The agent known as the Moonflower blended into the crowd, just one anonymous man among many, just another sullen face beneath the brim of a hat pulled down low against the December rain. The crowd grumbled and shifted as the Portuguese royal standard made its slow descent from the pinnacle of São João Castle, but the six thousand French soldiers massed in the square put an effective stop to louder expressions of discontent. In the windows of the tall houses that framed the square, the Moonflower could see curtains twitch, as hostile eyes looked down on the display put on by the conqueror.

The French claimed to come as liberators, but the liberated didn't seem any too happy about it.

As the royal standard disappeared from view and the tricolore rose triumphant above the square, the Moonflower heard a woman sob and a man mutter something rather uncomplimentary about his new French overlords.

The Moonflower might have stayed to listen—listening, after all, was his job—but he had another task today.

He was here to meet his new contact.

That was all he had been told: Proceed to Rossio Square and await further instructions. He would know his contact by the code phrase: "The eagle nests only once."

Who in the hell came up with these lines?

Once, just once, he would appreciate a phrase that didn't involve dogs barking at midnight or doves flying by day.

The message had given no hint as to the new agent's identity; it never did. Names were dangerous in their line of work.

The Moonflower had gone by many names in his twenty-seven years.

Jaisal, his mother had called him, when she had called him anything at all. The French had called him Moonflower, just one of their many flower-named spies, a web of agents stretching from Madras to Calcutta, from London to Lyons. He'd counted himself lucky; he might as easily have been the Hydrangea. Moonflower, at least, had a certain ring to it. In Lisbon, he was Alarico, a wastrel who tossed dice by the waterfront; in the Portuguese provinces, he went by Rodrigo, Rodrigo the seller of baubles and trader of horses.

His father's people knew him as Jack. Jack Reid, black sheep, turncoat, and renegade.

Jack turned up the collar of his jacket, surveying the scene, keeping an eye out for likely faces.

Might it be the dangerous-looking bravo with the knife he was using to pick his teeth?

No. He looked too much like a spy to be a spy. In Jack's line of work, anonymity was key. Smoldering machismo and resentment tended to attract unwanted attention.

There was a great deal of smoldering in the crowd. Since the French had marched into Lisbon, two weeks since, with a ragtag force that could scarcely have conquered a missionary society, they had proceeded to make themselves unpleasant, requisitioning houses, looting stores, demanding free drinks.

The people of Lisbon simmered and stewed. This lowering of the standard, this public exhibition of dominance, was all that was needed to place torch to tinder. Jack wouldn't be surprised if there were riots before the day was out.

Riots, yes. Rebellion, no. For rebellion, one needed not just a cause, but a leader, and that was exactly what they didn't have right now. The Portuguese court had hopped on board the remaining ships of their fleet and scurried off to the Americas, well out of the way of danger, leaving their people to suffer the indignities of invasion.

Not that it was any of his business. Jack didn't get into the rights and wrongs of it all, not these days. Not anymore. He was a hired gun, and it just so happened that the Brits paid, if not better than the French, at least more reliably.

There was a cluster of French officers in the square, standing behind General Junot. They did go in for flashy uniforms, these imperial officers. Flashy uniforms and even flashier women. The richly dressed women hanging off the arms of the officers were earning dark stares from the members of the crowd, stares and mutterings.

Some were local girls, making up to the conqueror. Others were undoubtedly French imports, like the woman who stood to the far left of the huddled group, her dark hair a mass of bunched curls beneath the brim of a bonnet from which pale purple feathers molted with carefree abandon. Her clothes were all that was currently à la mode in Paris, her pelisse elaborately frogged, the fingers of her gloves crammed with rings.

A well-paid courtesan, at the top of her trade.

But there was something about her that caught Jack's eye. It wasn't the flashing rings. He'd seen far grander jewels in his time. No. It was the aura of stillness about her. She stood with an easy elegance of carriage at odds with all her frills and fripperies, and it seemed that the nervous energy of the crowd eddied and ebbed around her without touching her in the slightest.

Her features had the classical elegance that was all the rage. High cheekbones. Porcelain pale skin, tinted delicately pink at the cheeks. Jack had been around enough to know that it wouldn't take long for the ravages of her trade to begin to show. Those clear eyes would become shadowed; that pale skin would be replaced with white lead and other cosmetics, in a desperate simulacrum of youth, a desperate attempt to catch and hold the affections of first one man and then another, until there was nothing left but the bottle—or the river.

Better, thought Jack grimly, to be a washerwoman or a fishwife, a tavern keeper or a maid. Those occupations might be hell on the hands, but the other was hell on the heart.

Not that it was any of his lookout.

The courtesan's eyes met Jack's across the crowd. Met and held. Ridiculous, of course. There was a square full of people between them, and he was just another rough rustic in a shapeless brown jacket.

But he could have sworn, for that moment, she was looking fully at him. Looking and sizing him up.

For what? He was hardly a likely protector for a French courtesan.

Go away, princess, Jack thought. *There's nothing here for you.*

The French might hold Portugal, but not for long. Rumors were spinning through the crowd. The British navy was sending ships. . . . There were British spies throughout Lisbon. . . . The royal family was returning to raise their army. . . . There were troops massing on the Northern frontier. . . . Rumor upon rumor, but who knew what might have a breath of truth?

It would all go into Jack's report. Provided he ever found his bloody contact, who appeared to be late. The review was almost over, and still, no one had made contact.

That did not bode well.

The soldiers began to filter out of the square, marching beneath the baroque splendor of the Arco de Bandeira, the cheerful yellow of the facade in stark contrast to the bleak weather and even bleaker mood of the populace.

"Pig!" a woman hissed, and tossed a stone.

"Portugal forever!" rose another voice from the crowd.

The officers milled uneasily, looking to their leader. Junot turned, speaking urgently to the man at his side, one of the members of the Portuguese Regency Council, the nominal government that had replaced the Queen and Regent.

A bottle shattered against the tiles, between the feet of the departing soldiers, spraying glass.

"Death to the French!" shouted one bold soul, and then another took it up, and another.

Projectiles were hailing down from every direction, stones and bottles and whole cobbles pried from the street. Abuse rattled down with the stones. The French troops ducked and milled, looking anxiously to their leader, who appeared to be in the middle of a fight with the Portuguese Regency Council.

And then, the sound that could turn a riot into a massacre. The crack of an old-fashioned musket, shot right into the ranks of French soldiers.

It was, Jack judged, not a healthy time to stay in the square.

Any moment now, the French were going to start firing back,

and he didn't want to be in the middle of it. If his contact hadn't appeared by now, he wasn't coming. One thing Jack had learned after years in the game: Saving one's own skin came first.

He slipped off, through the heaving, shouting crowd. The various approaches to the square were already crammed with people, people surging forward, people fleeing, people fainting, people shouting, mothers grabbing their children out of the way, fishwives scrabbling at the cobbles, old men running for ancient weapons, French émigrés and sympathizers running for their lives as the crowd hurled abuse and missiles at the collaborators. Rioters were fighting hand to hand with French soldiers; Junot's face was red with anger as he shouted, trying to be heard above the square. A runner was making for the French barracks, undoubtedly to call up reinforcements.

Jack ducked sideways, down the Rua Áurea.

A hand grabbed at his arm. Jack automatically dodged out of the way. This wasn't his fight. And then a musical voice said, "Wait!"

It was the courtesan, the courtesan he had noticed across the square, her curls flying, her bonnet askew.

"Please," she said, and she spoke in French, a cultured, aristocratic French that caught the attention of the mob around them, made them stop and stare and growl low in their throats. "I need an escort back to my lodgings."

He'd say she did. Her voice was already attracting unwanted attention.

But Jack didn't do rescues of maidens, fair or fallen. *Don't get involved*—that was the only way to survive. Even when they had a figure like a statue of Aphrodite and lips painted a luscious pink.

"Sorry, princess," he drawled, his own French heavily accented, but serviceable. "I'm no one's lackey." He nodded towards the embattled French soldiers. "There's your escort."

"They can't even escort themselves." Her pose was appropriately beseeching, the epitome of ladylike desperation, but there was, even now, in the midst of all the tumult, that strange calm about her. It was the eyes, Jack realized. Cool. Assessing. She lifted those eyes to his, in a calculated gesture of supplication, her gloved hands against the breast of his rough coat. "Please. You know that the eagle nests only once."

All around them, the hectic exodus continued. In the distance, Jack could hear the ominous clatter of horses' hooves against the cobbles, signaling the arrival of the cavalry.

But Jack stood where he was, frozen in the middle of the street, locked in tableau with a French courtesan. And a very pretty tableau it was. Pretty, and completely for show.

Beneath the heavy tracing of kohl that lined her eyes and darkened her lashes, her gray eyes were shrewd and more than a little bit amused.

She raised her brows, waiting for him, giving him the chance to speak first. It was a damnable tactic, and one Jack used himself with some frequency.

He didn't much appreciate being on the other end of it.

"The eagle," said Jack, his gaze traveling from the plunging depths of her décolletage to her painted face, "sometimes nests in uncommon strange places."

The woman didn't squirm or color. She said calmly, "The more remote the nest, the more secure the eggs."

"*Puta!*" taunted one of the crowd, jostling towards them.

The woman raised her voice, putting on a convincing display of arrogance tinged with fear. "I will pay for your escort. My Colonel will reward you well for seeing me safely home."

"I'll see her—," shouted one man, and made a graphic hand gesture.

Loudly, in Portuguese, Jack said, "When coin is lying in the gutter, it would be foolishness not to take it, eh?" Under his breath, in French, he added, "Squeal."

Without waiting for a response, he scooped her up, over his shoulder. A ragged cheer rose up from their viewers, combined with some rather graphic suggestions. Jack waved his free hand and then hastily had to clap it back over her bottom as she squirmed and bucked and squealed, putting on, he had to admit, an excellent show. That is, if she didn't unbalance them both.

"Easy there, princess," called Jack, with a wink for the crowd, and, with a hard hand on her bottom, hoisted her more securely over his shoulder.

Something hard banged into his collarbone, making him wince.

Not all flounces, then. He'd eat his hat if that wasn't a pistol tucked into her stays.

Who—or what—in the devil was she?

"Where to?" he asked beneath his breath, staggering just a little. The woman was slim, but she was nearly as tall as he was, and burdened with a superfluity of flounces and ruffles. The street was slick beneath his feet with mud and offal.

"Down Rua Áurea and turn left on the Rua Assunção," she said, as briskly as though she were giving directions to her coachman. And then she began whacking him on the back with her parasol, screaming for help.

"Right," Jack said under his breath, and took off. Bloody hell, did she need to hit so hard? "You might be a little less convincing," he muttered.

"And ruin the deception?" Amused. The woman sounded amused.

They were past the mob now, out of the way of the men who had witnessed their little scene. Jack set her down with a thunk, right in a patch of something unmentionable. It did not do wonders for the lilac satin on her slippers.

"Sorry, princess. I'm not your sedan chair. You can walk the rest of the way."

He half expected her to argue, but she cast a look up and down the street and nodded. "Follow me."

She knew how to stay in character—Jack had to give her that. She minced along, constantly readjusting her bonnet, fidgeting with the buttons of her pelisse. Jack followed, in the slouch he'd developed in his role as Alarico the drunk, keeping an eye out for pursuers, and trying to figure out what to make of the woman trip-trapping ahead of him, making moues of distaste as she picked her way through the sodden street, her flashing rings practically an invitation to a knife at her throat.

But there was an alertness to her that suggested her attacker wouldn't fare well.

Jack remembered the hard feel of the pistol beneath her stays. That, he realized, explained the fiddling with buttons. And the hat? Jack regarded the woman in front of him with new interest. He'd be willing to wager that there was a stiletto attached to that bunch of feathers on her hat.

As for those rings, those foolish flashing rings . . . most would-be assailants would be so dazzled by the gleam of gems on her hands that they wouldn't notice that those hands were holding a knife until it was too late.

Grudgingly, Jack had to admit, whoever the woman was, she knew what she was doing.

Which made her both very intriguing and very, very dangerous.

The house to which she led him was a private residence. Jack followed her through a gate, across a courtyard, and up a flight of stairs, to a narrow iron door. His fingers briefly touched the point of the knife he kept in a sheath at his wrist. The woman might have known the code phrase, but that didn't mean this wasn't an ambush. No secret organization was inviolable, no code unbreakable. The woman's French was impeccable, her clothes Paris-made.

Which could mean anything or nothing.

How far did her masquerade go? Jack wondered. Was there

a Colonel who had her in keeping? It had been done before. Sleeping with the enemy was the surest way of securing information. A man might share with a mistress what he wouldn't with a friend.

Jack's imagination painted a picture of the rooms they were about to enter: lush carpets on the floor, a gilded mirror above a dressing table laden with mysterious creams and powders, a hip bath in one corner, silk draperies falling around a wide bed. The perfect nest for a French Colonel's woman.

Jack didn't consider himself prudish or squeamish; a job was a job, and they all got it done as best they could. So why the instinctive feeling of distaste, that this woman, this particular woman, might sell her body for information?

From a reticule that looked too small to contain anything of use, the woman took a heavy key and fitted it into the door.

It opened onto a spartan room, the walls whitewashed, the only furniture a table, a chair, and a divan that looked as though it doubled as a bed. There was no dressing table, no gilded mirror, no bed draped with curtains.

"Surely," said Jack mockingly, "the Colonel could afford better."

The woman closed the door behind them with a snap. "There is no Colonel."

Now that they were inside, her movements were brisk and businesslike, with no hint of coquetry. She tossed the key on the table and crossed the room, testing the shutters on the window.

"No?" Jack lounged back against the doorframe, his hands thrust in his pockets. "You surprise me."

"I doubt that." The woman plucked the bonnet off her head, taking the dark curls with it.

Beneath it, her own hair was a pale brown, brushed to a sheen and braided tightly around and around. Without the coquettish curls, her face had the purity of a profile on a coin, the sort of face to which men ascribed abstract sentiments: Liberty, Honor, Beauty. All she needed was some Grecian draperies and a flag.

She dropped the bonnet on the table. "You have a reputation for keeping a cool head. Or have we been mistaken in you . . . Mr. Reid?"

Jack straightened, slowly. "I am afraid you have the advantage of me."

No names. That was the rule. Never names. Only aliases.

One by one, the lady plucked the rings off her fingers, setting them each in a bowl on the table. "Your full name is Ian Reid, but no one has ever called you that. Your family calls you Jack. You were born in Madras and served for some years in the army of the Maratha chieftain, Scindia, before Scindia's French allies recruited you and renamed you the Moonflower."

Years of taking hard knocks kept Jack's face wooden. The only reaction was his very stillness, a stillness he knew betrayed him as much as any response.

"You fell out with the French three years ago." The last ring clattered into the bowl. The woman stretched her bare fingers, like a pianist preparing to play, before glancing over at Jack. "People tend not to like it when you work for someone else while pretending to work for them. They like it even less when you abscond with a rajah's hoard of jewels."

Jack shrugged. "All's fair, they say."

The woman raised a pale brow. "In love or in war?"

From his limited experience, Jack didn't see much difference between the two. Except that those one loved might hurt one the most. "They're one and the same, princess." His eyes lingered on her décolletage with deliberate insolence. "I had thought you would know."

The woman brushed that aside, continuing with her dossier. "As a result of your little escapade with the jewels, you relocated to Portugal, where you have been positioned ever since."

Jack tilted his hat lazily over his eyes. "You are well-informed," he drawled. "Brava."

The woman's lips turned up in a Sphinx-like smile. "It *is* what I do."

She sounded so pleased with herself, that Jack decided that turn and turn about was only fair play. He'd see how she liked it with the shoe on the other foot.

"We've ascertained that you know all about me." Jack straightened to his full height, favoring her with a wolfish smile. "Now let's talk about you."

"I don't—," she began imperiously, but Jack held up a hand.

Pushing back from the wall, he prowled in a slow circle around her. "You speak French beautifully, but it's not your native tongue. You wear your French clothes well, but they're a

481 costume, not a personal choice. Left to yourself, you don't go in

costume, not a personal choice. Left to yourself, you don't go in for furbelows."

His eyes went to her neck, where she wore a gold locket on a silk ribbon. The rest of her jewelry was showy and undoubtedly made of paste. The locket was simple, and it was real. Jack nodded at her neck. "Except, perhaps, one. That locket."

The woman's hand closed over the bauble, a small but telling gesture. "Very nice, Mr. Reid. You are quite perceptive."

Jack smiled lazily. "That's what they pay me for, princess. Now, do I go on—or are you going to tell me who you are?"

He half expected her to demur. Any other woman would have. Any other woman would have teased and played.

Instead, this woman, with her elaborate rings and plain locket, looked him in the eye and said simply, "You may know me as the Carnation. The Pink Carnation."

Jack stared at her for a moment, and then he broke out in a laugh. "Pull the other one, sweetheart."